The Scientists

OTHER BOOKS BY THE SAME AUTHOR:

Lincoln McKeever

The Kiss Of Death
Murder One
The People Against O'Hara

The Scientists

ELEAZAR LIPSKY

APPLETON-CENTURY-CROFTS, INC.
NEW YORK

March 1959

Library of Congress Card Number: 58–13806

PRINTED IN THE UNITED STATES OF AMERICA

W

To my wife

*Peril lurks in definition, so runs
an ancient maxim of law.*

—Benjamin N. Cardozo

AUTHOR'S NOTE

So far as I know, no substance like biocin is yet known to science, but its properties, I am told on good authority, have validity as hypothesis. No connection is intended with any substance which may in fact exist. All events and personalities in this work are fictional, except for actual persons and institutions to whom occasional reference is made.

I am profoundly grateful for information, advice and guidance to more generous friends than I can properly mention in this space. Any departures from accuracy are unintended and rest wholly at my door.

The First Day

Chapter 1

THE TAP ON THE DOOR WAS REPEATED.

Freda Stahl put aside a cigarette with a surreptitious motion. Her stubby hands raced on and when the letter had been typed with no more than three errors, she called out permission to enter. A student with an impudent grin came in and placed a letter on her desk.

"I've got an appointment," he said.

Freda methodically finished her erasures. "I'm afraid you're out of luck," she said in a tart upstate accent.

"In conference?" asked the youth.

"He's not in yet," she replied.

"Ah, hum," said the youth, tugging at a sleeveless sweater. "Can I wait here?"

"Suit yourself."

The youth took a chair to a window overlooking the university grounds where he sat, tapping his teeth with a pencil, staring at woolly clouds drifting across a soft blue sky. Freda gathered herself uneasily and continued to type, glancing up with annoyance, until finally she stopped. "Don't sit there," she said, pressing her lips tightly.

"Pardon?"

"Not behind my back," she said sharply. "Take the other chair."

"Excuse me," said the student with an air of concern. He slouched into the other chair and pulled out a paperback commentary on the Kinsey Report and turned to a controversial chapter on the incidence of bestiality in rural communities. His grunts of amazement disturbed the peace. Freda gazed longingly at her cigarette and then at the clock. With mounting irritation, she made corrections and added the letter to a tray marked OUT.

"Please don't do that," she said sharply.

"Do what?"

"Jiggling your knee. It disconcerts me. I've made a dozen mistakes since you began."

"Oh, I am so sorry," he said apologetically. "But then maybe you can help me meanwhile."

She stared suspiciously. "If you're looking for permission to take Professor Luzzatto's course, you'll have to take it up with him directly. I can't help you."

"Oh, no. Nothing like that." The student's head was oversized, bony, topped with a crew-cut stubble of red hair. "As a matter of fact, I'm here to do him a favor. I'd like an interview for *Patroon*."

Freda pursed her mouth acidly. "We've given *Patroon* an interview already. One should be enough."

"If I didn't have the interests of the university at heart," said the student calmly, "I'd run that interview as written. But—well, I'm the responsible editor."

Freda pushed up her reading glasses and stared at a replusive insect on a pin. "Are you James Henschel?"

The student placed a hand to his heart. "I am indeed."

"What do you want?"

"I'd like to check a few points before the article goes to the printer." Henschel fished into a pocket for a sheaf of yellow papers. "Now, let's see, Madeleine wrote—"

"Madeleine Thorne? That child who was tagging at Professor Luzzatto's heels all last week?"

"That 'child' is an English major at Burland." Henschel grinned. "Straight A's and a good reporter. She describes you, Miss Stahl, as the Professor's strong right hand and—"

Freda sniffed.

"—and watchdog and devoted employee."

"Correct that, please."

"In what respect?"

"I am not employed by Professor Luzzatto. I am employed by the graduate faculty of science. I'm assigned to this department, but I'm paid by the university."

"Why the science faculty? That's something I don't quite understand, Miss Stahl. The graduate faculties were combined about five years ago. How does that work out?"

"I'm one of the hangovers," said Freda tartly.

4

Henschel made a note. "Madeleine describes Luzzatto—"

"Professor Luzzatto," she corrected.

Henschel accepted the correction sweetly. "Madeleine describes Professor Luzzatto as an attractive young family man with a pleasant smile and discerning gray eyes. Would you like to comment?"

"No."

"I quite—ah—understand," Henschel went on blandly, although indeed there was nothing in Freda's manner but correct coldness in the face of impudence. "She goes on to write that Professor Luzzatto does not feel that he will let affluence change a simple way of life. Is that a thing that he'd be likely to say?"

"Mebbe."

"It gives the impression that Professor Luzzatto wants us to believe that he doesn't care about money. In fact, she has a quote that he regards money as helpful only to enable him to devote his life to research. Would you believe a thing like that?"

"Why not?"

"Doesn't it sound a little farfetched to you?"

"It does not."

"Oh, come on, Miss Stahl! I mean, even for a secretary?"

Freda contained herself with an effort. "Henschel, I know that the college gives *Patroon* a lot of latitude. Professor Luzzatto realizes that his discovery of biocin is important, not only to the world, but to the university, and we've been told to give the student press our co-operation. But I think you're a spoiled brat. I intend to report this."

Henschel let his head tilt back. "I don't suppose," he said gently, "that I can stop you?"

"You could apologize," she said acidly.

"I'm awfully sorry," he replied. "*Patroon* has a definite function to perform, and when something sensational like biocin comes along, we've got to handle the story on a journalistic level. The stuff was discovered right here in this lab, wasn't it?" The thin neck craned about. "University facilities were used and we've got some obligations to ask questions. If your boss wants to button up, I'll print that we got No Comment. But the fact is, he volunteered a statement to our reporter—"

"Little wrigglin' bitch," muttered Freda under her breath.

Henschel waited, but the mutter failed to develop into intelligible discourse. "Did you know that he bought a pretty expensive split-level house in the Heights last winter?"

"It's not a split level. It's the old Wessels House."

"With two-car garage?"

5

"He'll need two cars out there in the woods. One for himself, one for his wife."

"Including an expensive station wagon? I'm entitled to raise my scanty eyebrows. Or don't you think so?"

A gong rang and a shuffling of feet passed the office door as classes began to assemble. Freda glanced at the door expectantly. "A lot of rumors are going around," said Henschel, pursuing the matter. "One can't help hearing things, and there you are."

"Where's that?" asked Freda icily.

Henschel leaned forward confidentially. "If I print a statement which lets the Professor picture himself as a starry-eyed goof, a sort of laboratory recluse, and if a contrary set of facts ever comes out, he'll be embarrassed. I want to get the story straight for his sake."

"What rumors?" asked Freda.

Henschel waggled his hand wisely. "You know, the usual thing—"

"I don't know!" she said decidedly. Her desk was a jumble of nose drops, tissues, chocolates, pills, and copies of obscure religious tracts, under which she found a cigarette. Her heart, she noticed, was beating faster than usual. "Henschel, I have the impression that you've got some motive for making these snide remarks against Professor Luzzatto behind his back. I swear I don't know why!"

"I don't know where you get that impression," the student objected smoothly, seemingly surprised. "I'm sorry if I've given you a false—"

Freda tapped the desk with her fingernails. "You know very well that Professor Luzzatto donated the bulk of those royalties from biocin to the university. You printed the story on the Center yourself in your commencement issue last May. I've got a copy in the scrapbook."

"I wrote the article," Henschel conceded.

"Then there's absolutely no excuse for these insinuations, is there? Especially now, when we're making so much of the Center?" Freda's eyes strayed to a drawing on the wall, showing the architect's vision of the twelve-story science building clad in an apron of black marble against the north quadrant of the campus. "Professor Luzzatto's been working day and night on those plans. I can't imagine a more devoted man."

Henschel's sandy eyes widened, but he refused to be diverted. "Insinuations?" he exclaimed, hurt.

Freda went on, "Unless you claim that the statement released by the university was a lie? Is that what you're hinting?"

"A lie? I'd never print a thing like that about the administration. No, I don't doubt that Professor Luzzatto assigned royalties, but—" He hesitated tantalizingly.

"But what?" Freda demanded.

Henschel studied the flushed plump face. "I'd rather not speculate," he said calmly. "It's simply that a press release does not have to be complete, does it? What's easier than an omission?"

"What possible omission? What makes you think so?"

"I see a cherub that tells me," quoted the youth inaccurately.

The telephone rang. It was a frog-voiced man, Si Podell, at Strollo Hall, the Administration Building, talking out of the side of his mouth. "Freda? Is the boss there yet?"

"I'm afraid not."

"Oh!" A pause. "Kid there from *Patroon* name of Henschel?"

"Ayeh. Yes, why?"

"Can he hear me?"

"I should think so. The way you're growling, you'll take my ear off." Freda held the hearing piece tight to her ear with a suspicious glance at Henschel. Podell seemed to be talking to someone else in his office; a driving voice went on and off as though he were covering the mouthpiece intermittently. If she was not mistaken, the other voice was that of the president of Haverstraw University, James Fitzherbert Foxx, B.A., Oberlin, 1924; M.A., Wayne, 1926; Ph.D., Iowa, 1931; E.C.A., Washington, 1943. Podell came back, "Freda, I don't want that snot-nosed quiz kid putting questions to your boss before I get to him first. Something's come up."

"May I know what? Can I take a message?"

"Not yet."

"I see," she said tightly, letting the inflection rise.

"Now don't get offended, Freda kid, not for now. Where's your boss likely to be this time of morning? We're trying to set up a conference."

Henschel's elaborate interest in the steel engraving of Darwin—the classic portrait of 1881 complete with inky cloak and gentle benign face —was hardly deceptive. Freda suggested, "Suppose you ask me?"

Podell chuckled with appreciation. "Okay. Now—will he stop in first at the office?"

She assumed a blank face. "Maybe not."

"If not, then someplace else?"

"Exactly."

"Could he still be at home?"

"Mebbe."

"Can we call him there now?"

"I don't see why not. I think you might trust me, Mr. Podell," said Freda sharply.

"Next time," said Podell, and rang off. The receiver whirred and her gaze went around the sunny office, picking out a vase with its single rose, an array of cabinets, a chest for slides, a display of shells including a spectacular *Terebra flammea,* iridescent and spiraled like a sea god's phallus; a skeleton of *Seymouria,* a primitive amphibian; a portrait of a group of graduate students in which a thin youth with lank black hair and gray serious eyes towered above his fellows.

Freda opened a drawer for a towel and soap. "Henschel, in this department we think a lot of Professor Luzzatto," she said, arising with all the dignity of a pouter pigeon, panting with anger and high blood pressure. "He's a fine and brilliant scientist, and he's done more than any man on the faculty to bring credit to the university. His discovery of biocin was a blessing to humanity. I can't imagine why anyone, let alone one of our students, would want to raise sneaky inferences."

"Ah," cried Henschel with dismay, "I've offended you. I see my mistake."

"Do you?" Freda studied the goblin leer. "I'm going to lock the door now," she said firmly. "You can leave."

"After you," said Henschel.

Freda wrapped towel about soap. "I don't like anyone breathing down my neck," she said sharply. "Go on ahead."

"Why, of course," Henschel replied amiably, glancing at a wrist watch. "I'm late now for a seminar in Goodness of Heart. It's an advanced course. It's been so nice." He stuck his hands in his pockets and sauntered out, bearing his grin of impudence like a badge of honor. The gong rang three times.

Sometime during the night David Luzzatto had already come to a decision—or rather formulated a conviction which had lain in his mind over the summer months—to take a fresh position regarding the royalties accruing from the discovery of biocin.

It had been distressing his mind for a year. He knew there had been speculation in faculty circles for some time, especially after the magnitude of the revenues had become common knowledge. A sensitivity to faculty gossip had some bearing on the decision, not because of any regard for public opinion—on the contrary, in these matters he felt committed only to conscience—but because he had reached the conclusion that his position had become untenable, so that there were many nights he could not sleep.

There was a sigh from the next bed. "Can't you sleep, dear?" Eva whispered.

8

"No," he answered, "I'm not asleep."

He sensed that she had arisen in her bed and resting on her elbow, she was gazing at him in the dark. The light of a full moon fell through the window, picking out patterns in the carpet. "I can't sleep either," she confessed.

He turned his head and saw the outline of her figure. In the moonlight her reddish hair, tumbling over naked shoulders, was black. Her eyes were in shadows. He said softly, "I'd like to come into your bed."

She sank back as he entered the bed; the linens were warm and crisp. They embraced and even as they held each other the thought of the biocin patent and its Pandora's box of troubles intruded and persisted; he cursed himself for letting his mind run on such things even at moments like this. He put his hand lightly on her belly. For some moments under his silent question she waited. Finally she said, "It's alive."

"How can you know? Isn't it too soon?"

"Oh, I know," she whispered. "I'm sure."

"Have you seen the doctor?"

She shook her head. "Not yet."

"Isn't that silly, dear? Why not?"

"I don't want to hear the verdict. If there's anything wrong this time, I want to put it off. I want to set my mind on its life."

"Isn't it better to know the truth?"

"I think not." In the darkness her eyes seemed to glisten. "I know that this child will live. I have no doubts. I don't want to go through that other business again."

At her vehemence he hesitated, considering all this in silence. She had gone through a dreadful pregnancy before; she had carried the child dead within her almost to term. He did not like the way her latest had begun. He held her gently.

"All right, dear," he agreed. "But in the morning, I want you to see the doctor."

"I'll think of it," she promised.

They lay comforting each other with their bodies, their thoughts in different worlds. He kissed her mouth and his breath was whistling in her ear when she thrust him aside. "No!" She flung her head away. "Go away, darling! No!"

"Let me," he whispered urgently.

"No!"

He waited a sterile moment, angered and hateful, feeling the blood at his throat. He was surprised. He had not wanted or expected this, but

9

something elemental had triggered the reaction. He withdrew slowly. "I'm sorry, darling."

She kissed his hand.

"Don't you see, dear?" she pleaded. "I can't take a chance."

He smiled faintly, recovering his breath, and stroked her hair. "But you're being unreasonable," he said gently. "Now that you're pregnant, this can't possibly do any harm. You know all that."

"I know, but there's something——" She paused in despair. "I can't help it. Not after what happened last time."

He got up and went to the window where he stared into the night. Against Orion low on the horizon, an apple tree was silhouetted and he could hear the trilling of crickets. Her voice came from the bed.

"I love you," she whispered. "All this will come to a good end, I promise you. This time I'll give life. Wonderful things are happening for us both. Come to sleep?"

To his chagrin, he found his mind divided. In the midst of her anguish, his thoughts were still on the excitement and frustrations raised by the biocin patents. Ruefully he decided that this was not the time to disturb her with this matter. In silence, he returned to his own bed, feeling the stiff nap of the carpet under his bare feet. When her breathing was again soft and regular he arose and went up to the study and lit a cigarette. It was dawn when he finally returned and fell into troubled sleep.

Suddenly he was awake.

A dull boom told him that somewhere along Tynesdale Road workmen were dynamiting an outcropping of granite. A fresh breeze was blowing the bedroom curtains and the next bed was empty. After a moment he threw back the covers and went to the door and called out into the house.

"Evvie?"

Her rich contralto replied. "That you, Davey? Did you finally get to sleep?"

"Not really."

"What was wrong this time?"

Luzzatto hesitated. "Biocin," he confessed.

"Oh, darling! No!"

"Supposed to help the whole human race and it's killing my sleep. Can't seem to let go of the subject."

"Really, darling, you've got to learn to control that obsession."

Something about her voice, a note of detachment, loving but distant, struck a chord of wonder. He looked out into the hall. "Where are you?"

10

"Here in the nursery. I'm wondering how to paper the room. It's so sunny and the river's glorious. Come look!"

"Not now. I've got to bathroom first. Say, why so early?"

"The light got me up. You ought to invent something against that—a pill to desensitize the retina or something. Anyway you were asleep, snoring like a bandsaw."

He waited a moment at the door, visualizing Eva in the nursery below. Too much of her days was spent in that room. He heard her step—not quick and light as in their first years of marriage, but slow, careful, deliberate on flat heels, concerned for the life within her.

"Honey—" he began.

"Yes?"

Her voice at any rate was cheerful. He said, "Oh, nothing. I'll take a shower."

"I'll get your breakfast," she called lightly. "What about a stack of wheats with that good ole southern molasses?" Her voice was explosive and positive and to his taste delightfully accented and foreign. She mouthed the locutions of American slang with a special touch.

"No, not that," he yawned. "You know what I always want and don't disappoint me. Hear?"

"My God, yes!" she agreed. "I hear! Sunnyside-up eggs and bacon?"

"Right!"

"Will you ever change your routine?"

"Why should I?"

But there was only the sound of her slow step, going down the stairs, and he closed the door. Some dim recollection of an unpleasant dream swam to the surface and dissolved. It was the tension under which he lived, he decided, rubbing his chest. He shook his head in impatient disregard.

The Luzzattos lived in a sprawling reconverted farmhouse once known as the Wessels House. Since it stood on a hill overlooking the Hudson River where it widened into Haverstraw Bay, they could depend on a breeze and it was comfortable in summer. On any clear day one could see river craft plying the blue waters. In winter the house was warm and insulated under its low ceilings; one might imagine past generations roasting apples around the Franklin stove which, polished, gleaming, restored to working order, still stood before the whitewashed hearth of rough-dressed native granite. What once had served the Wessels family for household activities—carding and spinning and occasional nursing of farrows born out of season—was now the living room. It was decep-

11

tively simple. The hardwood floors were bare, but the pine walls glowed with color. Comb ware pottery of Colonial design stood in a scalloped open cupboard. Tall slat-backed chairs of slim design reared their boldly curved backs. At the hearth a settle bed faced a polished oak cask. The heavily beamed ceiling was low, but when the shutters were flung back the room was flooded with light. All this represented some years of work and a sharp nose for a bargain. Eva had patiently assembled the pieces dirt cheap, and even after the biocin royalties had begun to mount, she had played a tight-fisted game with scores of antique dealers within a radius of hundreds of miles. It was a game in which her husband joined in a subordinate role: his own taste was thought to be atrocious, yet he took too much pleasure in the rude trestle table which divided the room for that to be entirely true.

The bedroom was Eva's, it was agreed, from Dufy reproductions to white candlewick spreads. His own presence hardly counted. His bed was undisturbed as though during the night his long rangy body had barely stirred the covers. Except for military brushes on his bureau (representing his father's idea of a wedding gift) his clothes were stowed away in bureau and closet. But his wife was all over the place. Her bedclothes were in a heap, a stack of novels had fallen in disorder between the beds. He restored the lot to a neat pile, marveling that she could in one week digest a range from Trollope and Sukhanov to English thrillers. One slim, tattered book was his own: Erwin Schrödinger's lectures delivered in Dublin during the war on physical aspects of the living cell. *What Is Life?* He studied the title, frowned and considered the last pages which had been underscored by his wife. The subtlety of the argument enchanted him, but the final leap into Berkleyism struck him as preposterous. Where was the proof? "Quatch!" he muttered, using an Ullmanism. Unsatisfied, he stepped into the needle shower and danced and gasped at the icy spray.

Breakfast was the attractive time of day for the Luzzattos. It was cozy and bright in the dining alcove and here they loved to sit in the morning, reviewing matters of common interest, gloating over their new house and the exciting developments at the university. Whatever Eva's fears in the night, they were not evident as she worked the orange juicer. He glanced at her covertly with pleasure. Every motion was strong and competent; her long white arms were instruments of grace. Her face was translucent and pale, shining with delicately balanced happiness, marred only by blue circles under magnificent large green eyes. She cracked a pair of eggs in a bowl and glanced up almost shyly.

12

"Why do you look at me like that?" she asked, smiling.

He said seriously, "I love your hair. I never want you to cut it short. Promise?"

Still smiling, she looped a ribbon and brought her hair into a pony tail. At once she was typical, one might suppose, of the several score of bright young faculty wives in the development, all healthy and knowledgeable and alert. Her waist was still slender, but she walked in these first days of pregnancy like a brimming vessel, he thought, as though in dread to spill a drop of vital liquid. Under a loose morning robe, her breasts, still lovely, had not yet begun to change, their tips were pink and simple. She was beautiful.

"Not too hot a flame," he reminded. "Eggs!"

"I know," she said patiently.

She half-expected comment to follow on the denaturing effects of heat on the polypeptide molecular structure of ovalbumin, but on this morning the valuable fact was withheld. She brought the platter of eggs, moist and country-style with nut-brown bacon, and a pot of hot coffee to the table, and sat so that they were facing each other in sunlight. She said, "Darling?"

"Yes?"

She sighed contentedly. "I'm happy."

He smiled and kissed her palm, sniffing its pleasant morning smell. Her remark meant much to both of them, he reflected, more than anyone else might suspect. It had been long since this mood of tranquility and fulfillment, precarious as it was, was on her. Eva looked up to notice the lines of fatigue about his eyes. "I'm sorry I fell asleep on you last night, Davey. What time did you finally get to bed?"

"Late enough."

"What were you doing up in the study?"

He grinned sheepishly. "Going over plans for the Center," he confessed. "Couldn't figure out the best spot for the plant pathology lab. Trouble is Monckton wants the skylight but so would I. It's like trying to push an extra domino into a full box. Something's always popping up. Scientists! They're jealous as cats. What makes it tough is that Monckton's giving me first pick. Subtle?"

A sniff of disapproval was amused. "Can't you leave the details to the architects? It's only a building."

"This building is too important," he paraphrased neatly, "to leave to architects."

"Ho!" she laughed, patting his cheek.

Smiling fondly, they chatted with deep pleasure in each other while

13

he explored the back pages of the *Times*. Systematically, he hunted out each item related to scientific developments in all parts of the world. As a geneticist, he turned first to the debate raging on the effects of radio-active fallout on the future of humanity, impatient with political interests that obscured the purely scientific observation that the world was already poisoned beyond remedy—that death was loose upon the planet. Beneath the table, their knees met with the warmth of wool against silk.

"Nothing on biocin," he muttered disappointedly.

Eva looked up from an item in the *East Haverstraw News* on a new shopping center in town. "Oh, darling!" she exclaimed with mock dolor. "Are we off the best seller list?"

"Something like that." A faint smile appeared. "Oh, it's a good thing, I suppose. Shows we're out of short supply. No more black market, thank God! Used to give me the willies, those stories about smuggling and scandals about the stuff. Didn't look good for us or for the country. When the rest of the world can't get its hands on a vital medicine, it creates resentments. I'm glad the controls are finally off. Remind me!"

"About what?"

"Ought to drop a line to Eddie Fitzpatrick in the Surgeon General's Office. I'd like him to get one of their top personalities for the dedication."

"Oh? Who?"

"I was thinking of the Secretary."

Eva looked doubtful. "Would a Cabinet member come to Haverstraw? Isn't she too busy?"

He touched his rimless glasses reprovingly. "Why not? It's an important occasion and besides," he added humorously, "she's quite a dish, and Eddie has all that Irish charm. He might persuade her. After all, what is she? A newspaperwoman, and this is a story that ought to go all over the world. It's worth a try."

Her lips pursed with deadly maturity. "Isn't there a committee in charge? Will they accept a thing like this dumped in their laps?"

Luzzatto paused. "They ought to be pleased."

"People resent any invasion of their prerogatives. Why not let Foxx handle the invitations in the regular way?"

He sat thinking. "Well, I see your point," he acknowledged, "but it seems funny not to be able to suggest a speaker. Everyone's so damn sensitive! I swear, it feels as though the whole thing's slipping through my fingers."

She lowered her cup. "Really, dear," she said sensibly, "you must stop breathing down everyone's neck. You've got to face up to the fact that administration's not your field."

14

He frowned at this. "I completely disagree. I don't want to brag, but I'm as crafty and devious and political as any man in the shop." They laughed together with good humor. "It is ridiculous," he confessed and then, feeling foolish, he returned to the *Times,* wondering at himself. Well, that question of royalties would hold till later. "You'd think they'd send this stuff to my office," he murmured, skimming through begging letters and advertisements. "How they manage to get this address, I swear I don't know. Junk, all junk!"

"Lend me a pencil," said Eva.

"Um? Sure."

He passed over a pencil and continued to slit envelopes. A bureau in New York soliciting a month's lecture tour of the Midwest promised substantial fees. A request of the East Haverstraw Community Chest to attend a Big Gifts parlor meeting. "You handle this, dear." A letter from Mrs. George MacKay, widow of the mathematician, advising that subscriptions to *Vogue, House Beautiful, Science, American Scientist, Saturday Review, American Decorator,* and *Manchester Guardian* were due for renewal. "Gosh, I don't really want all these, but I guess we've got to help the old girl out. Damn shame. MacKay didn't leave her a dime. Handle it, dear." Blue Cross. "Your department." Letter requesting appearance on television, and then he glanced at the next item dubiously. "How do we owe £20 to Fred Kellogg?" He was referring to their grocer in Bimini Island. During the summer, Bimini housed a colony of scientists whose appearance in the Bahamas was ensured by the attractions of the marine laboratories maintained by the American Museum of Natural History in New York. Seas of colbalt blue and emerald green, sport fishing, shop talk, everlasting disputations, off-season prices were lures to the select handful who flocked annually to the island like migrant waterfowl between semesters. He said, "I thought you paid this bill."

She studied the postmark with all the respect due to Her Majesty's Service. "Fred Kellogg's a nice man," she observed, "but maybe he's trying to put something over. Didn't I give this bill to you?"

"You handle the accounts," he reminded her. "I haven't made out ten checks in the past three years. That reminds me, I'll need my allowance. Haircut."

She nodded. "I have some money for you. But about Fred—" Shortly before their return to the mainland, she recalled, she had gone, checkbook in hand, settling accounts with shopkeepers. "Didn't I get around to Fred Kellogg?" she wondered. "I'm in such a damn muddle."

He shook his head deploringly. "You've got to be more methodical," he observed.

15

Eva reheated the pot of coffee and brought it back to the table. "Methodical?" she queried with ironic self-knowledge. "Well, I'm not and I'll never be. Let's see that stupid bill. I'll send an offer to settle for half. And if that doesn't work—" She paused.

"Yes?" he prodded.

"I'll pay the whole thing," she said firmly. "How's that? Businesslike enough for your blood?"

She waited hopefully for a smile but he had already drifted away from the amiable conversation. It was one of his exasperating traits: this ability to lose the thread of an argument at its height.

"Oh, say!" he cried.

"Um?" She looked up patiently.

"Listen to this!" His sallow face lit up with sudden enthusiasm. "Leo Katz-Moebius down at Brandywine."

"Yes, I saw the return address."

"Oh? Well, Leo has got a line for me on that program for digging up materials for retarding growth of transplanted neoplasms in animals. They're trying a crude filtrate of this new purine pyrimidine antagonist with biocin against Crocker mouse sarcoma 180. Just a few milliliters of the combined filtrate knocked the hell out of that sarcoma's resistance. But that's not the point. It's the method they're working out to speed up the whole line of research. It's based on showing high correlation between the capacity of the filtrate to inhibit this Kloeckera brevis yeast and its ability to inhibit the tumor."

"What's the specific value? Let's see?" she asked, frowning.

The letter was handed over. "You can see for yourself, dear. The idea is economy. The crude filtrate is tried out on yeast. If it looks good, the stuff gets purified, isolated, characterized, and anti-tumor tests in the animal are limited to the important steps. It's the animal tumor you're trying to destroy." His eyes lit up with enthusiasm as the technical implications appeared.

"Is that all?" Eva returned the letter, losing interest. "I thought you had something more spectacular. Leo's always off in a burst of enthusiasm." She looked up. "How many can we invite, d'you suppose?"

"What?"

She gnawed her pencil critically. "What's the limit of this house? I'd know in our poor little old flat, but here? Aren't we in danger?"

"Of what?"

"Spilling over?"

"Oh!" he said as comprehension dawned. She was checking her guest list, he saw, against the Haverstraw General Catalogue. He had no high

16

opinion of that book. It reflected not his own austere thinking, but Si Podell's values. Its emphasis on the social doings of the undergraduate body—for example, the picture of a pretty Maid of Honor adjusting the crown of the Queen of the Senior Prom—struck him as an affront to Haverstraw's standards, such as they were, nor did his own full portrait on the cover—peering sternly through rimless glasses into an empty Erlenmeyer flask—diminish his disdain for the product.

"How many is many?" he asked.

"Fifty couples. Maybe more."

"Is that so much?"

"*Much?* I'm scared to death. I didn't mind the partying at Bimini this summer, it was so informal, but here? It's a responsibility."

He was not too pleased with her worrisome tone. He now saw the blue shadows under her eyes; her white skin was drawn and translucent. "Who would you like to omit?" he asked drily.

She laughed and smoothed back a wisp of hair. "Oh, you know me," she acknowledged, and a slight measure of tension seemed to diminish. "Must we have the Puces?" she asked wistfully. "Just this once?"

"Gordie Puce? Oh? Well!" Professor George Gordimer Puce was a luminary at Haverstraw. In the catalogue, his photograph, white-haired and satanic, standing at the stone fireplace in his comfortable Georgian house on the outskirts of the campus, facing a circle of women students, lent distinction to an otherwise prosaic faculty. His seminar in Contemporary Morals was a feature of the new streamlined curriculum of the current administration. This held a measure of irony, considering his turbulent and naughty past. Puce had been the *enfant terrible* of the Twenties, comrade-in-arms of Schmalhausen, casualty in forgotten clashes with the Watch and Ward Society, Apostle of Sex to the freedom-loving nations; he was now heir to the mantle of Irving Babbitt. "Gordie Puce is a good friend," he observed, "and besides, he's chairman of the Senate Council. I wouldn't want to leave him out."

She studied his troubled face. "Is something up?" she asked. "You sound calculating."

"Do I?"

"Yes. It's not like you."

"Well—" He hesitated. "I like Gordie."

"So do I," she protested. "He's silly but charming. It's Hilda that scares me. She's bound to burst out in that peacock soprano, or do something horrible, and I'll either start to laugh or to cry or something. Remember that party when she proved that a dancing girl could wear a diamond in her navel? We found the natural color of her hair that night!"

17

Luzzatto grinned. "Hilda's whacky," he admitted, "but that should put you on your mettle."

"She's a mess. It's a big event, Davey, the dedication and a house-warming, and I don't want the woman to screw it up. She's been good to me, but I've had her."

Luzzatto lowered his eyes and did some thinking. "I'll ask Gordie my-self," he decided. "Now what's so funny?"

Eva was now resting her chin in her palm, her elbow on the alcove table; the sleeve of her robe slid down to expose the curve of her forearm. She was smiling at him fondly.

"I'm just thinking what a long way we've come," she sighed con-tentedly. "Did I tell you that Nadine Foxx offered to lend us extra knives and forks? What a damn tuft hunter!" Her eyes sparkled with relish for the turn of events. "I'd like to pass her over if I could. Yesterday I was just a graduate student, baby-sitting for the Puces, then wife of a lowly instructor without tenure. Dirt! Today? You should have heard the woman on the telephone. Cooing like a dove. Imagine that—knives and forks! I'm proud of you, Davey."

He chuckled sympathetically. "Did you take the offer?"

"Most certainly I did not."

"Now why not?"

"Because I hate insincerity." Eva's accent sharpened with European idealism. "I will not use the silverware of another woman unless it comes from the heart. It's simply that she recognizes that your star is rising." Large green eyes narrowed to sinister slits. "She's a sheer opportunist."

"Opportunist? She's the Frau President," he scoffed. "What's she after with us?"

Eva pursed her lips wisely and raised one shoulder. "It's the contagion of fame," she said darkly. "Yesterday we were less than nothing to Nadine. Now there's all this talk about the Nobel Prize. She wants to get in on the ground floor on that day."

"What day?"

"The day you get too big for this place. It's a shitty world," said Eva brightly.

Luzzatto winced. "Darling, don't," he murmured.

Her eyes went wide. "Don't what?"

"In French, it's permissible, yes. *Merde,* yes. But not in English. You've got to find some euphemism."

She weighed the word delicately. "But I hear it everywhere," she protested logically.

"You're not the type," he said decisively. "Anyway it makes me uncomfortable."

"I shall try to remember."

She closed her eyes in concentration. "But I know it will pop out," she murmured worriedly. "However I shall try. I must say, I have discovered that the English language is not quite what I was led to expect when I studied in Poland. What did they give us at the *Gymnasium*? *Huckleberry Finn* and *Hamlet*. I cannot tell you how misleading that was. In a foreign tongue, it is so hard to master the nuances. Do you think there's a chance?"

He had returned to the *Times*. "Chance of what?" he asked vaguely.

"The Nobel," she said patiently.

"Oh, *please*." He rattled the newspaper. "Of course not."

"It's not so silly as all that," she argued, "After all, people do. How many discoveries like biocin ever get made? Even my butcher's been asking when you're going to Stockholm."

"It's that publicity nonsense," Luzzatto grumbled, secretly pleased. "It isn't of the slightest importance."

"Isn't it?" she asked wisely.

"No."

Luzzatto raised his eyes to the lovely countryside. The house sat fairly high on Tynesdale Road commanding a view of the valley where clumps of houses were springing up in the development. Workmen were planting a poplar where earlier that year a bulldozer had destroyed a fine maple. "Anyway it's a long way off," he said speculatively. "Too many older men have been waiting for years. How do you make fifty couples?"

"Oh! Easily," she said, laughing. "I've cut to the bone, but I can't work miracles. We may have to go to a hundred. Thank God for this big house."

He was astonished. "That many?"

"You have become a big frog in a small pond," she said, smiling. "I've kept as many of your friends as possible, but it is a bread-and-butter list. Or isn't it?"

He rubbed his jaw with sudden gloom. "Guess so," he admitted. "We've got a lot of obligations, come to think."

"Can we possibly omit administration? I mean, assistant deans are so terribly sensitive. Then in our own department"—she ticked off on her fingers—"I'm not including anyone at the non-tenure level, and we're up to thirty. Right?"

"I suppose so."

"Suppose? Ah, I've counted heads down to the last man," she assured

19

him, "and their wives. By the way, we've got bachelor boys for the bachelor girls so that's no problem."

"If we throw a big party and we omit the younger guys I lunch with? How will they feel?"

She stared accusingly at the list. "But we simply won't have room. Won't they understand?"

"Maybe. Even so I feel funny."

"Suppose I throw another party for the younger crowd? What about Thanksgiving recess?"

There was too much gaiety for his liking. He was distressed at her tendency these days to rattle on almost with garrulity. Instinctively, he noticed, she had slipped a hand into her robe to rest on living flesh. "Take it easy, dear," he murmured. "It's just a party. Not the Mardi Gras."

She caught herself. "Oh? Yes, sorry!" She made a notation and came up squinting earnestly. "Tell me, what is Thanksgiving? Catholic or Protestant?"

"What? Neither." He almost laughed. "It's a national holiday."

"Ah? I have never quite understood. Ever since I came to this country I have wondered and I never thought to ask." He was not quite sure about a smile at the corners of her mouth. "We've got your family—"

He pulled down his glasses. "Did you get Papa to agree to come?"

She smiled cleverly. "I've been working on Nella, and she promises to deliver him, no matter what. Then there's the old bunch."

"Who does that include?"

"Ah? Well, the old crowd who were in on biocin. Leo Katz-Moebius and Joe Wodzick and those. Could we possibly leave them out? And Victor Ullman, naturally, and Sophie. She can drive Victor in from New London if her leg mends. They can stay with us overnight." Eva hesitated imperceptibly. "And Jo, if she can be persuaded to leave Florida. Then if Will Tewksbury is up to it—"

"Tewksbury?" he murmured. "I'm not sure."

Eva removed her spectacles, tortoise-shell harlequins which she used for reading. "Why not Will Tewksbury?" she demanded. "I don't see why you want to worry about Victor's feelings. You're not still in the man's shadow. Darling, when will you realize that you are Luzzatto?" Her voice had risen in appeal. He looked aside and shrugged.

"All right, Tewksbury."

"Good!" With a look of triumph she made a note, for an idealistic point had been scored. "Now you won't crab about this later?"

"No, it's a good idea," he said finally.

"Then that's the list!" she said decisively. She put her notes in a sta-

20

tionery box. "Thank God we can afford to live! Now you'd better get cracking. You're late to class."

Luzzatto arose to leave and paused at the door. "Um. Honey?"

"Yes?"

He took a breath and came to the decision he had reached in the early hours of the morning.

"How would you feel if I were to assign more of the biocin royalties to the university?" There, he felt, it was out! He sat waiting with a queer sense of the moment, as though something had been said which could not be retracted.

She stared at him sharply. "More royalties?"

"Yes."

"Why? Has anyone suggested that you should?"

"No."

"Then what brings this up?"

He shrugged. "It's something I've been thinking of. No one has said anything to me about it."

She lit a cigarette, deeply disturbed, and held the match fluttering. "Then I don't understand. You've given away over a million dollars already. How much is left to give?"

He smiled faintly. "Oh, enough."

Suddenly the cigarette was nothing. "What can I say, Davey? It's yours to give." She filled the dishpan and turned the tap and stared into the gush of steam. The pleasant mood had vanished.

"It affects us both," he said. "I wouldn't act without you."

He was appealing to her, she was quite aware, to make the decision for him, but she could not help. They had discussed the proposal many times before. She began to scrape dishes.

"I always understood that first gift," she said despondently. "After all, it was the right thing. It made the Center possible and I suppose you owed that much to the university, although there was no conception of how big it would turn out. But you can't keep this up, can you? How many more discoveries like biocin can you hope to make in your lifetime? Maybe none?"

"Maybe not," he agreed.

She studied the lean, intelligent face with its stubborn mouth.

"Davey! Why?" she asked quietly.

"I feel in a false position, Evvie," he said simply. "It was never my idea to make money out of science. There oughtn't be any profit factor at all, and here I'm making more than I can feel comfortable with. It's too much money."

21

"Oh, Davey," she said wearily.

He halted with rueful self-knowledge. "You think I'm a fool?"

"Not a fool," she said realistically. "A coward. Oh, in a nice way, I suppose. I simply wonder why you're so squeamish about this thing. How much have you decided to give away?"

She repeated the question and in the silence the doorbell rang and the moment was lost. Not till long after was he able to tell the answer then on his tongue. She said, "I'll get it."

Eva was always to remember that moment, and the view of Tynesdale Road, a pleasant street shaded with trees, alive with children going off to school. Tom Adderly, a shaggy instructor in physics, waved cheerfully as he drove past. She made a mental note to add the Adderlys to her guest list for the housewarming; Barbara Adderly was a quiet and energetic neighbor whose second pregnancy was advancing with her own and part of her mind was planning a joint first birthday party as she opened the door.

"You're looking mighty pretty this morning, Mrs. Luzzatto," said the postman. "Hope it's good news."

Luzzatto returned to the living room, hatless, briefcase in hand. He was mentally reviewing an opening witticism for the first lecture of the semester when he saw Eva returning from the doorway, frowning at a special delivery letter.

"For me?" he asked.

"I don't understand it." She was staring apprehensively at a creamy envelope. "Why wasn't it sent to your office? Why would they spend the postage?"

"Well, let's see," he responded.

The envelope bore the return address of the office of the president. The seal of the university, designed by public relations experts on Madison Avenue, was as traditional as ingenuity could devise.

There were two items.

A covering letter advised that the photostat enclosure had been received the previous day. Would Professor Luzzatto call for an appointment? The summons was icily and indifferently phrased. Luzzatto turned to the enclosure and a half-smile formed. "Some joker—" he began. A flush mounted, then color drained, leaving his sallow skin dirty gray.

"What is it, Davey?" asked Eva anxiously.

The enclosure was a copy of a letter addressed to Dr. James Fitzher-

22

bert Foxx as president of the Haverstraw Foundation, Inc. It was quite simple.

Dear Dr. Foxx:

I am writing in a personal vein so that my friendly concern for Haverstraw University and the Haverstraw Foundation, Inc. may not be misunderstood.

I have decided to rescind all rights which the university or which the foundation has purported to exercise with respect to the exploitation of biocin and which rights fully belong to me.

I give notice that I will not recognize the position in this matter which apparently has been usurped by one David Luzzatto whom I recall as a former student of mine.

I reserve all rights and will at the appropriate time demand an accounting of all monies and revenues received to date.

My kindest personal regards to Mrs. Foxx.

The letter was signed with the characteristic neat, precise lettering of Victor Frederick Ullman, Ph.D., Sc.D. The dateline was New London.

Chapter 2

USUALLY HE PICKED UP A RIDER OR TWO AT THE BUS STOP ON TYNES-dale Avenue—these informal car pools were a pleasant aspect of life in the university town—but today he felt a desperate need to be alone. Instead he decided to take the back road through the hills. He was driving at a fair speed, sunk in thought, when something brown crossed his line of vision.

The dog yelped.

"Oh, Christ!"

He jammed his brakes and sat trembling at the wheel. The heavy Mercury convertible had rolled the animal like a pat of wet clay under a sculptor's thumb. He felt sick and queasy. Then to his intense relief the howls of agony diminished and an undistinguished mild brown mongrel with white paws limped into the underbrush without a backward glance.

Luzzatto after some failure managed to light a cigarette.

What was he doing here? The road was quiet and no one was in sight. Blackberry bushes laden with ripe fruit nodded over the roadway; around the bend cowbells were clanking and he judged that a milch herd was jogging across the road to pasture. That would be Pacciardi's farm, he decided, a landmark from which he and Eva had wandered as students, sighting birds, collecting minerals, talking endlessly, mostly of himself and his ambitions in science. In the first touch of autumn, the hills were in flames.

It was fantastic, he told himself, utterly impossible that the morning's earlier events should have happened. Ullman had a heavy, almost perverted, sense of humor, he well knew, an awkward and cruel sense of

24

fun, and he was not above a practical joke. But even a bad joke would not allow that letter to the president of the university, not with the dedication of the Center only a few short weeks off.

Yet what was the answer?

With a shudder he drove on. The road dipped and climbed and then a rattletrap truck hauling a load of chickens to the great markets in New York was blocking his way. Impatiently he reduced speed and crawled in the lee of a foul barnyard smell. Bright gallinaceous eyes and soft anxious clucklings brought the thought that Eva's heart would have bled for the captives. Especially these days, he reflected, when her emotions were in precarious balance, and the sight would be too vivid a reminder of Poland to endure. On the last such occasion she had made this clear.

"I have no objection to quick death, Davey, I've seen too much of it, but I simply cannot stand suffering. The smell makes me sick."

The least thing set her off. At such times she paled and withdrew, passive and silent, behind a wall he dreaded and could not penetrate. She had taken Ullman's letter rather well, he thought, better than he would have expected, but how long could she hold the pose? In the first moment of incredulity, he recalled, she had sunk to a hassock in the living room where, hands crossed protectively over her burden, she had waited in silence, struggling to understand.

"Oh, God," she had whispered. "What a thing to happen."

They had talked for some time, trying to grasp the fact, and he had reacted with his deepest instincts as a scientist. In the way of the investigator, the raw fact could not be taken for granted. Never simple, it shimmered through opaque layers of illusive meanings, misleading in the extreme, a trap for the unwary. The difficulty was shock. In the first impact of the letter—reeking with malice, crashing into their world like a disaster among tenpins—his reactions were wholly cerebral. Later, perhaps, other reponses, more primitive, more adequate, would take over, but for the moment he strove desperately to grasp the event on its most meaningless level. His first thought, he realized, should have been for Eva.

"Evvie, please! You musn't," he had begged.

She looked up with an angered smile. "Oh, I'll be good," she promised tightly. "I'm concerned for you, Davey. I'm not sure this is really happening." She stared at the letter with hatred darkening her eyes. "Give me a cigarette."

"Yes. Oh, sure."

Cigarettes were in a small stinkwood box, a memento of a scientific congress in South Africa. She smoked hungrily, then flung back her head and looked up—and a certain graceful flair caught his heart. "About

25

that letter—" It was impossible, she burst out almost with incoherence, to accept. It must be returned at once. It could not remain in the house another moment. It—

"This is only a copy," he said.

"Oh? Yes, I see."

She caught herself in mid-flight. It was the original that held the capacity for mischief, she agreed; this was no time for nonsense. She managed a grim smile of compassion. "I'm not helping too much, I can see that, but my mind still won't function. It's so hard to grasp that Victor would do this to you."

"Of course you're a help," he protested.

"Am I?" she asked cynically.

She pressed her fingertips to her temples. "What does it mean, Davey?"

He turned the letter over for some hidden message. "I don't know. It's got to be some kind of mistake. That's all I can think."

For a brief moment their glances met before he turned away, taking the letter to the window. It was no good, he reflected; her insight at times was rather terrifying, far more penetrating than his own. She had no capacity for illusion. He added unconvincingly, "Or somebody's put him up to it. This isn't really his language."

"No one ever put Victor up to anything," Eva replied, shaking her head. She arose and began to pace the room. "This could only be his own idea."

A grandfather clock struck the hour.

She looked up with surprise. "My God! How long have we been talking? You've got a ten o'clock, Davey. Shouldn't you get started?"

"Yes, I suppose." He hesitated, biting his mouth with indecision. "I don't know if I should leave you."

She said quickly, "You can't be late for class."

"I'm not sure—" he worried.

With an effort she composed herself and crossed the room, still shaken. For a moment he expected an embrace but instead, with a firm tug, she straightened his tie. "I'm not a child," she reminded him. "Now! There, you look beautiful." She patted his chest lightly. "Poached sole tonight. I'll expect you for dinner."

"Are you sure it's all right?" he asked dubiously.

"I wish you wouldn't hover, Davey." Suddenly impatient, she returned to the fireplace and slipped hands inside quilted sleeves. She shivered violently. "I'll be perfectly all right and I'm better off alone. If I need company, I've always got Barbara next door. I'd rather have you find

26

out what this means. Anyhow," she added impulsively, "I've got to see the doctor today."

He looked up with surprise. "You didn't tell me that last night."

"I know," she agreed, biting her mouth.

"It's not Dottie Applegate?" he demanded. Dr. Applegate had been Eva's first obstetrician. Aside from her specialty, she plied a roaring trade among the modern young faculty women, fitting contraceptives and retailing premarital advice in a shabby mansion on the outskirts of town. He scowled at the recollection of a large room with medical certificates and a sour British West Indian nurse traipsing past with biological specimens for analysis. Even in retrospect a repellent case-hardened psychiatric lingo made his gorge rise. Dottie Applegate was an intense, wiry woman with lank hair, thyroid eyes, and—surprisingly—a brusque masculine cruelty which Eva held responsible for the loss of her baby. But that was another matter. "You're not going back to that abattoir?" he cried with alarm.

Eva threw back her head and laughed. "No, it's not Dottie. I'm in the hands of a good solid male obstetrician this time, darling. Don't trouble your head—you've got your own worries."

He paused suspiciously. "I've got to know about this. What doctor is that?"

"Well, Barbara finally got me to Sinclair Hawkins," she said, laughing with a trace of hysteria. "Sinful old man with the dirtiest jokes in town. I must say the examination was an experience, but at least he inspires confidence. Told me he saw no reason why I couldn't have this child. I meant to tell you tonight."

"Why not sooner?" he demanded.

"I thought I'd wait for the tests," she said, sobering under a scrutiny of intense concern. "I wanted to be sure he wasn't merely bolstering my morale after that callous line of deceit and indifference I got from Dottie. According to that woman, this baby shouldn't be happening at all. Hawkins promised to let me read the lab reports myself this afternoon. I was feeling so good," she added bitterly, "until this damn thing had to come along."

He liked this hectic air of banter even less than her first mood. She was being good so far, he reminded himself, but these days she was always on a fine edge. Well, the important thing was not to exaggerate the matter.

"Let me cut that class, Evvie," he urged. "I'm really in no mood to lecture. This whole thing has just hit me. It might be a good thing to stay home and think it through."

27

"Darling—" she began argumentatively and broke off as her glance fell on the portrait of Victor Ullman, affectionately inscribed, resting on her spinet. "Davey, would he cut?"

"I don't see the connection," said Luzzatto.

"Victor never cut a class in his life," she said. "I could kill him for this letter, but in your place he'd stand up in class and begin on the dot. You can't do less!" Her voice took on a sharp edge of anxiety. "You mustn't give him the satisfaction. Is that so hard to understand?"

"I'm not Victor Ullman," he muttered.

She studied the white, sensitive face. He was deeply upset, she saw, more disturbed than herself, but there was also something more than she understood. They exchanged stares in silence and suddenly the telephone rang.

"I'll get it," she said.

When she returned from the kitchen extension, Luzzatto was striding about the room. He paused at her entrance.

Eva said slowly. "That was Mrs. Haggerty. Foxx has called a meeting at twelve."

He was silent a moment, looking at the touch of autumn in the hills. "Twelve? I've got an appointment with this man from Tulane. Cunningham," he said slowly. "I'd rather not attend a meeting, not until I've got this thing clear in my mind."

She shook her head. "I told her you'd be on time."

"Why didn't you ask me first?"

"I assumed you'd put everything else aside." She paused. "They'll want to ask questions. You can't avoid that. Or are you afraid to face them?"

His eyes dropped. "Of course not. Oh, I suppose you're right," he conceded, and came back to the basic issue. "But I still don't see the picture. Victor can be funny sometimes—I don't have to tell you. Only last month we had the friendliest talk on the telephone. I thought I could spot him as the featured speaker at the dedication. I made it clear I'd pull every possible wire for him. I didn't hear any complaints at the time, just small talk about an experiment he's trying to persuade those people at Beltsville to undertake."

He studied the blaze of light on the window curtains. "If he's got some grievance, if something I've done or said is bothering him, if I've hurt his feelings, if it's some question of protocol—why didn't he write to me before sending this damned thing to Foxx?"

She had no answer. Her deep grave eyes followed him with a look at once careful and intent.

28

He shook his head ruefully. "Funny!"

"What is?"

"Oh!" He made a vague gesture. "The capacity for the irrelevant."

"What does that mean?"

"I was just thinking of Victor," he said, visualizing Ullman at the old-fashioned roll-top desk in his private laboratory. "Life follows a pattern," he intoned bitterly, mimicking the grave harsh voice, "mathematical in nature, and therefore it must work out." Rimless glasses were raised, eyes peered earnestly in imitation. "All events however small or remote have meaning. It is for us to decipher the sense."

"Oh, Davey," said Eva exhaustedly. "I'm fed up with all this Ullman-ismus. I don't think it's in the least appropriate."

"I suppose not," he said, and found himself staring at the flooring. After a moment, he looked up. "Evvie? Have you any idea what might have sparked this off?"

"No, I haven't," she said in a low voice.

"Could it be anything you said or did inadvertently? Is there anything I ought to know?"

She shook her head slowly. She could imagine nothing. She had not been in touch with Victor Ullman for several years and then on a matter of no consequence.

"What was that?"

"I endorsed a note for him for some money. Or perhaps it was a check. You were at that congress in Johannesburg, you recall? But that shouldn't have had this effect, should it?"

He stared with surprise. "You never told me."

"Of course I did," she said sharply. "While we were driving back from Idlewild."

"I completely forgot," he murmured.

She shrugged. "Anyway, it's not important."

"You're funny, Eva."

"Why?"

"You always do these things without consulting me. I wouldn't have minded helping Victor out but why did you have to assume a thing like that?"

"Does it matter now?" she wondered. "How could I have refused?"

"No. Well—" He did not like the dangerous look of rising anxiety in her face. It was no time for this sort of thing and he went on. "What about Sophie?"

"I haven't talked to her for years. Just a few letters."

"And Jo?"

29

"Just a post card from Florida. Let's see, it was Easter."

"Have we neglected them in any way?"

"Not that I know, Davey."

"Then what?" he wondered helplessly. "Could some sneak have put something in his mind? A poison pen letter or anything on that line?"

"It's possible. I don't know," she said.

He rubbed his neck with despair. "Evvie, why wouldn't he contact me first? There's not a thing we couldn't straighten out between us if we just had a chance to talk. He's never before hesitated to bawl the hell out of me. All he had to do was to pick up the telephone. It's not even as though he didn't know the number by heart."

"Perhaps he didn't dare to call," she suggested.

He looked up. "Not dare?"

"If he let you talk to him for five minutes, it would have become an impossible thing."

"That sounds ridiculous," he observed after a pause.

"Why so?"

"Because he knows this letter is a lie!" he muttered.

"All the more reason," she said. "I think that's the whole point. He can't face you."

"No. That's not like Victor," he replied doggedly.

He paused to consider a difficult problem. "I could call him to find out," he suggested.

"Davey! You can't!" she cried aghast.

"Well, I've got to know what's on his mind. I can't just accept this. If there's any possible explanation, I'd rather get it now before this thing gets out of hand."

She stared with anxiety. "Davey, listen to me. You can't possibly make such a telephone call in the face of this letter. You're no longer a student and you can't afford to make a mistake. How long will it take you to see through Victor Ullman? What must he do before you take a position? Don't you see that the relationship changed a long time ago?"

"You're not thinking," he said abruptly.

She drew a breath. "I'm not so sure this requires thinking. It calls for something else, Davey. An instinct for survival, a protective sense that includes us both."

"That's not fair!"

They exchanged looks of deepest anger. She strove for control and then as she searched the pale troubled face, she turned to the spinet and tore the picture from its frame.

"If you want to, call Victor," she said in a shaking voice, "I can't

30

tell you what to do, but it'll be a terrible mistake. In the meantime," she cried passionately, "take this picture out of our house. The man's trying to destroy you. Don't you see that?"

They remained staring and every detail of the room seemed clearer than reality. His eye was attracted to an ornamental rifle over the hearth with its muzzle pointed at a rack of copper utensils. It had once been a good weapon, fashioned by gunmakers who had taken pains to keep lines clean, butt thin, trigger guard graceful, decorations refined. It was now useless, a collector's piece and quite expensive. It seemed to typify all the things collected by Eva to decorate their home. It was not his idea surely; it was a present, unsolicited, bought by her, like everything else, with a lavish hand. My God! he thought irrelevantly. How much *had* the house cost? Now why did that seem to have a bearing? He could not face the anger and dry fear glistening suddenly in her eyes and he looked away.

"Why would he want to do a thing like that?" he muttered, tasting incredulity. "Destroy me?"

"Why else did he send that letter?"

Again the clock sounded its deep tone. He blew out his breath dejectedly and knew their talk was at an end.

In looking back, he could have wished for more anger against Ullman, more resentment in himself. It might have been better for Eva, he thought, a sounder basis for the hours to come, but in all honesty the fact, disappointingly, was simple enough. In the moment of crisis he felt nothing but dim wonder and bewilderment.

That and utter desolation.

His shoulders sagged and he asked her to see him to the car. Perhaps anger would come in its own time.

"Of course," she said tightly.

She picked up his briefcase and slipped her arm in his and walked him out to the garage. Above them a maple cast its shade and they embraced.

"Oh, Davey," she whispered. "I love you. I'm always with you."

He kissed her hungrily and the smell of her loose hair was fresh. "Don't be afraid, dearest," he said urgently. "It's nothing I can't straighten out. You'll be good?"

Her hands on his neck were cold.

"Biocin is yours, Davey," she said starkly. "Remember that. It belongs to no one else. No one! Will you keep that clear? And you'll let me know what happens?"

As he drove off into the highway, her smile followed and when he was out of sight, she turned back to the house, scuffing the gravel path at her

31

feet. Her step was thoughtful and slow as she seemed to hug her breasts for comfort. In the living room, cigarette smoke was still swirling, acrid in smell, escaping in tendrils in the hearth.

The room suddenly seemed less colorful, less splendid. As her eyes traversed its details, picking out ornaments and pieces painfully gathered, it was suddenly small, meager, empty of her young husband's presence. She thought of him affectionately with twisted pride in his far-ranging, speculative mind—that, and a growing fear. It was not fair, she cried, clenching her fists, it was not deserved.

Work, she decided, that was the thing.

The breakfast plates in the kitchen were cold and eggy, disagreeable to the touch, but the gush of steam was welcome. When she lowered her hands into a scum of soap powder, the scalding pain was a blessed interruption. Her morning sickness, a faint haunting nausea, seemed to subside and she was left with the reminder of the coming child.

With an effort of will she picked up a sponge and began to wash the dishes.

The road widened and Luzzatto pulled ahead of the chicken truck with a rattle of gravel and he came at last into view of East Haverstraw. Down below the road along the railroad tracks led him to his destination—the sickly green rooftops of Haverstraw University.

Chapter 3

LUZZATTO PARKED THE HEAVY CONVERTIBLE IN AN AREA RESERVED FOR faculty on Renfrew Street. Chapel bells were tolling and from all directions students were strolling into the university grounds. He locked the ignition and hastened along.

Mackenzie Hall stood on a quadrangle formed with St. Paul's, a romanesque chapel proud of its windows by Maitland Strong and native woods carved by Coppede; Philosophy Hall, its twin in decrepitude, and Davenport Library with its concrete dome and the largest collection of books in Merton County. Lost in shabbiness, Mackenzie Hall gazed apologetically across a thin patch of lawn.

"Hop in, sir." Danny Foy, the elevator man, was unusually cheerful. "Lots of room in the back."

Luzzatto followed a crowd into the elevator and stood to the side, head and shoulders above the jam, abstracted and still shaken, barely aware of a pretty girl whose hair was exuding a delightful washed smell. On this first day, the women were sly and observant with anticipation; there was joviality among the men; before him was the familiar view of a reddish head with out-sticking ears and sun-baked neck.

Foy demanded, "D'ye think it'll rain, Professor?"

Luzzatto came out of his thoughts with an effort.

"I do not," he said curtly.

Foy looked startled. "Why not?"

With suppressed annoyance, Luzzatto went through an expected ritual, and pointed out reasons in the same meteorological exchange which had greeted him every day since his first arrival at Mackenzie Hall.

33

The door opened on the third floor and he followed the surge of students who immediately dispersed to their classes, chatting and laughing. At the familiar sight, he paused to get his bearings. A long, dim hall filled with zoological exhibits was alive with morning activity. With a nervous sigh, he turned to the offices of Professor Alfred Tobiansky, secretary of the graduate faculty of pure sciences, where a neat, middle-aged woman was involved in a task remembered from that first day.

"Oh, Dave! How nice!" said Mrs. Renée Nakamura, looking up with a cheerful face from a vase of flowers. "Did you have a good summer? Everyone's come back full of tan and high accomplishment."

"Oh. It was all right," said Luzzatto abruptly. "Is your boss in yet, Renée?"

"Him? Gosh, no. He'll drift in at ten. Would you like to leave a message?" She patted the colorful mass and stood back with a critical eye.

Luzzatto said, "Is there any news around?"

Mrs. Nakamura glanced up at the odd tone. "News? No. Should there be? What did you have in mind?"

"Nothing special," he said uncomfortably.

He was still at the door when she had finished the task to her satisfaction. She said, "Will we have you at cocktails next Thursday? I just tacked a notice on the bulletin board." She set the vase at the window and called his attention to a card posted by the door. Professor Alfred Tobiansky and Mrs. Elena Tobiansky would serve cocktails at home in honor of Dr. Gustav van Plattin of the Institut Karolinska of Stockholm the following week. Faculty and graduate students were invited. Dr. van Plattin would discuss recent observations made in Stockholm on structure and functions of something called mitochondria—

"Wives are invited," said Mrs. Nakamura, flashing her teeth attractively. She was a tiny thing in a gray sweater, friendly to the rising young professor and mindful that she had been his first acquaintance in the university. She ran an informal canteen from her office, complete with water cooler stocked with cokes and chocolate milks and sandwiches, which featured a dating bureau on the side. In earlier years, while Luzzatto was still a student, she had confided something of Nisei difficulties raising children in the hostile war years and the warm feeling remained. "Mrs. Luzzatto would love it. Oh, by the way,"—her voice dropped sympathetically—"how is she?"

"Oh, fine, fine," he said vaguely.

"Good thoughts?"

"Sure!"

Evidently the grapevine had the story. It struck him, peering at the announcement, that no love was ever lost between Alfred Tobiansky and Victor Ullman. Now what had that been about? Some spat between their wives? Renée Nakamura might know, he reflected, and suppressed an impulse to ask the origins of a feud lost in the mists of departmental prehistory. It was an item, he thought grimly, to file away for future reference. "Mitochondria?" he murmured in a wave of unwonted boredom.

"We'll try to get there," he promised aloud. "Mrs. Luzzatto doesn't get out much these days, you know."

"Oh, I know, I know," Mrs. Nakamura replied sympathetically. The dedication of the Center, she thought, would, however, be even more splendid; she had every hope that Eva, Mrs. Luzzatto, would be fit for the occasion. Acceptances were pouring in, it would be a day to remember.

"Um. Yes," he said uncomfortably in the torrent of good will. "Do-so," he added in Japanese.

"Do-so," she replied, smiling.

With a brisk air, she turned back to work. The rest of the notices caught his eye. A baby sitter service was recruiting personnel. The Co-op offered to buy, sell and exchange textbooks. Candidates for Ph.D. degrees were reminded that doctoral dissertations were to be filed three weeks prior to oral examinations the last week in November. The announcement was signed by Dr. Henry Polk, dean of the graduate faculties.

A deep voice broke in. "Think Hubbard can make the run in November, Dave?"

"Hello, Bronco," said Luzzatto, looking up abstractedly. Bronco Joe Wodzick was one of the refreshing features of the building—a placid blond giant in worsteds, bucking for a full professorship in biometrics. Unluckily, a thrice-broken nose, sacrificed in football days, a humorous tongue, and a realistic eye of disenchantment were less than helpful in the murderous game of faculty politics at Haverstraw. The two men shook hands warmly and Luzzatto managed a smile as they caught up after the summer's vacation. "What have you got against poor Hubbard?"

"Nothing, nothing," said Wodzick equably. "I don't think the man can make it. I got a look at his dissertation. Horrible!" He wiped a finger across his throat.

Luzzatto was torn by impatience to get on to his office, but the problem of Hubbard might conceivably cross his desk, and he was automatically interested. Erskine Hubbard was a graduate student from somewhere in the Ozarks, a raw-boned dullard toiling at forty for a doctorate which should have been earned at thirty. How his application

35

had been accepted at Haverstraw was something of a mystery. Luzzatto frowned. "I heard he was coming along nicely."

"Propaganda, Dave," said Wodzick. "Someone's trying to create a favorable climate of opinion for the poor bastard." He went on to describe a doctoral thesis of six hundred pages. *The Topology of Cultural Dynamics*. It was a real bitch, he drawled, but prolixity was not the main offense. In their time, they too had jacked through equally slovenly jobs, and they could both name names. But this? It was the worst flatus yet.

"Dave, listen to Wodzick," he said. "We're headed for trouble. We can't let the jerk get to that exam. On the basis of that manuscript he'll be slaughtered."

Luzzatto looked up with surprise. "Isn't that his lookout?"

Wodzick waited for a group of women students to pass. His friend, he observed, was not thinking of the human factor. Everyone knew Hubbard's marital situation. Surely Luzzatto recalled a bony little woman with an infant in arms and another in the oven? No? It was the old grim struggle to qualify for better than a starvation future. How could anyone with feelings deny the man his degree—passport to a decent living in the academic world. The dilemma was real, said Wodzick.

"I don't see the problem." Luzzatto found the discussion suddenly oppressive. "The schools are filled with guys like Hubbard. How have we got a choice? Either we set a standard, Bronco, and stick with it, or we don't."

Wodzick studied his pipe meditatively. "Oh, sure, I'm all for that," he said calmly, "and that's why the guy ought to be stopped now. Once he gets to the defense of that thesis, the pressure to jack him through will get terrific. Who's going to cut the guy's throat? Me? You? Can we hold the line? It's not fair to put us in that spot, Dave. Why let it get that far?"

"I thought you were for this man?"

"I have two minds," Wodzick grinned, stretching his muscles. "If we fake the guy out, it's a disaster for the rest of his life. Why impose that on the family unit? On the other hand, I'm tired of watching everybody else's pet getting out on the market with our stamp of approval on his rump—just because no one's got the guts to vote him down. Or to cross the sponsor," he added wickedly. "It makes a bad impression for the rest of us, Dave. Lowers those standards of yours. I'm surprised you don't agree."

Luzzatto was bored and annoyed. His own problem was gnawing and he was tempted to confide about the letter from Ullman, but a voice of caution within stopped his mouth. Aloud he said, "What's your angle, Bronco?"

36

Wodzick laughed. "Dave, I think you ought to take this up with Lizzie Batchelor. She ought to kill the thesis now. Sidetrack the deal in her own interests."

"Is she sponsoring this man personally?" asked Luzzatto sharply.

Wodzick tamped his pipe, puffing thoughtfully. "Very much so," he said.

"Um!" said Luzzatto. Here was an awkward problem in human and faculty relationships. The formidable Elizabeth Batchelor, author of *Sexuality in Micronesia, Prostitution Sacred and Profane, A Comparative Approach to Kinsey,* and other best sellers, was head of the Department of Psychology and a woman of dimensions with pipelines of influence into the board of trustees.

"I wouldn't like to make a campaign against the guy," said Wodzick, growing serious. "I think it's entirely Lizzie's fault. The poor son of a bitch is so easily dominated, I think she's led him astray for some purpose of her own. Otherwise how could he pile up all of this crap? Lizzie's shrewd!" he added meaningfully. "So what's her game with this guinea pig? Personally, I think she's trying to snag him for that girl friend of hers, Helen Montgomery."

Luzzatto laughed uncertainly, not quite sure how to take this extravagance. Helen Montgomery, who taught group psychology in Lizzie Batchelor's department, seemed a plain enough biddy of a schoolteacher. "Bronco, you're wild!"

Wodzick pulled down an eyelid. "Listen to Wodzick, Dave. Five gets you ten Cynthia Hubbard gets booted back to the Ozarks, and Montgomery winds up with a wedding ring. Someday I'll tell you about Lizzie."

Luzzatto glanced at the clock. He said irritably, "Let Hubbard take his chances with the committee. Wouldn't that be the cleanest way out of his misery?"

"Oh, oh!" said Wodzick warningly.

The elevator had opened and a fresh load of passengers had emerged with Professor Elizabeth Batchelor in the fore, thrusting forward like the prow of a windjammer. She was one of those small, resolute women who give the impression of size by combining resonance of voice with the weight of enormous breasts. She was laughing heartily, amused by an anthropological jest. Professor Helen Montgomery, a willowy blond woman, was listening with a submissive smile. Both women were tanned.

"Lizzie—Helen." Wodzick grinned. "Have a good summer?"

"Fair." Lizzie flashed a glance of suspicion at the men. They shook hands and chatted briefly. It appeared that the women had spent three months in Greece in the study of local mores, from fly-infested slit-trench

37

privies to courting customs of the peasantry. On their return, they were chagrined to learn that plans for a major paper had been forestalled by *The Greek Village,* a work to be published by a Fulbright husband-and-wife team of scholars. Lizzie concentrated with intensity on the Luzzattos and their summer at Bimini Island. "How's Eva coming?" she demanded heartily. "Feeling well?"

"Oh, yes, Lizzie, she's fine," Luzzatto replied vaguely.

"Wonderful, wonderful!" sang the hoarse contralto throatily. "Charming woman, Eva. Ought to see each other more this year. Give her my best. When's the baby due?"

"Oh, April," he said uncomfortably. "Or May."

Lizzie trained her guns on Wodzick. "On a question of common decency, Professor?" she said poisonously.

"Yes, Lizzie?" Wodzick grinned.

Her breasts swelled aggressively. "Professor, I've been getting some nasty rumors about your attitude to Erskine Hubbard's thesis. I hope they're not true, because I'd hate to believe that any colleague would be destructive and unfair to my candidate."

Wodzick returned the woman's stare. "Lizzie, you know that Hubbard's thesis is a total mess. What made you approve it?"

"That's for me to judge," she said evenly. "Erskine's not brilliant, but he's qualified, as much as any candidate you ever sponsored. I expect him to do well."

"I'd think twice if I were you, Lizzie."

"What do you mean?" she asked.

Wodzick said, "Because it may not work. If you're not careful, it's likely to wind up in embarrassment for you and the candidate, or for the committee. You can do as you please," he added with annoyance.

Helen Montgomery had been smiling at the floor, demure, little interested. She murmured, "Lizzie, we'll be late."

"In a minute, dear," Lizzie said fondly, then stared speculatively at the men. "We're all vulnerable," she remarked cryptically. "Come, dear." She flashed dislike at Wodzick, smiled at Luzzatto, linked arms with the other woman, and strode off on military heels to her office.

"And you want me to bell that cat, Bronco?" said Luzzatto.

"Yes."

"Why me?"

Wodzick laughed. "You're the only man who carries weight with Lizzie. She'll listen because you talk the language. Power. With the Center looming, there's not a man or woman in this shop who isn't looking for some bone you might want to toss his or her way. What else?"

"Is that how people feel about me?" asked Luzzatto queerly, taken aback by a sudden unpleasant image of himself as seen by others.

"Haven't you noticed significant silences when you enter rooms?" asked Wodzick.

"I'm not sure I like that," said Luzzatto sharply.

"What else do you want?" asked Wodzick patiently. "Jealousy's a fundamental part of human nature, an evolutionary factor of survival value. Lizzie might hate your guts, but if you'll scratch her back, she'll scratch yours. You're a biologist. What do you expect from human nature?"

"Oh, don't ask me," said Luzzatto in a troubled voice. "I don't know any more. I doubt if I ever did."

Wodzick stared with closer attention. "Dave? Is something wrong?"

Luzzatto hesitated, watching the busy morning scene with a gloomy sense of unreality. Little had changed, he reflected, in the eight years since his arrival as a student at Mackenzie Hall, except that walls seemed shabbier, exhibits dustier, competition fiercer, students cockier, and the void left behind by Victor Ullman deeper than ever. The morning's events were still difficult to grasp.

"Nothing at all," he said.

It was remarkable, he thought, how his instincts had become adapted to danger—how quickly and how unpleasantly. "I've got something waiting at my office." Abruptly he left for the sanctuary of his desk in the old wing.

Wodzick followed the departure with a thoughtful expression. "Renée," he said, stalking into Mrs. Nakamura's office and flopping his great frame into a chair, "what's biting Dave this fine morning? After a romantic and expensive summer at Bimini? Is he being crossed in love?"

Mrs. Nakamura looked up, most impassive, most Japanese. "I have no idea, Joseph," she said politely.

Luzzatto had a way of stalking about the laboratory, muttering with vexation. He strode about in the security of familiar walls, surrounded by physical things of which he was master, until finally a measure of unreality drained off.

He wondered frozenly what to do next. It would be a serious mistake to call Victor Ullman. It was precisely what he had promised Eva not to do. The important thing, he reminded himself, was not to betray the impact of the shock he had received.

There was a light spinsterish tap on frosted glass and Freda Stahl peered in crossly. "Good morning, Professor." The upstate rr's came rolling through a grinder. "Will you want me na-ow?"

"Oh? What?" He looked up. "All right, Freda," he said heavily. "You can come in." She trotted in, starched and spectacled and smelling of peppermint. She placed her back to the protective wall, flopped a notebook on her knee, and began in a nasal busy-busy voice to run through the morning routine.

He strode about restlessly. This had been the inner office of Ullman's private laboratory. By craning his neck he could see a mousehole behind the radiator—a tribute to the ingenuity, persistence and fortitude of the mouse population of Mackenzie Hall. Morally they owed much to Eva, for in the past they had fed on her bounty, since one of the room's charms lay in the opportunity to lock its doors for surreptitious lunches and midnight suppers. Eva's excuse in the early days for breaking in on his work had always been simply stated—she wanted to! She had never acquired any taste for the social activity of the university and reading and music had their limits. In those first years, she had managed regularly to break in on him, bearing gifts of moist, pungent Italian bread, ripe olives and strong cheeses with oranges for drink and dessert. It had become a ritual between them, recognized and accepted by his fellows. The food was something he had introduced; it was a habit rooted in the poor days before the biocin discoveries. It recalled that period of his life when he had first begun to visit his father's editorial offices in Broome Street. He had a vision suddenly of a dim room smelling of hot metal and printer's ink; in those days—he was perhaps ten—he was repelled by the food his father ate, the tearing of chunks of bread with his workmen, the noisy chewing of olives in the banter of the shop. "Papa, that's for poor people," he had complained. The twinkling eyes had shrewdly measured his distaste. "Davido, Davido," his father had laughed, shaking with amusement. "You skinny shrimp, you don't know how to eat. The best thing in the world is the food of peasants. Open the mouth. Here!" Well, thought Luzzatto, rousing himself, his sensibilities as a child had gagged on coarse food and boisterous manners, but in time he had come to adopt them both. Now why, he wondered, had his thoughts gone back to his father's old office? He looked up and saw that Freda had paused inquiringly.

"Sorry," he muttered, taking his chair. "Go on."

She stared at him sharply and continued. Something about a microbiologist from Ohio State looking for a job. Undergraduates trying to line up appointments. Form D was still unfinished. Vouchers for laboratory animals needed signing. Requisitions for supplies. Paper promised for the *Journal of Immunology*. Committee meetings.

40

He frowned. "Damn it, Freda, can't we buy a paper cup without calling for a vote? What was that last one?"

She paused with surprise. His deep voice had its usual pleasant masculine timbre, but there were gray patches in the flat sallow cheeks. She raised her brows and flipped back a page. Joint Committee on Graduate Instruction. Four o'clock. He pulled down his mouth in a grimace. "Oh, that! Guess there's no way out of that one!"

"No, Professor."

Freda bent her head to make a notation, showing a fuzz of blond hairs on her neck. He eyed her dubiously and began a cigarette, goaded by suppressed irritation. He liked Freda Stahl well enough but she was not always easy to take. There emanated from the crosspatch little woman a mephitic though faint menstrual odor like that of a piano teacher he had learned to hate at the age of six. He was too fair-minded or too modern to allow a mere childhood association to condemn a diligent office worker, especially one with a form of tenure almost equal to his own, but the sad fact was that in a closed room Freda could be insufferable. Fortunately the windows now were open to the warm winds of Indian summer. No, he decided grimly, it was not Freda who disturbed him—it was this other thing in his mind. He struck the match again twice, broke off its head and threw aside the stick of wood. "Freda?"

"Yes?"

He tried to smile. "Don't hate me for this, but could you get me out of all that goop?"

She put down her book. "Professor, aren't you feeling well? Would you like an aspirin?"

"No, no, no!" he said. "I'm all right, but— It's just that—" He paused. "Well, go on."

She sniffed with disapproval. "It doesn't make a good impression," she observed acidly and marked a notation. Edwin Cunningham, a prospective graduate student, was in the outer office.

"That man from Tulane? So early?" Luzzatto unbent with sudden interest. "Oh, well? He had a terrific record at Berkeley before he went down to New Orleans. Oh, sure! If we get him for the Center, it'd be a real feather in our cap. Cunningham! I'd trade him any time for the best three psychologists we've got." He drummed the desk in indecision. "I've just got time to say hello. I'll see him later."

She reminded him of his ten o'clock class and gathered her notes and trotted off pigeon-toed, but almost as she reached the door he called her back. "Could you give me another moment?"

"You haven't much time," she reminded him crossly.

41

"Please—"

How far, he wondered, could he go with Freda Stahl? What really did he know of her? Little enough, he supposed. She was an ordinary diligent little woman with no great skill or competence outside her own groove. She kept a parakeet and a television set and her own counsel and professed a set of religious beliefs he could not fathom, and she seemed to have organized the emotional structure of her life around a fussy dread of rape creeping up from the rear. It was not much to go by. He paused uncomfortably, thinking that what he had in mind was wrong, wrong! He had no business opening up to Freda, or to anyone else for that matter, at least not yet. So much had been agreed upon with Eva before he had left home, but still he felt the need of reassurance.

He said abruptly, "Freda, there's something I ought to tell you." He told her about the letter.

She listened intently and she took it, he thought, rather quietly. She resumed her seat and darted a quick glance at him and averted her eyes. "Oh, dear," she muttered. "This is dreadful!"

"It's not too pleasant," he conceded. "But since you're bound to hear of it, I wouldn't want you to be the last to know." He managed a false smile although in truth he felt acutely embarrassed. "Freda, has any talk been going around?"

Freda looked startled. "Talk?"

He made a vague gesture. "Gossip! You know, powder-room stuff. Have you heard rumors of, any, well, differences, let's say, between me and Dr. Ullman?" In the tightly pressed mouth he read nothing.

She shifted uneasily. There was always malicious talk, she said slowly, especially since Dr. Ullman had, well, left the university so abruptly. It was only natural since the place was a hotbed of jealousy and spite, quite unlike any other establishment in the world—but specifically? No, nothing like this—at least nothing she had heard.

"I can't tell you how badly I feel," Luzzatto said, "but there's something else I ought to know. Freda, will you feel at all embarrassed to keep on here with me? Because if you do, I'll quite understand."

"Embarrassed?" she exclaimed nervously. "Why should I be?"

"You were with Dr. Ullman a long time. Wouldn't it be natural not to want to be caught in the middle of a quarrel?"

"Me?" Her mouth dropped at the appalling thought. "Really, Professor! It's none of my business."

He said reasonably, "I've got to do something about this situation, you see, and I may need your support. I simply want to know how you feel."

Freda arose in agitation. "Professor, I'll do anything of course, but I

42

don't see how I can help." She faced him worriedly. "I'd rather not become involved. I—I— Now I've really got a lot of work to do!" Patches of red were flaming in her cheeks, he noticed. Her blood pressure had shot up, he guessed, twenty points. She scurried for the door and there paused with her mouth open.

"Will this mean a scandal?"

"I don't know, Freda," he said uncertainly. "I hope not. It's the last thing Dr. Ullman should want. I'm quite sure all this is a mistake." Strangely enough, although her question was practical as a paper clip, this obvious aspect had not yet struck him with any force. "You will keep this in confidence?"

She drew herself up primly. "I should hope so."

Luzzatto twisted his mouth in a forced smile. "Because when he has a chance to reflect, he'll certainly want to retract that letter."

She stood for the moment breathing noisily. "It's not for me to say this, but are you sure?"

"Oh, yes! Oh, yes!" he said with conviction.

She glanced up with an odd expression. "This isn't like Dr. Ullman," she said slowly. "He'd never have sent that letter unless he thought he was in the right."

Luzzatto touched his glasses. "Did you ever know him to be in the wrong?" he asked grimly.

There was no answer.

He smiled bleakly and let his hand slide over the huge oak roll-top desk at which he was seated. It was a monster of a prior era with a dozen pigeonholes and a brass plate showing its manufacture in Hamburg early in the century. When he had moved into this laboratory he had inherited this chattel from Ullman, some of whose effects were still strewn about a room occupied for twenty years. It was strange, he mused, how that man's shadow still lay over the room.

"Okay, Freda," he said. "Send Mr. Cunningham in now. Perhaps he'll want to audit the lecture before we talk."

"Yes, Professor," she said with relief.

"No, wait!" he exclaimed. "Before I do anything else, I'd like you to put a call through to New London."

The staccato musical tones sang as the East Haverstraw operator dialed. A bell rang twice and a woman's voice with a cool flavor answered. "Yes?"

The operator asked, "Is this New London 1342? East Haverstraw, New York, calling Dr. Victor Ullman. Is Dr. Ullman there?"

43

"Who is calling him?" The voice was uncommitted.

Luzzatto cut in. "Sophie? This is Dave Luzzatto."

"Oh, yes? How are you, Dave?"

It was a modulated voice without curiosity and accented with good breeding. It betrayed neither surprise nor pleasure and it had that hushed remoteness he had always associated with the frail, rather chalky woman.

"Is your leg better?" he asked, louder than necessary.

She answered precisely, "It will take another few weeks. I never expect to leave this wretched bed. But as long as I can read I am not uncomfortable. Did you call about something special?"

Luzzatto hesitated. "I thought you might like to know, Sophie. Eva's pregnant again."

"Is she? I'm so glad for her."

"Yes. She's quite hopeful this time."

But there it stood. Sophie Ullman waited passively without comment for his next move. He wondered what perverse impulse had gotten him off into this area. It was wrong to strike a note of weakness. He said, "Is Victor there? I'd like to talk to him."

"No, Dave. I'm afraid not. Is there a message?"

"Do you know where to reach him?"

"I'm sorry. No."

"Shall I call again later?"

He heard her say aside, "No, dear, put the pillow higher. Thank you." She returned to the telephone. "Dave? I really don't know if it would help. I've got no idea when he might come home."

"Sophie?"

"Yes?"

"Last Friday Victor sent a letter to Dr. Foxx. Do you have any idea what that was about?"

"No, Dave," she said finally. "I don't."

Her voice was queerly reserved, he felt, quite unconvincing and nervous. Now how, he wondered, did one handle this sort of thing? Of course she would feign ignorance. His business was properly with her husband.

The corridor gong sounded a warning. He wondered whether the sound might carry to Sophie Ullman in New London. What was she thinking?

"That letter was about me," he said slowly.

"Oh?"

"Didn't Victor tell you what he wrote?"

"No-o?"

How oddly she made everything sound like a question, he thought. He had an impulse to hang up but reconsidered. Beneath the surface he sensed a new element. Discomfort? Guilt? In the background he heard a familiar cough. He said, "Yes. About me, and he wrote some shocking things. Frankly, I feel quite angry, Sophie. If it were anyone else, I wouldn't be making this call. But I thought if I could talk to him directly—" He paused.

"I'm sorry I can't help you," she said.

"Are you sure? Hello? Are you on the line?"

"Yes. I'm listening."

"I had the impression you put your hand over the telephone."

"No."

"I wish you'd tell Victor for me that he's making a serious mistake—"

Her voice came back again, cool and withdrawn. "If it's some business between you," she said softly, "you'll have to take it up with him. I really don't know what else to tell you."

"Will you give him a message? I called to tell Victor I'm expecting to see Dr. Foxx later today. I'd like—" He paused. "I imagine Foxx wants an explanation. I mean, a thing like this? Well, it's so incredible. What can I tell him?"

"I don't think I should be talking about this," she said slowly.

He interrupted. "Sophie, you've got to talk to Victor. You're the only one who can. I want to be able to tell Foxx that the whole thing is a misunderstanding. I want a promise that a letter of retraction will go out today. Can you do that much?"

She said crisply, "I don't see how I could possibly."

"Really that's not good enough," he protested, shifting his grip. "A thing like this can get ugly."

"I'll tell Victor you called," she said firmly. "That's all I can say."

"Is anything wrong with Victor?"

"Why do you ask?"

He found his voice suddenly rising. "Why is he afraid to talk to me? Because I'd like you to know one thing, Sophie. I'm sure he's in the room there with you. I don't believe a word you've said. I don't deserve this from you!"

The cool modulated voice hesitated. "I'll deliver your message. Thank you. Goodbye."

He was left staring at an empty telephone. There was a burst of static and the operator cut in to remind him that he was no longer connected.

Slightly delayed, chapel bells reverberated for his first lecture of the semester—a reminder of the disciplines of the larger organism of which he was part.

"Oh, my God," he whispered. "What did I step into?"

45

Chapter 4

Si Podell clamped his teeth on a cold cigar and swiveled about with a sense of satisfaction. He had been drafting the new edition of the Haverstraw *Bulletin* to appear in dashing crimson and gold with a profusion of photographs. He was pleased with the job; it was dignified, catchy, subtly academic.

With some disquiet, he glanced at the clock and sat back, patting his thigh. His desk was shabby oak littered with newspaper clippings and pencil stubs; a decrepit Woodstock waited at his elbow. It was a writing instrument he had dismantled and repaired many times in an inverted form of snobbery all his own. Faced by the new order at Haverstraw, he clung with pride to his origins in the liquor industry in the depths of the depression. In an institution striving for the hush and polish of richer, older rivals, it pleased him to keep to older ways. His office had less grace than a prizefighter's dressing room. A spittoon was his gonfalon. He shifted the cigar and addressed his secretary.

"Let's hear what it sounds like, Letty," he grunted.

Letty Rodgers, who had spent many years as an actress, read back the copy expressively. " . . . low student-faculty ratio . . . potential . . . superior intellectual climate . . . areas of study . . . in terms of maturation . . . rapidly changing world . . . percentile . . . methodological . . . societal values . . . goals . . . frames of reference . . . integrity of learning . . . exploration of truth to innermost . . . the whole man . . . unyielding in face of contemporary . . . permanent human values which . . . significant in terms of . . . dynamics . . . traditions . . . beauty . . . the Ideal . . . "

Podell listened with pleasure and lit the cigar. After some things he had done for a living, this was only too elementary. The ease with which he tossed off the borrowed academic jargon tickled his sense of craftsmanship.

He glanced at his secretary humorously. "Like it?"

"Love it!" breathed Letty.

Podell turned and stared through the window at a lone runner practicing sprints on a cinder track in South Field. Suddenly he sat up. Hastening across the Green in a rumpled gray suit was young Luzzatto; bareheaded, unkempt, self-absorbed. A woman student paced him for a distance, talking earnestly, but the professorial figure shrugged and she dropped back. Podell arose and for a heavy-set man of large girth moved with remarkable speed.

Luzzatto looked up to find his path blocked.

"Well, Professor!" growled Podell. "What took so long? Did one of those Burland cuties get you in a closet? Or didn't you think it's important to get here on time?"

"Pardon," a young voice interrupted.

They stood aside as a group of students passed with curious glances. Oleander bushes flanked the stone flagging of the steps. A new beech cast its shade on a doric porch coming to life behind a facade of scaffolding. Cut into the stone lintel was the building's new name: STROLLO HALL.

"Please, Si," said Luzzatto anxiously. "I'm due to see Foxx. I'm late now."

"I know all about it," said Podell. "Come on."

Peremptorily, he grasped the younger man's arm. Strollo Hall was still incomplete; some of its features, especially a new south wing, were in the process of building; the smell of wet cement hung heavy in the central hall. Plasterers were at work on marble stairs where an arrow pointed to the Office of the President. They walked on in silence.

Podell said, "You were due here for twelve sharp. Your lecture broke at eleven. You spent an hour up at the Center. Was that smart?"

Luzzatto explained seriously that he had been showing off the Center to a prospective graduate student.

Podell stared. "That's more important than your appointment with Foxx?"

Luzzatto guiltily adjusted his glasses. "I hope I haven't pulled anything, Si, but this applicant, Ed Cunningham, has a terrific potential as a biochemist. He's been working with Finnerty at Tulane on the specificity of mutagenic chemicals. He could give us a lot of inside dope on that project. The whole problem of mutagenic stability—"

Podell cut into the flow. "You mean you were working on the man to switch to Haverstraw?" he asked with incredulity. "*Haverstraw?*"

"Of course," said Luzzatto.

"Why would he do a thing like that?" Podell marveled.

"I promised him the moon," Luzzatto confessed with a faint grin. "Fellowship to cover all expenses. Enough salary for a married man to live on. By the time he gets his degree, we'll have the Center ready with its full program. All research and no time wasted in teaching. He was impressed, Si, really impressed with our program for studying control mechanisms in intermediary metabolism and all those factors affecting induced biosynthesis. You know?"

"Know?" said Podell with grudging respect. "Hell, I wrote a release on that. I don't know what it means, but it got me a page in *Newsweek*." He made a mental note to start a file on Cunningham.

Luzzatto said, "He'll let me know next week after he talks it over with his wife. It's a big question, you see, because he's got to switch from medicine, which means less money for him. I went through that routine once myself. Of course that's a point I didn't stress."

Podell whistled softly. "It sounds like a real snow job on the man, Dave. I didn't know you had it in you."

"I was talking pretty fast," Luzzatto confessed, with a touch of complacency, "but it wasn't just that. Who wouldn't like to get in on the ground floor? Why, he could be a full fellow by thirty!" He paused. "I simply lost track of the time."

"Suppose you tell that to Foxx," said Podell drily. "He loves explanations. Let's step into my office first. I want a minute with you alone."

Once seated Podell cut off all calls and stared angrily at the younger man's uneasy expression. In many ways Luzzatto was the press agent's darling. He was courteous and modest with reporters, unassuming with laymen. He was responsive to questions when he wished, and when not, his evasions were graceful and humorous. His gaunt face was immensely expressive, from worry lines cleft between watchful eyes to deep parentheses cutting down to a sensitive obstinate mouth. Podell's liking for the young scientist was more than journalistic instinct, for he sensed that the warm feeling was returned. This response, he surmised, was the fascination felt by the scholar for the rude man of action, for Luzzatto seemed attracted to dockwallopers, truck drivers, farmers, steel workers, mechanics, short order cooks, cops and muscular worldlings like himself. Was it the attraction of opposites? The principle of polarity? He drummed the table and shook aside these thoughts. "I got akvavit, Professor," he growled. "What about it?"

"I couldn't touch it," said Luzzatto.

"No? Well, skoal!"

With his back to the light, Podell could see the gray irises of the younger man's eyes expand, as they grew accustomed to dimness. So far, so good, thought Podell, the guy's under control. He lowered an empty tumbler. "A–a–h!" he sighed heavily, blowing his mouth. "There's a cellar in Stockholm six hundred years old called *Den Gyldene Freden* where I got a taste for this stuff. Have a chair?"

Luzzatto shook his head impatiently. "Si, I'm in no mood for chewing the fat."

"Hold your water, Professor," said Podell calmly. He placed a tender hand over his belly. "You know, this stuff's smooth sliding down. Then it collects here and burns like a candle. Whah!" He fixed the younger man with cold purposeful eyes and let the silence grow.

"What's this about, Si?" said Luzzatto. "Some damn question about plans for the dedication?"

"Is that what you think?" asked Podell skeptically.

"Well, I can tell you that the last campaign was all wrong, Si. We were splashed all over the place. Frankly I thought it was horrible."

"You didn't say a word at the time. Not a mumbling word."

"I've been thinking it over."

Podell grunted. "You mean it took six months to formulate these objections? What's your real beef, Dave? Don't you want publicity?"

"I'm not a monkey in a zoo. I've told you this before, Si," Luzzatto retorted. Every move, he explained angrily, stirred up tremendous amounts of talk in scientific circles. It might be hard for the layman to grasp, but the world of science was small, highly competitive, charged with emotion. Even the first announcement of the discovery of biocin through Podell's office had left a bad taste.

Podell smoked quietly, unmoved. All this was a diversion, he thought, but one he was ready to follow to its conclusion. "I don't see why, Dave. I got more space for you than a fan dancer at a world's fair. Here's this stuff, biocin, that's mixed with every dose of antibiotics, and it's been saving human lives." He went on to recall picturesque stories of lightning humanitarian dashes to distant parts of the world in the days of scarcity. "Isn't that what you want? Recognition?"

"I've told you before, Si," said Luzzatto angrily. "I resent the gossip and backbiting that your kind of publicity has been getting me all over

49

the country. All I want is not to lose the esteem of the few guys in my own field who know and value my work. If you can't understand that, let's get somebody who can!"

Podell's ideal was the smooth operation, the hidden control, the getting of 'space,' and, owing these duties to the university, he was honestly bewildered by the show of indignation. The biocin operation, he argued, had been a first-class job which had successfully focused the world's attention on the modest young student and his mentor, Professor Victor Ullman, in whose laboratory the discovery had been made. Was that so bad? he wondered.

Luzzatto arose, unable to contain himself. "If you don't see it now, Si, you never will. I'm simply going to have to do something about this whole question."

Podell glanced at his cigar. "Dave, I ought to tell you something. Der Fuchs will be ready in a few minutes, but he won't be seeing you alone."

Luzzatto halted. "Oh?"

"There's a group waiting to see you. I wanted you to catch your breath first."

Luzzatto stared. "Group? Who?"

"You'll see."

"Let's go in then," said Luzzatto.

"No, no! Sit down. Take only a minute." Podell brought his cigar to life and let a moment pass. "I imagine Eva knows all about this," he said carelessly, waving out a match.

"Knows about what?" asked Luzzatto.

Podell nodded appreciatively. "Why, that letter from Ullman," he said sweetly. "What else?"

"Just what inference—" Luzzatto began angrily.

The older man held up a paw. "Oh, please! I know all about it, Dave. More than you think." He sat forward on the desk and folded his massive arms. "Fact is, I'm doing my best to keep the story inside these four walls. It's a question if I can succeed. That's why I'm taking all this time from my more creative duties. You're today's headache."

Luzzatto digested these remarks before he raised his eyes in a strained look. "Si?"

"Yeah?"

"It's nonsense, you know."

"Ullman's letter? Oh, sure it is! A lot of crap!" said Podell with heavy sarcasm. "No question about it—"

Luzzatto searched his pockets for a cigarette. He glanced up resentfully. "Whose idea was it to send that letter to my home this morning? Why not to my office?"

"I had nothing to do with it," said Podell heavily. "Personally I'd have called you up with orders to drag your arse over on the double. Maybe the idea was to give you time to think."

"About what?"

Podell smiled like a wolf. "I imagine it was a legal point."

They exchanged stares.

"Yes, Eva knows," said Luzzatto abruptly, answering the earlier question. "What about it?"

"How's she taking it?" Podell was solicitous.

"How would she take it? She went through a major war, didn't she?" asked Luzzatto bitterly. "Why would a little thing like this bother her?"

Podell said drily, "When a man's been called a thief, his wife's entitled to get upset."

"Thief?"

"Does that surprise you?" Podell studied the depths of the younger man's pallor. "Yeah, yeah," he said thoughtfully. "I guess it does."

Luzzatto stared at the carpeting. The word had struck with a shock. The morning had been filled with disagreeable new perspectives, but on the whole, he thought, he had recovered his balance. It was only now that he was beginning to see the path ahead in harsh new outline. He thought back to an earlier implication. "What did you mean by a legal point?"

"Oh, that? You were being put on notice, I imagine," said Podell. "It's usually sent to a man's residence."

"Was that necessary?"

The older man folded his arms and sighed. "I told you, Dave, I'm trying to keep this situation under wraps. I'm not sure I can. Have you any idea what's going on?"

Luzzatto shook his head, bewildered.

"Professor, you're up to your neck in shit," said Podell with animal simplicity. "When you get into that room, watch yourself."

"What does that mean?" Luzzatto exclaimed in rising alarm. "I'm here because Foxx wants to see me. I don't have to watch myself."

"Ah, sure," said Podell.

"I don't like this. You can tell Foxx—"

Podell raised a hand. "Dave, you act as though I'm accusing you of something, but that's not the case. Get sore at Ullman, he's your hero, but not at me. Officially, you're a hundred per cent. I just want to give you one bit of personal advice. Of course," he added tolerantly, "I'm no lawyer." Thus claiming a rather commonplace virtue.

51

"I don't need advice," said Luzzatto angrily. "I'll just—"

"Just what?"

"I'll tell the truth, that's all. Foxx knows the facts. So does Gussett. So does everyone. There's nothing in this charge!"

Podell studied the long ash he had managed to cultivate. "All right, Dave," he said heavily. "You go in like a good boy and tell the truth. Whatever you tell 'em, they'll want to believe because it's for the record. Only—"

Luzzatto turned. "Only what?"

"Oh, they're highly ethical people in there," said Podell grimly, "and an awful lot is riding on that truth. Be sure to make it good. *Capish?*"

"I'm not sure that I do," said Luzzatto angrily.

Podell arose with an air of decision. "All right, Professor," he said amiably, "you're on your own. Don't say more than you've got to—and remember that I'm on your side. Not everybody else will be. Let's go!"

With a cold meaningful stare, he opened the door leading to the presidential offices.

Chapter 5

"SHALL WE BEGIN?"

James Fitzherbert Foxx gave the order. The group of men stirred, settled back, ended the murmur of conversation as R. Major Gussett, secretary of the university, a small obsequious man with feral eyes, opened a minute book and requested directions as to the taking of minutes. Foxx failed to answer directly. Instead he pressed a lever of an intercom box. "Mrs. Haggerty?"

"Yes, Dr. Foxx?"

"Is there any word from Dean Mackenzie?"

"Not yet, I'm afraid."

"Have you tried his home?"

"His housekeeper says he left at noon."

Foxx let the lever snap back and glanced up after a moment of hesitation. His plump face wore a manner of reserve and behind rimless spectacles his eyes stared like agates, milky with egotism. Six men were seated at the long refectory table. One could see a woman's touch, for his wife, Nadine Foxx, was responsible for dark paneling, Holbein reproductions, ornate chests and tudor chairs fitted with red cushions. "Minutes? If you wish, Major," he murmured. His peremptory voice, rich, pleasant, choir-trained, resounded musically.

"Is that wise?" Philip Seixas said.

Foxx turned to consider the point. Philip Seixas, a lawyer of sixty with dark aristocratic features, added, "Do you wish to take minutes?"

Foxx turned to the others. "Dean Polk?"

Henry Polk, Ph.D., dean of the graduate faculties, fumbled at a goatee

53

like a mild elderly Lenin, a likeness accentuated by a bald intellectual shovel dome and pouchy mongolian eyes. "Well, I rather think—" he offered vaguely, losing himself somewhere in time and space.

"The suggestion is to dispense with minutes. May we have that as a motion?"

"I so move," said Polk, finally comprehending the requirement. With an air of control, Foxx turned to Gussett. "Merely note the attendance of those present. You, me, Mr. Seixas, Dean Polk, Professor Luzzatto and, by invitation, Mr. Podell." He paused politely. "Yes, Professor Luzzatto?"

Luzzatto was aware that one never came directly to the point in the presidential offices or stated the issues simply. For the working scientist, deep in research, or harassed by teaching, it was not easy to master the arts of the courtier. He was seated at the foot of the table, facing the president of the university, conscious of the clutch of fear. Lying on the table was the letter from Victor Ullman.

"Can't we go on?" he said with outward calm. "I really have no objection to keeping minutes."

Foxx made no immediate reply. Among his affectations—which included rough tweeds, lack of gubernatorial ambitions, democracy, concern for refugees, musical taste, Jackson Pollock—was a briar pipe. He scraped the bowl thoughtfully, sucked tentatively. "I'm afraid, Professor, that you'd better leave that to the judgment of others. It's an awkward situation, you see."

Luzzatto flushed. "It's no less awkward for me," he said unnecessarily, instantly reminded of Eva's injunction to curb his tongue. With suppressed feeling, he turned to a scratch pad and made a pretense of scribbling notes. There was a moment of silence.

"We'll dispense with minutes." Foxx tapped with an air of precision and glanced about the table. His rich voice brought the group to order. "If counsel is ready? It was generous of him to give his valuable time."

At the note of deference, Philip Seixas glanced up with a pleasant smile. "Not at all," he said gravely. "I feel that this problem is my reponsibility, not yours. It might have been wiser to take this up with Professor Luzzatto in my office, not here." He glanced at the object of discussion. "Come, Professor," he added, smiling faintly. "It's not as bad as all that."

Luzzatto looked aside.

"I expect," Foxx resumed, tamping his pipe, "that you've all noticed that Dr. Ullman's letter of claim is addressed to me as president of Haverstraw Foundation, Inc." A match was allowed to hover for dramatic effect. "Now I might point out that this letter could not be less timely.

54

Our financial efforts this year turn on the dedication of the Center, which of course Professor Luzzatto's assignment of the biocin patent has made possible."

Foxx picked up the letter from Ullman and glanced over it thoughtfully. Grateful as they were to Professor Luzzatto, other financial burdens remained unsatisfied, he pointed out, and in fact had been increased by the expansion program of his administration. "Special gifts, general solicitation, our position with the Ford people, our total program to augment our cash and endowment position could be badly hit." A thumbnail pressed against a wrinkled forehead as the mood of uneasiness grew. "There's also a knotty problem in Albany—"

Luzzatto cast his eyes down as the rich voice resounded in the room. An intricate bit of lobbying was going forward in Albany in the hope that the state would assume the budget of the School of Agriculture while leaving control as before to the university, a condition which would be an educator's dream. Only now, Foxx seemed to be saying, were these efforts within sight of recognition by the legislature. Now where, Luzzatto wondered, was all this leading?

"This letter is not only disagreeable," the president concluded regretfully. "It could not be less opportune. It could become extremely embarrassing." He favored Luzzatto with thoughtful scrutiny.

"Oh, dear," murmured Dean Polk with distress.

Foxx placed the letter aside with a fastidious touch. "Let me make clear that Professor Luzzatto enjoys our confidence in his integrity. And that, I believe, is the crux of the matter. I'm sure that's the consensus?" He looked about inquiringly.

A murmur of approval went about.

Foxx hesitated and fingered his pipe with an air of regret. "Obviously Professor Luzzatto is uniquely and unfortunately affected by this letter. At this stage, it's not clear exactly what Dr. Ullman has in mind, but some things are evident. Mr. Seixas will correct me if I'm wrong. The letter charges that Professor Luzzatto has usurped some special position with respect to biocin to which he is not entitled. Standing alone this would merely create a personal issue between Professor Luzzatto and Dr. Ullman in which—" He broke off to consider a disagreeable point. "I was about to say, a personal issue in which as a body we would have no interest. No! I'm not sure I can go that far. Obviously we would be deeply concerned in any such controversy. However, this letter goes beyond all that. Dr. Ullman now seeks to rescind all rights to biocin which are held by the foundation. I'm not sure whether he has the right to make any such attempt. In any case, we've asked Professor Luzzatto to attend because of the relationships involved. Without the biocin revenues, the foundation has no real existence, while the Center, which means so much to us, would merely be a financial embarrassment. Professor Luzzatto is here as managing director of the Center. He is also here to satisfy us that this scandalous charge is without substance." Foxx coughed into his fist with a curious hardness of smile. "I'm sure he'll have no trouble on that score. Let me now read the letter."

Foxx read slowly and with full dramatic effect. Luzzatto's pallor deepened. His own copy lay before him, but he had no need to read, for the words were burned in memory. He still felt slow in his reactions, stunned by the growing sense of disaster, striving to grasp what was happening. He was going down a path of no return, he felt, like one of those dreams of infancy; something dreadful and irretrievable was about to happen. He glanced up covertly, feeling the eyes of others on him but this was not so. Gussett was chewing his cheeks disagreeably, Dean Polk seemed stricken by the enormity of the situation; Seixas was gazing off, his long dark face expressive of superior insight into the matter. One side of Luzzatto's mind was forced to admire the economy of style. It was wholly like Victor Ullman, he reflected grimly, to conform even in this letter to the fundamental laws of nature. Like a particle traveling through a field of force, he came to a point with least expenditure of energy.

Foxx placed the letter aside and restored the pipe to his mouth. "There it is, I'm afraid. It's a disgraceful charge but it's got to be met. Professor Luzzatto, did you have any reason to expect this letter?"

The question was not wholly unexpected. Luzzatto shook his head. "None whatever. I'm completely surprised."

"Were you and Dr. Ullman on good terms?"

"When?"

"Before this letter?"

"I'm not sure."

"What does that mean?"

"I thought we were friends. Evidently we were not."

"Is there any reason for his present lack of friendship?" Foxx smiled. "If I may put it so mildly?"

"I can't think of any."

"Then can you possibly account for this situation?"

Although this last question was put in a friendly way, the accent had sharpened. Podell coughed warningly. At these affairs he usually managed to shove his chair back from the table where he teetered with folded arms, cigar festering at a sardonic angle, eyes fixed at a pewter plate hung on the oak paneling. By this stance, he indicated his role as guest and specialist

56

in hard common sense among the savants. Luzzatto caught the flick of an eyelid, hesitated, shook his head. "Really, Dr. Foxx," he said in a strained voice, "I can't tell you what's on Victor Ullman's mind."

"Would you like time to consider your answer?"

"Perhaps later. I don't believe I ought to say anything until I know exactly what's involved here."

The lawyer turned with a glance of approval.

Foxx sank back, nursing a thumbnail with a faint air of doubt and mistrust, an expression instantly submerged in a genial encouraging smile. "Can we assume that you're prepared to deny this charge of usurpation? Whatever that may mean?"

"Of course I deny it," said Luzzatto resentfully. "Isn't that taken for granted?"

Foxx let a moment of tension accumulate. "Yes. Yes, of course," he said finally. "I put the question badly. But you do see, Professor Luzzatto, that while you enjoy our complete confidence, this matter may not rest in our hands? Can we safely take anything for granted? Isn't that what's called in your field the error of untested assumption?"

An enormous Siamese cat arose from the hearth, yawned, exposed its claws, padded across the room. It proceeded to lick the dangling hand of the president of the university.

The door opened.

"Hello, Foxx," said Dean Mackenzie ungraciously. "Can an old man come in?"

"Mackenzie!" Foxx leaped to his feet and hastened forward with an expression of pleasure. "We're so gratified you could attend. We were forced to start without you."

Lackland Mackenzie, B.A., Edinburgh, 1900; Sc.D. (*hon.*), São Paulo, Brazil, 1933; Sc.D. (*hon.*), Princeton, 1949; swayed slightly as he entered the dim chamber and let his hand be pumped. His strong roman features were tattered with age; and although one blurred eye was without vision his glance was keen. At seventy-six he was tallest in the room and without effort he radiated dominating intellectual force. With some impatience he withdrew an elbow from Foxx's solicitous guiding touch.

"Ah? Polk? How's that gout?"

Henry Polk rose benignly and extended a soft brown-speckled paw. "Delighted, Mackenzie," he murmured with pleasure. "Simply delighted. Did you ever get that book I sent over?"

Mackenzie grimaced sourly. "Hump! Can't make the slightest sense out of Whitehead. Why don't the man express himself in English? I'm afraid these days I'm reduced to television and detective stories. I've got no patience left for hard thought and as for novels— Well, the highest praise is that they read like detective stories so why not read the real thing? No, thank you, Foxx, I can manage," he said irritably, coming finally to the foot of the table. "Davey Luzzatto? Sitting below the salt, hey? Incongruous to find you on the carpet."

Luzzatto awkwardly extended an icy hand. "I'm sorry about all this, sir," he said, flushing. "I'd have been glad to call on you if I'd known of your interest."

The old man peered closely and a strong smell of tobacco wafted up like a cloud. "Save it, Davey," he grunted. "You're just at the beginning. Now is there tea?" He was settled in a leather chair off to the side. A table was put beside him with a pot of black English tea. "Good, this tea! I see Martha Haggerty still remembers me tastes." He sucked noisily and turned his glare to the council table. "Now! What's all this?"

Concisely, plainly, without dramatic effects, Foxx summarized the proceedings.

"Well, well!" Mackenzie drew down the lines of his mouth disagreeably. Some moments of meditation passed before his brows rose. "Tell me, Davey? Are ye surprised?"

"Yes, sir, I am," said Luzzatto simply.

"Hump! Will somebody tell why it's always the predictable that's never expected? Could have told you this might happen years ago. Well, nobody asked me advice. Why bring me out of me burrow, Foxx? It's not groundhog day."

Foxx pointed out that Lackland Mackenzie was still dean emeritus of the graduate faculty of pure science.

"Am I? What the hell does that imply?"

"Your advice is valuable," Foxx remarked with deference. "I'm sure you appreciate our respect for your experience."

"What's the legal mind got to say?"

Seixas smiled pleasantly. "Oh, at this point, Dean, we've simply got a letter," he said. "While it's embarrassing, I can't take it too seriously from the legal point of view. Not yet."

"Oh? Why not?"

"Primarily because I'm acquainted with this transaction, Dean Mackenzie. I'm perfectly satisfied with the purely legal aspects. As a matter of fact, the patent assignment was delivered to my office. Am I correct, Professor?" He turned back to the foot of the table.

"I believe so," said Luzzatto. "I wasn't present. That aspect was handled by Dr. Ullman."

"Yes. Well, it was something like that." Seixas thought back, puzzled by a blind spot in his recollection. "The position is simple. May I have that folder?"

Gussett handed over a folder stamped with the firm name of Seixas & Wyandotte. "My file tells me that biocon was discovered about eight years ago while Professor Luzzatto was working as a graduate student in the department of zoology under Dr. Ullman." The lawyer wiped his glasses with a linen handkerchief. "After the discovery, Dr. Ullman and Professor Luzzatto jointly applied for letters patent to the United States Patent Office. About five years ago, both parties assigned their rights in the patent application to Haverstraw Foundation, Inc. which now holds the patent for the benefit of the university. Dr. Ullman retained no benefits for himself, nor, strictly speaking, did Professor Luzzatto. However, Professor Luzzatto has a separate contract with the foundation to direct its affairs and under this contract a percentage of all revenues are payable to him during the lifetime of the patent. Dr. Ullman's signature appears on the patent assignment.

"Under these documents," Seixas went on, modulating his tones subtly, "it's rather difficult to see the basis of any claim. But in fact, Dr. Ullman's letter calls for no action. He merely states a position and tells what he intends to do at a future time. I'm afraid," the lawyer concluded, smiling faintly, "that anyone can write a letter in a free country."

Foxx said, "What do you propose?"

Seixas replied thoughtfully. "Acknowledge receipt, I imagine, then wait for the next move. Of course one must reply."

"Reply how?" asked Mackenzie drily.

Seixas turned. "As counsel, I daresay I can answer for the foundation, Dean, to advise that this item will be brought to the next regular meeting of the trustees in February. That might keep it spinning and at that time we'll reject the claim."

"And then?"

"I'm afraid," said the lawyer, "that we'll consider other measures then. After all, Dr. Ullman has not yet advised us of the nature of his grievance. His next communication will undoubtedly be more precise, and"—he paused lightly, significantly—"in more public form."

The silence was uncomfortable. Having allowed the discussion a free rein, Foxx sat back, scraping the bowl of his pipe, estimating the forces at play across the table. "Would you care to comment, Professor Luzzatto?"

Luzzatto felt his cheeks redden. "I'll have something to say later, sir," he replied and studied his notes.

59

"Very well," said Foxx quietly. "Dean Polk?"

Polk laughed deprecatingly. He had no legal training, he readily acknowledged, but on the other hand, years of intra-mural disputations had taught him something of the contentious ways of scholars. "We must remember that there are other considerations besides the strictly legal. This is not the market place. Dr. Ullman was part of the university for many years; he expresses no animus; in fact he takes pains to show a friendly concern. He could hardly relish a scandal—" Some of the discourse was lost in the inarticulate mumble which had made his seminar in medieval philosophy infamous among undergraduates until finally the low bubbling tones emerged into the vehemence of the moralist. "I don't believe we ought to accept this letter as a challenge. That's never the way to peace. It ought to be our aim to understand what he has in mind. Dr. Ullman's a fine man, you know," he added with a penetrating stare, "a fine scholar. It ought to be possible to invite him to meet with the rest of us. Mr. Seixas, Dr. Foxx, myself, Professor Luzzatto, or anyone else for that matter. Once we know the facts, I'm sure we could work out this grievance. Don't you think so, Professor?"

Luzzatto looked up with suppressed anger.

"What would you expect from such a meeting?" he asked in a strained voice.

"Better understanding," the dean replied after a pause. "If we could talk this matter over? I can't say where it will lead, but surely we've got to make the effort? I'm confident Dr. Ullman would welcome an invitation from Dr. Foxx to come up for a conference."

Podell removed a cigar to make his first point. "Dean, suppose he won't accept the invitation?"

"Not accept? He must." Polk looked startled.

"But if he won't?"

"I refuse to consider that possibility."

Podell narrowed his eyes cunningly. "Not even hypothetically?"

Dean Polk could no more resist an hypothesis than he could creamy, indigestible food. "I cannot believe that Victor Ullman would refuse to confer in the spirit of friendship," he answered with decision.

Much enlightened, Podell resumed his cigar and stared at the ceiling.

"Thank you, Dean," said Foxx drily. "I have no doubt that Dr. Ullman is a fine man—as you say—but so is Professor Luzzatto. I wonder if you fully appreciate Professor Luzzatto's position?" He paused for effect. "I hope that esteem for one colleague will persuade no one to do less than justice to another."

Polk managed to look startled and stricken together. "Oh, my dear

60

fellow," he exclaimed with contrition. "Of course not! I meant no—I mean, not the slightest intention. I'd feel awful if you felt that I had less than the highest regard for—"

Luzzatto flushed. "Quite all right," he said. Polk was a dear old boy, he thought acidly, who dwelt on high among the monads, as far beyond evil as an infant, but even so his guileless reaction to the letter was not to his own liking; he managed a frozen smile. "Oh, Dr. Ullman's all you say, Dean. He's a fine scholar. Still, I'd like to ask a question."

"Yes?" said Polk warily.

"If you were the subject of this letter," Luzzatto asked, "would you hold to your same high forgiveness?"

"Ah!" Polk thoughtfully considered a question which brought him back to familiar moralistic fields. "I think that's the only possible approach to a difficult situation like this."

"I'll try to remember," said Luzzatto.

Foxx tapped his pencil for attention. "Professor Luzzatto, I'd like to express myself frankly. Dr. Ullman left the university at his own request, without any official grievance, so far as we know. Indeed, he declined an offer to continue on as professor emeritus on a year-to-year basis. There seems to be no reason for animosity against the university." A quick glance went to Gussett and then he went on with a trace of hardness. "Now the letter can be handled in several ways. I can reject it out of hand. Or I can send it to Mr. Seixas as a legal matter. Finally I can leave it with you to handle on a personal basis."

"I don't think that would be wise," murmured Seixas.

"Perhaps not," Foxx agreed quickly. In the silence which followed, the cat leaped upon a carved chest and curled up as a silent watcher of events beyond his ken, paws extended, blue eyes slitted with adoration.

"Not that we accept the imputation," Foxx went on with vigor. "Not for one moment. I want to make that clear, Professor Luzzatto, but there's no use wearing blinders. If this matter should get out of hand, it might become highly unpleasant. Public airing of dirty linen. It can hardly do the university any good. Or anyone else for that matter." He paused a long significant moment. "Now with that in mind let me say that we will back up any statement you may care to make."

Luzzatto stirred restively, sensing that no one else intended to fill the silence. The presidential statement was fair enough. It was carte blanche, an acceptance of any position he might choose to defend; it was even couched in those resonant tones of sincerity which were the badge of high administrative office. But something elusive was disturbing. What was expected of him? He wet his lips.

61

"I'm not sure that I follow everything that's been said across this table, Dr. Foxx. Except that I can tell you flatly that there's nothing to this whole thing. As I understand it, everything involving this patent here is a matter of record. Mr. Seixas has told us that he's satisfied with the legal position. What else can I add?"

Seixas and Foxx exchanged glances. "We were rather hoping that you might have some suggestion for us, Professor Luzzatto," said Foxx.

"Me?" said Luzzatto stupidly.

"You're the only one who might know the facts at this stage. We thought you might have some notion."

"But to what effect?"

"Oh—" Foxx nibbled his pipe stem reflectively, but getting no satisfaction glanced up meaningfully. "We're hopeful, I imagine, that you can come up with some sort of solution. No one's closer than you to Dr. Ullman. After all, we face a distinct threat of a lawsuit. Even if it doesn't get to that point, a thing like this can get, well, ugly and difficult. Surely, for a man of your discriminating intelligence, that's not hard to see?"

"I still don't understand what's expected of me," said Luzzatto stubbornly.

Foxx sat back nursing his pipe. "I'm afraid that's as far as I can go, Professor," he said abruptly, after a pause. "I did hope for a suggestion that might dispose of this matter with good will and common sense. We can still view this as a misunderstanding, nothing worse, between two men whose contributions to this university are equally valued. Perhaps that ought to be our guiding principle: the higher interests of the university. Otherwise? Well, Dr. Ullman's next move might throw the fat in the fire." A glance went to the lawyer whose dark eyes reserved comment. "On the other hand, we can adopt Dean Polk's suggestion and ask Dr. Ullman to confer with us in a friendly spirit. I was rather hoping that you might propose something along these lines."

Luzzatto flushed uncomfortably. So there it was, he thought grimly, the explanation for Henry Polk's presence—reliable peacemaker, born pacifier, steadying force of goodness and light. What was that damn phrase? *The higher interests of the university.*

Mackenzie lowered his cup and addressed the chair. "If everything's so simple, Foxx, why bring me out of mothballs? I'm supposed to be on a high dry shelf, out of sight, out of mind. Hey?"

Foxx drew a cold glance away from Luzzatto. "Someone's got to talk to Dr. Ullman," he said simply.

"Why me?"

"I think he might listen to you," confessed Foxx with a candid air.

"Certainly not to me. Or anyone else. After all, your position here is unique. Oh, it's always possible to fight it out in public but why let it come to that? I'd like you to attend the conference."

"So that's it! Hah!"

Mackenzie stretched a bony hand for the letter. "Mind if I look at that? I couldn't quite make it out on the telephone."

"Here you are," said Foxx.

Mackenzie affixed a pair of horn-rimmed spectacles and glared with his good eye at Ullman's letter. "Hump!" he grunted. " 'Purported to exercise . . . usurped by one David Luzzatto . . . monies and revenues'!" He tossed the letter back and turned his craggy brows. "Davey?"

"Sir?"

"What kind of language?" Mackenzie snorted. " 'Monies and revenues'! Some damn lawyer framed that letter. It's got that smell of lurking connivance. 'Monies and revenues'!" The phase was turned with loathing. "D'ye know what would send Victor Ullman running after lawyers?"

"No, sir," said Luzzatto.

"Have you 'usurped' anything from Ullman? Hey?"

The younger man flushed. "Of course not."

"Well, don't get huffy. Do any rights whatever to biocin belong to the man?"

"None."

Mackenzie extended a warning finger. "He claims they do."

"I'm aware of his claim."

"Then who owns the rights?"

"I've conveyed all rights to the university."

"When?"

"Oh, four-five years ago."

"How?"

"I made a formal assignment. I believe that's what it was called."

Mackenzie paused and with some meaning went on. "Were those rights yours to give?"

"Now look here, sir!" said Luzzatto angrily. "I don't see why I've got to go through this sort of interrogation! If they weren't, I would never have executed the assignment papers."

"Are you prepared with proof?"

"Certainly," said Luzzatto impatiently. "The whole world knows I discovered biocin. Up to this moment my claim has never been questioned. I've got my original notes to go by. Then there are my contributions to the literature. I've published over forty-two, no, forty-three major

63

papers on the stuff. There's my doctor's thesis on file at the library. In addition—" he halted.

"Yes?"

Luzzatto exchanged a glance with Seixas. He had been rattling along too fast for proper effect. "There's the patent."

Mackenzie sank back in his deep chair. "Has that finally been issued?"

"Oh yes. Five months ago."

"Who now holds the patent?"

"Why, the foundation. I assigned rights to the patent application about fourteen months after it was filed. Dr. Ullman also executed an assignment, but that was purely a formal matter. I thought you knew all that?"

"No," growled Mackenzie. "I hadn't known. In my day it was publish the results and be damned to all this patenting nonsense."

Luzzatto folded his arms and waited but surprisingly Mackenzie remained suspended in thought. "Davey, I seem to recall your original paper. *Biocin, a New Bacterial-Resistance Inhibitory Substance.* Wasn't that it?"

"Oh, yes. That was eight years ago."

"Now wasn't that signed with more than one name?"

"Yes."

"Whose name appeared first?"

Luzzatto said slowly, "Dr. Ullman's."

"How did that happen?"

"I felt it was the fair thing. After all he'd been my chief at the time. I got a good deal of knowledge and guidance from him."

Mackenzie's deep voice dropped a tone. "One might take it from the order of names that Dr. Ullman was in fact the senior author."

"Oh, no!" cried Luzzatto. "I was."

"Yet his name precedes yours?" Mackenzie demanded. "Was that at his request?"

A tempting door had been opened. Luzzatto frowned and thought back and shook his head. "No. It was at my insistence."

"You were senior author—?"

"Yes."

"And yet you put Ullman's name first?" Mackenzie's brows shot up. "Isn't that surprising?"

"Not at all," said Luzzatto warmly. "As a matter of fact, I distinctly recall that we had a stiff argument. I might even be able to give you the date. It was a few weeks before Christmas recess. We met in front of Mackenzie Hall. Jo was there. Jo Ullman," he added unnecessarily. "She might remember because she'd brought her Chevvie to pick her father

64

up and to get me to the barber. I wouldn't have paid attention except that Jo said I looked like a wet owl with feathers sticking out around my ears and she was so bossy about the whole thing that—" He paused. "Now that I think, Jo made an entry in my diary, so it's still there, I guess, in her handwriting. In any case, we were all in the car. I told Victor, I mean, that is, Dr. Ullman that I'd got a call about the paper. It was a question of the credit line. Jo would remember."

"A call? What about?"

"Oh? Well, you see, Frank Higby, who was editing the *Journal of Cytology* had gotten a note from Dr. Ullman to take his name off the paper. Didn't think he deserved the credit or something like that, and Dr. Higby wanted to know if the note was on the level. I told him I had put down Dr. Ullman's name and to let it ride. Well, Dr. Ullman definitely stated to me that he didn't want his name to go on the paper."

"Why not?"

Luzzatto hesitated for a moment—barely the skip of a heartbeat—and went on. "At the time I thought it was modesty. Or something. Later I got to wonder whether or not he was offended with me."

"Why?"

Luzzatto drew a breath. "I simply don't know. I just assumed it was one of those unpredictable things and that he had his reasons. I told him, Nonsense! I owed him a lot. The fact was he helped to draft the paper. I was so damn fagged out at the time, I was practically neurasthenic. I think the records might show I'd been working steadily around the clock for months. I finally reached the point where I couldn't even take readings. I had double vision, spots, oh, the works. I had to rely on Will Tewksbury for that and a lot of things.

"I mean, when the time came I had to have help. I was mentally blocked and we were anxious to publish before we could be forestalled. Victor had a shrewd idea that something like biocin was being cooked up at McGurk and we couldn't stall.

"Anyhow, I had my notes but I couldn't seem to get off the ground. After ten versions, I gave up and went to Dr. Ullman. At that time I had no experience in writing for publication and his style was first-class. He was very nice about it and told me how to arrange for publication, with his permission. Anyway when he found I had put his name on the paper, he ordered me to get it off."

"But you didn't?" said Mackenzie.

"Well, I flatly refused and I suppose I got stubborn and angry. I wouldn't vouch for my emotional state at that time. Jo thought we were both getting recriminatory and ridiculous, and finally he threw up his

65

hands and told me I could do whatever I pleased. That's about it except that I was conscious all the time that—I don't want to sound precious but, well—I felt that something pretty important was happening. I was in a state of exaltation. Not too responsible. Maybe I went overboard."

"But the fact remains," said Mackenzie caustically, "that Ullman's name came first?"

Luzzatto paused with a sense of intolerable dryness in his throat. He had been rushing pell-mell against the old man's disbelieving frown and in the gush of tumbling words he found control impossible. "Yes. Dr. Ullman's name came first."

"Yet you want us to understand that you alone were making these important decisions?"

"I didn't mean to give that impression."

"Hump! Why would he give you all that authority? You've got to admit it's hard to swallow."

"It was because he knew I was entirely and solely responsible for the discovery. You can ask anyone in the old crowd."

"You give him no credit at all?"

Luzzatto hesitated and glanced about. "Only in the most general way. Only for background support and the kind of help any teacher gives a student. As for the discovery *qua* discovery? He had absolutely nothing—" He paused.

"Nothing to do with it at all?" Mackenzie supplied.

"Exactly."

"Can you possibly explain that state of affairs to the satisfaction of this group of intelligent men?"

In the long watchful silence Dean Polk's whistling breath was loud. Luzzatto closed his eyes and a vision of the old laboratory, mysterious and promethean, quickening in the dark of night, came unbidden. He was conscious of a deepening scowl, almost of dislike.

Mackenzie demanded harshly. "Is the patent itself here?"

Seixas glanced up. "Just a moment," he said quietly. "This is exactly what I didn't want, Dr. Foxx. I don't think this line of questioning is advisable."

Foxx cut this short. "Mr. Seixas," he said, "let Dean Mackenzie see the patent."

The closely printed document was handed over to Mackenzie who held the paper to the light. Almost four years had passed, he observed, between date of application and final grant of letters patent. No drawings and six tables of data of which only the first four attracted his serious attention.

Four species of bacteria tested by gradient plating in the presence and

66

absence of biocin had been classified in the order of resistance to a score of antibiotic drugs ranging from penicillin to the barbarously named nicotinaldehyde thiosemicarbazone. In the presence of biocin the antibiotic drugs were uniformly effective; in its absence an ominous phenomenon was noted:

". . . the rapid development of resistant and possibly virulent populations of cells negates a measure of safety in any program of therapy where the rise of exceptional mutants must be taken into account. Dispersion of resistant and virulent mutants of pathogenic species among the human population must therefore eventually impair the usefulness of antibiotic drugs in current use. It is against this danger that biocin may be prescribed."

He came next to countervailing language:

"The novelty of the present invention includes use of biocin and the process of preparing the same . . ."

The concluding claim was sublime:

"Claim 17. Biocin."

Mackenzie meditated citations of prior patents and the literature which included, he noted with interest, an article of his own published in 1912 in the *Proceedings of the Society of Experimental Genetics and Medicine.* It baffled and disconcerted him that he had forgotten the paper entirely.

Seixas put a question. "Professor Luzzatto, is biocin an antibiotic?"
Luzzatto turned. "No, sir."
"Why not?"
Luzzatto hesitated. "It's not bacteriostatic."
"Is it bacteriocidic?"
"Only in concentration," said Luzzatto. "But that's true of almost anything. It's a matter of definition."
"What do you call it?"
"I've called it, um, a biochemical additive."
"*Add*-itive?" Mackenzie broke in, looking sick. "What the hell are ye? A gasoline chemist?" He snorted with disgust. "Add-i-tive! Why?"
Luzzatto laughed suddenly. "Because it's something you add, Dean," he grinned impulsively, "but I'll relieve your mind. At one time I intended to call the stuff a co-antibiotic."
Mackenzie looked his horror. "Ye didn't! Well, anything's better than that, Davey," he conceded grudgingly. "Additive, hey?" He tapped the

67

paper. "But on the clinical side, I gather it's being used like an antibiotic?"

"Not at all. It's got no lethal or inhibitive biological activity of its own. At least none that we know of yet." Luzzatto turned to the others. "But, in conjunction with most of the known antibiotics, it precludes the emergence of organisms resistant to the major drug with which it's given. It has tremendous public health significance. It's pretty well unique because it creates no resistance to itself so far as we can detect. Its clinical value is to increase the safety of the antibiotic with which it's mixed. However, if you don't like the word additive," he concluded restively, coming back to Mackenzie, "you can call it anything you please. Really, though, Dean, I don't see where this is leading. I'm not adding to your knowledge, I'm sure."

"Oh, but you are." Mackenzie turned back to the letters patent and examined legend and signatures. "Davey, you've explained how you came—I'm accepting your version for the moment—to put Ullman's name on your first publication of discovery. But, if he was not a discoverer with you, will you please now account for the fact that, one year later, the man's name appears with yours on the patent?"

Luzzatto looked about the table. "Well, I don't know why you adopt that tone," he said impatiently. "I did that under legal advice."

Mackenzie made a full turn. "Mr. Seixas's?"

"Not exactly. I was told that the patent lawyers had decided that it was technically necessary."

"Why so?"

"Well, because Victor Ullman's name had appeared on the first paper announcing the discovery. I didn't question it. I assumed the lawyers knew what they were doing."

Mackenzie stared. "Were they your lawyers?" he asked pointedly. "Did you pay 'em?"

"Oh, no. Of course not. They were lawyers for Brandywine Laboratories. I understood that Brandywine was handling the technical details. It was a relief to get rid of those problems. I wasn't too interested."

"And you let yourself be guided by an outside company?" Mackenzie demanded. "Without independent advice?"

Luzzatto considered the point. "Well, you see," he said slowly, "Mr. Strollo took a personal interest in the operation. He's a friend of the family. In fact, he got me my appointment with Victor Ullman in the first place. Naturally I assumed it would be all right."

"Didn't you talk to these lawyers personally to determine that point of law?"

"Not about this point. Dr. Ullman took care of that."

"He told you that it would be legally necessary to include his name on the patent?"

"He did."

"Why?"

Luzzatto paused uncertainly. He failed to answer directly. "You'd better ask him. He handled all contacts with the lawyers."

Seixas intervened. "Must we dwell on this aspect, Dean Mackenzie? The patent lawyers handled the matter with our consent."

Mackenzie turned back to Luzzatto.

"Was anyone else present when Ullman brought the news that his name had to go on the patent?"

"No one." Luzzatto felt his cheeks flush under the penetrating stare. "I'd have to search my memory further. I can't be positive because it was a time of intense excitement, you see?" He paused. "If it's a witness you want, I'll have to think about it."

Mackenzie studied the patent in detail. "I seem to recall that Will Tewksbury did a bit of work on this discovery, Davey?"

"Yes," said Luzzatto warily.

"In your first paper of discovery in the *Journal of Cytology,* you gave him a handsome acknowledgment for his help. Ye didn't make him an author? Why?"

"Tewksbury had nothing to do with the discovery. He was simply acting as lab assistant to me, and later he helped to fix standards, working out techniques for growing the stuff under my direction. I don't see the relevance."

"Don't you really?"

"Certainly not!"

"Oh, Davey!" sighed the old man reproachfully. "Ye now say that Tewksbury got no credit as author because he had no part in the discovery. But Victor Ullman's name was included. Then isn't the converse true? Don't it follow that in fact Ullman had some part in the discovery? Or what would you call his contribution? An additive factor?"

"I can't follow that reasoning," Luzzatto retorted. "I don't know why Dr. Ullman went on the patent. I was working constantly on biocin. They brought me papers and I signed 'em. I had no interest in technicalities."

"They've done pretty well by you, Davey Luzzatto," said Mackenzie. "Don't turn on 'em now. Pots of money are involved. Don't that mean anything?"

"No!" said Luzzatto strongly.

"Indeed?"

Mackenzie's glare was more saturnine than ever. "Well, Davey, a lot of hinting's been thrown at you the past hour, but I wonder if you get the drift? No, no! Let's get it into the open, Foxx. Davey," he continued meditatively, "you're the brilliant young man who's bringing cash and fame to this anemic institution, and suddenly, in the midst of adulation and festivities, a malignant outsider is casting mud. What can the people around this table say? The only possible attitude is official solidarity— close ranks, make the right noises till the last gob has been flung—but they're uneasy, and they'd like a way out. D'ye see?"

"I'm afraid not," said Luzzatto grimly.

"Hey? Well, if you need a finger in your eye, I'll oblige," Mackenzie snarled. "Ullman's out, Davey, and you're in. Apparently he wants to share what you've got. Would you like to volunteer to divide it up? Because that's the hint that's lingering in the air."

With some effort Luzzatto kept himself in control. "None of this was my idea," he said tightly. "If I were out for money, would I ever have gone into science? Or teaching? Biocin was the fruit of my labors. I have some pretty deep convictions about the social obligations of scientists regarding anything related to human life. I didn't want any part of the profit side. Now you're treating me like some commercial hack out to grab a buck. Well, that's not the case.

"Let me tell you something." He rubbed his aching eyes, affixed his glasses firmly, drove on. "It was Dr. Ullman who persuaded me to apply for the patent. I couldn't see that. I wanted to keep the price down to ensure the wide use of the stuff, but then he made it pretty clear that without a patent we would be completely vulnerable against the big houses. With a patent in our names, we could look out for the public interest. That was the premise on which I was talked into the whole thing. I had no idea it would ever turn into a squabble over loot.

"As a matter of fact I've been ready all along to hand over my entire interest to the university. Only this morning at breakfast I told my wife—" He paused, brimming with emotion. "Only this morning I told her I wanted to hand over my entire interest to the university. You act as though I'm defending a financial position. I'm not. I don't give a damn about that side and, when I entered this room, that was my feeling. I was prepared to make that offer to this group. Now?" He gazed about the dim room with its ornate furnishings and impassive older men. A small yellow bird, a prothonotary warbler, was flitting at the window, and suddenly the clutch of deep anger, unbidden, massive, welling from the depths of emotion, was a surprise. Oh God! he thought with boredom and vast distaste and a sense of terror, how long could this drag out? He folded

70

his arms defiantly and shook his head, feeling isolated and unbelieved. "I'm no longer sure I can."

Foxx tapped a pencil. "Dean Mackenzie, are you finished?"

"Not quite."

The old man rubbed his white brows and scurf fell in flurries on a pepper-and-salt jacket. "Davey, d'you think I've been too hard?"

Luzzatto glowered. "You haven't been easy."

"I'm being asked to talk to Victor Ullman about this thing. Is that all right with you?"

"I can't stop you," said Luzzatto sullenly.

"Now don't be difficult. In this letter he's talking primarily about moneys and revenues. Are you prepared to let me go into that question on your behalf?"

"No. Why should I?"

"Because if in fact it's finally a question of splitting up your royalties, Davey," said Mackenzie grimly, "your high-minded pose might be a leetle hard to swallow. Some people at least might draw unfavorable inferences. Under the circumstances, I can't see that it's my affair."

Luzzatto turned to the head of the table. "What do you want me to do, Dr. Foxx?"

The president said evenly, "It's entirely up to you, Professor Luzzatto. I'm not prepared to indicate my final position."

Si Podell, teetering stolidly with folded arms, was staring at the ceiling through a cloud of smoke. No comfort was there. Luzzatto said slowly, "I won't let the question of money stand in the way. I'll do anything reasonable."

The sighs of relief were audible. Gussett grinned widely and cracked his knuckles. The lawyer, whose impulse to interfere had been held in restraint, broke into advise that he had certain points of conduct to suggest.

Luzzatto interrupted. "However, I intend to lay down some conditions."

Foxx looked up. "Yes?"

Luzzatto ticked off his terms. "I want Victor Ullman to retract his letter. I want a formal apology and an expression of regret. I want this matter kept quiet under any circumstances. If any of this becomes public for any reason all bets are off. In that case, I'll want an expression of confidence from the university."

Foxx stared over his pipe, sucking the flame of a fresh match into the bowl. "Oh? What else?"

Luzzatto's jaw went out. "If I agree to share royalties—and I'm making

71

no commitments—that's only a matter of expediency. I don't care about money. But under these circumstances, I won't share the credit for biocin. It's a matter that affects my conduct as a scientist and there, well, I want no compromise. I want Victor Ullman to concede that I alone discovered biocin. Nobody else!" He paused with heart thudding. "Unless that's agreed there's no point in going ahead."

"Let me understand you, Davey." Mackenzie broke the silence with a sardonic question. "Does that mean you want Ullman to withdraw any claim of his own to that discovery?"

Luzzatto nodded grimly. "Yes."

The old man studied a tangle of chalky knuckles for a long moment. "That's not negotiating at all, Davey. That's putting a gun to the man's head."

"He put the gun first!" Luzzatto said bitterly. "He's put my integrity as a scientist in question. He's got to retract that letter."

"And if he won't?"

Luzzatto slowly shook his head. "In that case, Dean Mackenzie, I'm sorry," he said simply. "I didn't come to negotiate anything. I don't feel like that. I feel angry. Is that a surprise?"

"No," said Mackenzie gently.

Luzzatto stared about the room and sighed. "Well, that's it. Except that nobody seems to want the facts."

There was a long uncertain pause.

Mackenzie asked curiously, "Davey, d'you know what you're asking? D'you actually want a fight with an older man of his standing?"

"I won't run away from it," Luzzatto retorted. "He made a reckless and unfounded charge. It's false and he knows it to be false. Let him retract or make it stick."

"Well, what d'ye want of me?"

"Nothing. Except to convince him that he's making a horrible mistake. Tell him that he'd better watch out. That's all I can say." Luzzatto paused and added vindictively, "Or if he wants to be bribed by cutting into the biocin royalties, let him say so."

After a disagreeable silence, Philip Seixas put aside his cigar and remarked that a certain amount of background preparation was in order. "Tell me, Professor Luzzatto," he said curiously. "Do you agree with Dean Mackenzie? Do you think it's money that Dr. Ullman wants?"

"I don't know," said Luzzatto bitterly—

—and felt unclean. The warm rubbing at his ankles was the Siamese cat.

72

Chapter 6

WHEN LUZZATTO FAILED TO SHOW UP FOR DINNER, EVA, WHO HAD BEEN considering the problem of a sole on the brink of ruin, decided not to wait. She was almost disciplined to his habits, but now she found it impossible to control the anxiety twisting her heart. She put out her good madeira cloth on the trestle table and lit a pair of tapers. The candlelight on the reddish pine paneling was warm.

"Let's begin," she said to the maid.

She did well enough with a clear soup, but at the next course her appetite failed, and she found herself staring blindly at the fish. The maid cleared the table.

"Trouble with His Majesty?" she asked acidly.

Clara Stokes, a self-styled jewel from North Carolina, came to the Luzzattos four days a week. She was well paid and emotionally identified with her mistress whom she treated on a basis of equality.

Eva looked up vaguely. "Clara, could he be working at the lab?"

"Maybe. Why doesn't he call?" asked Clara practically.

Eva shrugged. "I don't know. He gets so absorbed in his work—"

Clara glanced at her mistress keenly. "No, honey. It's not that. Something's on your mind besides His Royal Whereabouts. Why not ring him up?"

Eva shook her head slowly. "He doesn't like me to do that. I'd better wait."

"Suit yourself." Clara left and returned with a wedge of cheese. "He gasses me, honey, he really does," she said firmly. "What's the matter with the man? How can he stay away when you look so lovely tonight?"

Eva looked up with pleased surprise. "Why, thank you, dear." A sleeveless gown of black velvet set off her white skin to full effect. She said, "Clara, have a drink with me?"

"Why certainly," said Clara promptly.

Clara had a hearty laugh, a fund of wisdom, a capacity for work, a palate for plum brandy. With the demitasse, she brought a decanter of slivovitz and goblets and went to work on the academic community. Ordinarily Eva had an amused interest in Clara's gossip, but tonight it was no good.

The clock struck eight.

"Call the man," said Clara peremptorily, "or I will!"

The lab failed to answer.

"You want me to sit with you?" asked Clara.

Eva shook her head.

"No, of course not," she said sharply. She was striding about the living room, twisting her hands and shivering. "No. I'll be quite all right. You go home."

"If you're sure?" said Clara doubtfully.

Eva closed the door after the maid and threw the bolt and then locked the windows. She dialed a number.

"Barbara, dear?"

"Oh, yes. Eva? Is something the matter?" Barbara Adderly's voice sounded muffled as though her mouth were full. "Are you all right?"

"I've got a pair of tickets for the concert I thought you might like to use," said Eva. "Dave's not coming home, it seems. One of those late nights."

"Can't," said Barbara.

"Why not?"

"Oh, the baby's got the sniffles and I'm so tired with this damn pregnancy. I've been sick every morning. Why not come and spend an hour with me?"

"I'd be miserable company. No," sighed Eva.

"What'll you do, Evvie? Go alone? I might scare up someone for you—"

"God, no!" Eva paused. "I'll just curl up with a heating pad and hope that Dave'll come home in time. Poor suffering bloke! He's bored stiff by anything that's not Mozart or Beethoven. How long can one live on that?"

"Beethoven? Mozart?"

"He's a musical moron, you see? It takes a giant with a sledgehammer to make an impression. I'm quoting, by the way."

"Doesn't Dave like music?"

74

"Only good music. That's not the same thing."

"Guess not."

"Still, he's very good about it for my sake. Docile, tractable. I'm weaning him on the Goldberg sequence and teaching him to tolerate Bach. I guarantee nothing. Men are wonderful, Barbara, don't you think?"

"I've got to ring off," said Barbara Adderly with an amused chuckle. "I've got my own catalogue of woes with Tom, but we'll set aside an afternoon for that colloquy. Baby's calling. Bye!" There was a click.

"My poor Davey," said Eva slowly.

She hung up and stared out of the window. Lights were on along Tynesdale Road—islands of comfort and security in the night. Some miles away a faint glow marked the township. A light was shining at the university.

"God! Oh, God!" she muttered. She returned to the telephone and called the university. No answer came from office or lab.

"Can't help it, Mrs. Luzzatto," said the girl at the switchboard. "He's not there at all."

"Keep trying," said Eva.

She prowled the house, noting a score of minor blemishes which had not before disturbed her sense of riches and possession. Her trestle table had two pegs missing; at the time of purchase these errors had added to the flavor of age; now they were vexatious. The television was no help. Ordinarily she was fascinated by the emotional problems of the strange race of television beings, but this night her nerves were taut. In desperation she switched channels. Long-haired blond wrestlers tore and bit and gouged at the St. Nicholas Arena in New York. A panel of sophisticates were convulsed by their own inanities. Finally it was past eleven.

The private line rang.

She ran upstairs to her husband's study on the second floor.

"Hello? Davey?" Her voice was breathless.

An unexpected voice responded.

"Oh, hello, Eva," said Podell casually. "Is Dave around? I want to go over some copy with him before I turn in. Say," he paused contritely, "I didn't wake you up, kid?"

"Dave's not here," she said stupidly.

Podell was no help. It was his impression that Luzzatto had left the conference at Foxx's office with some routine tasks in mind at his office, and that he had meant to spend the evening at home.

"Well, I wouldn't worry too much. You know how he gets."

She paused, staring at her husband's desk. Behind this item of curly

75

maple and undoubted authenticity lay a trip to Freehold in New Jersey that hot July shortly after their marriage.

The four of them—Eva, David, Victor Ullman and Jo—had made the trip in Jo's Chevrolet into Monmouth County in a hunt for bargains. As it stood among the English pieces in the display room, the Winthrop desk had seemed modest enough in price, but on an instructor's salary the thought was madness. Yet somehow title had passed. It seemed to have turned on a quiet conversation in German back in the workshop between Ullman and Mr. Friedrich Mühlbach, dealer in antiques, a gruff man with a pitted skin. The dealer had peered closely at the young people, questioned David about his work, allowed the Winthrop desk to go for two hundred dollars. Driving back, Eva had hugged herself in ecstacy. "I didn't dream," she marveled. "Incredible! Two hundred dollars! How did you persuade him, Dr. Ullman?"

"How did I persuade?" Ullman echoed. "I simply reminded the man Mühlbach to remember that he came to this country from Heidelberg." Reverence for intellectual achievement, he added, was clearly incumbent on the offspring of that ancient city. "A Heidelberger? How could he refuse?" Ullman concluded ironically. "It would be a major scan-*dal*."

"Dr. Ullman, are you from Heidelberg?" she asked.

Ullman shook his head and raised an amused finger. He said with precision, "Lindorf. But now you must call me Victor."

"Well, it's a lovely piece, Victor," Eva gloated, "and we'll build the room around it. I've got the chairs picked out, and the table, and with a day bed—" She went rattling ahead with grandiose plans and concluded, "I think we can pay you back by December. I'm so grateful I could cry."

Jo turned from the wheel and flashed a smile. "Oh, shut up, Eva. You're making too much of it. The man wanted cash and Dad was glad to help out. I wish you'd take the desk as a gift from us both," she added, reverting to an earlier argument.

Eva shook her head firmly. "No."

"Why not? We haven't given you kids a thing, not really," said Jo persuasively. "A household's a big investment, and we'd be delighted to help out. What's money?"

Eva went on emotionally, "I'll never forget your kindness, Dr. Ullman. Never." She blew her nose. "Nor yours either, Jo."

"Never is a long time," Ullman observed drily. "I'm glad he took my check. Of course he knew who I was." He nodded as though resolving a point of perplexity. It had seemed odd to Eva to call her former teacher by his given name.

76

The telephone was shaking in her hands. "Si? Could you tell me what happened at the meeting?" she asked finally.

"Well, kid, it's too late now," he replied evasively. "It wasn't much. Just kicking it around, you know."

"What made Victor write that letter?" she asked in a low voice. "Does anybody know?"

"Later, kid. Take it easy," said Podell, and hung up. She replaced the receiver and remained seated, dreading to move. On an impulse, she switched on every light till the house blazed from cellar to attic and then went to the nursery and squatted on a hassock, hugging her knees and staring at the window. Past midnight, with an exclamation of despair, she put on a coat and went out into the night.

The campus was dark. Eva paused in front of Mackenzie Hall and stared up at the building. All this was only too familiar but now in the fog she heard footsteps and her heart was cold.

A bullseye flashing around the building struck her eyes. "Yup, Miss?" asked an incurious voice. She identified herself. "Mrs. Luzzatto? Okay, go ahead," said the voice hoarsely. "Far as I know, Mackenzie's all buttoned up. But you can try."

"No, look up," she said.

High up under the eaves a light glimmered. It meant, she thought, that her husband was somewhere in the building. The voice was amused. "I wouldn't take that for granted, Mrs. Luzzatto. I kin recall when they kept a light burning all night just to give the impression they were working around the clock. Ought to know because in those days I had strict orders from the Professor not to touch the switch. Burned a lot of juice."

"Oh, no," said Eva, "they *worked*. I was there."

The light flashed into her eyes.

"Oh, yeah. Miss Bronowski. I recall you now." The voice seemed equable, even pleased. "You put on a little weight since those days. You changed your hair?"

"Oh, never the hair." Instinctively her hand flew up and touched it.

"Well, if you'll wait, I'll get the elevator key."

Suddenly this was too tiresome. "Thank you, no," said Eva, "it won't be necessary. I'll walk up."

"Sure you don't mind? It's quite a climb."

"I know the way. I'm not afraid," she said. But she was afraid, she realized, with a cold constriction of her heart. In the dark foyer, silence lurked. Oh, absurd! she told herself sternly. Nothing can touch me.

She turned to the stairs and passed the directory—names, titles, vanities smoothed out by the alphabetical order of listings—and began the climb. Dim night bulbs glowing at alternate landings accentuated the gloom. On these steps legend had it that a student had once cut his throat to protest a flunking grade. She hastened on.

"Davey?" she called.

His office on the third floor was deserted and the night wind was blowing through an open window. She retreated back into the hall.

"Davey?" she cried. "Oh, where are you?"

Her voice went echoing in distant places and somewhere a door slammed. A whistling clamor of guinea pigs in the animal room arose and she fled on and up.

"Oh, Davey?"

The recollection of darkness and fear, the scurrying of rats in a Warsaw cellar was on her. In the distance the enemy with the—

"Where are you, Davey? For God's sake?"

—shells crashing and death everywhere. Hunger and—

"Is that you?"

—thirst and a girl insane in the cellar and in the streets men in gray uniforms hunting people and safety only in the—

"Oh, please! Where?"

—huddled darkness with the shivering bodies of the Polish women—

"Oh, my God!" Eva stood trembling. She was on the top floor. With an effort she quelled rising panic. She was simply exploring a deserted building, she reminded herself with common sense. She was in no danger. This was America. She was safe. She had a husband and he was somewhere near. But—

She was standing before a familiar door under the eaves of the roof. A streak of light was shining through the sill; her shoes, she saw, were streaked with mud.

With an effort she clenched her teeth and turned the knob and then in a hot and fetid room littered with cigarette stubs, crowded with records and storage files, she flung herself into the safety of her husband's arms.

"Oh, Davey," she gasped. "Thank God! I didn't think I would ever find you."

And as he looked from the haggard depths of misery and exhaustion, she burst into tears.

Chapter 7

THE ONLY HAVEN OF FOOD AND COMFORT AFTER MIDNIGHT IN EAST Haverstraw was the diner on Route 25 which plunged through the outskirts of the city. Its neon sign was not without pathos:

GUS APOSTOLICO'S DIN R ELENIKON

In the state of exhaustion, Luzzatto stared glumly at the sign, wondering at his longing for bright lights and noise. The hours in the dead files at Mackenzie Hall had exhausted his emotions more than he had believed. In the damp fog he shivered and turned off the ignition.

"You're sure you don't mind?" he asked.

"It's quite all right," said Eva.

The diner was empty except for two man in leather jackets at the counter who looked up with appreciation and wonder at Eva's entrance. Luzzatto found a booth and ran down a bill of fare in two languages: one Greek and the other not quite English. "Do you see anything you want?"

Eva was applying lipstick and studying a wan face in a compact mirror. "Nothing but coffee, Davey. I don't mind watching you." She closed her eyes and waited. Luzzatto snapped his fingers.

"One moments," said the counterman.

Hippocrates Pappas was selling a policy slip to a state trooper under the motto of the house: *They Also Serve Who Only Stand and Wait*. He finished the transaction and hobbled to the occupied table. "Colleges people," he decided as he brought an order blank to the firing position. "Yuppa?"

Luzzatto looked up. "Does Gus still come around?"

79

"Oh, yes. But not by nights," said Hippocrates. "Too old, too riches, too fats. Now what's to be?"

The cuisine implied traditions going back to antiquity and the division of the world between two Romes, East and West, Greek and Latin, Papacy and Patriarchate. Two ways to God, two civilizations of thought, art, taste, architecture, songs, dress, cookery were evoked in the concentration on mutton and lamb.

Luzzatto said, "Coffee, black, for my wife. Cream and sugar for me. Tell me," he added, glancing up gravely, "I understand you serve a special Greek salad."

"Oh, sure. Is finest."

Luzzatto said, "Is it still one olive to the customer, Mr. Pappas?"

Hippocrates pointed a finger of joy. "David Luzzatts!" he cried incredulously.

Luzzatto smiled. "Hello, Mr. Pappas. Did you ever get that wig for your wife?" It was an old and feeble joke to which the counterman responded. "Oh, Luzzatts! Oh, Luzzatts! Still one black olivus! Still the wig! I read about an I hear about an I wonder when I see you again." He was distraught with the sense of reunion. "Now I read about you big riches man? Famous?"

"This is my wife," said Luzzatto. "Mr. Pappas."

Eva managed a smile.

"How do you do? Am most please!" Hippocrates danced from one painful arch to the other. "Whats a long time you not been around now? Whats can I get you? Oh, I tell you, Mrs. Luzzatts, this boy used to be skinny kid big eyes wrinkled stomach. Oh, my! No money in pockets but how many grick salats an black bread and olivus he eat here onna cuff? Oh, my!" Hippocrates earnestly expounded Luzzatto's hardships as a student at the university. It was only in his second year, Hippocrates recalled, that the hungry student had paid off a line of credit, appearing in new and splendid clothes for the occasion.

"Victor got me that suit," Luzzatto murmured to Eva.

Hippocrates went on happily, gratified that the young scholar had vindicated the confidence of Mr. Apostolico, the kindest of men. Always Professor Luzzatts the book book book, he recalled. A most remarkable mind! Only one thing— He paused. "About this biocinus. I think I grasp its propertchies from common gossip, you know, but last April I read explanation you write for this magazine in New York. I must say I am now entirely in a state of confusion."

Luzzatto considered the statement. "Oh, then," he remarked quite seriously, "it must have been a very bad article, Mr. Pappas. What about that food?"

The dark face wrinkled with delight. "Ah! Professor Luzzatts, you are still an extremely nice person. Truly modests. An American in the finest sense of the word." Hippocrates left and returned with gifts evocative of wine-dark Aegean seas.

Eva lifted the mug, drawing comfort from its bitterness, studying her husband over its rim. The diner was clean and comfortable, but suddenly her senses were taut, unpleasantly exquisite. Resting on the table, her elbows were acutely aware of a slight film of grease. Music was strident, lights garish, faintly her nostrils quivered at the smells. She shuddered.

Luzzatto looked up from a plate of food. "I used to live on this stuff, you know."

Patiently she closed her eyes. "I know."

He was avoiding the issue, she thought bleakly. When would he come to the point? Aloud, she reminded him that she had heard the story many times.

"Oh, did you? Sorry. Bad habit." He sank back rebuffed, infected by her mood.

After a moment she said, "Your Mr. Pappas is sweet. I'm glad I finally met him." She sighed and leaned forward on her elbows. "I want to talk about this morning. Give me a cigarette, Davey."

He struck a match, steadied her hand. Her fingers were fragile, mere featherweights of bones, the palm felt icy and wet. "Oh, honey, what's this?" he exclaimed. "You're not letting this business get you?"

"Guess not," she sighed. "I'm being bitchy. Only—"

"Evvie. I love you," he said softly.

"Do you?" she asked curiously. "Yes. I suppose you do." She withdrew her hand, studying his face in the harsh light. His nails, splintered, were filthy, dust streaked his collar, an unpleasant fleck hung from a nostril—she felt an impulse of distaste, instantly regretted. She stared at the table, tracing its network of faint blue lines. "Why didn't you come home for dinner?" she asked in a low voice of pain.

"Darling, I didn't—" He paused under her bitter glance.

Her eyes remained level. "I've been in agony all day. Ever since that letter came," she went on in the same low tones. "If you love me, how could you stay away?" Suddenly tears were coursing down her cheeks.

"Oh, Evvie! Darling, please!" he cried in dismay.

After a time she smiled weakly and wiped her eyes. "I seem to be a woman suddenly. I promised myself not to do this to you. It's because I'm tired, I suppose." She blew her nose apologetically. "Well, now! Let's

81

forget it!" She waited, knowing it would come in its own time, his own way. He was not an easy man, this young husband of hers, but then, her own hateful mood was impossible to understand. She said, "What were you actually looking for in that room?"

Luzzatto hesitated. "I'm not sure. Every scrap I could lay my hands on. A lot of records are up there I've forgotten. It was going to be only five minutes, I swear, to find an item. Then I started to hunt through old files, but one damn thing led to another. I completely forgot the time. I'm sorry."

"Forgot? Oh, Davey!"

"I know, I know," he agreed wearily, showing some irritation. "I was wrong, Evvie, but I certainly wasn't frivolous."

Eva looked up. "Davey, will this come to court?"

He waited a moment to answer. "No, Evvie," he said patiently. "It won't come to court. Now you've simply got to trust my judgment. Can I be more specific?"

"I suppose not," she agreed and then, "I feel so unsure," she said miserably. "Tell me again."

Patiently, concisely, more amply than before, he described the meeting in Foxx's office earlier that day, laying special stress on the legal opinion voiced by Philip Seixas. "If the lawyer's satisfied, I'm certainly not going to worry about court at this stage. He doesn't give Victor a prayer, Evvie. Why isn't that good enough for you?" There was a tired, nagging quality in his voice.

She lifted a shoulder unhappily. "Because I'm not your lawyer, Davey. I'm your wife. This isn't merely a legal matter to me. I don't think you should be subjected to this—this conference. I don't like it."

"What's disturbing you?"

"Foxx," she said finally.

"What about him?"

"Can you trust that man?" she asked with a cynical grimace. "Or any of them? Oh, Davey! I've got such a cold feeling about this whole matter. Why are they so insistent that you meet Victor?"

"You don't seem to understand," he said impatiently. "It was the feeling that every attempt to head this thing off has got to be made. Could I refuse to sit down and talk?"

She had no reply.

"It would look as though I were afraid. Well, I'm not. Besides, the idea is to get Victor to retract. If he doesn't, Foxx agreed to back me one hundred per cent. Victor always said that when it comes to a matter of principle, I—"

"I wish you'd learn not to quote Victor," Eva said.

"Oh, I guess you're right," he agreed uncomfortably.

"If he refuses to retract? Then what?"

"He'll retract, Evvie. I promise you that much." He paused. "The problem is to get him to that conference. That's up to Mackenzie."

"Mackenzie? Is he willing?" she asked sharply.

He faced her squarely, feeling the constriction in his throat. He said evenly, "He'll be entirely with me, Evvie."

Eva looked up quietly, unconvinced. "Yes, they tell you things," she muttered. "Things they want you to hear, but have they given you their true thoughts?" Her speech was suddenly more foreign than usual. "I'll ask you about your Mackenzie? Why must they bring him into this?"

Luzzatto waited for a rumble of traffic outside in the black night to die. "He's not my Mackenzie, Evvie, but I'll tell you this again. The thought is that he can get Victor to that conference to talk this thing over."

"What is there to talk?" she burst out. "What?"

Luzzatto summoned all control. "One idea is to make Victor understand how much harm he can do," he said patiently, then waited to recover. "I don't mean only to us, I mean to himself. That's something only Mackenzie can accomplish. It's good of him to be willing."

She remained in thought. "Where will it take place?"

"It's not set yet."

"Will you be there?" she asked pointedly.

He paused to study a tendril of smoke. "I might be. I can't be sure until Victor gives his consent."

"Will he refuse to meet you?"

"He might."

"Then what?"

"Mackenzie will meet him alone. But I don't see why Victor should refuse. Of course, a sneaky letter is one thing—meeting me face to face is another. He might not have the gall."

Eva rubbed her knuckles nervously, huddling the coat about her shoulders. "Davey?"

"Yes, dear?"

"Have you thought that the purpose might be the reverse of what you imagine?"

"What does that mean?" he asked sharply.

"You think to influence Victor to retract? To withdraw? Ah?" She slipped into her coat. "But perhaps the purpose calls for Victor to influence you?"

"That's nonsense!"

83

"Is it? Why? From their viewpoint, isn't it logical? They can't expect to get rid of Victor so easily as all that. But you?" Her glance had the appraisal of hard, pitiless realism. "Isn't it more likely they're hoping for you to give in?" She finished the buttons with an ironical smile. "Do you know what they're saying among themselves? This fellow Luzzatto? Bright? Oh, yes. But such a damn bloody nuisance. Why not jolly him along until he becomes reasonable? So much better for the higher interests of the university." Her voice mimicked the suave tones of the president.

"Stop it," he said uneasily.

"They're afraid of this threat," she retorted flatly, "and they're letting you walk into dangerous conversations without telling you what they've said among themselves. You're still the outsider, Davey." Her glance was suddenly desperate. "They don't care about you. All that counts with them are outward appearances. You'll be sacrificed."

"How?" he demanded.

"I don't know."

And because the probe was cruel, he responded with anger. "I've got to assume good faith," he retorted. "In any case, Victor knows me well enough. If we meet, he knows I won't budge unless he retracts completely, without reservation. It's got to be on those terms."

"You say that now," she observed cynically, "but when you face Victor, will you stick?"

A dismal moment of silence passed.

No use, no use, she thought. In hurting this man, she was achieving nothing.

"What shall I do?" he asked.

She lifted a shoulder hopelessly. "I don't know, Davey. You must follow your own judgment, I imagine."

The radio signed off for the night. Hippocrates came forward, slopping a rag along the counter. "H'everything's okay?" he cried cheerfully. Luzzatto blew out his breath and nodded. "We're leaving, Mr. Pappas. Coming, Evvie?"

Eva looked up. "I didn't know Victor ever gave you a suit," she said oddly.

Luzzatto stared. "Oh, that? Yes."

"Don't you want to tell me about it?"

He did not like her expression one bit. "I think there was also an overcoat, but what's the point?" he demanded irritably. "What significance does it have?"

"None, I suppose."

She huddled under her coat and looked up with dry, shining eyes.

"Only, Davey, don't you see? It's these things that stick in the mind. Suppose it should finally come to court?"

"It won't!" He threw down change, exasperated.

"Oh, please!" she replied with dreadful realism. "Could you possibly explain to strangers how this man who did you so much kindness should suddenly become your enemy unless—" She paused.

"Unless what?"

She concluded in a low voice. "Unless in fact you had done him an injury? That's how it will appear to people, even if it never gets that far. Davey," she whispered starkly, "I'm terribly afraid."

Luzzatto drew a breath. "Keep out of this, Evvie," he said in a shaking voice. "You musn't be affected. Keep your mind off this matter, have the baby, concentrate on that. Victor won't press this to a conclusion. You've got my promise."

"Have you got Victor's?" she asked cynically.

"I know, I know." He paused unhappily. "Evvie, we're angry with Victor, terribly angry, but we can't let that blind our understanding. He can't let this thing erupt in court. Because—" He was silent.

"Yes?"

"Because that's the last thing he can possibly want. It could only destroy him. Now, that's the truth, Evvie."

"Take me home," said Eva abruptly, desperately. "I don't want to know more. Not tonight."

Slowly, stiff in every joint, Luzzatto picked up a valise of papers collected in the record room. Its weight was surprising.

The convertible was wet with dew, but the engine responded richly, instantly. Fog was clinging to the roads. They crept through the dark town, and drove into the hills in silence. On the long sweep up Tynesdale Road no word passed between them.

Eva put aside a silver-backed hairbrush and got into bed in silence while her husband turned out the light.

They lay in darkness while the events of the day raged through their minds, poisoned their thoughts.

"Can you sleep, Evvie?"

"No."

A creak sounded, and his weight was on her bed. He said, "I shouldn't have run off on you this afternoon. I'm so terribly sorry."

"You couldn't help it," she said.

She added in a low voice, "Don't expect too much of me either, darling.

85

I ought to be better for you, especially now, and I'll try, but I can't always help these moods." A pause. "I don't want it this way."

"Oh, darling," he cried in pain.

The mood of estrangement melted in a surge of love. He spoke her name, and held her, trembling in every limb, and then as warmth arose began to kiss her body with vehemence.

There was sadness and desolation in a wilderness of ice and cruelty.

In the end, he withdrew, shaking and sweating in the cold night air. "Oh, Jesus!" he gasped.

Her head was thrown back on the pillow. Her throat was exposed and naked, her breasts were blue circles against the sheets, he could taste blood of her bruised mouth. After a time the hoarse breathing diminished.

"I don't know what happened. I never meant to—" He trailed off.

"Don't talk," she said.

He took her hand and marveled at the papery texture of skin. His senses were sharpened to animal keenness. Faint whispering sounds came in a pitch never before heard. And smells of paint and carpet dust and linens and over this medley the warm odors of coupling—semen and vital slippery fluids salt as the sea.

"But it wasn't your fault," she said. "I wanted you and I tried to make it happen but I couldn't. It's something I can't help. There will be another time."

Luzzatto was silent.

"No. I don't think so, darling," he said finally, painfully, summoning all his tenderness. He forced the tone, feeling unstrung, dissatisfied by her dreadful remoteness. "I couldn't do this to you again."

"There was so much love this summer," she said. "It will come again."

"I know," said Luzzatto.

She touched his cheek. "I love you so very much, Davey. I want to do everything I can. But you understand?" A kiss rested on his mouth.

"Now you must try to sleep," he said softly. He smoothed the blankets. When her breathing had diminished, he went up to the study. There he opened the valise with its contents retrieved from the record room at Mackenzie Hall. None of the items was helpful. He stood in perplexity, and then the attic came to mind.

There he gazed at a confusion of oddments inherited from the past—iron bedsteads, *Leslie's Weekly,* a cranberry rake, almanacs. Wedged behind the massive stone chimney, a carton gave up a notebook:

Immediately below was a date in September.

Deeper search brought him to a large manila envelope. His handwriting, precise and minute, slanted:

Misc. Personal (Ull)

Thoughtfully he blew off the dust of years and emptied the contents on a trunk. Old letters and postcards from São Paulo, Martha's Vineyard, Lake Marah, Miami, La Jolla and Lake Lucerne. Photographs. Jo in Gloucester at the Fisherman's Statue. A post card: "Sailing tomorrow with *Captains Courageous*. Will write again. Luck to Eva. Love to both. Jo." Her signature was bold.

And a chart three by five inches in an odd design of seven candles supported on pyramids and engraved with selected verses. The curious design trembled as the events of the past came flooding back to mind. At sunrise he was still at work in the recovery of the past.

Less than twenty-four hours had passed since the postman had knocked to deliver the letter from Victor Ullman.

The Year of Discovery

Chapter 8

FROM THE MOMENT LUZZATTO ANNOUNCED HIS INTENTION TO QUIT medical school, down to the moment of departure for the university, his mother had waged a campaign against the decision.

Nella Luzzatto was a pretty and energetic woman of fifty with sparkling black eyes and a manner of utmost practicality and she was, in her son's opinion, the best mother in the world. He teetered maddeningly on the kitchen chair and studied her through lidded eyes. She had disapproved of his tie—an egg stain had disappeared under her scraping thumb nail—a change of shirt had been demanded, and finally she had insisted on a full breakfast. Even the best of mothers could be exasperating.

"Mama," he pleaded, "for God's sake!"

She said coldly, "Yes?"

It was a humid morning in September with a hot sun peeping from behind obscuring clouds. At ground level, the kitchen had a view of a garden enclosed by a wooden fence badly in need of paint. Nella banged the coffeepot on the stove and cracked a pair of eggs into the skillet with suppressed anger.

"All right, Mama," he demanded. "What? What?"

She turned on her son in anger. "I don't want you to leave medical school in the middle. You've got three years to go and I simply can't see why you want to break it off. I want you to go back."

Luzzatto shook his head. He was a thin, intensely ambitious youth at the time, with an obstinate mouth and keen gray eyes. He suffered from awkward manners, fitless clothes, self-absorption, lack of pocket money, rebellious hair, a sense of shame, unrequited loves, unpublished sonnets,

91

intense ambition, uncertainty of the future and an abashed grin which gave no hint of these turbulences within.

It could not be done, he said roughly. He had already notified the medical school that he had no intention to return that semester.

She was stupefied. "But why burn your bridges?" she cried. "You don't know yet if you can get into this other school, this whatever-it's-called. This—" She snatched at the air with vexation. "Oh, what is it?"

"Haverstraw," he supplied.

"Haverstraw, Haverstraw." She mouthed the syllables with disrelish. Any word she disliked was incapable of correct enunciation. "Who ever heard of it? Some third-rate farm school for country idiots? Eh?"

As she stood, arms akimbo, eyes flashing with scorn, he almost grinned at the picture of wrath and contempt. "Mama, I can name two dozen good schools you never heard of. It may not be Harvard but I can get my doctorate there and it's the best I could do on short notice."

She raised her hands in supplication.

"Ah! Wonderful!" she exclaimed. "Why not first take your medical degree and then decide? What harm would it do? You could have a good calling—a worthwhile profession. You could make a decent living. What can science do for you? What will you do? Teach? They starve. How much can you hope to make?"

He closed his eyes with the hopelessness of the argument. He had had his taste of medical school and he wanted to stop wasting his time and his parents' money. He was going into science.

"Ah! My God! When I think of how I'm ready to go down and scrub floors. Struggling to keep the business going." She was referring to a small antique shop in Greenwich Village from which basically the family revenues came. "What is so important about science?"

He sighed wearily and because he loved her he was cruel and punished her for probing his weakness. "Mama, why not drop it? You're just not educated enough to understand. Either that or the house has warped your sense of values. Anyway it's too late to argue."

The Cesare Luzzattos lived in a large whitestone on a quiet street in the West Side of New York City not far from the Hudson River. It was a monster to manage and a hopeless investment, for the neighborhood was in decline. Other owners had cut their losses and fled to the suburbs. Nella however had for twenty years kept up a stubborn rear-guard action. In her opinion the West Side was still the choice residential section of the city. Where else, she demanded, could one get stout walls and high ceilings and such solid and true values? Or for that matter the finest harbor view in the world?

"Look at the River!" she would demand hotly, with a gesture encompassing the scene from the bridge to the bay. "The View! The Cliffs! The Park! The Air! A Man Can Breathe!" She took cognizance of the rivalry of an upstart neighborhood across town. "What's that other river? What do they call it? The East?" She sneered. "A dirty ditch from which they fish out bodies? Eh?"

In any case she was convinced that real estate values would return and she lived in the hope of a glorious resurrection of the West Side when interest rates would once again be proclaimed by the Central Savings Bank at 3 per cent with second mortgage money for the asking, and in this faith she had clung to her investment and rented out her spare rooms and waited for a better day.

Luzzatto stared gloomily at soot settling in the garden. One of his earliest memories came to mind. He was then five years old, a timid child with saucer eyes, peering into a room where his mother was struggling with bills and bank statements and tax demands, desperate to make the figures come out right. It must have been summer for her hair lay clammy on her shoulders—and then, the quarrel, not loud, not high in pitch, but passionate in the extreme. He had waited on the stairs in a nightmare without end—and glimpsed Papa Luzzatto, much younger then, muttering guilty excuses like a boy who had lost pocket money on the way to school. It was the house! It wasted her substance, weakened her strength, devoured her business; he could recall a time of collapse when she lay stricken, shaking with anxiety, clinging nevertheless with a strong instinct for property. Her drive, her anxieties, her unhappiness, it now seemed to him, had cut deep into his soul. He sighed and faced her gloomily.

"Mama? What do you want from me?" he asked simply.

She held up a hand of appeal. "You were training for medicine. Finish!"

"It can cost a lot of money."

"Something will turn up. I'll manage."

They exchanged glances. "I saw the bank statement," he said finally.

"Oh? You read my mail? Davey!"

"Stop it, Mama." He was not embarrassed. "It was open on your desk. Papa won't make sense and I can't see you carrying me on your back forever. How long can I be a drain?"

She touched his face questioningly. "How can you talk like that?" His brows were those of a young hawk, she thought, smoldering with resentment, stubborn and without compromise. He had outgrown her, she thought, this son of hers, escaping into a world she could not enter or understand.

93

"Oh, Davey, Davey," she muttered bitterly, "you're your Papa's son! Go! Finish your breakfast!"

"Mom, cut it out!" he appealed uneasily. "What's your objection to Haverstraw?"

"I've got a feeling," she said in a low voice. "Something. How can I say?"

"Am I supposed to choose a school by your feelings, Mama?" he demanded irritably. "Does that make sense?"

"No. I suppose not," she sighed. "I see there's nothing I can do. It's your life. All right—live it."

In the meantime, upstairs, Cesare Luzzatto had passed a fruitful morning in his study overlooking the garden.

He had been working over an editorial for *Il Nuovo Mondo,* a small weekly newspaper with a cosmic range of political interest and a voice of thunder. With quick, crabbed strokes, he inserted a string of fiery adjectives in the margin—he had no patience with the thinner schools of rhetoric. The diatribe drafted against the Middle East policies of the State Department— "imbecilic" was his lightest animadversion— met with his own severe standards. A slash of crayon cut the piece to size. He encircled a bold "30". His handwriting was indecipherable, the city's worst since Horace Greeley's. An accomplishment, he noted with pleasure, not easily attained.

His grin faded as he was brought back to a much less satisfactory world. He put on a faded dressing gown and went down to the kitchen, jovial and handrubbing, singing:

La donna e mobile . . .

"Mama! Davido!" He kissed each in turn and settled in his accustomed place facing the stove and opened the *News* to the crime reports. In his expert opinion, the reporters of the tabloid press represented the flowering of American journalism—their gaiety, their irreverence, their flair for the seamy side had the flavor of the Renaissance. A bank robbery was a feast and a mucky divorce held special delights. "Oh, listen to this—" he chuckled.

"The boy's decided to quit medical school," said Nella.

Reluctantly Cesare put aside the paper. "Yes, yes," he said guiltily. "I know. Medical school."

Luzzatto watched his father's evasiveness grimly. "I told you about

94

it last July, Papa," he said coldly. "You promised to get me a letter from Jim Strollo."

"I remember," Cesare muttered, lowering his eyes under Nella's accusing stare.

"Papa!" she cried.

"Have you got the letter?" their son demanded skeptically.

Cesare flung down his napkin with vexation. "If I say I have it then I have it," he replied testily. "It's in my study. Is it so important?"

"It might be," young Luzzatto replied. "Can I take it?"

Cesare nodded. "You'll find it in the right hand pigeonhole. I have it among some papers for the Committee for Basque Justice. I don't understand"—he stirred his coffee slowly—"what is this about? Why is Mama unhappy?"

"Ah! My God in Heaven!" Nella exclaimed, raising eyes to invoke Deity. Very much to the point she forcibly and completely set forth the situation at this place—what-was-it-called? Hertapan?

"Haverstraw," said her son.

Cesare digested the situation. "This school. Haverstraw? Is it the best you could find?"

Luzzatto shrugged. "It'll do."

"Wouldn't you be better off, let's say, at Harvard? Or one of the better-known schools?"

Luzzatto sighed deeply. He loved his father devotedly, but how many times need one traverse the ground? "Papa," he demanded reasonably, "where would we find the money?"

Cesare was offended. "The money is no question."

"Ah! Papa!" his son said. "I know that story. You'll lay your hands on a few dollars and every one of those panhandlers around the office will get to it before Mama can pay the milk bill. I'm settling for Haverstraw because that's where I can still grab off this Fleischer fellowship. At any first-class school I'm too late. I'm not trying to be nasty, Papa, but I don't see any other way."

Cesare sat quietly with sudden pain and let his eyes slide guiltily toward the morning paper. After a life of polemics against property, it was melancholy to endure its inexorable revenge.

What was Papa Luzzatto?

No one could quite find the precise word. From behind square spectacles, flat pouchy eyes stared imperturbably at the world, teeth clenched a pipe and a homburg sat at a jaunty angle. He had the nefarious bland look of an art dealer who had graduated from the secondhand furniture business.

95

"What is Papa Luzzatto?" he would roar. "I will answer easily enough. He is irreconcilable!"

And it was true. He was a free radical floating in solution affected by the thermal agitation of his environment. He found the universe imperfect and its exudate—mankind—absurd. But if his field was the universe, politics was his garden. He rejected all hypocrisies from Emma Goldman to Stalin.

But if his own views held a pattern, it was outwardly unknown. He was a whirling dervish, a kaleidoscope, a quixotic tilter of windmills. Only in the secrecy of his home did his family know that he devoured Jefferson. He had annotated the *Collected Works,* scribbling notes for a commentary which never would be published. But this did not matter for in truth he loved liberty.

This was the light which guided his life—liberty!

Not, he would hasten to protest, that slovenly misgovernment and loose arrangement of affairs which America was pleased to call "liberty," but rather that true liberty which vanished when the first republic was formed and when the first law was passed. All men were knaves and fools, he contended, and so he opposed all men. In former days he had had a finger in every pie from the waterfront to City Hall. Union officials and racket men, capitalists and publishers, lawyers, physicians and thieves, intellectuals and the worldly brightened in his exuberance. Wherever he stuck his massive roman nose, he upset orderly meetings, offered impossible resolutions, demanded marches, demonstrations, collections or protests for this or that—yet he was still popularity itself in these dwindling circles. His laughter and wit supplied the only opposition for many weary and flaccid outmoded political splinter movements which had run their courses.

He had no friends, only followers. He had no cause, only dreams. He had no program, only love for man. He had no direction, no future, no goal. To the Right he was Left. To the Left he was Right. He was not at the Center. He was nothing. He was Papa Luzzatto. He had his pen and that was all he had.

The years had fled and now he sat sipping the dregs of coffee in a shabby old kitchen smelling of soap, longing to escape into the busy turmoil of public affairs—longing for anything but this matter of dealing with a family problem. Nella arose and went to the sink and scraped the breakfast dishes.

"Talk to the boy, Papa!" she cried.

Cesare sat drumming his fingers. "Tell me, Davido? You were doing well at your medical studies?"

96

David Luzzatto smiled ironically. "Papa, how many times? I was in the top tenth, I told you. I was doing all right."

Cesare lit an evil, cheap cigar. "Well," he finally said, "it seems we had this discussion two years ago, Davido. We agreed that medical school would be the practical thing even though we saw that it might have money difficulties." His face clouded uneasily. "Now suddenly you want to enter something else?"

"Yes."

"I—I simply don't understand."

"I made a mistake."

"I thought you knew your mind, Davido. What mistake?"

"I went into medicine," said Luzzatto in a low voice, "because I was afraid I wasn't good enough for research."

"Not good enough? How?" Cesare was puzzled.

Young Luzzatto straddled a chair awkwardly and studied his hands. "In scientific research the problem is that to get out of mediocrity, to get anywhere at all you've got to be brilliant. The competition is frightful. Even the bright guys in my class were afraid they weren't sufficiently outstanding. I shouldn't have paid any attention to that feeling but you both were hammering at me to play it safe and I did. I'm not the only one."

"And now? Are you specially qualified for science?"

"I don't know."

"Isn't that important then? To know if you have the talent? If you are not highly talented, what can you hope for? Can you expect a big career? Can you become what? A head of something? A professor? Tell me?"

"I might not amount to anything," said young Luzzatto. "How can I tell? I can only go into the field and get as far as I can. I don't want to wind up dragging my tail at forty. I've seen those guys. I want to make a big contribution and if I don't make it before I'm thirty I never will. Papa, I'm twenty-two."

Cesare smiled sadly and his fleshy shoulders sagged. "I don't know, Davido," he said. "I know nothing of science but I've met scientists and I've been able to take their measure. As far as I can see, success isn't only a matter of intellectual capacities. There's a question of luck and so many things. Have you carefully thought of all the problems?"

"Papa," said his son simply, "I'm committed."

Cesare gazed at his angered wife who was wiping dishes with a ragged towel. He nodded slowly. "If this is the wrong decision, isn't it possible one day you'll wish you hadn't let your life turn on a gesture?"

"Papa, are you in a position to give me lectures?"

Cesare lowered his eyes. "Go! You'll find Jim Strollo's letter on my desk. I hope you know what you're doing."

Luzzatto hesitated, then ran up to the study. His footsteps shook the building. Nella glanced up and clenched her fists.

"He's a good kid!" she cried. "A good kid! Why won't he listen?" Tears of exasperation mingled with those of pride. "Papa, can't you say something to him?"

But Cesare Luzzatto was already ruminating through the obituary page of the *Times,* pleased with the thought that on this page all strings were tied, all loose ends disposed of. "Eh?" He peered up. "What?"

"Nothing, Papa," she sighed. "Read your paper." Unaccountably she found herself in tears.

"Havemeyer!" she muttered. "What kind of a name is *that?*"

Luzzatto boarded the Poughkeepsie local at Grand Central Station. The coach was smelly and hot but he settled down with a sack of peanuts and opened the small recently published volume of Schrödinger's lectures and became critically absorbed in the argument. It was only as they rattled into East Haverstraw that some of the text struck him as out of date.

He picked up his bag and descended to the platform. There was a sense of serenity that day in the small industrial town asleep on the Hudson. A taxi was waiting at the weathered station.

The driver chewed a toothpick. "Goin' to the college?"

"Oh, yes."

Luzzatto felt himself flush under the critical stare directed at his threadbare sleeves. He stood insecure on worn heels with gravel sharp under thin soles.

"Ain't you a little late for registerin'?"

Luzzatto gazed about. "Isn't there a bus?"

"You just missed the connection. Next bus ought to come along in forty-five minutes. Well?"

Luzzatto fingered a wallet with a vision of its contents—draft registration card, return ticket to New York, driver's license, social security card and fifteen dollars in tattered bills. Keys and sixty cents in a pocket with a torn lining.

The driver sucked his toothpick and spat. "Get in," he commanded. "On me."

"I can't pay—" said Luzzatto.

The driver grinned. "Forget it. I'm an old West Side boy myself. I know what it is to get lost amongst the chickens. What brings you up from the big city?"

Luzzatto settled back expectantly. He looked about eagerly absorbing the sights of a busy industrial town. J. C. Penney and Sears and Woolworths dominated the shopping district with only such names as M. Friedlander (specialty shop featuring a $14 ready-to-wear dress line) to give a familiar touch among the alien corn.

"Know where you're staying?" The driver rolled a fattish eye; he was enormously muscled and dark as a Mexican with ruddy cheeks and a hearty laugh and he had in the few minutes managed to cover the fact of his service with the armed forces of his country in India, Burma and Assam. Based on his observations he was convinced that there was a gentile conspiracy to control the world—they were everywhere, he hinted darkly, London, India, Tokyo, Washington and even the Gold Coast was about to be taken over. No getting away from the scientific fact. He came back to his question. "If you like good cooking and a place to stay, give me a call. Tiny Feinberg. I can find you a nice spot and cheap. Maybe you can do some baby sitting? Now who you looking for on the Heights?"

"Oh, one of the faculty," said Luzzatto briefly.

"Bud, I been hackin' here since I come back from the war. What's the name?"

"Um. Mackenzie," said Luzzatto dubiously. "He's the dean up there."

"Dean?" Feinberg cocked an eye.

"Isn't he?"

"Not any more. The old gentleman's been on the shelf since when he took that fall on the ice and cracked his hip. You know that?"

Luzzatto felt a twinge of dismay. "No. I didn't. I mean, I've been getting some letters from a man named Ullman to come up for an interview but I had no idea Mackenzie was out. You're sure?"

"Terrible thing. Mr. Mackenzie's a fine old gentleman and it's only that way he's got that sets people off. He can get nasty with the arthritis and stuff but still he's got a lot of common sense and we got along. He made a lot of history around here in his time, he built this place, and this cracked hip and the pneumonia come as a shock. It took place along here. Cobb's Hill."

Cobb's Hill ran steeply to the Heights past an array of older houses surrounded by lawns and wide verandas. "Mr. Mackenzie's got that old house on the corner which meant he climbed the hill twice each day, up and down, to the college. I can still see him stompin' through the snow. Big shawl wropped around his neck. Thinking about another world. I was using chains at the time and I got him to the hospital. Real freezing

99

weather. Not a peep out of the old gentleman but with complications set-tin' in there was no question, although he kept going officially till the summer. So now Ullman has got the chance to be acting dean though he ain't the man the old gentleman was and he never will be. I mean, a man who can give a nickel tip when the clock reads three dollars—what kind of a man is that?"

The news had been decidedly unpleasant. Lackland Mackenzie had played an important role in his special field since its beginning. As a boy he had worked in the great gardens at Kew, and after taking his degree at Edinburgh, he had come to America to establish an experi-mental farm at East Haverstraw. His earliest contribution had turned on the application of the new insights of genetics to plant breeding. He was naturally gifted in the field, and his impossible hybrids, novel mutations, useful fruits and hardy grains were known throughout the world. But more to the point had been a steady flow of technical and philosophical papers which had made East Haverstraw as familiar to the world as Menlo Park and Burbank. Early in the century he had been invited to direct the School of Agriculture which later, under his control and in-spiration, had grown into the university's graduate faculty of pure science. Now suddenly, Luzzatto reflected with dismay, this towering figure was gone. The taxi bounced to a stop.

"Here it is, bud. Smell that air. A-a-h!" Feinberg set his brakes and relaxed, grinning possessively. He lit a cigar stub with an expansive, ad-miring gesture that encompassed sky and buildings.

"Pretty, ain't it?" he demanded.

Chapter 9

HAVERSTRAW UNIVERSITY WAS ANYTHING BUT PRETTY, THOUGHT LUZ-zatto on that first day. Her ugly green roofs were far from the idealized projections of the bulletin. He was unfavorably impressed by rows of quonset huts beyond Davenport Library. The sound of trip hammers was everywhere. Even Mackenzie Hall, which was his goal, seemed shabby, second-rate, desultory of purpose after medical school. With a sense of disappointment, he brought his problem to the elevator man on duty.

"Try the Information, sir," said the man. "Always start with the Japanese lady."

Mrs. Nakamura was married to a hard-working Buddhist priest of a poor temple in White Plains. She had little time or interest for anything beyond her strict duties which did not include Luzzatto's problem, but something awkward and helpless in the gaunt young man, perhaps the frayed collar and worn shoes, appealed to her motherly instinct.

"Gee, I'm sorry about the mix-up," she exclaimed, flashing her teeth. "Dean Mackenzie's retirement was a tough break. Still, you can take it up with Dr. Ullman."

"Can I see him now?" asked Luzzatto.

"Oh! He's got a ten o'clock. Why not go in and audit that first lecture?" She called out. "Eva?"

"Half a sec," said a muffled voice.

Eva had been poring through an index to periodicals in Dr. Tobian-sky's office. At the summons, she closed the book, and came out with a light step.

"Follow, please," said Eva, and strode off.

Of that first moment, there was to remain most vividly in Luzzatto's memory, Eva's slender nervous wrists and her musical voice, low-pitched, slightly husky, belling with a rich quality. Its foreign timbre was slight but pleasing. For some indefinable reason, her inflection brought to mind Natasha, the delightful heroine of *War and Peace,* with whom, at fourteen, he had fallen violently in love. In the clean lines of her firm chin, her low intelligent brow, long neck and abundant hair coiled in braids about her ears, Eva fulfilled a vision of a high-minded, idealistic and ardent young woman of Tolstoyan dimensions. A white shirtwaist with starched cuffs seemed altogether appropriate.

"Come along!" she ordered peremptorily.

Like the Red Queen, Luzzatto thought wryly. His eyes were busy picking out details as she led him down a hall filled with exhibits of local and foreign fauna including a series of prehistoric horses in evolutionary order. It was hardly impressive.

"Do you work here?" he asked inquisitively.

Her shoulder lifted in the foreign shrug he was to know so well. No, not exactly; she had some office and laboratory duties but that was in connection with her fellowship, she replied, and strode on in silence.

"What fellowship is that?"

Her brows went up. "Are you interested?"

"Why, sure."

It was rather early for tactless questions, she thought, but he seemed more anxious than presuming. She held a fellowship in biology, she advised, the Fleischer Meat Products Corporation Fellowship in Biology.

A sickly expression suffused his face. "The Fleischer?"

"Oh?" Her inflection rose. "Were you interested in that?"

"Oh, no," he said hastily. "No."

She sniffed. "It's not much but it keeps me going."

They strode past the library in silence.

"What's your special field?" he asked finally.

She squinted at a point in space. Really, she thought, this country! One showed off bathrooms and asked rents and priced clothes and questioned fellowships and next, no doubt, the bloke would ask if she were a virgin. A Polish word for uncivilized boor came to her mind before she reminded herself that in a free country manners were free. She held a sharp retort in check.

"I am still wavering, sir." The 'sir' put a nice distance between them. "My courses are not too specialized yet. Who knows?" she asked darkly. "I may never get past my master's."

"Why not?"

102

"It takes a bit of talent."

"Oh, that?"

In his mild and worried eyes she saw a naive expectation that—on the whole—anyone at all could qualify for a mere doctorate in science. "Yes, that," said Eva slowly. "Sometimes I feel like such a dunce."

"Oh, sure, you'll make it, Miss—uh—" He paused seriously. "Say, gosh! I guess I'm being a pest. My name's Dave Luzzatto."

"Bronowski," she said formally, "Eva."

They faced each other like strange colts in a pasture, sniffing with velvet muzzles. A firm cool hand gripped his own in a European handshake—once up, once down—and a loose button caught her glance of disapproval.

"Well," said Eva coolly, "here you are."

She opened a door which led to an anteroom where a dark, hairy man of forty was distributing forms to students. A buzz of voices could be heard within.

Luzzatto approached. "Is this Zoology 125?"

The older man glanced up. "Are you taking the course?"

Luzzatto shook his head. "I don't know yet. I'm trying to get to see Dr. Ullman. I had an appointment, I thought, with Dean Mackenzie."

"Oh, yes." The older man scratched a heavy jaw and glanced at Eva. "Let me know what happens. Katz-Moebius. I've got an office on the fifth floor. In the meantime, take any seat you like. Free, on the house. Say, Miss Bronowski, we're showing those movies today."

Leo Katz-Moebius winked at Luzzatto. Confidentially, he remarked, he had promised the puritanical Miss Bronowski a film which showed a tribe of New Guinea monkeys at sexual play in their native wild. Miss Bronowski, he observed gaily, drawing Luzzatto into the discussion unabashed, was not interested. "And yet," he observed, "it raises a question for science. Where do monkeys learn these human delights? Who teaches them? Pygmies perhaps? You see the implications? Yet Miss Bronowski doesn't care. Incredible. In-credible!"

Eva's brows rose frostily. "You must not excite yourself unduly, Mr. Katz-Moebius. Luzzatto, good luck." She nodded curtly and strode off. Katz-Moebius handed a form to a latecomer and turned back to Luzzatto. "Just find any seat at all."

With a glum heart Luzzatto climbed to a high tier from which he could survey the class. It was damn sickening, he thought, to learn so offhandedly that a strange woman had jumped his claim to the Fleischer. He flapped open a notebook and automatically set down the date and course and waited for the lecture to begin.

103

Two raps sounded and someone coughed.

Victor Frederick Ullman entered and took a position behind the table which traversed the room. He waited for silence and turned and wrote his name across the blackboard in flowing European script. Under this he wrote the course: *Zoology 125,* and returned to the class, dusting chalk from his fingertips with a fastidious air.

"Now, let me see," said Ullman.

His harsh voice was high-pitched and guttural, yet despite a slight lisp, it brought the class to order. Pens and notebooks came to the ready; women students from Burland tucked in stray wisps of hair. With pinched fingers he affixed a rimless pince-nez and picked up a set of cards. "I should get acquainted," he remarked in a strong Germanic accent. "Hendrix?"

A pale youth looked up. "Here."

"Prescott?"

"Present."

Thirty or so names later he looked up.

"Wodzick?"

A deep, good-humored voice arose. "Correct."

Ullman wiped the corners of liverish, almost Egyptian, protruding lips. He sniffed and stared up with magnetic blue eyes. "Not Bronco Joseph Wodzick?" he asked ironically. "All Up-State?"

"Correct."

"What are you doing in this course?"

"To tell you the truth, Professor, it's convenient," said the blond young giant.

"To what?"

"My training schedule."

Wodzick grinned engagingly and the Professor sighed. "Candid enough," Ullman admitted. "Are you interested in this field of science?"

"I'm interested in behavior." Wodzick enjoyed the craned necks, the covert support and sympathy from a loyal following.

"But this is not," said Ullman, "a course in behavior."

"Isn't it?"

"No. This is a course in genetics."

Ullman took a position closer to the blaze of sunlight. From one of his coat pockets—he wore a cheap black suit with a pin-stripe effect and a polka dot tie—he brought out a packet of brown cigarettes and began to smoke through flaring nostrils.

"Wodzick, we are concerned here with problems of heredity," he said instructively. "If you will read your catalogue, page 120, you will see that we cover an introduction to the principles of the science. Such things as Mendel's principles, meiosis and the physical basis of heredity, linkage, genetical and cytological mapping of chromosomes, mutation, introduction to population genetics, the heredity of sex— Ah," he broke off, "I see a smile?"

"Sorry, Professor."

Ullman studied the youth for several moments and then without expression wiped back a shock of iron-gray hair. It was a queer, almost preening gesture.

"Wodzick," he queried, "you're planning a career in science?"

"I'm not sure, sir."

"Ah? Why not?"

"I'd like to but my father's got a big dairy farm that needs attention."

Ullman pushed the cigarette into his mouth, European style, holding the brown paper from below and sucking smoke over a protruding lower lip. "I would be more impressed," he observed finally, "with this pose of stupidity, Wodzick, if I did not know of a set of excellent marks in every subject but Public Speaking. How did you fall down in that?"

Wodzick flushed with embarrassment. "I guess I'm not interested in speech," he grinned.

"Ah! It might be well, Wodzick, to show less conceit, less complacency with this philistine pose," Ullman commented. "You deceive no one. You're a plain simple superior intellect like the rest of us." He gazed about hopefully but the pedantic jest failed to take. The class waited stolidly for the next queer remark.

Except that in an upper tier, he noticed, a thin hungry-looking youth had flashed a winning smile. Smoking thoughtfully Ullman walked to the window and lifted the sash. He returned rubbing a strongly molded nose as though meditating how to dive into the sea of knowledge.

"Who knows the Mendelian laws?" he asked, staring through his pince-nez. A scattering of hands went aloft, then others followed reluctantly. He asked, "Does anyone wish to state the principles of Mendel?"

No hands were raised.

Luzzatto shifted uneasily. He had an impulse to stick up his hand but he felt strange and illegitimate—not yet entitled to the franchise. What was the matter with this crowd? The Mendelian laws were simple enough, elementary.

Ullman strode about, chewing his cheeks, and tapping ashes on the floor, and proceeded to a circuitous joke. His hand was stained a deep yellow, either nicotine or nitric acid in origin, and it moved muscularly with a life of its own. "Who knows 'The Young Lady From Starkey'?" he asked, smiling broadly.

There was a moment of silence. Ullman's lectures followed an invariant line—the same points, the same jests, the same sequence. In the third row, Roy Hendrix, a crop-haired weedy youth in spectacles, underscored a paragraph in a mimeographed set of notes—published in the Beta Sig house by an entrepreneur of an earlier generation.

"Here it comes," groaned Hendrix, lifting his eyes. "On the dot."

A hand went up finally.

Then another.

Scarcely gratified, Ullman called on the first hand up.

Jack Prescott, a grizzled navy veteran, hitched his belt and recalled the well-known verse:

> "There was a young lady named Starkey,
> Who fell in love with a darky,
> The result of her sins
> Was quadruplets, not twins,
> One black, one white, and two khaki."

There was some tittering, a groan or two, but Ullman's heavy manner left the class cold and embarrassed. "Is that verse in good taste?" he asked gutturally.

Prescott scratched his chin. "Guess not," he shrugged, annoyed. He had been called on to recite, his manner said, and he had complied. Why the moralizing?

Ullman glanced about at the men, then the women. "No. It is in execrable taste. I imagine, gentlemen, ladies," he said harshly, "you are thinking the teacher is telling his usual joke to be a good fellow? To give a little life to a dry set of lectures? Or perhaps there is one here who thinks the teacher likes to shock?"

Some shock! thought Luzzatto ironically.

"No!" Ullman went on, examining his cigarette critically. "It is to illustrate a number of points—first, that all human beings are not alike. Miss Starkey is white. The darky is not white. In pigment they are not alike. Perhaps in other things they are not alike—in temperament? In spiritual elevation? In emotional capacities?"

He looked about, staring with deliberation. "Is there perhaps one in this room who wishes to comment?

"No?

106

"Have I said something that's not liberal? Well, why? Isn't it merely a political article of faith that all men are born equal? That they are endowed by their Creator with inalienable rights?"

He snapped his fingers and pointed challengingly. "Who believes that all men are equal?"

A blond girl raised her hand and others followed. They were off on an uneasy tangent, wondering what would follow.

"Who is authority for that notion?" he demanded harshly. "Does anyone know?"

"Lincoln," said the blond girl faintly.

"Jefferson."

"The Declaration of Independence."

"The Constitution."

"Montesquieu."

"Locke."

Ullman received the diverse opinions with thoughtful appreciation. "Isn't it clear, gentlemen," he said finally, "*transparently* clear that we are in a state of hopeless confusion?" It was another professorial joke, but as no one seemed to respond, he went to the next point.

"It is only an assumption," he went on gutturally, "that all men are equal. Whether or not they are in fact measurably so? Ah! That is a scientific question." He grasped his lapels and frowned. "I will make a statement. From the beginning of time all living things have shown profound and measurable inequalities." He paused for emphasis. "*In*-equalities! Is there anyone who wishes to challenge?"

No one wished to challenge.

He gazed about hopefully, then sighed and looked up. "Mr. Tewksbury? Are you ready?"

On an upper tier, a bald man of fifty looked up from a slide projector, and nodded slowly, wiping a hairless pate at the summons. His features were dull, sluggish, devoid of expression.

Ullman pressed a clicker. "Let's have your first three slides, Mr. Tewksbury. Will someone lower the shades? Ah! Thank you!" Green blinds cast the room in darkness, and then, with a hiss and sputter a picture of the Aphrodite of Cnidus was thrown on a screen. The naked loveliness was unexpected and embarrassing.

"We will call her Miss Starkey," said Ullman drily, and proceeded to draw an outline of the picture on the blackboard.

At the next click, the slide danced and settled on an old Chinese merchant smoking an opium pipe.

"Let us call this gentleman Chang," said Ullman, drawing a second outline.

The last figure was the Negro janitor of Mackenzie Hall. "We will call this gentleman Stephen," said Ullman, "because that is his name. Now! We will have discussion." As the shades went up, he turned and pointed. "Miss? You will state your name?"

Self-consciously the blond girl acknowledged that she was Mabel Olcott.

Ullman pointed to the first outline. "What color is Miss Starkey?"

"White, I guess," the girl responded squeakily.

"And Mr. Chang?"

"Yellow."

"And Stephen?"

"Black."

"Can you suggest another such division?

"Um. Brown, I suppose. Hawaiian. Polynesian."

"Good." Ullman drew another figure in a grass skirt. "Any other?"

The girl licked her lips nervously. "Well, not by color, Professor. Pygmy?"

"Excellent." Another figure, gluteally magnificent, got drawn. "Why not red?" Ullman demanded. "The American Indian?"

"Aren't they supposed to be Mongolian? I mean in origin?" the girl wondered.

Ullman nodded, pursing his lips. "Are all these alike in physical structure?"

The girl hesitated, as her hand unconsciously went to a small crucifix at her breast. "No," she said reluctantly.

"In what respects not?"

"Pigmentation," she said faintly. "Bone structure. Height. Hair." She paused self-consciously.

"Perhaps blood groupings?" Ullman prodded.

"I don't know about that," she confessed.

"I will tell you." Ullman turned and wrote a series of fractions under each figure. "Different ratios of blood groupings are found in different groups of mankind. I will not," he frowned, "designate these groups as racial, or ethnic, or anything, but X and Y and Z. But does this not suggest anything?"

The girl shook her head mutely.

Ullman nodded slowly in disappointment. "Note this, gentlemen," he remarked to the class. "From the beginning of time there have been wise

108

men and fools, big men and small, philosophers and football players, thieves and their victims. Since the divisions of mankind are diverse in such physical details as skeleton structure, and pigmentation, and susceptibility to cancer, *and* diabetes, why may we not expect it in moral and spiritual and mental structures? Miss Olcott?"

Every sound in the class ceased. There was a sense of shock as the harsh opinion rolled to the rear and back again.

"I—I don't know, sir," the girl whispered.

"But you dislike the thought?" The slight lisp was now marked through the Germanic gutturals.

"Yes, sir."

"Why?" Ullman demanded.

"Well—" The girl cast her eyes down. Her lips, Luzzatto noticed, exquisitely penciled in like a Giorgione, petulant but primitive, were bright with orange lipstick. She looked up defiantly.

"It sounds undemocratic," she said hesitantly. "And besides—" She meant to add, "Unchristian," but blushed and bit her lip.

"Why?" Ullman's eyes widened. "Is it undemocratic to conjecture differences among men?"

"Yes, sir," she said. "I think so."

"Is this an opinion of fact? Or a moral attitude, Miss Olcott?" The girl had no answer.

"Why? Because you fear that to acknowledge physical differences will lead next to a politically unpleasant conclusion? Yes? Let me give you an instance. You know of sickle-cell anemia?"

The girl shook her head.

Ullman smiled ironically, and went on to explain in a precise dry manner an obscure hereditary disease of interest to physiologists, biochemists, physical chemists, anthropologists and above all to the geneticist. Because of a slight variation in a single molecule in the structure of its hemoglobin, he went on, the sickle cell is susceptible to a peculiar reaction. Under certain conditions it forms long rods which clog the body vessels and induce anemia and possibly death.

"A disease! No?" Ullman demanded.

The girl nodded.

"Now! In this respect, is not the victim biologically inferior to one free of the defect?"

"Inferior," said the girl reluctantly. "I guess. At least physically," she added.

Ullman accepted this as a point gained. Among certain tribes in Africa, he went on, the incidence of the trait was not less than forty per cent, and of the disease itself, induced by the trait, not less than four per cent. Then —as to this trait—were not such tribes in the biological sense inferior?

The girl had no answer.

But yet, Ullman went on, the trait was not without its biological advantages. Studies had been made of the area of sickle-cell incidence in Africa. It was also an area infested with malaria and in some unknown and mysterious way it appeared that the sickle-cell trait strongly protected young children against the parasite of malaria—the scourge of mankind.

So that, Ullman concluded neatly, in the malarial belt of the African continent could one properly call the sickle-cell trait a sign of biological inferiority? Were not such persons in fact gifted with biological or survival superiority? Eh?

The girl flickered a pale tongue and plumped for the biological superiority of the African native in the terms stated.

Ullman remained rocking on his feet. Now why, he demanded dryly, *why* the reluctance to extend the train of logic to other hereditary traits— sunniness of temperament? Passion for justice? Intelligence? Flair for drumbeats? Spiritual insight? Capacity for cultural adaptability?

The blond girl stared in wordless dismay. Ullman drew a heavy breath of smoke. The sardonic lines at his nostrils deepened. "Tell me, Miss Olcott. In forming such an opinion, do you feel insecure merely to rest on a moral judgment?"

"Not exactly, sir."

"You would prefer a more objective basis?"

"Yes, sir. But I think it's wrong," she said with a rush, "to talk about the differences between people as though they mattered. That's where all the war and misery come from. I mean, Hitler and all that. Killing people because of race. I mean—well, gee! Maybe people are different in some traits but we're all human. If people weren't fundamentally similar," she added as inspiration struck, "they couldn't interbreed, could they? I mean—" She hesitated and took refuge in her notebook, blushing furiously.

"Aha!"

Ullman clapped his hands with pleasure and lengthened his stride. He ran his hands over his hair as he digested the girl's happy response. "*Not* opinion, gentlemen, ladies," he noted, raising a finger. "*Not* sentiment, but an appeal to fact—the demonstrable universal capacity of the human race to interbreed. Yes! Here finally is proof on which judgment may rest." He paused at the blackboard and wrote a sequence of block letters:

"Miss Olcott," said Ullman quietly.

"Yes, sir?" she answered weakly.

"What is 'Knowing'?"

She frowned. "I don't know, sir."

"Isn't it equivalent to another vital word?"

"I—I'm sorry." The poor girl was lost.

Ullman completed the design:

K N O W I N G

S C I E N C E

He then repeated the design vertically:

K	S
N	C
O	I
W	E
I	N
N	C
G	E

"Now," he remarked, "you will not forget." He dropped the chalk in a pocket and stared around the class, lingering briefly as Luzzatto's alert face fell under his glance.

"Gentleman, do you see now?" he asked. "Mr. MacIntyre? Prescott? Wodzick?" He completed the rounds and came back to the unhappy Mabel Olcott with some impatience. "Science is Knowing. And Knowing is Science. Not opinion. Not wish fulfillment. Not good taste or bad. Not even democracy." He studied his cigarette. "This means something. It means that what we seek here is Truth."

He sighed and looked up. "Truth, Miss Olcott. Do you read Scripture?"

"Why, yes," she agreed, startled. "Not much."

"Have you any idea how many commandments there are in Scripture regarding the pursuit of Truth?"

"Gee, no," said the girl uneasily.

The class stirred with embarrassment. The teacher had violated a cardinal rule that he keep to the subject advertised in the catalogue. The switch to theological speculation was a breach of contract. Would that question come up in the finals? If not, it was a waste of time—an imposition, if not a cheat.

Ullman sighed and removed his glasses. His reddish lids were suddenly naked in the common gaze. "In Scripture there are thirty-five commandments to pursue Truth," he said, pinching his eyes. "Why should we take those directives seriously? Can anyone say?" He paused questioningly.

"Because Scripture joins Science in the single command. Scripture says, 'Know the one true God.' Science says, 'Know thyself.' These are commands to know. What can that mean to this class? Eh?

"It would seem evident," he continued, restoring his glasses and walking stolidly to the window, "that a principle is involved. It is an assumption that the universe has a single design. From the farthest galaxies, remote in space, distant in time, down to the microcosm here and now, this universe is governed by uniform cosmic law. Well!"

He seemed to be talking almost to himself. The sun picked out deep lines in a high forehead, glinting against silver threads in the gray coarse hair. The handsome face was strongly molded on Teutonic lines, the firm heavy features were those of Goethe at the same age, except that the mouth was clamped like a line. In repose the face was without humor. He turned back to the bemused class, frowning heavily.

"Because, you see," he went on, continuing a private train of thought, "the universe is too vast to be understood by the human mind—but if, if we snip the fabric for study, if we learn the part, we will know the whole. Eh?" He gazed at the array of well-nourished young faces and raised a finger. "A drop of water comprehends the sea.

"It is a postulate of the Higher Indeterminacy," he continued sardonically, "that one can never know simultaneously with accuracy both the position and direction and speed of a particle at the same time. In the physical sciences, this is thought to place a limitation on the boundaries of our knowledge.

"But is this so?" He smiled with amusement, smelling the chalk at his fingertips. "This rule obtains only if we limit ourselves to the function of reason, not when we expand our conception beyond those boundaries. No such limitation should be assumed when we command all the resources of the human mind, human intuition, human knowledge. *All* the resources, gentlemen," he added weightily.

"We are not here to memorize details, facts, tables. We are here to learn Truth. Gentlemen, ladies, when we know the Truth—when we can define with the words of our mouths, with the meditation of our hearts—we will serve the purpose of Knowing—of Science. Let us return to Miss Starkey."

The class stretched uneasily. The performance was queer—grotesque. It was as though he had bared something of almost extreme intimacy to them.

"The limerick implies one truth," said Ullman, exhaling a lungful of smoke, "and two untruths. Can anyone state them?" asked Ullman. Throughout the discourse his glance had been attracted to the face in the rear—the young man whose quick grin had seemed responsive to his sallies and who now was thoughtfully digesting the summation. Ullman raised his chin. "Your name?"

Luzzatto sat up, startled. "Me?"

"Yes, sir."

Luzzatto was surprised at the thin quality of his voice in the strange room.

"Well." Ullman returned to his position behind the table. "Mr. Luzzatto, is the limerick a correct statement of Mendelian law?"

"No, sir." The class turned with vague hostility.

"Why not?" Ullman demanded.

"Because the ratio would not result from that cross."

"How do you know?"

Luzzatto hesitated. "Because observation tells us so."

"And what else?"

"Theory."

"Good! But what did Mendel find? What truth?"

Luzzatto unwound his bony legs and sat erect. "Mendel established the law of heredity known as the law of segregation." He struck and held a note of confidence. "That rule that the factors of heredity, derived from the parents, do not mix in the offspring. On the contrary, those factors are segregated in the different sex cells of the hybrid offspring."

Ullman smiled with pleasure. "Yes. The truth," he conceded, rubbing his hands. "What are the untruths?"

"Well, Miss Starkey ought to be a Negro herself. The one-one-two ratio appears only when the parents are similar hybrids. Aside from that, the transmission of skin color is complicated by a series of factors—more than one, that is. That's why the offspring would be an in-between shade, not black, not white. Mendel worked with plants." He stopped abruptly.

"Kindly explain."

Luzzatto cleared a dry throat. In the first thrust and parry, he had felt the older man's steel. "Mendel crossed different varieties of peas with clear characteristics such as the color of their flowers. Mostly traits which were obvious."

"And?"

113

"The ancestral qualities refused to mix. They turned up uncontaminated in the second generation."

"Uncontaminated?"

"Yes, sir. When he crossed yellow with green, some offspring were yellow, some green—but none turned up in-between." Luzzatto searched for a simile. "Not like mixing paints, sir."

Ullman nodded. "And what did he conclude?"

"That the ratios were fixed. He determined that the mechanism of heredity was controlled by discrete units, or particles, of some living substance within the cell, transmitted to the offspring and reassorted in each generation without change. It was an atomistic theory." Luzzatto was conscious of an impulse to talk well, to win a point. It struck him as absurd that his voice was rising in pitch under the intensity of the older man's stare.

"Have these atomistic particles a name?" Ullman demanded.

"Yes, sir." Luzzatto waited.

"Well, go on."

"Later investigators named these units genes."

"Stop there!"

Ullman fished out a piece of chalk and wrote across the blackboard:

GENE——from *genos* (Gr.)——GENETICS

He then wrote with deliberation:

2,200,000,000 human beings!

He stood back and nodded at his handiwork. "Mr. Luzzatto, if the egg cells from which all the human beings on earth have developed were contained in a vessel, what volume would that comprise?"

Luzzatto hesitated, reluctant to appear clever on his first day. He had a good notion of the original estimates made at Indiana University. "Oh, about a gallon pitcher."

"And the equivalent sperm cells?"

"A thimble."

"And the naked genes stripped of cellular materials?"

"Two aspirin pills. Maybe less."

"Incredible," said Ullman. "Is it not?"

The class meditated that all the bits of matter that account for the heriditary make-up of the human species, with all its infinite variety and complexities, would compress to a tablet of unbelievable potency and

114

complexity. Ullman broke the chalk and came back to the discussion, nodding appreciatively.

"Very good, Luzzatto," he remarked, stroking a smile of satisfaction. "Where did you pick all this up? Perhaps you bought the same set of notes for this course that I see in Mr. Hendrix's possession?"

Luzzatto hesitated under a mischievous impulse. "To tell you the truth, sir, I began to learn all this when I was about ten years old. I read *The Book of Knowledge.*"

There was a titter of laughter.

Ullman's face slowly darkened with displeasure. "It would be better for those who laugh to realize that one cannot read *The Book of Knowledge* too early in life." A deeper meaning was underscored. "The science of genetics deals with man's deepest urge to understand himself—to know his place in the universe. Man must to know," he went on heavily, his intonation thickening, "his own nature as a living organism. He must to fathom the mechanism that shapes the development of body—the flowering of mind—the assumption of spirit. If anyone disagrees with this"—he paused to grasp his lapels— "let him leave now. The bursar is prepared to remit all fees.

"Who disagrees has no place in science.

"It must be understood!" The harsh voice rose in pitch. "Here is the science of life. Here is the most philosophical of all sciences since it deals with genesis—the beginning of man and possibly the end of all life. This donkey laughter is simply foolish. The sense of wonder in the infant can not appear too early.

"For this is the essence," he concluded somberly, rocking on his toes. "The thirst for knowledge. Who lacks this thirst may withdraw."

A bell marked the end of the period.

Ullman sighed and relaxed. "Next session we will take up the first basic problem of heredity—the mechanism by which the living cell reproduces itself." He went on with a few brief announcements. Assignments would be followed according to a short guide published by the department. Supplementary materials for the textbook of the course, Ullman's *Principle of Genetics,* were on sale at the Co-op. He concluded, "Mr. Luzzatto, I would like to see you in my office in ten minutes."

Chairs banged and the class dispersed. Luzzatto's earlier dissatisfaction was forgotten in the thrill of the older man's restatement of the loftiest ideals of science and the human spirit.

Chapter 10

"OH, HELLO!"

A friendly woman with dark flashing eyes came forward wiping her hands on a laboratory smock and introduced herself as Professor Ullman's daughter.

"Come in, Luzzatto," she said cheerfully. "I'm Jo Ullman. Guillotine's ready. We're waiting for the headsman. Dr. Ullman's in conference. Do you mind?"

"Guess not," he muttered.

He let his eyes grow accustomed to the light. The laboratory was crowded with books and equipment and furnished with a number of tables. Toward the rear an inner office door was closed. Two smells were detectable to his trained nose, a stink of tobacco stronger than anything from beaker or flask, and, like the musk of gardenias, the body smell of a woman in close quarters.

"It's pretty late," he remarked sorely. "I've been waiting since eleven."

"Have you had lunch?"

"No. Guess not."

"Well, my God! Why not? You might have knocked."

"That secretary didn't tell me I could."

Jo Ullman thrust her fists into the pockets of her smock and squinted at the thin face. "Luzzatto, if you haven't got the nerve to knock on the door, turn around and leave right now. The door's still open. Eh?" she drawled. "Dr. Ullman will be with you in a minute."

She winked and strode back to a table covered with wine bottles of pint size. Luzzatto put down his briefcase and glanced about.

"You can sit," she suggested.

"I've been sitting," he replied. Curiosity prevailed. "Can you tell me what you're doing?"

The woman explained pleasantly that she was preparing a fixed stain mount of a selected strain of yeast. A smear of the culture had been spread on the glass slide with a sterile needle and allowed to dry.

"What culture's that?" he asked.

"Um. Let's see." She consulted a note. "*Saccharomyces ellipsoideus.* It's a strain used by vintners." She passed the slide through a flame and poured a dye with quick skill. After a minute the slide was washed in water and dried on absorbent paper. "Would you like to look?"

"Why, thanks."

Luzzatto bent over to a familiar shimmering picture. A number of cells had been arrested in a moment of reproduction and their nuclei, lovely in color against a clear background, were distorted; the distribution of vacuoles was clear. It was a good workmanlike job, he murmured. Jo Ullman sat back with a relaxed air and offered a cigarette. "Luzzatto," she asked curiously, striking a match, "what brings you to Haverstraw?"

"That's a funny question. Why not?"

She smiled pleasantly. "Why not, indeed? Well, that's a question my dad's bound to ask you and you ought to have an answer. He's strong on getting down to brass tacks. I've been looking through your application. You might have tried any number of other schools." She lit her cigarette and observed him coolly. "You've got a sour look on your face. Why?"

"Have I? Well, I don't think it's exactly courteous to keep me waiting outside," he replied stiffly. "A lot of other people were coming and going. He could have seen me—or sent out word."

"My dad's got more than one thing on his mind, Luzzatto," she retorted equably, raising her brows, "especially after registration's closed. You should have been up here last June."

"Well, I couldn't—"

"Why not?"

"Because Dean Mackenzie wrote me not to come in June. That's why I waited till the last moment. It wasn't my fault. I thought I was set."

"Dean Mackenzie?" She eyed him sharply. "What did he tell you?"

Luzzatto shrugged. "Oh. It was about the fellowship. I had my application in last April. Said it looked favorable, but subject to personal interview. He couldn't see me till September and he'd let me know. Well, he never did and now some woman's got that grant. I'm back where I was six months ago." He stared with concentrated uncertainty. Jo Ullman's speech seemed vaguely British or Canadian. She was a small woman with

117

lustrous black hair, older than himself, he thought, by ten years; he was struck by the tan of her flat olive cheeks and a sinewy humor in her glance. She was quite unexpected. He said glumly, "Guess I'm on a spot."

"Loosen up," she commanded, smiling. "It's not that bad. Just take it easy and present your case."

The door to the inner office opened. Ullman stepped into the laboratory proper, accompanied by a well-groomed man of his own age. His face lit up.

"Ah, Luzzatto! You've met my daughter?" he said abruptly. "Have I kept you waiting? I am so sorry. Oh," he added, recalling the situation, "this is Dr. Beekman. Mr. Luzzatto is a candidate for admission to our poor school." Handclasps were exchanged and the information given that Dr. Douglas Beekman was director of research at Brandywine Laboratories.

Luzzatto looked up with interest. "Do you know Mr. Strollo?"

Beekman seemed amused. "Hardly. Mr. Strollo's president of Brandywine Industries. The Laboratories are, or is, only one small part of the whole. Of course we're very much aware of Mr. Strollo. Why?" Luzzatto explained the family connection. "Yes. Well, when you're finished here, Luzzatto," said Beekman affably, "call on me in New York if you've got plans along industrial lines. We're interested in anyone with Professor Ullman's imprimatur. Goodbye!" And Douglas Beekman, whose manner seemed more brisk and businesslike than academic, nodded pleasantly and left. Ullman relaxed imperceptibly and assumed an air of geniality. "Nah! Come inside. Here by the window. Good! If you don't mind the broken springs? So! Maintenance is in a dreadful state. Now then?" He rubbed his hands briskly. With a reassuring wink, Jo went back to work.

"Well now!" Ullman sank back in a deep swivel chair and selected a brown cigarette. "An old habit," he remarked informatively. "Your folder, please?"

Luzzatto began impulsively on a note louder than intended. "Oh, Professor Ullman, my background's a B.A., City College, and I've done a year at Pennington Med. I realize I'm late but I've had a lot of background and my interest is basically—" He halted abruptly. None of this was quite as planned and his voice felt hollow.

"Yes, yes," Ullman frowned. "I remember some correspondence." His eyes traversed the record with an air of dissatisfaction. "I should have expected a B.S. with these courses?"

"No, sir."

Ullman snapped his fingers. "Ah! Yes, it comes back. You started an

118

arts course in college? Yet you elected to major in science? Four years of chemistry, I think?"

Luzzatto nodded and the teacher went on. "Yes. Now after a year of medicine, you would like to be accepted as a candidate for a doctorate in—?" The heavy brows rose.

"Zoology, sir. Genetics, to be exact," Luzzatto supplied. "I guess it took some time to figure things out. I'd always had a drive for science, even as a kid, but I never quite saw myself in the role. I always expected to be a writer or something like that, you see? I never thought I could be a scientist."

"Why not?"

"I had too much respect for science. I doubted that I had the ability."

"That interests me." Ullman lit the cigarette and sat back. "A writer? Why?"

"Oh." Luzatto hesitated under the sharp glance. "My father's a writer, you see. Well, not so much a writer as a newspaper man. Sort of an agitator. Political theory, that sort of thing. He gets out a paper, *Il Nuovo Mondo,* you know."

"Ah, yes!" said Ullman intelligently.

Luzzatto smiled faintly. "It took some time to know what I really wanted to do. Medicine was my family's idea, not mine. It was supposed to be the practical thing and I went along with that."

"You thought to be practical? Why?"

Luzzatto hesitated. "I was bothered by money problems. How to make a living. I've seen a lot of that in my family. But medicine's not for me. I've had it, sir," he said decisively. "That year at Pennington convinced me to get into research."

Ullman accepted the explanation with a cold stare as though it conveyed a world of meaning—as indeed it did. The dilemma of these sensitive science majors, torn by uncertainties, was a recurrent problem. "Tell me, Luzzatto," he suggested finally. "Your father, mother, the background has interest. In this country, the intelligentsia is so small, one rarely meets their children. I should like to hear about them."

"Um. Well—"

Luzzatto went on to talk of his parents with some freedom, fondly, almost with indulgence. The older man ran on through the documents, glancing up at times appreciatively during the earnest discourse. His questions were shrewdly put; he nodded attentively and finally tapped the documentation.

"Luzzatto, where is the pattern?"

"Pattern, sir?" asked Luzzatto.

119

Ullman placed an instructive finger along the flat of his cheek. "Science assumes that life has form, purpose, design, a continuing pattern which molds and guides all things. If you lack this understanding, you cannot grasp the underlying symmetry." He returned to a photostat of the younger man's college record. "You were pre-medical. What made you elect cultural anthropology in your senior year?"

Luzzatto's grin was boyish. "I'm afraid, sir, it was a snap course. Professor Quarles—" he blurted humorously, unable to resist the impulse. "Oh, I'm sorry." He subsided under a level stare.

Ullman let a moment of silence pass. "Quite all right. I'm not a prig," he remarked coldly, then made an effort at geniality. "How is Harry Quarles? By the way," he added pleasantly, "Quarles is one of my dearest friends, you know."

Luzzatto said, "Oh, he's fine, sir. Still goes in for those horrible puns."

Ullman laughed indulgently at the mere notion of Professor Harry Quarles. He ran down the list of courses, noting other dear friends and old comrades, then raised his brows. "Engineering physics?"

"Oh, that?"

"Was that another 'snap' course?"

"Hardly." It was a tough optional course, Luzzatto recalled ruefully, three semesters jammed into two; and although supposedly geared for the pre-med student, it covered quantum mechanics, nuclear physics and relativity. Perhaps it had called for undue effort, but he had been unable to pass it up. Why? Well, because once out of college, he might not have gotten another crack at that field of study. Ullman sank back, swinging a gold key. "You thought this remote area important to your special field? Why?" he demanded dryly with rising inflection. "Because it might prove helpful in the practice of medicine? To take X-rays? To repair encephalographs? To manipulate radiation dosages? To fix the television set?" His tone was laden with irony.

Luzzatto was taken aback by the challenge. He shook his head doggedly. "No, sir. I don't object to those practical reasons, and they might be valid for the next guy, but for me? Those weren't my reasons."

"Then what?"

"Look here, Professor,"—Luzzatto sat forward earnestly— "when we get down to the most basic processes of life, aren't we dealing with the electro-chemical functions of the cell and of aggregations of cells? No question in my mind we'll finally be forced to write our explanations in terms of purely physical systems. I mean—" He paused, disconcerted by a sudden expression of alert interest. "Take the distribution of electrical charges within the living cell. A lot of recent studies seem to go a long

120

way to explain and predict the life functions of all organisms. How else can they proceed meaningfully except in terms of purely physical systems? You raised that question yourself in our lecture this morning regarding the structure and function of the gene. Well, let's take those latest reports from Cambridge. I don't have to tell you that the picture that's been deduced of the helix structure of the DNA molecule in the gene actually has the most far-reaching implications for a whole line of research—" He struggled forward, gesticulating stiffly, absorbed in his train of thought.

Ullman listened attentively, occasionally bringing his brown cigarette to his mouth. "You say, Luzzatto," he murmured dryly, "that the physical is the only way by which the gene ultimately determines the organism?"

The younger man sat back. Something new and bleak had entered the discourse. What indeed explained this genetic power? Evolved in thin chemical soups of primordial seas, by what powerful mystery did the units of heredity still, after a billion years, retain their capacity to live, reproduce and function with higher intensity than in the beginning of time? He answered cautiously. "The only known way, Professor. I don't feel I can go beyond that position. Excuse me, sir. I guess I'm talking too much." He sat back, outwardly serious, but inwardly warmed by the pleased conviction that all this had been neatly put indeed.

Ullman failed to answer directly. "It is an analysis," he nodded. His glance fell to the slender book peeping from Luzzatto's briefcase.

"You have been reading this fellow Schrödinger?"

"I've just finished," said Luzzatto cautiously.

"Your opinion?"

Luzzatto cast his eyes down, not knowing quite what was behind the question. "I'd say this, sir," he ventured carefully. "I'll go along with the physical laws Schrödinger concedes, I mean, the role of the statistical principal in explaining the size and stability of the genetic unit. But then he leaps off into the notion that it's not the body that organizes and determines the mind—but rather mind that creates and directs body. In fact that the human mind is equivalent to Godhead itself. For a scientist?" A wry grimace was expressive.

"You object? Why?" Ullman's hands were motionless, his eyes were watchful.

Luzzatto grinned impulsively. "I simply think those mystical doctrines are not proved. Or rather, they're not provable—"

"You mean, by scientific methods?" Ullman interrupted.

Luzzatto considered the amendment. "If there are other methods of proof, what are they?" he asked with disdain.

121

"There are, perhaps, other methods, " Ullman suggested quietly. It was a popular notion, he pointed out instructively, that scientists apply their formidable intellects in the simple, logical induction of new general principles from known laboratory facts. But was this correct? He was inclined to think not. Far greater advances had been made in science by mental processes remote from mere logic—in large part by subconscious processes. For example, the classic experience of Henri Poincaré, who, putting his foot to the step of an omnibus, had felt the exultation of an idea, bursting from intuitive, subconscious depths, that certain mathematical transformations used to define Fuchsian functions were identical with others of non-Euclidean geometry. "In fact, Luzzatto," he went on ironically, "Poincaré later verified his discovery to his complete satisfaction. The flash of intuition, which preceded logical deduction, was thus proved correct. The hypothesis was at once displaced by the fact." He paused and twirled his gold key, sunk in inner thought. "This sort of hypothesis," he resumed heavily, "which predicts the probable existence of facts, or orders of facts, is recognized in the literature. It has recently been named the stochastic method—which means to divine truth by conjecture. Look in the literature, Luzzatto!"

"Yes, sir," said the younger man.

The blue eyes widened with irony. "Nah, nah! You must concede the value, Luzzatto. The problems in our field are of great importance to mankind, and they are so refractory, so resistant to penetration, that we cannot afford to overlook any possible pathway into the unknown." Ullman glanced up with mistrust. "Perhaps I am disturbing you?"

Luzzatto shook his head. "Sir, we all have hunches, flashes of insight, intuition, what not? But what does that prove? Logic's not a description of how we think. It's a method for determining the correctness of inferences drawn from established facts." He added with certitude, "I can't see how mere intuition can guarantee the superior attainment of truth."

Ullman seemed to be thinking deeply. After a long moment, he glanced up gravely, sighed and arose. So far, Luzzatto thought, there had been no discussion of credits, courses, a stipend—the guts and sinews of an academic career. The teacher strode about the room and came to a halt rocking on his feet. "Luzzatto, when you abandoned medicine, what was your idea?" he demanded abruptly. "Didn't you regard medicine as science?"

Luzzatto hesitated. "No, I did not, sir."

"What is medicine?"

"In its present stage? An art. One day? It may become a science. I've got nothing against medicine but I feel that one vital discovery in the laboratory can do more to advance the frontiers of knowledge than ten thousand practitioners pumping penicillin." Luzzatto hesitated, feeling now on firmer ground. "I mean, take the transformation in the past fifty years—Loeb and Warburg and Meyerhof and Lackland Mackenzie and what they represent. They've changed the whole picture. Fifty years ago we were concerned with single organisms—the differences between species and groups. Now? The idea that all living beings share the essential processes of life has tremendous implications. I can't imagine a more fruitful approach than through investigation of the universal functions and substances common to all things. I don't see why we can't continue to get tremendous insights into all mammals—that includes man, of course—by getting into the chemistry, let's say, even of unlikely organisms that seem unrelated to us. I want to work with anything that can reveal the processes of life at the most fundamental and universal level. Now how could I do that in the practise of medicine? Gosh, no! I can't see any attraction in that."

He paused for breath, feeling queerly divided as he awaited judgment. Under the piercing blue stare, so much of this suddenly seemed pretentious, inflated, windy, diffuse, conceited. Yet underneath he felt a measure of elation. Whatever the outcome he felt unburdened and relieved.

The older man favored the younger with an enigmatic, almost calculating glance. His next remark was unexpected. "It was artful of you, Luzzatto, to include Dean Mackenzie in your pantheon," he observed, smiling gently. "The one glory of this university. Have you read his book? *A Field Theory of Life Sciences?* I seem to recognize some of his ideas in your, ah, discourse."

"Yes, sir," Luzzatto agreed readily. "It was Mackenzie's book that gave me the impetus to apply here. Tremendous, sir. Just great. One unified field of all the biological sciences. It seems the key, doesn't it? But I wasn't trying to be artful," he added quickly.

"I daresay not." Ullman meditatively resumed his pacing in a cloud of smoke. "Dean Mackenzie's wish to retire was a blow to us all, but in some ways, I may confide, Luzzatto, it comes as a relief to his friends. He was not happy as an administrator. It was not his strong point—the practical handling of budget, appointments, staff. Oh, I could tell you." He smiled tolerantly and a thought struck him. He turned and called out through the open door. "Josephine?"

"Yes, Dad?"

Jo Ullman was smiling as she entered. "Well? Are you making the team?" she asked humorously. "My dad's been talking about you, Luzzatto, you might as well know. We're always on the lookout for talent."

123

"Really?" Luzzatto wondered, pleased and flustered by the unexpected assist from the sidelines.

Ullman smiled. "I'm afraid that Dr. Ullman," he emphasized her title gently, "forgets sometimes that what is said within these walls is in confidence." He put his arms about her shoulders and squeezed. "My assistant, you see? She gives me several hours a day with, ah, a branch of my work. Invaluable. Deficient in theory, of course," he added indulgently, "but a good technician."

Jo Ullman made a face.

Luzzatto laughed uncertainly.

"Later, I may ask my daughter to show you the ropes," said Ullman, returning to business. "Josephine, dear. I'd like you to fetch Will Tewksbury. Would you mind?"

"Nah!" said Ullman abruptly when they were alone. He erased a cigarette, frowning heavily, extended an arm. "Luzzatto, let's understand certain things. How much do you know of conditions here?"

"In what respect, sir?"

"Well! We've been slack, I concede. I won't say where the fault lies," —a formal smile was without mirth—"but the fact is that even under Dean Mackenzie not all of our graduates have been to our credit. There's a chance now for a new dispensation. Up till now our advanced degree has called, for example, for a research dissertation on a level suitable for publication in a recognized journal. I need not tell you, this is of course the usual yardstick of merit, but in our case '. . . *ist's ein Gebrauch, Wovon der Bruch mehr ehrt, als die Befolgung!*' A custom more honored in the breach, Luzzatto, than in the observance. This standard is not high enough. I propose to require actual—not putative—publication. Does this intimidate?"

There was challenge in the dry glance, the harsh tone. Luzzatto felt a quickening response.

"I don't see how you can demand too much," he said emphatically.

Ullman smiled. "Perhaps you know, Luzzatto, that a large part of a university's research program is given to problems submitted by industry and government. I am not sure I entirely approve. It diverts time and effort from pure research. Frequently it gobbles us up, and we find ourselves committed to methods of financing ourselves which divert us from the main task—the search of truth.

"For that," he added somberly, raising a finger, "is our entire justification, the fact that we serve one mistress—truth. Truth, Luzzatto. Nothing else. That is why a proper research project has such extraordinary importance. Unluckily," he sighed, "in this respect we have a restricted freedom of choice." He paused, fixing a somber gaze on a rain cloud piling up in the humid sky. A sense of exhilaration in the younger man was mixed with growing uneasiness.

"I shall be entirely frank," Ullman went on. "It may be that you've come at an opportune moment, Luzzatto. For quite some time now I've had such a research project available of extraordinary interest. You may know that I've had a long experience in fermentation processes? It is one of my conceits that I was in that field from the very beginning." Smiling modestly, he described his early years at Manchester in the first World War under the great Weizmann who had devised the first practical method for the production of acetone and butyl alcohol. "So you see," he concluded, smiling, "I'm an old fermentation man. Come back here." They strolled back to the microscope together. "Do you see what we're trying to do?"

Luzzatto nodded. "Dr. Ullman's classifying some kind of yeast."

"A special strain, Luzzatto." Ullman reverted to his classroom manner. "Now here"—he picked a glass slide from a case—"she has been staining and fixing an example of vintner's yeast, *S. ellipsoideus*. I needn't tell you, Luzzatto, that today only selected strains of this organism are used by the wine maker. What do you think?"

"I—I'm not sure I get all this."

"Several years ago Dr. Beekman brought to us a genetic problem on behalf of his people at Brandywine. Can one modify this organism so as to produce entirely new kinds of local wines of superior body and novel flavor? Eh?" During the last war, he pointed out, genetic knowledge had been used to increase the harvest of penicillin several thousandfold by manipulation of the organism *P. notatum*—an achievement of staggering importance. Here now was an equally exciting vista. Not only was it practical, but a solution might lead to important future relationships with the sponsoring industry.

"Well, Luzzatto? What do you think? Would you be interested in such a problem?" He waited expectantly.

The younger man failed to answer immediately. The project had been outlined with a force and enthusiasm he could not share.

Luzzatto rubbed his mouth. "It sounds fine, Professor, really fascinating. But if you'll excuse me—well, isn't it a bit commercial?"

Ullman stiffened. "Perhaps. Why?"

"Nothing, I guess. Except that I've already got a project I'd like to discuss. It's something I began to run down over the summer." He paused, suddenly aware of a chill.

"Project?" A fixed stare deepened into a scowl. "What project? Who's been talking to you?"

"No one's been talking, sir. I've had this idea for the longest time."

Ullman stared with a trace of anger, noting the clear gray eyes and obstinate mouth as though for the first time. "Tell me, Luzzatto," he asked. "You feel qualified to make a decision like this?"

"It's not that, Professor," said Luzzatto slowly. "I'm sure your own project is exciting, and I'm really flattered, but that's not the point. It's just that I feel committed to see it through. My own project, I mean. I thought you'd want me to feel free to discuss my ideas?"

"Go on," Ullman invited ungraciously. "I'm prepared to discuss. Of course. Now! What is this project?"

Luzzatto drew a breath and stated simply that he had in mind to explore the resistance of bacteria to antibiotics and other drugs. It was a field of rising value, he felt, that promised to throw light on the basic mechanisms of evolution.

Ullman received the proposal with astonishment. "In your first year you hope to start a program of this magnitude?" he demanded ironically. "In the laboratory at our disposal? *Um Gottes Willen,* Luzzatto, have you yet got the training? The technique? Can you run before you learn to walk? This is a lifetime study!" His smile was incredulous, angered.

"But I've already begun," said Luzzatto simply.

"So?" Ullman considered the younger man, now shaken by the drastic change of mood. "Begun how?" he demanded.

Luzzatto described a series of experiments begun six months earlier at home. "I've been thinking about this for a long time. Of course I haven't got the right materials or equipment—"

Ullman interrupted. "Equipment is nothing. Have you kept records?"

"Certainly. I brought them with me."

Ullman put out his hand. "May I?" He opened the book with a cool air of professional skepticism. It was an ordinary journal for laboratory purposes, sturdily bound and numbered, worn with use. The pages were ruled off for graph purposes.

Bacterial Resistance

The first experiment was entitled:

Classification of representative bacteria strains by gradient plate techniques with reference to antibiotic sensitivity.

126

Lines of disdain deepened as he traversed the pages digesting the data in a powerful, orderly mind.

"Was this work supervised?" Ullman demanded.

"No, sir."

Fourteen experiments had been done, Ullman noted, comprehending their purport at a glance. "Luzzatto, I'd be unjust if I were less than frank," he said harshly. "Your handwriting is a miserable scrawl." The book closed with a sharp clap. "What's all this supposed to get you? Eh?"

Luzzatto looked sick. "Insight, I guess," he replied slowly. "Something basic might turn up. Or maybe nothing. That's the chance I take. But isn't it a legitimate field for the study of genetics?"

"Something basic? Hundreds of papers are in the literature," Ullman remarked coldly, sucking a lungful of smoke. "Some work of this order has been done," he added angrily.

"Sure. But, gosh, is the field closed? Up till now we've estimated the rate of mutation, the flow of evolution purely on the basis of chance."

"The Poisson function. Well?"

"Must we accept that concept of mere chance?" asked Luzzatto simply. "Isn't it possible to sharpen our insight into causality?"

Ullman resumed his smoking, obscurely offended. "What would you suggest?" he asked harshly.

"Well—" Luzzatto hesitated, disturbed by the challenge. This was either sublime, or absurd; he could not tell how it was going down; in any case he felt the compulsion to go on. Perhaps if they knew more, he suggested, they could base the emergence of mutant organisms, the flow of evolution, the origins of new forms of life—not on random factors but on more classical concepts of law. "It's a chance to experiment with evolution," he pointed out. "I just can't accept the idea of a universe based on principles of uncertainty."

Ullman stared peculiarly at the younger man. "You imagine to refute the fundamental assumptions of modern science? To upset the concept of the indeterminacy of matter? Either you're fifty years behind or a thousand years ahead." A grimace of incredulity drew the corners of his mouth. "Or perhaps," he added, "there's another explanation? Well, Luzzatto?" He sat back frowning suspiciously.

"Gosh, no! Not of all matter," said Luzzatto hastily. "I can't go as far as all that, Professor. But you've got to admit that the principle of indeterminacy operates basically on the nuclear level—where we're dealing with theoretical points in time and space. When we get to living organisms, we're faced with larger structures that differ in scale entirely from any piece of matter handled by the physicist or chemist. Why must we assume that the same laws apply? I'm sorry," he concluded, "living matter is an orderly thing—at some point in the scale the amount of indeterminacy becomes negligible—"

Ullman interrupted. "Luzzatto, leave this area or explain yourself more concretely," he said. "Who advised you to pursue this line with me?" He seemed disturbed.

"No one, sir."

"These are your own ideas?"

"Of course."

"Well, well," Ullman considered the matter with a scowl of disbelief. "You've shown me your lab book. What else?"

In the face of unwavering blue eyes, Luzzatto went on to express the thought that, like a sublime master key, the science of genetics might unlock the ultimate mysteries of growth and evolution and even permit an attack on the major ills of mankind. Might it not be possible one day to control cell heredity by direct manipulation of genetic units? Such notions were in the air. Why not in their laboratory as well as any other in the world—?

Well, there it was, he thought, breathlessly, excitedly, committed. It was stated and done and he had no idea of the effect of these speculations. Ullman removed a cigarette and nodded.

"It is original," he conceded sardonically.

"Oh? I didn't think of it that way." Luzzatto was taken aback by the dry and ungenerous tone.

"Are you sure it is not *too* original?" Ullman studied the sudden pallor of the obstinate young face. "True originality?" he intoned rhetorically. "It is priceless. But too often, Luzzatto, it masks something else. Can you be sure that you are not choosing this plan because in fact secretly you hope it too grandiose ever to reach a point of proof? Eh?" He sat back, pursing his lips with anger.

If the question was meant to cause Luzzatto to shrink within himself it was effective. He had been rattling on, almost oblivious to the older man's reactions and now—this! What had he said wrong? The impression of a neurotic young man drawn to science for the wrong reasons—likely to be torn by phobic indecision—was too damaging to risk.

"I don't believe so, Professor," said Luzzatto slowly. "I've got no false concern in originality for its own sake. Just now I'm interested only in a specific area of study for my dissertation."

"Tsah!" said Ullman abruptly. He turned his back and plunged into the signing of letters. He glanced up with an air of decision. "Luzzatto, you must accept a premise. You seem to know your mind. Good! This is desirable. It is equally clear that this department must know its mind. Here research is not hit-or-miss for the student to decide. It is a disciplined co-ordinated effort in which the student works completely subordinated to the teacher's direction. Is that agreed?"

"Of course," said Luzzatto slowly.

Ullman scowled disagreeably. "I have offered you a problem. It is I who must supervise—I who must decide. You think this arbitrary? Ah, my God! If one dared at Göttingen to address the teacher in this fashion?" Upraised eyes were eloquent. "Of course this is not Göttingen and we make allowances. But as to your so-called project?" Slowly he shook his head. "Out of the question. I regard my own suggestion as more practical—more suited to your needs at the moment. Eventually—"

Luzzatto was dismayed. "Sir!"

"Yes?"

"I feel pretty strong about my project," he said stubbornly. His heart was thudding. "I really wish you'd give it more consideration."

Their glances met and neither wavered.

"Mis-ter Luzzatto!" Ullman began with deep anger. "If it is your idea —Nah!" With an effort he strode to the window, flexing powerful hands, and regarded the campus below. After a moment he turned and regarded the younger man somberly.

"I must be frank, Luzzatto. I find this situation disconcerting and I simply wonder why I allow the discussion to continue. However, I must admit to a feeling about you this morning in class. I was impressed by your response. We were dealing back there, I realize, with trifles, but what struck me was not the substance but your manner. There was something about you. You see—"

He hesitated, frowned painfully, then resumed on a curious, thoughtful note.

"Luzzatto, Luzzatto," he murmured, shaking his head. "A teacher has a sixth sense for these things. As one enters the classroom, almost instantly as one turns to that assortment of faces, in that moment—one knows. Ah, how one knows! It is a lump—or one feels intelligence that reaches out. What does our Shakespeare say?

Wer ist es im Gedräng, der mich begehrt?

How is your German?"

"Fair," said Luzzatto, taken aback by the abrupt change. "German and French are my languages. Nothing much to speak of."

Without transition Ullman resumed the quotation in declamatory style:

"Wer ist es im Gedräng, der mich begehrt?
Durch die Musik dringt gellend eine Stimme . . .

How does it go in English? 'Who is it in the press that calls on me? I hear a tongue, shriller than all the music . . .' So! This morning, Luzzatto, I heard a voice. Eh? *A voice!* Do you understand?" The hot, blue eyes widened to their fullest extent.

In the disconcerting moment Luzzatto was queerly elated. Something of intimacy had been expressed. He licked his lips. "I think so. You're talking about a feeling?"

"Am I? Perhaps!" Ullman said somberly. "Luzzatto, Luzzatto! A teacher learns these things. He earns his place in life by the talent he brings to flower. I have such a feeling—a sense of—well, excitement, intuition. As you observed, we are here to extend the limits of reason, but do not limits suggest something beyond—limitation? It is Horatio who says:

> There are more things in Heaven and Earth,
> Than are dreamt of in your philosophy . . .

Wouldn't you agree? For the first time since I came to this God-forsaken place I feel that together—" He made a strong gesture. "My God! Why am I going on? It is only that these feelings are not to be disregarded."

"Hamlet," murmured Luzzatto deprecatingly.

"What? Of course, it is *Hamlet.*" Ullman frowned with displeasure, then suddenly patted his hands, and laughed noiselessly and immoderately. It was an orgasmic explosion of mirth, until finally, wiping tears and gasping for breath, he recovered. "Yes, yes," he nodded. "To be sure! It is Hamlet who expresses that thought. Not Horatio. I was thinking of the version in German." He replaced the pince-nez and blew his nose refreshingly and sighed with amusement. "I've never forgotten my first *Hamlet* which as a student I saw at Göttingen. Moissi played the part. Or was it Sonnenthal? No, I am sure Moissi. In those days," he added nostalgically, "the German stage was the finest in the world. Our Shakespeare? Ah, dear! Magnificent! Although I must admit that the English translation is not bad—not bad at all." At the classical jest he laughed again under forced draft. "Nah! We must talk of this another time, Luzzatto. As you see, nothing is out of context. Everything is relevant to truth—spirit as well as reason. It would be unscientific, certainly unrealistic, to exclude either one.

Es gibt mehr Ding' im Himmel und auf Erden,
Als Eure Schulweisheit sich Träumt—Horatio!"

130

He laughed freely, refreshingly, still not quite accurate, but of this seemingly unaware. "You see?" he asked gaily, "I have accepted your emendation as perhaps you might accept mine. Isn't that the test? Fidelity to truth?" He rubbed his hands briskly. "And now let us return to practical considerations. We publish of course jointly with credit on the most generous possible basis to the student—"

Striding the room, he swept Luzzatto along in the excitement of future plans. He halted suddenly, a shadow crossed his face. "Luzzatto, if we are to work together, certain rules must be accepted." He glanced sidewise at the younger man, hope mixed with trepidation and suspicion. "I must ask for extreme caution with respect to what goes on in this laboratory. A certain give-and-take is permissible but outside this room our work is not discussed. It may seem disagreeable but it is necessary. I detest gossip and a great deal of harm can be done by loose discussion of work in progress. I don't want to go into the question of factionalism and jealousy, Luzzatto, except to remark that the situation here is delicate—extremely so. After a time you will perhaps understand—"

Luzzatto grinned. "You're talking about faculty politics?"

"Oh, my God!" Ullman permitted a glance of amusement. "Unbelievable! As acting dean I must to make painful decisions. Questions of budget, advancement, papers, honors, assistants, equipment and God knows what. One cannot satisfy them all and one's position gets painful, but then who else should fill the position of dean?

"Mackenzie himself agrees," he argued, pacing about with bowed head. "It is not only logical, it is necessary that I should assume the direction. Yet it is the last thing I want. I should want to play with red tape? To shuffle papers for those—those *administrators?*" he demanded rhetorically. "It is only that a responsibility is involved. Nah! I've said too much!" He paused and stared meaningfully. "Leave your notes with me and I'll make a decision. Eh?"

Luzzatto said a stupid thing. "I—I'm accepted?"

Ullman struck his forehead and laughed heartily. "Am I accepted?" he mimicked. "I thought that was clear."

"Well—" Luzzatto hesitated.

"What is it? Yes?"

"It's just this one thing, sir. You haven't mentioned my stipend. That's pretty important."

"Stipend? Nonsense! You've got the Fleischer.'" Ullman exclaimed irritably.

"No, sir. I haven't."

Ullman frowned. "But surely? Oh, yes!" He halted in surprise. "That went to Bronowski. Yes, yes. Of course! But then when you got no favorable response didn't you understand?"

They exchanged glances.

All this, thought Luzzatto unhappily, had been too good to be true. "I—I was counting on something like that stipend, Professor. I need a job. I really do."

Ullman pressed his mouth thoughtfully. "I see. Well, I didn't quite understand—" The door opened and Jo Ullman looked in with a serious face. "Dad?"

Ullman looked up impatiently. "Yes, yes?"

"Willie Tewk's not feeling too well," she said worriedly. "I'm not sure you ought to see him now."

"Quatch!" Ullman frowned. "Send him in."

Tewksbury entered and waited for orders, utterly without expression. The man's lemon-colored skin was completely hairless even to brows and lashes.

Ullman introduced Luzzatto as a new student who would require locker and equipment privileges. "See that he gets what he needs, Will?"

"Ayeh," said Tewksbury in a flat apprehensive voice. A slack mouth trembled as he turned to go.

"Oh, Will?" said Ullman casually. "We are out of sugar and tea. Would you mind, at your convenience, to fill the cupboard?"

Jo Ullman looked up. "Dad, I'll do that," she said sharply.

"No, no, no!" said Ullman indulgently. "You tend to forget, Josephine. I'm sure Will won't mind. Eh?"

" 'Course not," said Tewksbury.

"Domino size will do," Ullman went on pleasantly. "And, oh yes,"— his fingers bunched in perplexity—"tell me, Will? Did you sterilize the Waring blendor for Dr. Patterson?"

Tewksbury licked his lips. "I did that Monday. I entered it on the chart."

"Do you recall the steps?"

Tewksbury described the protocol haltingly—wash in hot water, wash in cleaning fluid, rinse in hot water, rinse in distilled. A standard detergent had been used.

"I see. Yes," said Ullman gently. "I wouldn't mention this, Will, except that Dr. Patterson reported a contamination of his last culture. He thought a step had been omitted. It's of no importance, I'm sure. Let Dr. Patterson see the chart." His nod was a dismissal.

Tewksbury hesitated, glanced anxiously at Luzzatto and left. His shuffling footsteps paused in the anteroom.

Freda's hysterical scream came as a shock. "Oh, God! No! Not here, Will!"

Ullman strode through the laboratory and flung open the door. In the outer office Tewsbury was standing, pigeon-breasted, at Freda's desk, and in the bright autumn sunlight his face was purple. Hoarse sounds rose from a slack mouth, fishlike in a pout of horror. Freda covered her face.

"Tewksbury!" Ullman shouted. "I order you not to lose control!"

Although Luzzatto knew what was happening, his bowels turned to water. Tewksbury's hands curled into talons and in a split second, although it seemed forever, the spine formed a rigid arc and the man pitched forward with an unearthly rising yell, smashing his skull against the desk. A froth of blood bubbled from slack lips. A knot of students stared with disgust and terror.

The man's eyes rolled back in his skull and his face turned livid as a corpse. A fecal smell arose. Ullman took command. "Josephine! Back to the lab and close the door," he ordered. "Freda, don't be an idiot! Luzzatto!"

Jo Ullman with her face pale and tense closed the door. Luzzatto knelt beside the stricken man. "Sir?"

"The ruler!" Ullman ordered. "Now your handkerchief. Hold up the man's head. We protect the tongue. Good, good! Unloose the tie—the belt. Hold the wrists. He'll be all right presently, poor devil. Ah, my God! I warned him to take his medicine. Nah, nah! There we are—"

Muttering encouragement, Ullman gradually reduced the uncanny to the commonplace. He was quite good—direct and authoritative and in control, and full of kindness—and gradually the tension abated. There was pity from the women students, nervous comments from the men. Eva Bronowski was a pale face of compassion at the door. The body felt warm and muscular, radiating heat as its functions went on, and this was somehow strange. Medical help finally arrived.

When it was over, Ullman sighed and blinked encouragingly over a cigarette. "Luzzatto, in the morning we will come to an agreement. I'll find something to your satisfaction. Eh? You'll assist?"

"Thank you," said Luzzatto gratefully.

In this odd moment he felt a part in the fellowship of Mackenzie Hall and it was a good warm feeling. It perplexed him that a trifle hovered in his mind. Why, he wondered, had Ullman had recourse to the German version of *Hamlet* to justify a misquote? Were not all the versions alike?

It was a point he resolved one day to check.

And never did.

Chapter 11

LUZZATTO WAS ASSIGNED TO A BARE AND UGLY ROOM OVERLOOKING South Field in Buckley Hall. He stacked his books and hung his cherished portrait of Darwin. Once settled, he got down to a hard routine, departing early for Mackenzie Hall, returning late to self-imposed tasks beyond the call of duty. Lobbies were noisy with the caterwauling of undergraduates, but his own floor was given over to students from the three graduate faculties, a quiet, toiling lot whom he got to know in the fellowship of common showers and stalls. Down the hall lived Leo Katz-Moebius.

A week after matriculation, the door was opened toward midnight by a genial, naked figure wrapped in a towel.

"Telephone," said Katz-Moebius.

Luzzatto looked up from a text. "This late?" But Katz-Moebius was off to his own room down the hall. Luzzatto marked his place and went to the telephone. The dramatic rumble was familiar. "Davido?"

"Yes, Papa? Is something wrong?"

"Why must it always be something wrong?" Cesare complained. "Mama tells me you have finally settled this business of yours. Yes?"

"It looks so. I'm sticking here." In the background, Luzzatto detected the clack and whirr of a flat-bed press. His father, he reflected, would be stalking the shop with Tullio, his foreman, slapping metal into frames, joking, scribbling last minute fillers. "Papa? You there?"

"Yes, Davido. Tell me about the fellowship? About this woman, it doesn't sound fair. You had a promise."

"Dog eat dog, Papa. I can't complain. If I could have gotten that deal over her dead body, believe me, I would. Anyway, it's all blown over."

"How do you manage financially?"

Luzzatto hesitated. "Dr. Ullman got me a sort of stipend."

"A fellowship?" Cesare's voice rose with hope.

"No." Luzzatto was silent. "It's out of a fund at his disposal. I'm acting as his personal assistant. We're doing a piece of work for Brandywine."

"Brandywine? Is that Jim Strollo's outfit?"

"Papa!" Luzzatto had returned late from the laboratory, and his eyes were burning with fatigue. He clung to the telephone for a moment. "If it lets me do my work? What difference does it make? Dr. Ullman's letting me work on my own project in my spare time. It's quite a break."

Cesare said slowly, "Well, I'm so glad, Davido. I know how these obsessions give one no rest. If this is how you can accomplish your purpose, it's exactly what we want for you. Only I regret that you did not come to me for help. I can always raise a few thousand dollars."

"Not necessary, Papa. I manage to get by."

There was cold silence and a heavy sigh floated over the wire. "We'll miss you Thanksgiving. Will you be home for Christmas?"

Luzzatto hesitated. The holidays meant nothing in the bohemian household. This was a bid for sympathy, a plea for his return. "I'm not sure. I've got such a load of work here." He paused guiltily. "I don't know if I ought to take off the time. Suppose we see?"

Cesare's voice detained him. "This Ullman?"

"Yes?"

"I should like to meet him some time. I'd like to thank him myself for us. Also, I would like to know something of your work, your future. Perhaps if I were to call on him?"

Luzzatto paused. "Sure! If you want to, it can't do any harm."

Now why, he wondered, had he hesitated? His feeling for his father was one of pride, of affection, and yet he felt discomfort at the prospect. Cesare was himself too shrewd in common affairs to be taken in by pedagogues. Over the years, few of his son's enthusiasms had withstood his critical, rather jealous evaluations. No, it would be wiser to keep the two men, father and teacher, apart. He said slowly, "He's really been wonderful to me, Papa. I think he likes me."

"Why should he not?" said Cesare.

Luzzatto hung up finally, regretful of his meager response. His deeper feelings were warm, protective, but the futile offer of money, as remote from reality as the moon, had excited old resentments. He returned to his room, guilty and ashamed, but convinced that the meeting was not worth the risk.

135

When next he looked up, sodden with fatigue, it was three o'clock in the morning. In all its immensity, Ullman's *Principles of Genetics* lay before him, a mountain of toil to be conquered.

"Oh, God Almighty!" He yawned, touched with panic.

It was a typical text, ponderous with certitudes derived from accepted principles. The smell of authority was Germanic, and related to developments of the past.

What of the future, he wondered, still hidden by dark clouds, waiting the penetration of investigators yet to come? He made a batch of coffee and worked till dawn.

As much as he wished to, Luzzatto had little part in the social life of the building. Hours were long and intense, and despite the informality, he worked too hard to develop friendships outside the classroom. He was closest to the group assigned to the small lab on the fifth floor—Joe Wodzick, Roy Hendrix, Mabel Olcott, and Eva Bronowski. He shared a bench with Wodzick, whose practiced ease with the women students was a source of wistful, secret envy. Occasionally, Leo Katz-Moebius, who had an office on the floor, would drop in to supervise the work and to joke lewdly with the women. At five Wodzick would give the signal to down tools and adjourn to the canteen. Invariably Luzzatto would decline.

"Come on, Dave!" commanded Wodzick. "Time off for a coke can't kill that brilliance."

"Don't bother me," Luzzatto said impatiently. "Horse around, but don't waste my time." It was a pose not conducive to popularity.

It took Katz-Moebius to surmise—broken shoes, lack of barbering, frayed cuffs, hollow cheeks—that the problem was pride and economics. The student was living on nut bars and apples with occasional sorties to the Greek diner just off campus. Katz-Moebius had a sensitive streak, and he kept these speculations to himself.

Luzzatto looked up wearily from a battered microscope, attracted by the gurgle of a pipette cleaner. The October sky was overcast and it felt late in the laboratory on the fifth floor. A sluggish voice sounded at his ear.

"Plan to work much longer?" asked Tewksbury. "I'd like to close up."

"I'll do that myself," said Luzzatto briefly.

Despite his best intentions, a note of irritability crept into Luzzatto's voice. Tewksbury's dragging manner of deprecation and dull beaten

136

timidity set his teeth on edge. Nevertheless he forced a smile. "What's on your mind, Mr. Tewksbury?"

Tewksbury blinked lashless reddish lids. "I just wonder—" he began. "Yes?"

Tewksbury picked up courage. "I hope you don't mind me too much?" he asked on a rising note.

Luzzatto could not meet the mournful stare. "Mind what?" He understood the question only too well.

Tewksbury paused. "About that—that attack back in September," he said finally. "Being with me in the same room. I hope it doesn't make you uncomfortable?"

"Oh? Of course not!" said Luzzatto emphatically. "Why should it? It's like anything else, nothing you can help." He broke off and forced a smile. "It's understandable that you might be sensitive, Mr. Tewksbury, but no one else gives it a second thought. Forget it." He gave a friendly nod of dismissal and shuffled his notes, but as the older man lingered dolefully he looked up. "Is there anything more?"

"Well, it's just—I don't know how to put this. I just wonder—how does the Professor feel about me since that last attack?"

"I have no idea." Luzzatto sat back from the desk not liking this turn of conversation one bit. "No, why should he discuss you with me?"

"I thought he might. You're with him a lot and maybe—"

Luzzatto shook his head. "Your name hasn't come up in any special way. Not with me, anyhow." Now where was this leading? he wondered.

"The thing is," said Tewksbury, "since that—that last one happened—no, even before that, ever since Dean Mackenzie went, the Professor's changed a lot toward me. He used to talk to me. Little things, I guess, about my family, my little girl—I've got a problem there, you know." Tewksbury licked pendulous lips in wonderment. "He's silent to me all the time. I don't know what I've done."

"What can I tell you?" asked Luzzatto. "I'm new here myself, Mr. Tewksbury."

"Yes, I see that," said Tewksbury. "Excuse me for raising the point." He returned to the pipette cleaner and the rhythmic gurgle and suck filled the room. The pores of his nose gleamed with sweat.

It should have been a poignant moment, yet Luzzatto returned to work with a shudder of distaste.

Shortly before the Christmas holidays, Luzzatto found himself at work in the private laboratory on the wine process. Ullman's tuneless whistle

137

could be heard from the inner office. At the window, Jo turned from drifting snow and slate clouds.

"Are you sore about something, Dave?" she asked.

"No. Why?"

"You seem to be. Do you resent something?"

"Nothing to resent," he said briefly.

In the winter light, her long, slightly horsy face was melancholy, and her olive cheeks, flat and creamy, were taut. It was not her usual mood. "You look so damn intense, Dave. Are you fighting this work?"

"I don't know," he sighed. "Oh, damn!"

A pipette slipped from his fingers, shattered, and sprayed the laboratory with splinters. He cursed, kneeled to pick up the slivers with his fingers.

She knelt down beside him, picking at splinters, and her mouth parted with a smile, showing boxlike, almost monkey teeth, gleaming white, small, delicate. Small breasts showed their points under a dress of red wool. "Tell Auntie Jo your troubles?"

Unexpectedly, his heart turned over. Over the months, he had become highly conscious of Jo Ullman. He was used to her presence in the lab, but he had no clear idea how to treat her, an older woman, his teacher's daughter. On occasion, she lapsed into this mood, silent, abstracted, sunk in gloom, but more often she was cheerful, bantering, restless, almost frenetic, much the indulgent, older woman, and his awkward response to her raillery seemed only to amuse her. For lack of small talk, he took refuge in erudition, and in this she had no interest. She had laughed aside more than once such clumsy attempts—as, for example, a persistent effort to discuss the impact of August Weismann's historical prediction of meiosis—that process by which the number of chromosomes in the body cells becomes reduced by half in the formation of sex cells as a preliminary to the later doubling in sexual conjugation. It was hardly her idea of small talk. "Oh, Dave! Tell that to my dad," she had teased. "He's the intellectual. I'm simply a pair of hands." Luzzatto could never quite square this blank lack of intellectuality with her doctorate in anthropology. Blinking like a fool, he persisted. She yawned and shook her head deploringly. "Please, Dave, I just don't give a damn. I know enough about Weismann."

Discontentedly, she had sauntered back to her own bench, leaving him to his devices. He found himself bursting to get on a personal basis, but this never seemed possible. Partly it was inexperience, partly a sense of inadequacy, partly an uneasy feeling that friendly chaffer was a barrier beyond which he was not to step. She was not always in the laboratory, and her absences were a source of concern to her father. Ullman was a stickler for method, for punctuality, for reliability, and her irregularity of attendance left him silent, pinched as he gazed with hurt eyes at the clutter of neglected work. "Nah, Luzzatto! Be a good fellow? Remind her to enter her findings at once. I would be deeply obliged." Jo never explained these absences. She was a good athlete, devoted to sports and long walks; in early fall her ringing cry could be heard on the tennis courts below, or her flat-heeled shoes, encrusted with mud, would point to a ramble in the hills. At such times, Luzzatto found himself doing her dirty work, a task not less annoying because of careless apologies.

"Sorry, Dave," she would gasp, sweeping in from the brisk outdoors, glowing with her exertions. "I'll do as much for you. There's a good guy! Is Dad sore?" Under the awful, bold temptation to suggest a date, to make a pass, to entrap the woman into intimate talk, he could not maintain a pose of vexation, and each such episode would end with a shrug. How did one go about these maneuvers? He had no clear idea. On this occasion, her direct interest had a shattering effect.

"Dr. Ullman—"

"Jo," she corrected.

"Uh. Yes. Jo." He flushed, fumbling at the minor intimacy. "Here it's almost Christmas, and I'm still working on this wine deal. It wasn't supposed to take all my time."

She thrust her fists into her pockets and sauntered close enough for her perfume to engulf him. It was heavy scent, cloying with musk and over-ripe gardenias, which he thought incongruous to her vigorous personality. She stood quite close and looked up.

"My, my! We're bitchy," she drawled with amusement. "I'd imagine you'd be grateful. Maybe it's tedious work, and monotonous, but on the other hand, isn't it giving you a solid background in something without the slightest practical value? Work for work's sake!"

"You're kidding," he said suspiciously.

She laughed grimly. "Oh, Dave! You're such an amusing specimen. You take yourself so damn seriously and you can't see the absurdity of the situation. Priceless!"

"I don't get it," he said grumpily.

"You're not meant to." She patted his cheek lightly, and turned to the window with folded arms, staring at a darkening sky, and suddenly his cheek burned with her touch, his spirit expanded to yearning, cosmic dimensions. Except for a hissing radiator, the laboratory was suddenly quiet and he realized that the whistle in the inner office had stopped. Ullman's toneless voice came from the inner office:

> *"Freude, schöner Götterfunken*
> *Töchter aus Elysium,*
> *Wir betraten, feuertrunken,*
> *Himmlische, dein Heiligthum!"*

Schiller's words were a reminder of an era of simpler hopes, the naive political idealisms of another century which the melodic line of the *Ninth* expressed. Abruptly, the singing ended, and heavy feet paced behind the door. Luzzatto turned back to Jo, whose dark eyes were fixed on the door with strange hostility. As he caught the glance, it vanished and she smiled.

"Why not go in and talk it over with my dad?" she asked ironically. "If you feel exploited, speak up, lad. You've got a standing invitation to bring him all your gripes, you know."

"Um. Well, another time," he said uncomfortably. "I don't know just how to go about it. He hates to be disturbed." He paused irresolutely. "When he comes out, maybe."

"Can't get your hand to knock on the door? Eh?" she remarked drily. He lowered his eyes. "Maybe not."

In fact, he was dissatisfied. Hundreds of Petri dishes filled the racks about him, assorted flasks were awaiting inspection in a closet used for constant temperature control, and a yeasty smell pervaded the room. It was dogged, laborious work, hit or miss, purely empirical in nature, which challenged his imagination not at all. The method laid down for isolation and development of these cultures was out of date, over eighty years old, devised originally by the great Danish botanist, Emil Hansen, whose innovations had dominated the industry for decades. Other methods had since arisen.

Luzzatto surveyed the equipment with discontent. "Why can't he let me use a single cell technique?" he complained. "At least I'd be building up some skills. Like finger exercises." He was referring to an advanced technique for picking up single cells by use of capillary pipettes under the microscope. It was a delicate operation that called for special training, and was used when pure cultures based on progeny of single known cells were needed.

Jo smiled ironically.

"Don't tell me. Tell him," she said, and jerked a thumb at the inner door. She sauntered back to his work table. "What are you doing upstairs in the old lab? Have you accomplished anything?"

Luzzatto set aside a glass cover for observation. He was nervously conscious of her body heat. He shrugged. "Nothing much. I haven't had the time."

140

She studied him sharply. "Is that the big gripe you're nursing, Dave? That you've been kept too busy on this project?"

"Something like that," he admitted. Morosely, he transferred a loopful of inoculum to a sterile solution of grape sugar, and took the flask to the closetlike constant temperature room. His motions were skilled and dexterous as he went through the operations and this—the work of his hands—was pleasurable. He was not thinking, he reflected, but like Candide at least he was cultivating a garden of sorts.

Jo followed him into the closet and shut the door. It was a small dark room, eight by ten, governed by moisture controls and a mercury thermostat, agitated by a fan set in the ceiling. A cheese box drum was rotating scores of cultures in tubes plugged with cotton. A red lamp was burning.

"You are angry!" she cried with surprise.

He shrugged. "I thought you knew."

Beneath a laboratory coat, he wore nothing but a thin shirt. In the close quarters, humid and warm, her face tilted, ruddy in lamplight, and as she stepped forward, his heart's blood thickened. Through the thin fabric, the tips of her breasts touched, light as feathers, cool against his heated skin, convulsive in effect. Their glances met and held.

Oh, God! he thought in panic. Does this mean anything? Do I hold her, kiss her, rape her? Is that what she wants? What am I supposed to do now?

All dimensions of his universe—sun, moon, stars, nebulae, trackless wastes of space—collapsed into one point in space and time. She was studying him gravely, he saw, with dark eyes curiously somber and questioning. He could think of nothing but the smell of gardenias, and the scalp furrow in her glossy black hair. Her mouth had parted, her breath was quick and shallow, and with its own dreadful volition his hand sought to move forward. He was transfixed and terrified. What actually did she want? How far might he go?

She'll despise me, he thought in agony. Her head was thrown back, exposing her throat, her eyes were closed. What makes me such an idiot? What would Joe Wodzick do? I mustn't. I shouldn't. Oh, God! I am!

The harsh voice could be heard:

> *"Wem der grosse Wurf gelungen,*
> *Eines Freundes Freund zu sein,*
> *Wer ein holdes Weib errungen,*
> *Mische seinen Jubel ein!"*

"Not here," said Jo quietly.

She stalked back into the laboratory before the implication sank in. He hastened after and found her engaged at the microscope, head bent, apparently absorbed in the image focused in the oil immersion objective she favored. Wordless, trembling, he waited for something to happen. She glanced up quizzically.

"Got any plans to go home for Christmas, Dave?"

He hesitated. His conversation with his father was much in mind, the half-promise, the evasion. But these were suddenly nothing as Jo folded her arms. He shook his head as a great hope formed itself.

"Um. No. I don't think so."

"I wonder why not?" she asked coolly.

He looked about the laboratory. It was dark now, the windows were black, a rattle of hail struck a warning of dirty weather to come. "I thought I'd use Christmas recess to organize my work upstairs," he said slowly. "I'm terribly impatient to get something started. I haven't found it possible since I hit this place."

"Now, really," she said impatiently, "whose fault is that?"

> *"Brüder! Brüder!*
> *Uber'm Sternenzelt*
> *Muss ein leiber Vater wohnen!"*

Her glance shifted to the inner door, enigmatic, inviolable. The hymn resounded unmusically.

"Above the stars a loving Father must dwell," she murmured oddly, translating. She continued to listen, then cocked her head. "He's got a remarkable talent for inspiring devotion." She smiled faintly. "It's his real genius, you see?"

"Oh, yes."

"But only for a select few." She drew thoughtfully on her cigarette. "It can get pretty bleak here in recess, Dave. Think it over?" She glanced up from her reverie curiously. "I'd like to see what you're doing upstairs. Eh? Mind if I invade the sanctum? Maybe we can talk up there."

Promptly at five, Ullman came out, calling for tea in a glass.

"Nah! Luzzatto!" he cried cheerily. "Jo, dear? Free-dah—?"

As he glanced about an empty room, a look of profound disappointment darkened his face.

Luzzatto spent the week before Christmas in turmoil. Faculty and students began to disperse for the holidays, while he wandered the icy streets, concocting imaginary conversations, staring at the moon in the winter sky. Eva left for the Laurentians on an invitation from the Puces,

142

bearing skis and winter togs, and the fifth floor laboratory was suddenly empty. In a most roundabout way he took his problem to Leo Katz-Moebius.

"If some woman wants to bunker off with you for the weekend," said Katz-Moebius judiciously, "my scientific advice is to act before she withdraws the offer. You're old enough, Dave. My God!"

"I don't know if I should," worried Luzzatto.

"Why not?"

"Qualms, I guess."

"Don't you want to get tossed in a blanket?" Katz-Moebius wondered. "Incredible. In-credible! Or does something else disturb you?"

Luzzatto hesitated. His parents wanted him home for Christmas, he observed, and he had no idea what excuse to give his mother.

Katz-Moebius exploded. "Excuse? Come right out with it, Dave. You're about to have a heterosexual experience. As things are headed in this country, they can only be thankful and relieved at the glad news. I never heard of such damn nonsense."

"I guess you're right," said Luzzatto.

With an air of concern Katz-Moebius kindled a meerschaum pipe. "Don't look so worried, Dave. A hell of a lot of young scientists go through this lopsided development. These bookish types hardly skid through supercharged intellectual puberty before they hit delayed emotional maturity, and the effects can be disastrous. This guy at Yale has made a study of the phenomenon, but I can tell you from personal experience that it all comes in cases like ours from being more highly sexed in fact than one ever supposes. This inflames the imagination, floods the carburetor, so to speak, and not all women understand the powerful, yet sensitive, mechanism with which they must deal. It may today seem unbelievable, but at your age I had the same problems. Sorrows of Werther—" and he was off on an earthy tale of a farm woman in Bavaria where in pre-Hitler days the Katz-Moebius family had spent their vacations. It was a romance that ended abruptly in a hay loft. He sighed ponderously. "Don't make my mistakes, Dave. Strike while the iron is hot. You cannot do better than Bronowski. A smashing beauty."

Luzzatto's mouth dropped with surprise. "Eva? I didn't mention names."

"Have I jumped to the wrong conclusion? I thought you meant to follow her to the mountains. You're both using the lab upstairs? You're in each other's pockets when you're not working for Ullman? What could be more natural?"

"Other women use the lab, too," said Luzzatto slowly.

"I see," said Katz-Moebius.

Luzzatto stared at the grinning mask with the realization of his folly. "I give you my solemn word you're wrong," he said after a pause. "I don't want you to speculate, Leo."

"I'm an oyster. I'm a clam," replied Katz-Moebius.

It was only after Luzzatto had returned to his own room that another possibility struck the mind of Leo Katz-Moebius. A lewd and commiserating grin spread. His young friend was in for a most interesting experience.

"Incredible," he murmured. "In-credible!"

The bewildered Chevrolet had turned off the main highway and now it waited, panting and exhausted, in the country lane. Headlights were approaching in the distance.

"What now?" said Jo.

Luzzatto studied the road map under the dashboard. "I think we're on the Taconic Parkway. You should have taken Route 6 at the intersection."

"I didn't see the sign," she said bad-temperedly. "You were talking a blue streak. You're really terribly distracting, Dave."

"Oh, thanks!"

"Don't sulk," she exclaimed. "Just find the directions." She huddled in her coat. Snow was glazing the windshield. It was a lonely place on a second grade back road. She looked up in alarm as the headlights stopped. "Dave!" she said warningly.

He caught some of her anxiety as the man in boots and fur parka approached in the swirling snow. A flashlight peered into the car, picking out the anxious couple.

"Any trouble?" boomed the state trooper.

It was one of Jo's disconcerting talents that she could without transition melt instantly from mood to mood. She rallied at once. "Oh, officer,"—she flashed her most enchanting smile—"I'm afraid I'm in a terrible muddle. We're trying to get to Brewster. Are we off course?"

The trooper said ponderously, "Oh, lady! Are *you* in a muddle!" He gazed at the wonder of her. "*Are* you in a muddle! Are you in a *muddle!* Whoo-hee!" He played on the theme, drawing out the agony. "You're fixing to hit Troy." He gave directions, and then with a fat amiable chuckle drove off in the icy glaze. Jo relaxed into her foul mood and started the car.

Luzzatto reached back and touched her ear.

She shook her head, annoyed. "Please, don't."

144

They crept between granite ridges through an area marked "Falling Rock Zone."

"What am I doing that's wrong?"

"Nothing."

"I feel that something's my fault. But I don't know what. Please, Jo?" he pleaded.

"Oh, Dave, don't be so bothersome. Watch the road."

He studied the dim outline of her profile. Her brows were thick, knitted in a frown, and she was peering ahead into the gathering blizzard. At a cloverleaf intersection the heater died. "Oh, damn!" she cried.

"Dearest," he said tentatively, humbly, shivering with cold and pleasure. "Whatever it is that's irritating you, I'm sorry."

She drew up and set the brakes. He lit a cigarette for her, marveling at the delicate mouth and nostrils in the glow.

"It's got nothing to do with you, Dave. It's simply that I'm a bitch. I should have known better than to talk you into this."

"Talk me into what?"

Her gesture encompassed the frozen scene. "This. Everything. What I'm doing to you." She paused. "We can still turn back, you know."

He stared with consternation, aware of the touch of fur under his hand. It was a rough fur coat whose lines, like everything about her, from the toss of her head to her accent, filled him with delight and approval. It went somehow with her swagger and jaunty personality. A forbidden picture flashed to mind. Jo had been wearing this coat, sportily open, on a sunny afternoon outing across the river to West Point. On a Sunday the fields were deserted except for cadets marching off to chapel. At the statue of Kosciusko, Jo had stopped to fix a garter—and the flash of white skin in cold sunlight, the coat flung back, her breath in plumes, her cheery lipstick grin, were cause for exaltation and joy. Her tone now struck him with alarm. It had a cold decisive quality he had not expected. "Turn back? Oh, no! This is something I want to do."

"All right, we'll go ahead," she sighed. "Only don't be such a pain in the neck about it. I'll make a deal?"

"Oh, sure!"

"You take care of yourself, Dave. I'll take care of myself. Agreed?"

"Agreed. Say, Jo? Am I really such a goof?"

She studied him carefully, a mischievous grin lit up, and she patted his hand. "Too soon to tell, Dave," she said gaily. "I'll let you know in the morning." Her glance was half-teasing, half-contemptuous.

He hesitated and knew suddenly a moment of decision. "Jo?" He took

145

her head, feeling the yield of her nape, digging into warm curls, and drew her over. She flung her mouth aside. "No, not—"

"Oh, yes! Jo! Darling," he whispered hoarsely. Cruelly he dug his claws and his mouth went into hers with a taste like snow and within the limits of clumsy wraps and freezing cold he explored her with rising ferocity while their breaths mixed like smoke.

"God, Dave!" Gasping and breathless, she tore away and thrust his hand from her breasts. "You almost killed me!" She shrank back, wincing with pain, and stared with reluctant respect. "All right, Dave," she gasped finally. "You've made your point. But if you apologize for that, I'll murder you."

He said nothing. She started the car and they drove along the deserted highway. Her mood became as frenetic and rollicking as earlier it had been foul and gloomy. Evidently the surprise of his attack had done something. She drove recklessly, humming to herself, glancing occasionally with good humor at Luzzatto. "Oh, say? Do you know this one, Dave?

> The minstrels sing of a British king,
> Of a thousand years ago,
> Who ruled the land, with an iron hand,
> Though his mind was lewd and low—"

Her gaiety rose as they drove deeper into the storm.

Luzzatto shivered with cold, nonplussed. He had a sense of delicious and intimate shock. The salacious touch, so contradictory of the image formed of Jo, was stirring, but coarsely, basely, not what he was prepared to admit. An affair? Yes! It was the normal, human thing, lovely, expected. But this garlicky stuff? He felt utterly confused, and obliged to support her mood. Out of his memory came something entitled 'Lil' which called for a French-Canadian dialect:

> "When he put his meat on Murphy's bar,
> I swore, by Gar! It stretched from thar—
> To thar!"

Jo burst into laughter. "Oh, Dave," she crowed, "you're priceless. Absolutely. You're getting more human with every mile. Oh, God, what a night!" She sighed with laughter and calmed down. Snow was streaming in the headlights and the road was dim. "Oh, dear! If only we could drive like this forever. Just alone, with the world blotted out, and nothing but a cocoon of ice like this. Why, we might stall here, and fall asleep, and never wake up, and in the morning they'd find our sinful bodies! Wouldn't that be a hell of a note back home?" She laughed harshly and lapsed into her earlier gloom.

She drove in silence through a shroud of white. Luzzatto accepted this change of mood, shivering in a thin coat. Somewhere they passed a stranded bus, empty of passengers.

It was almost ten o'clock before the Chevrolet found the end of the road. The rambling house, dark against luminous drifts, stood on a hill behind a stone fence. No light was showing. Jo switched off the engine and the motor died. Her teeth were chattering.

"Damn, I'm cold! Is this it?"

The snow had died and an icy wind from Canada was blowing.

"Well, let's get out. I'll carry the bags. It's a cinch we're here for the night." He helped her through snow up to her knees; it was immediately chilling.

"What's that?" she cried.

Down the lawn a huge dog came bounding, eyes gleaming, barking fiercely. A light showed.

"*Pierre! Tais toi!*" cried a woman's voice into the night. "He will not hurt you. Please! He is a good dog. *Tais toi, Pierre!*"

Mlle. Bailleul was waiting at the storm doors as the dog bounded onto the freezing porch, followed by the humans. She sniffed through a long intellectual nose, noting with wise, gallic eyes the couple that entered the foyer of her *pension*, stamping and rubbing against the cold. The tall young man whose wrists hung out in the raw cold was surely younger than the woman.

"Come in, come in. Ah! My God, what a night!" she cried. "The television is telling us it will go to twenty degress below zeh-rro. It is lower than that now. In, in, in! I 'ave got a pot of soup on the stove. Why did you not telephone you would be late?" She clapped her hands imperiously. "*Pierre! Va-t-en!* Out!"

"You're not putting that dog out into that cold?" asked Luzzatto, stamping his shoes.

"Oh, he loves it. He is such a good dog," Mlle. Bailleul crooned. "He is covered with the fur, and he does not mind it one bit. He will chase the deer, poor things," she sighed. "They come down out of the 'ills for the apples. Take off your coats."

"Are there deer about?" Luzzatto wondered.

"*Ah, oui!* Deer, foxes, wildcat, squirrels, rabbits. We can do nothing wit' them. I do not mind, except that they bring the 'unters, and also it is im-possible in summer to keep a gar-den."

147

Jo had slipped out of her coat and was stamping on the hot air register, blowing and rubbing her knuckles. Her cheeks were pale with fatigue. She glanced with distaste at a dark parlor in which a television set was booming. "I'd like to see our room," she said crossly. "Then we'd like something hot to eat. Would you mind?"

"Not at all. What sort of beds you like?"

"What sort?"

"I 'ave twin beds, or I can let you 'ave a beautiful double. In that case, you 'ave a fireplace."

"Twin, I guess. No, make it a double."

"Ver' good. You will like it, I am *certaine*."

Mlle. Bailleul showed off the room with vigor and dispatch. It was dowdy but large and gaily papered in Colonial design. A large brass bed with columns like organ pipes at the head stood against the wall. Washstand and mirror, extra wool blankets in bureau, hangers, fireplace, tasteful pictures, *La Revue Mondiale, Life, Readers Digest, Vu, Spectator,* potted cacti, a view of distant lakes, and down the hall, the W.C. Jo rubbed her neck doubtfully.

"Is it too late for a hot bath, mademoiselle?"

"It is the automatic! Of course!" Mlle. Bailleul observed that the salad was out, but the soup, the ragout, the sweet, the 'ot tea were waiting downstairs. In the morning, the breakfast in the room, but the lunch promptly at twelve and dinner at six, for which the bell would ring.

Luzzatto only half listened, testing the storm windows.

"How cold does it get, mademoiselle?" he asked.

" 'Ow do you mean?"

"Can you sleep with open windows? I mean, in winter?"

Mlle. Bailleul pursed her mouth. "It depends 'ow you like it. In this weather, maybe not. I find it gets very cold, but you can keep the 'ot air register going. It costs a bit, but I do not mind. Now then, in the morning will M'sieu—?" She paused officially. She had not caught the name quite exactly. "It is to sign the book."

Jo glanced at the mirror, fluffed her hair, and turned ironically with folded arms. Luzzatto was caught by an oddity, an unexpected reluctance to commit a small deception. He had always expected this moment to come as a consecration, and suddenly the room was shabby, unworthy. He hesitated and supplied the first name that popped into mind.

"Andrews," he said humorously. "Joseph Fielding Andrews."

Mlle. Henriette Bailleul raised her brows. She had lived in the Rue de la Pompe in Paris opposite Gestapo headquarters throughout the Occupation. Tortured screams had echoed in the street through five years of war.

148

Her group had spirited hundreds of French from German clutches to the Free Zone, thence to England. In all this she had taken part. Even more refined subtleties of behavior would have been transparent.

She closed the door and went down to 'ot the soup. Oh, la! she thought wistfully. If only I could catch a young one like that!

He was to remember the quiet of the hills, frozen in the moonlight, which crept on him slowly as he opened his eyes, attuned his senses. The blizzard had passed and he knew that the snow lay on the hills in absolute purity, under a sky brilliant with stars. Dimly he made out the room, outlines of washstand and mirror, hot air grating. Windows were open and a freezing draft was blowing. He crouched under the feather quilt, suffused with her scent.

They were lying in a brass bed between mended sheets of coarse muslin. Jo's head rested on his shoulder; hand flung down his length curled lightly at his hip, she might have been asleep but for the too-quiet of her breath. He dared not move. How far it was from the frenzy in which she had been caught up—an hour ago, was it? The moment of consummation was like nothing he had ever expected: in the midst of transport, he had wondered that some portion of his mind could still remain apart from the greater thing. He had expected an utter transformation of reality—more so than life, it suddenly became clear, would allow. And yet, for himself, the deeper currents had been stirring to the depths. What of her? He whispered tentatively. "Jo?"

A moment of silence passed.

"Yes, Dave?"

"Are you trying to sleep?"

"No."

A pause.

"Can I touch you then?"

"If you like."

He placed his hand in her armpit and lifted her breast. Earlier, its flesh had been humid and inciting, but the mass now was a cold unresponsive gland; the erectile retort failed to come. She threw back her head and stared at the ceiling. "I was driving too long through the blizzard. I got exhausted and cold. The hot bath didn't help." She was answering an unspoken question.

"Is there anything I can do?"

"No."

"I feel responsible. Oh, Jo! I wanted to take care of you. To make this good for you." An endearment seemed at the moment false to utter. She

149

turned and gazed across the pillow into his eyes. "If you blame yourself, Dave, I'll feel wretched. This is my business. It has nothing to do with you."

"How can you say that?" he wondered.

She smiled sadly. "I should have known better than to put you through this. Only it never struck me that this would be your first experience. Why didn't you tell me?"

"It's nothing to brag about," he said ruefully, and touched her hair. "I was clumsy, I guess."

"It isn't important," she said in a strained voice.

Her passion had astonished him. He could not believe the arching strength of her body, the ferocity of her demand, the nails raking furrows in his back, the obscenities. *Oh, damn you!* she had moaned, thrusting with sudden spasms, flinging from side to side. *Oh, do it! Do it!* Hoarse animal cries escaped and in consternation he had poured his strength and had withdrawn and diminished until she came back to the attack, grasping his face, biting his tongue until the taste was salt and blood. *Oh, Christ! It's no good!* she cried at last, flinging herself off exhaustedly. *Damn, damn, damn!* What had she been striving for? he wondered— dominance? absorption? fulfillment? He dared not move or think. "I'll make it better for you next time," he promised without conviction.

She closed her eyes. "Please. I don't want to talk."

He drew deeper into the quilts, overcome with intolerable pain for her, filled somehow with anger and confused by something that eluded understanding. It seemed impossible to be in this position. Her physical grace had caught at his heart; even her earlier salacious mood of abandon had supported his exaltation; and although her primitive responses were a shock, his own power and attack had been great. What then had failed in her? Suddenly, from what depths he knew not, he felt the surge to mount again, to plough her deeply, to compel response and fulfillment with dominating ferocity. The impulse filled him with trembling—and yet, and yet! Flesh on flesh, a yearning for her grew. He thought to take her fully, the vibrant, muscular body, to strike his teeth against hers, to kiss her whole mouth. "Jo, dearest, I love you." It was the first such declaration in his life, and he felt a queer thrill of daring, but even as he spoke, he sensed his own doubt.

She turned on the pillow, her eyes were speculative. "It's not your fault, Dave. You're sweet and you deserve something better. No!" She placed a hand on his mouth and held him back. "Let's not talk." She turned her back and stared at the wall.

He waited but nothing further came. He kissed her hair, sniffing delicious odors which continued to fill the bed. Through the window, he saw, the Seven Sisters, low on the horizon, were in flight from the Hunter. They were seven, he recalled, drifting finally to sleep, because they were not eight.

The room was freezing.

He opened his eyes. The windows were flung wide, inner sash and outer, and the cold was intense. Jo was silhouetted at the window, stark naked in the still, icy air of early dawn. Puzzled, he threw back the quilting and arose. "Jo? What's wrong?" he asked in alarm.

"I've been watching the deer," she said dully.

He glanced at her sharply. She was holding a clumsy pose with hands resting on the casement, shivering in the cold. Her flanks were taut and covered with bluish goose flesh, as sexless now as Rhinemaidens of an illustrated *Nibelungenlied* recalled from boyhood. He followed her gaze. "What deer?"

"At the fence," she replied in the same dull voice.

He squinted into the yard. A pair of jays, wagging electric blue tail feathers, were hopping about an apple tree. They were stabbing the un-picked, withered fruit and running through a series of calls—harsh cries mingled with trumpeting whistles. It was their clamor, he thought, which had awakened him. The far perimeter was marked by an old stone fence bearded with brush and young trees.

"There!" she said querulously.

A faint movement caught his eye. In the brush were black muzzles of a pair of does gazing at the food. One snorted and the other responded with a bound into the yard. She muttered, "They must be starving to come this close."

"This is a damn fool stunt," he said. "Don't you feel the cold?"

"Cold?" she asked vaguely.

He did not like her manner one bit. Something was odd, askew. She shivered violently. Her flesh was like marble. He felt her face, neck, arms, avoiding her breasts—in the light of morning the tips were wrinkled and wine-red. How long had she been at this? "You must be frozen solid," he exclaimed roughly. "What the hell are you out to prove?"

"Oh, look!" she cried. The other doe had bounded into the yard. Gingerly they approached the apple tree, stabbing the snow with their sharp hooves. Almost instantly, simulating hawklike screams, the jays swooped to the attack. The starving beasts lowered their heads and dodged and searched the snow for windfalls until a clamor of barking and the dog put them to bounding flight. The birds returned to their feeding with

151

soft warbles and twitters of triumph and satisfaction in a job well done.

"I could kill them," Jo said savagely.

She was shaking violently with cold, and tears came to her eyes. By now Luzzatto was frightened. The chill of her flesh and her distraction touched him with dread. What ought he to do? The quilting alone seemed useless and then a thought struck that the bath was down the hall, that perhaps its heat was worth a try. He said, "I'll be back soon."

Twenty minutes later a discreet knock was heard. "Is there trouble?" asked Mlle. Bailleul.

Luzzatto said, "Not at all."

"The pipes are so noisy, you see?" Mlle. Bailleul explained through the door. "I could not help but hear. The cold riser is frozen, and I will 'ave to call the plumber from Brewster. Is the 'ot all right?"

"Oh, yes. I was filling a hot water bottle."

"Madame Andrews"—Mlle. Bailleul hesitated—"is not sick?"

"No. Just a bit chilled."

"I am sorry."

"She'll be all right," Luzzatto promised.

Mlle. Bailleul hesitated and returned to her own room. Jo was lying in the bed with unfocused eyes turned vaguely to the ceiling, nursing a rubber bottle. He asked gently, "Are you warm yet?"

She made no reply.

He said gently, "Jo, dear. Give me your hand." He had no clear idea why he said this, except that he wanted to communicate a human touch to let her know—in a way that had nothing to do with what had gone before—that he was with her still, tender, compassionate. It was an odd sensation as she put a flaccid hand in his, the flesh still cold. She stared with troubled eyes. "I'm sorry, Dave."

"Why were you at the window?"

She frowned in perplexity. "I don't know."

"Is something the matter?" he asked gently.

She nodded.

"Would you like to tell me?"

"Can't."

"Why not?"

She was silent and he repeated the question. She opened her mouth, no words came. She glanced away and whispered in tones of despair, "It's too shameful."

He was taken aback by the phrase. After their earlier abandon, it seemed absurdly incongruous, and yet her face was dark with distress. He could not imagine what she might regard as too shameful for discussion. Surely not some disease? He squeezed her hand gently, then asked abruptly, "Are you pregnant, Jo?" It was a wild stab but the best that came to mind.

She looked surprised. "How can I be? I'm not married, am I?"

He almost laughed, but her piteous expression caught him up short. No, she was not married, he agreed, but then what was so shameful that they could not discuss?

"I'm going blind," she said.

There was a moment of silence.

"Blind? What makes you think so?"

"I *know*," she said with simple conviction.

He lit a cigarette and glanced at the window, deeply disturbed, for a dreadful suspicion had entered his mind. Her behavior was surely bizarre, far beyond ordinary limits. The sun was now above the hills, golden and warm, touching the clouds with glorious colors. Confused and not a little frightened by his responsibility, he turned back to the lovely creature whose glance was mournful and appealing. "Has any doctor told you that?"

She shook her head. "No doctor."

He had no clear idea what to say. "Then I don't see how you can be sure. I don't believe it, Jo," he managed finally, "but even if something's wrong with your sight, it's only a physical thing. It's not a —" he groped for a word—"a sin. How can it possibly be a cause for shame?"

She stared without answer.

He took her cold hand. "Jo, have you talked this over with your father?"

"Him?" Her eye rolled questingly.

He spoke gently as though to a child and pointed out that her father was a man of science who understood these matters and who would protect her against harm. If her sight was failing, surely she would need medical help. Slowly she shook her head. It was nothing she could discuss at home.

"Why not?"

There was a glance of bitter scorn. After a pause she asked, "Have you ever tried to talk to God?"

He felt a queer sense of shock at the naked revelation, although to be sure he had felt something like this to be coming. He entered the bed and held her rigid body to his own. He had nothing in mind but compassion and her dreadful need for warmth.

"It's all right, Jo," he whispered. "I'm holding you now. You'll be all right while you're with me."

153

When finally her quivering ceased and her breathing told him she was asleep, he felt weary to the bone, ragged for lack of sleep, troubled, not sure where all this would lead. But some things were now clear. This older woman, this managerial creature with her authoritative swagger, was in his care. Of the two, she was the more fragile with an emotional structure precarious in the extreme. It was a new burden in his life, one he was not ever to forget.

He was awakened by the tap on the door.

" 'Ere you are," announced Mlle. Bailleul.

Orange juice, hot cereal, slabs of butter on toast, yellow eggs and pig sausages, a pot of coffee, and bright sunlight. Luzzatto sighed finally and lit a cigarette, reflecting that no mood could last. "Jo?"

She patted his wrist. "It's all right," she said.

The hills were sparkling and frozen and suddenly he longed to throw himself into the snow. He said cautiously, "Would you rather stay in the room and rest? You might like to read?" She shook her head. "I was wondering if you'd like to get back home? I could get down to my folks for Christmas, then join you back in town."

"Is that what you'd like?" she asked.

He thought grimly of the harrowing night, but except for faint circles under wan eyes, no traces of distress could be seen. And now, with the challenge of the hills, something of salvage, he felt, might be done. He was sufficiently sensitive to perceive that he had walked into a serious situation, that retreat was indicated, but against this he had no protection. Something had been realized during the long hours. He was no longer a boy; a certain innocence had vanished forever; yet he was his father's son with warmth and tenderness and compassion for the woman he had loved that would endure. She had made no reference to the night and neither would he.

"Don't be an ass," he said amiably, forcing a light bullying tone. "I'm dying to get out for a walk. Look at those hills! I didn't come to mope around like an old man. Would you like to know something? I've never seen the countryside in winter."

A relieved smile lit up. "Oh, yes," she agreed, instantly responsive. "Suppose we drive into town and buy you some proper clothes? I can't wait to get out. Let's take that dog."

Luzzatto frowned. "I can't let you spend money on my clothes, Jo."

"Oh, don't be weak, Dave." She stared imperiously. "Just do as I say."

They laughed together and he gave in. While the cold snap held, they tramped the fields and back roads, studied the habits of winter birds.

Time seemed to stand still. Jo was again in high spirits, chaffing, teasing, playful in the snow, more so than he liked. He watched her anxiously, but except for one nasty experience with a farm dog—she was badly shaken by ferocious growls and bared fangs—hours passed in growing exuberance and physical delight and she seemed to make a recovery. Once a lynx bounded into a clump of birch, once an Arctic owl sailed past on silent wings, indicating a famine of lemmings in Northern Canada. They ate, slept, played, lived together, but not as lovers. By tacit consent they talked of everything but the thing between them. He measured his strength against the cold and late afternoons he was content to flop on the bed and read the works of science he had taken along. Jo groomed her hair and read French paperbacks which filled the bookcases. "Real nasty, the French," she said with relish. "They give you something to eat."

"Huh?"

She held up a book. Surely the soul of man, she remarked, was entitled to recoil from the problems of existence with more resourcefulness than relapse into anguish alone.

"Oh, that!" His muscles ached but the warmth of the room was sleep-inducing. The Christian existentialists, he thought, had resolved the problem of existence by escape into the plane of faith; their atheistic brethren had banished not only God, but the knowable physical universe as well. They were thus reduced to raw self-awareness as the sole knowable truth of human existence. It was from this self-imposed frustration that their anguish flowed. He dismissed the whole crowd with disdain—Kafka, Heidegger, Sartre, de Beauvoir—infants plucking lint from their navels.

"And you, my lad, are above all that?" Jo observed ironically.

"No scientist would fall into that trap," he said seriously.

"Too clever?"

Luzzatto grinned with good humor. "No, but the scientist has got to assume an objective universe that doesn't let him down. When he manipulates a crowd of electrons, he can always explode a bomb, and the blast of energy is pretty convincing. Anyway," he added somberly, "without that dependable universe he's got nothing to build on. I find it more reasonable to assume there's more out there"—he made a grabbing gesture—"than my own lonely ego."

"But you can't prove that?" she asked strangely.

"I don't have to." He did not like her mood. "It's an obstinate universe to tackle, enough to keep me busy. I'm not worried about proof." He forced a smile. "Not when I've got you in my clutches, Jo. You're here in that universe with me, you know."

"Poor lamb," said Jo grimly, turning to the book.

155

She was in a strange and restless mood, enjoying their last day, yet disturbed by her novel, a tale which led from Tahiti to a foul provincial morgue in France and a final scene of autopsy in which a corpse was dismembered. The dinner bell rang downstairs as she came to the final page. It left the question: where was the soul? A wretched storekeeper, dying of a foul disease, had uttered a faith in the wonder of the sea, and perhaps, the author suggested, mere identification with eternal processes of nature was sufficient to grant a form of immortality. Because the sea itself was deprived of something. Somewhere in Tahiti, an absence would be vaguely felt, a void, a passing away, a turbulence of disarrayed atoms. If indeed, there were another life or death of punishment or reward, the author suggested, much would be forgiven one who loved the sea.

Jo found herself staring at the passage with a wretched feeling of mortality. It was a strange and moody tale. Was there nothing more than this? An evanescence, a passing wave, a negation? She glanced up to catch Luzzatto's glance of alarm and surprise, and realized that helpless tears were falling down her cheeks.

"I'm so sorry," she whispered helplessly. "So damn sorry for the whole stupid mess. It couldn't possibly have worked out. It's just that this time I had so much hope."

They spent a last tranquil evening around the television set, cracking nuts, listening to tales of the Occupation. In the morning Luzzatto used Jo's money to pay the bill. To his surprise he carried it off without embarrassment and in a foyer heaped with boots made promises to return. Mlle. Bailleul shook her head.

"I am afraid you will not come back," she commented sadly, "but you both 'ave all my good wishes. Goodbye!"

As they drove off, the dog bounded after to the main highway, barking madly. They chatted briefly and then went silent. When they reached the university, the snow was melting in the road.

"Oh, Dave," she whispered.

They parted with a kiss. Nothing had turned out as expected, but for the first time in his life, he was aware of full strength as a man.

Chapter 12

"LUZZATTO, WHAT DO YOU SAY? IT'S FIVE O'CLOCK. WHAT ABOUT TEA IN a glass?"

It was a daily ritual. The sun across Haverstraw Bay was setting, filtering dull red rays through a bank of clouds in a winter sky. Snowdrifts were high on the campus, and from the window, rimmed with frost, they could see ice floes drifting in the river. As they sat in semidarkness, the hissing radiators gave a cozy warmth, and this was how Luzzatto was always to remember that period.

He got a box of tea from the cupboard and set a small copper kettle to boil on the Bunsen burner. Thick glass tumblers were inserted in metal rings. "Now why does it taste better in a glass?" he asked.

Ullman rarely answered a direct question. "Make the essence, eh?" he murmured. "Like a good fellow?"

"Right!"

The kettle had been fashioned by a smith of a past century in another country. It had come with Ullman's mother, as he was fond of recalling, brought with her dowry to the threadbare pastor whom she had married in a poor mining village in East Prussia. The kettle was the sole reminder of the place from which he came.

"Life follows a pattern," he would say gravely. "It must work out to some end, and therefore,"—raising his rimless glasses, he would peer earnestly at the younger man—"therefore all events, however remote, have meaning. It is for us to decipher the sense. Every event is a datum."

"Yes, Professor," Luzzatto would reply respectfully. At such times, Ullman's frigid manner thawed and in semidarkness, talking almost to

157

himself, he would discuss a hard and bitter struggle to rise in the academic world, the jealousies and bickerings of colleagues, publications refused and discoveries forestalled. And Luzzatto felt that he could only gain by listening.

Among his memories, for they were sharp, were grimy streets ending in slag heaps, miners trudging from the collieries at dusk, cheerless winter sabbaths, with cold winds blowing from the Baltic, a voice thundering from a high pulpit, preparations by a careworn woman in a draughty kitchen, the kettle gleaming on a coal stove for tea.

"What was my father like?" he would ask rhetorically. "He was too narrow, too rigid to understand the free winds of science blowing away the cobwebs of his world. The discipline was valuable, I admit, but I cannot say that I approved. I was always in rebellion against that narrow, constricting life. It was for that reason, I daresay, that I went to England after I completed my studies. I am a great believer in free inquiry, you see? Those other things are not in my nature, but some memories remain. Why tea in a glass? Because it satisfies something within. Isn't it remarkable how these patterns work out?"

Discovery and departure were linked. Often Luzzatto was to recall the voice in the inner office singing Luther's powerful hymn. He could always hear the words:

Ein feste Burg ist unser Gott!

So that the year of discovery was always associated with good talk in a darkened laboratory and hot tea in a glass and the copper kettle. Tea did taste better thus somehow; and this taste, like others absorbed from that period—occasional gutturals, pedantic impatience, a certain cast of thought—were to remain with him long after the older man had left the university.

Chapter 13

As Luzzatto opened the door to the fifth floor laboratory early in April, an aquarium crashed to the floor. Eva knelt in consternation and began to gather a dozen guppies flopping on the floor.

Luzzatto frowned. "Well, that's idiotic, Eva! That's a whole year's work."

"Give me a hand," said Eva.

The fish went into a glass bowl where their nervous dartings showed the effects of shock on elementary nervous systems. Luzzatto knelt and gathered glass splinters and observed that the fish would survive. He said, "Is something wrong?"

"No, no. Just a nasty experience this morning," said Eva, biting her mouth. While he turned to his table, she went back to restore the breeding experiment which occupied her time. Luzzatto turned to his own work, conscious of tension and rising agitation in the room. He said, "How did it happen?"

"Slipped!" Eva lit a cigarette, badly disturbed, and said suddenly, "Would you take me for a walk, Dave? It's so absolutely stupid to have nerveless hands."

"I'd like to—" said Luzzatto slowly. Eva's presence in the room was friendly, but her decisive manner and wall of reserve commanded respect. He knew little of her life beyond the fact that she lived as a sort of baby sitter with the Puces, that her political views seemed intense, that Joe Wodzick had given up all efforts to date her as a bad job, and that Katz-Moebius's rancid baiting set off in himself a reaction of intense discomfort out of all proportion to her own.

159

They struck out for the hills. Hours later, tired and footsore, they halted miles from town at a bus stop. He had learned nothing of her background, largely because he had talked steadily about himself, his hopes in science, his agreements and disagreements with Ullman, but he was aware of her troubled abstraction. He asked, "Am I talking too much?"

"No," she said, and added apologetically, "I hope you don't mind, but I'm thinking of other things."

"You don't have to explain," said Luzzatto sympathetically. "What happened this morning, Eva? Did you get some bad news from Poland?"

"Not exactly. Just a nasty experience," she sighed, looking up out of the haze. "Oh, say! You must be starved, Dave. The Puces are leaving for the weekend and I've got the kitchen. Let me fix some dinner?"

"Wouldn't they mind?" he asked doubtfully.

"Oh, no," said Eva soberly. "The arrangement calls for kitchen privileges. I must say it hardly compensates for those little monsters I take care of occasionally. What do you say?"

"Say? What can I say?" He grinned humorously in a surge of hope. "I'd love it, Eva. But it's got to be dutch," he added quickly.

"It's a deal," said Eva, smiling faintly.

When they arrived at the white Georgian house, the Puces were already gone. Luzzatto declined a drink, and while Eva went off to change, he prowled a formidable library, indulging in an old vice of reading book titles. Evidently Eva's luck in her surroundings was better than his own, he reflected, noting that time was passing. "Evvie?" he called. He went to the stairs and waited, listening under a crystal chandelier, but the house was quiet. An uncomfortable amount of time passed before Eva returned with an air of quiet exhaustion. "Sorry, Dave," she said mutely. She was lovely in a fresh blouse, but her eyes were reddish and he, even he, discerned that she had been weeping, but he said nothing and followed her to the kitchen. While she went to work on haddock fillets, he teetered on a kitchen chair, famished, still talking, much aware of the empty house. Eva went about her task, chain-smoking, silent.

"Well! Here we are," she said finally, presenting a savory dish bubbling with butter and paprika on aluminum foil. "I love good food."

"We walked far enough for it," he remarked, smiling.

"I'm used to that." Her smile was a frozen twitch, and then, something in the remark caused the mood to lapse and they ate without appetite. Eva stared at her plate, strangely still, paralyzed by something that demanded to be spoken. Abruptly, she remarked that her memory was filled with long walks taken during the war in Poland. He waited quietly, and then she went on, rapidly, nervously, yet speaking in dull, commonplace tones which filled him with mounting dread. It was a story for which he was unprepared by anything yet encountered in the security of his own mild and sheltered life.

"But what made you jump?" he asked with wonder some time later, appalled to learn that Eva's family—father, mother, herself—after the Russian army had engulfed eastern Poland, had been shipped back with hundreds of thousands of other Jews into the German-occupied zone. The question was absurdly naive, but her reply accepted it from the logic of a nightmare. During the night, she recalled, one of the prisoners had noticed by the stars that the train was en route back to Cracow in the German zone.

Her gaze was on the past. "Who would have thought that possible? Not my father, not my mother! The Polish government, you see, had encouraged us to evacuate to Lwow where we had property, and we felt safe enough because the Reds had overrun the border. They were thought to be a shield against the Germans, you see?" She swallowed without feeling. "But would you believe? Even in that cattle car, Jews still believed they were being sent deeper into Russia. You would think they'd have known better. The nights were clear, beautiful, and the fields were covered with snow. Prisoners were singing in all languages—Polish, Russian, Yiddish, Ruthenian—songs it would break your heart to hear. How could we not know where we were going? This was our Poland."

She looked down suddenly at shaking hands. "Only this boy and I understood the truth. He was a student in Cracow in one of the humanities, and he was attracted to me because my father had taught mathematics in the university. We decided to escape together."

Luzzatto was bewildered by the glimpse into horror. "What did your father think?"

"I don't know."

"How was that?"

"Because we had already been separated," she said simply, noting his pallor. "It was Russian policy to divide families. Perhaps that gave me the courage to jump from the train while in motion. If we reached Cracow, I thought, they would put me into a brothel, or something worse. I made up my mind, before they could kill me, I would have to know about my father, my mother."

Luzzatto thought of his own parents. "Were you very close to them?"

Her eyes went round with surprise. "I was an only child. Could it be otherwise? Just before Cracow," she went on with a shiver, "we jumped

161

from the train. I was badly hurt, but I hid in the woods until night, and then I stole some clothes from a peasant family." She went silent.

Luzzatto said, "What happened to the boy?"

Brows knitted painfully in the effort to recall. "He was killed when his head struck a stone," she said, "and I had to bury him. It was the first dead body I had to handle in my life." She thought back without apparent emotion. "I walked all the way into Cracow after dark. I was looking for a cousin who might help me to get papers. Fortunately, I could pass for a Pole. Ah! Your coffee is cold!" she exclaimed, and arose painfully and poured. He studied the high cheekbones, the pale, creamy skin, the broad slavic features and felt a globe of emotion in his throat. "What happened, Eva?"

She aroused herself. "Oh, yes! I found my cousin's house after dark, but there was no one there. I had had no food for three days, and nothing but a thin dress. I huddled in the doorway to wait for morning. I was afraid I would freeze to death, but about two o'clock, a door opened and a man looked out from the next doorway. He said in Polish, 'You can't sit there all night, Miss. No one will come back to that flat. You had better come in with me.' So I went in and stayed overnight.

"This man was a priest. He must have known about my condition, but he never asked my name, or papers, or anything like that. He didn't want to—to—" She searched for a word.

Luzzatto said, "To be put on notice?"

Eva nodded slowly. "Yes, if he were asked questions by the Germans, he would like truthfully to say that he did not know he was doing an illegal act. But of course he knew. He had an old housekeeper who made an outcry that he was risking his life. Her name was Elzbieta. Under the German law, it was not only a crime to shelter an illegal, but a crime not to denounce one who did. I stayed three days until I was clean and rested, but I could not get over my nervousness, and I wasn't sure of this old woman. I had to consider that she was a Pole."

Luzzatto was puzzled. "Wasn't the priest a Pole?"

Eva nodded somberly. "Oh, yes. But I felt the greatest confidence because he had something of goodness in the face. It was a handsome face, intellectual, serene, simple. Have you ever been deceived by looks?" she asked, glancing up inquiringly.

Luzzatto thought. "I don't know," he said slowly.

Eva lit a cigarette, thinking deeply. "I believe that people are what they seem. I have never really gone wrong on first impressions." She sat quietly, smoking, considering past events. "I had complete trust in this priest but I could not be sure how far he might control the old woman.

162

He wanted me to stay, but I had to find out about my father, my mother, and he agreed that I ought to go. I never explicitly told him about myself, but it had become obvious by then. I finally went out of the house."

"Where were you going?"

"I thought some cousins might still be alive who would know. Oh, I was careful. I kept off the main streets and I looked about for men in uniform, but on one of the main crossings I had to take cover in a chemist's shop and I was stopped by a man who called my name. I could have died of fright, I was so shaken, but I saw at once that he was a Jew—a man who knew our family." She resumed smoking, then shrugged.

"This man was conciliatory, ingratiating, and he wanted to know where I was staying. Well, I was new at this business of running and I told him my priest's address. I thought someone ought to know about me, you see, in case my parents came looking. No?" She paused. "Then he asked me about the diamonds."

"Diamonds?"

Eva laughed harshly. "The Germans were convinced that all Jews were hiding diamonds." Her face shadowed with distress. "I didn't like this man, even though he told me he could use the diamonds to bribe the Gestapo people for me, and I walked out of the shop. I was lucky enough to run into a woman who warned me not to go back to my priest. This Jew was an informer for the Gestapo.

"For a week this friend hid me and then I went back. This priest was sitting in his apartment that had been torn apart by people searching for diamonds—Gestapo people. I think they had tortured him. He had told the Germans that I was a niece and that I would turn myself in the next morning for questioning. The old woman was excited, crying that they would all be killed because of me, and I promised to visit the police in the morning."

"Did you mean that promise?"

"No." Eva stared up without expression. "It was a game, a comedy we were playing, where one thing was said, another meant. It was only to give him a proper surface story to which he could truthfully testify. I left the house the next morning supposedly for the police station, but actually for Warsaw. I felt, oh, so bad, but what could I do? I was young, he was old. No? And I had still to find my father, my mother. I am sure he quite understood."

A moment passed before Luzzatto looked up with a shiver. "Why Warsaw?"

"Could I stay in Cracow? They were circulating my description, I was sure. When I left my priest, we had no idea whether we would ever see

163

each other alive, but he did not bless me, except perhaps later, or to himself. I was sure he had the impulse, but this was a delicacy on his part. Elzbieta shut herself up, crying, so as not to say goodbye. In Warsaw there was a Jewish underground, I thought, who might help. I went through the bombardment."

She sat thinking, staring at other scenes. "Three weeks without food, two weeks without water in the cellar. I was with some women and a few children in a cellar. I had nothing, nothing but a water tumbler but there was no water in the city. At the end it rained and I put the glass out in the open where it might catch the water. In the morning, when I crept out to look, someone had stolen the glass. That moment, of all the things that happened to me, that was the very worst time when I came out for water and the glass was taken by a thief. I felt so bad, I cannot possibly describe it. It was a lucky thing, I suppose, because I saw the soldiers. I ran back through the cellar and out the back."

"Soldiers?"

"Two young boys in field gray. They had guns and they were hunting strays. I saw that they had spotted me, and I ran. But the others were too slow. I could hear the explosion behind me of a grenade and finally I found myself near the railroad station where a group of people were under guard. I went up to these people. Perhaps I would live, perhaps not, it was the chance to take. Also, I needed food, water. I really could not have lived much longer alone and the city was in ruins. Where I was hiding among the Poles, there was not even the fighting, the organization of the Jews. Did I have a choice?

"About midnight we were marched to the railroad yards," she went on. "This was a militarized area, a stockade surrounded by barbed wire. Soldiers in watchtowers had machine guns and freight cars being loaded with people. The worst of all was the hopelessness of the people. They were told to go and they went. The impulse to life is so strong. No?" She paused. "But I could not get into those cars. I knew I could not jump again, even if I had the chance. The shock of the first time was too great, you see? It was absolutely impossible, but I knew I had to do something.

"In the darkness, I crossed behind a train of cars and walked into one of the signal towers. The official was a German." She swallowed convulsively. "I was in frightful shape—the fires, you see, had burnt off all my hair. My face was black, I had only this thin dress, I was starved, freezing in the cold. He looked at me and I looked at him. We both understood, but we had to play out the comedy, I suppose. He asked me what I wanted. I told him I was a Jew and I wanted him to save my life. Thank God, I could talk to him in German! He was a soft, old man in

164

the uniform of some home guard and he was frightened by the situation. He started to stammer and then he told me to get out. He was shouting in German.

"I asked if he had any children? He told me he had two sons in the Wehrmacht, and he wanted to know why I asked. I told him that I wanted him to take my parents' name and address, and to let them know after the war that I had died because of him, this German, because he had turned me out into the night, because I was their only child and because they were entitled to know what had happened to me. He began to shake. 'Get out!' he told me. 'Get out! I cannot help you!' I refused to go until he had written down my name, because I saw that I had him, that he could not turn me in. He threatened to call the soldiers and I told him that I could not stop him, but I would not move."

"How did you feel toward this man?" said Luzzatto with wonder.

Eva brought her gaze to focus. "The German? I hated him," she said simply, "but I had to use him to keep my life. He was not human, only a thing to use. He was not even honest, because he had no pity for me—only for himself, only that he was too weak to pick up the telephone. He was spitting with fear and I had nothing for him but hate. I don't know how much time passed before he told me to wait till his shift was over. He showed me a place to hide.

"The German hid me in a closet and begged me to be quiet and I agreed, because now I had his life in my hands, just as he had mine in his. If I were discovered, I could denounce him and he knew it. I lived in that closet for ten days and all I had for my needs was a pail. I did not mind anything but the darkness." She waited without apparent emotion. "Finally the door was opened by a soldier in the Wehrmacht uniform, a blond man with a nice, young face. He told me to get out and I walked out with my arms and legs almost paralysed. I thought I was for it, but then he told me that he was the old man's son. The question was to kill me, or to help me to escape the yards, but the first way had become something intolerable to the father, and so the son was there to help me escape."

Luzzatto sat thinking. "How did you manage?"

"Manage? Oh, yes. Well, he had a peasant outfit for me and a shawl for my head because my hair had not yet begun to grow back, and my scalp was in patches. I washed at the tap and went out on his arm and tried to look stupid, like a peasant girl. I kept making remarks in Polish, oh, simple things like asking him about his medals, or how much bread cost in Germany—anything a peasant might say. He took me to the passenger station and we got on a train that was going west to Lodz. I had never

165

been to Lodz and I reasoned I would not be spotted there. It was on a line to Danzig where I thought I might get information of my father, my mother, through a family friend. He was a medical doctor, Julius Koch. I hoped he would know something, because the same idea, I knew, would occur to my father—to get in touch with Julius Koch. Someone, I thought, had still to be alive. Why not Lodz? One place in Poland was like another." She closed her eyes. "The train was full of soldiers. This fellow told the others that I was to help forage among the peasants for fresh meat and vegetables. They thought this clever to use a Polish girl as a— a decoy, would you say? Such ideas appeal to the German mind. Also, I looked like a sexual conquest, I suppose, and he had their sympathy. But it made no difference to me what Germans thought.

"At Lodz, this soldier gave me some food, about five marks in Occupation money, and told me I was on my own. He even saluted, which was quite gentlemanly. No? When he walked off, I felt so—so alone that I called after him but he never turned back. I stood wondering where to go, stunned. I had no papers. I could not talk to a soul without danger. I felt so weak that I sat in the gutter and looked at the dirty snow—and then I heard a woman call my name.

"I could not believe. I looked up and it was Elzbieta, the housekeeper of my priest. She was so glad to see me, I cannot tell you! She threw her arms around me and we laughed and cried together like crazy people. It was like—like something from Heaven."

Luzzatto stirred. "Did she know you would be there?"

"How could that be? Oh, no!"

"Was it merely a coincidence?"

Eva sat back with a strange expression. "I know only that of all the cities of Poland, my priest had chosen to move to Lodz. Partly it was because of the bad name I had given him in Cracow with the Gestapo, but also because of a—a feeling that something was calling him to that city. If you care to call that coincidence, I have no objection."

It was a moment of intimacy in the kitchen, yet it was almost as though she were telling the story to herself, and he felt deeply stirred by the peril to which she had been exposed. After a moment, he asked about Lodz.

In the same nervous monotone, Eva went on to describe three years under the German Occupation. Her priest had rented a villa where she had lived in hiding, passing as his niece, unable to make other arrangements for fear of betrayal everywhere, and this, the universal hatred— even more than thoughts of her parents—had undermined her spirit most. As time passed, she became convinced of their deaths. Toward the end, there was a young Pole with whom she struck up a friendship, a boy

166

named Jan who taught her mathematics in exchange for piano lessons. Luzzatto had the impression that the attachment was deeper than she was prepared to admit. This young Pole had taken her to a meeting of the Underground where a group of children had proposed a two-pronged attack of extermination, first, on the Germans, and, second, on the Jews.

"You can imagine how I felt," said Eva with a strained expression. "Millions had already died at the hands of the Germans, and these children had nothing in mind but more death, more killings. I felt, oh, so bad, and I made up my mind I would have to find out about my mother, my father. I thought my father's friend, Julius Koch, would have news where perhaps they had died and I left for Danzig the next morning.

"At the hospital a woman told me that Julius Koch had not been heard of for several months, and that he was possibly dead, and then she suggested his flat—perhaps the janitor might know. Could I talk to a janitor? A German? I walked down to the harbor and watched the shipping. Across the Baltic was Sweden. It would be lovely there in summer with decent people to take me in, but it was beyond my strength to think.

"Some sailors tried to talk to me, but I pretended to be a deaf mute, and idiotic, and they went off. It was a bad moment. How simple, I thought, to slip into the waters at night, to drift out to sea with the tide, to give up the fight. I have no idea what I might have done to myself, but then something inside awakened and told me that I could not kill myself, that my life was not my own to take. I felt then that God had kept me alive for a purpose. I have no belief in voices, but the voice that evening was quite real to me, you see? So many had been killed—so few of us were left."

Eva glanced up, troubled. "I am only trying to describe a state of mind, Dave. I've never discussed this before, not with anyone. I know only that suddenly I got up with a purpose. I bought food with my last money, and when I had gotten my strength, I walked across the city to the address they had given me at the hospital.

"I pressed the bell several times. Inside I heard footsteps approach and the door opened. It was my mother who looked out at me." Eva paused abruptly to smoke and continued with the same lack of emotion. "We could not to talk, Dave. She looked so small, so old, I could not believe. After a moment, she closed the door and took my hand to her mouth.

"She asked me if it was me, and she used a family name no one had called me in all that time, and I asked if my father was alive. After a moment, she called out to tell my father in another room that I was there —that I was alive, their only child. It was only then that she gave me a kiss."

167

The story seemed to end in a frozen smile without meaning and then Eva suggested that they move to the living room. The darkened room, lit only by the flames of the fire, seemed less real than the vivid scenes in Luzzatto's mind.

"I cannot tell you everything, Dave," she said apologetically, staring at the flames. "How they came alive to Danzig is another story. It is only that my father was put into an engineering unit, and when an order came to kill the women he tried to die with my mother, but instead his colonel connived that they should escape. It was some plot where he helped my father to steal his car to get to Danzig, to Julius Koch."

"A German officer did that?" Luzzatto asked slowly.

She nodded, troubled. "Oh, they are full of surprises, the Germans. I have never been able to formulate a consistent emotion toward them as a group, largely because I remember when we looked to them, the West, as the light of hope against the darkness of the East. That was, oh, seventy, eighty years ago when they presented the image of a dreamy people, full of sentiment, like—like the professor in Miss Alcott's novel, the one who marries Jo March. Ah?" She paused, biting her tongue as a fresh train of thought struck. "They are still the same people, the Germans—capable of terrible things, and wonderful, too. One of them, a soldier, had saved my father, my mother. I have always to take that fact into account. No?"

Luzzatto asked, "Where are your parents now?"

"Dead," she said briefly, returning to a cigarette. "I was already in Paris when I got a letter from my priest which told me that they had been killed with five other families by Endeks—Polish Nazis. What did I feel? I have no idea. I knew only that I had to quit Europe or go mad.

"I went that day to the Bois. It was a sunny morning and I felt—oh, quite detached, quite objective. All my people had been killed and I was the last. Yet I had a sense of illimitable vistas out of which my life had come—millions of years going back to the beginning of time, and I could not believe that it would end with me. I was a bit lightheaded, I suppose, but that was the feeling."

She was silent, then stirred. "My father, my mother had been free-thinkers—intelligentsia, you know? We had never anything of ceremonials, and I was at a loss—and yet when a father, a mother dies, something must be said. I had no words and then, suddenly, as I turned a path, I heard myself thank God for sustaining me and bringing me to that day alive. I said those words in Hebrew. It was quite strange. Where, how I learned them, I cannot tell you, because consciously I do not know the language—not one letter, not one syllable. Yet when I needed such a blessing, it was on my tongue.

168

"And then the mood vanished. I stood in the woods and I knew I was alone in the world. It is a feeling I am never without."

A smile without meaning formed, and suddenly her eyes, fixed, staring, were moist. He whispered her name. "Oh, Evvie!"

Wanting nothing for himself, his mouth pressed hers, warm with compassion. His heart, he felt, would burst.

A milk truck was in the street when he paused, hollow-eyed, at the door. "Evvie? What made you so upset this afternoon?" he asked curiously. "You said it had something to do with Poland."

"Nothing important. Really!"

"Tell me."

Eva drew a breath. "Well, I got a letter from my priest asking that I buy him a lace cloth that cannot be bought in Poland under this government. A vestment, I believe. This morning after the class in physiology I inquired at the Polish church in Hoe Avenue, and the caretaker advised me to shop in Poughkeepsie." She paused.

"Oh, why?" he wondered.

"Oh, don't you see? The local shop is owned by a Jew." she smiled bitterly. "It was a trifle, hardly an excuse for dropping that aquarium, but it reminded me of many things I thought were dead. Good night, Dave," she said softly. "I feel better for having told you."

He walked slowly through deserted streets, and when he reached the residence hall, it was dawn. He lay in his clothes and stared at the sky.

Chapter 14

FREDA STAHL WAS DEEP IN AMIABLE DISCUSSION ON THE TELEPHONE with her butcher when Ullman strode in, humming a jolly bit of nonsense.

"Hallo," he said gaily. "Miss Jo back yet?"

"Not yet, Professor."

An anxious shadow crossed his face. "Have you any idea?"

"Walking, maybe. Spring fever, I reckon."

Freda called attention to a backlog of work. On top of a pile of letters lay a request from the presidential offices. Ullman's ebullience gave way to fatigue. "Oh, Freda," he sighed in dismay. "Can't it wait?"

" 'Fraid not—"

But he had already left her presence. She found him in the inner office, almost hidden by the massive roll-top desk. "Come back later," he begged wearily. In the privacy of this office, his outward buoyancy had collapsed.

"What can I do, Professor?" she asked helplessly. "We're coming to the end of the year. You've simply got to attend to that memo to Dr. Foxx."

He put a hand to his brow and closed his eyes. "I am exhausted at the moment. Leave the papers and come back this afternoon. Be a good woman? Eh?"

The little woman observed tartly that supplementary budget proposals were overdue. Ullman made an impatient gesture.

"But it is not only the budget. It involves an entire table of organization. I can't pull that out of my sleeve like a rabbit. Didn't I make that clear?"

She shook her head stubbornly. "All you've got so far is the introduction, Professor. You haven't even begun the main part."

"You're sure?" He was surprised.

"At this rate, commencement will be on us first," she replied. "I must say!"

"Well, well!" He considered the situation with boredom and distaste. The procrastination was his own, the fault was not hers, and this fact made this neglect doubly vexatious. "Dok-tor Foxx!" he muttered with scorn. "A fund raiser, a jack-in-the-box! Who is he? Where did he come from? Why do we dance to his tune? Eh?"

"I wish you'd not talk like that," she urged reprovingly. "I know you don't mean a word, but you've got a tendency to express yourself like that before people. You ought to be more diplomatic."

He studied the plump, fussy face keenly. She was a limited and stupid woman, he reflected, but she had a point.

"Freda, what are they saying about me?" he murmured. "No, no! I would like to hear. Come? What's on their minds?" What had been the general reaction to his year as acting dean? His gutturals thickened as he assured her that the query was purely objective.

"I'm not sure—" she began reluctantly.

"Yes, yes?" His demand was peremptory.

She shrugged diffidently, and admitted finally that rumors had been flying since Christmas recess, and no one quite knew what to expect. People had heard of the plan of reorganization; everyone was wondering about the future; those on tenure level were worried for their junior colleagues. All this had bred fear and resentment.

"Fear? Resentment?" He looked pained. "Why should they assume I want to hurt? Some changes are long overdue—but otherwise? No one who makes a contribution need be afraid. Am I here to destroy? Or to fulfill? *Um Gottes Willen!* The smallness of these minds!"

Freda observed that one could hardly blame those who failed to understand. "After all, they can't read your mind, and lately you've been locking yourself behind that desk, Professor. It's not healthy."

"I have other work in progress," he said.

"Those little cards you're fussing with?" She sniffed.

"Freda!"

"Oh, all right! I'm sorry, but you're spending entirely too much time with those cards. It's simply not fair, and I get all the blame. I'm running out of excuses. What's it going to be? A book?"

"In due time," he said heavily, "you will know."

"Oh, sugar!"

171

He sank lower in the chair and made an effort at conciliation. "Freda, Freda," he sighed wearily. "Forgive me for imposing these black moods, but the truth is that I have such obligations, and I get little sleep these days. Perhaps I am unfair to Dr. Foxx. After all, he is what God made him." He nodded and blew out a lungful of smoke. "And I refuse to quarrel with Deity," he added humorously. "Not today, in any case. Have you yet heard from young Luzzatto?"

She shook her head.

"Again? Where does he keep himself?"

"He's very annoyed," she said briefly. "He returned your note."

"Nah? What's this?" He frowned with displeasure. "I haven't seen any note."

"You haven't looked." Almost with triumph, she rummaged through the pile and handed over a personal note written in his own hand.

My dear Luzzatto:

I was delighted to receive your card on the occasion of my birthday and to receive the generous expression of your sentiments. I grow increasingly depressed to pass these milestones and I have asked Mrs. Ullman to take as little notice as possible. Only our immediate family was present—Mrs. Ullman, Josephine and my brother, Thomas, and his family. You would have been welcome. You really must not work so hard that you neglect your friends.

Come again for a visit next Friday night? I will be glad to go over your notes with you anytime or help in any way possible. Your notebook is a fine piece of work. That thoroughness will carry you a long way. Although my attitude may seem hypercritical at times, I'm sure you know how much I enjoy being with you. I am making plans to move for the summer to Lake Marah earlier than usual, and you may be interested to join me there on some agreeable basis.

I have something to add.

Without my permission, you used your key to allow intruders to enter my private laboratory during my absence last week at Johns Hopkins. I presume you felt justified, but I regard the affront as intolerable. You will find your graceless action reflected in your final mark for the year, which will be posted in due course.

Yes, I saw the article and I am impressed by Pauling's reasoning. It is true that the average danger is small, but the total danger to some individuals is absolute and predictable. I do not see however that this political matter concerns us directly.

Yours, V. F. Ullman

Across this note, an angry scribble had spattered ink.

172

I refuse to accept this note. I did nothing which could be construed as an affront. I will not recognize any mark lower than I deserve. I am amazed to be condemned without a hearing.

David Luzzatto

"Well!" said Ullman with a curious smile. "The lamb finds his voice."

"If you'd have asked me, I'd have told you it was my fault," Freda said. "You told him to invite his parents to visit, and when they dropped in, I thought it would be a nice gesture to let him show off the laboratory. After all, he spends all his spare time on that wine project for you. He was real disappointed you weren't here to show off. Wanted his father to meet you in the worst way. I told him to go ahead."

"You know how I feel about my privacy," Ullman murmured coldly. He remained sunk in thought. "There are days, Freda," he murmured, "when the game seems hardly worth the candle, and then?" The heavy brows rose somberly. "Ah! Suddenly the door opens, and a clear wind blows through the house. I still have a feeling about that young man, Freda. We need fresh blood here, new ideas, young talent." He glanced more darkly at the ink-splattered anger across his letter. "Also, we need a disciplined and orderly approach. Talent is not enough."

Freda pursed her lips. "That note isn't too inviting. He'll need buttering up."

"That? Tush!" He shrugged. "We shall see what happens over the summer. I am looking forward to Lake Marah with more anticipation than I can say." Tendrils of smoke curled unheeded from his nostrils, and finally he nodded. "I'm a great fool," he decided with sardonic self-knowledge. "Nah! Let's see." He picked up the beginning of his memorandum and brought it to the light. An amused smile twisted his mouth. None of that crowd, fluttering, squawking, sycophantic about Foxx, would care for this—no, not one bit! He contemplated the vision with deep satisfaction, and then his face clouded.

"Freda, what shall I do?" he asked mildly.

She studied her hands—stubby fingers blunted by years of typing, but otherwise, she observed with pleasure, white, plump, soft as milk. She thought of this handsome man with his strongly molded features and magnetic blue eyes, as clever and learned, full of tricks and surprises, intellectually on a plane as far above her own as the seraphim. He commanded respect and loyalty, and in his shadow she felt stupid and clumsy, never sure what subtleties were involved, but some things, she told herself stubbornly, were within her own practical competence, not his.

"I'm in no position to advise you, Professor, but I can tell you what

Dean Mackenzie would have done. He'd first circulate a full draft plan to the faculty," she said pointedly. "He'd get a committee appointed, and invite suggestions, proposals, that sort of thing. Or better yet, he'd arrange for an outside survey. He'd never send anything affecting the school to Dr. Foxx without first getting that support. How can that be done now? The year's about over. You haven't even got the plan ready, just these few paragraphs. Why didn't you do this job over the winter? You promised."

Her strictures were equably, almost indulgently received. "Ah, but I have got the plan," he said with an air of surprise.

"Where?"

"*In meines Geistes Aug'!*" He tapped his forehead lightly. "In my mind's eye, Freda."

"Well, that doesn't get it down on paper," she retorted. "When will you dictate? Next winter?"

He arose stiffly and walked to the window, swinging his gold key. "It is clever of you, Freda. Yes, Mackenzie was a master tactician. In his way, he had certain devious qualities behind the mask, a certain skill in manipulation, techniques of indirection, of diplomacy, which one might well emulate. He was not quite so simple. Behind that great reserve, he had deep plans. I always thought he had a certain unfeeling quality, a lack of sensitivity. One never quite knew—"

He sighed, and resumed his thoughtful smoking. "Would you believe it, Freda? In twenty years, Mackenzie never once paid a visit to our home? Mrs. Ullman has always felt that very keenly."

She pursed her lips. "Did you ever invite him?"

"I?" He laughed harshly. "How? It was not possible! From him must to have come the first move! He was my chief and he never took the initiative. It was always we who called on him. Nah, nah!" he added quickly. "Don't tell me he was shy. I know about that one! No! It was that he did not see fit." He made a gesture of dismissal. "Leave now the draft and I'll think about it."

She arose. "Oh, stuff!" A door was slammed and locked, thus expressing a viewpoint.

"Freda! You will—"

But she was gone, and through two doors and across the laboratory came the rattle of errors and mistypings. He glanced at the clock, then swung about to the roll-top desk.

Each drawer was brass fitted. He unlocked a lower drawer, and removed a metal box from which he took a bundle of cards, tied with string. "Yes, yes, yes!" he murmured. Frowning heavily, he cleared a space and

174

laid out the cards in symmetrical display. He peered intently at each card, sucking his breath with doubt, hesitation, satisfaction.

"I think this one? No, this! Hah!"

His hand darted. With a hiss of decision, he played a game of solitaire, in which the rules were private, the cards cryptic in significance, the deck incomplete. The array held thirty cards—six rows, five ranks. It was not sufficient.

He arose and stood back, biting a thumbnail in thought. Finally in the top left corner position he placed a card on which a short verse was typed. He marked this card carefully in green ink as "1."

Know the true God!

He looked up suddenly. "Luzzatto? Is that you?"

The laboratory was however empty. After a moment, he returned to the cards.

Luzzatto stared with unbelieving eyes at the mark posted that morning in the lobby of Mackenzie Hall. He had received a jolting B.

"I swear I don't get this," he muttered. But of course he understood the cause at once. After the first incredible dismay, he strode from the building, choking with anger, not appeased by the string of A's racked up in his other courses. He had worked hard, carried more than his load, and this was not fair, he told himself bitterly.

"I'm God damned if I'll crawl!" he raged. "What kind of a mediocrity does he think I am?" The bitter sarcasm, flights of eloquence, monumental Philippics that assailed the older man were in the best family tradition, but like those of Demosthenes were spent upon the wind.

"Hi, there! Dave!"

Luzzatto looked up from angered abstraction. Eva was seated in the Green, a secluded corner of butternut trees and shrubbery. She was studying the underbrush while carrying on an earnest conversation with Wodzick. The two had their heads together like conspirators. Sheltered from the river breeze, the corner retained the warmth of late May.

"Sit here," she invited.

As always, Eva was dressed to crisp perfection. She had the habits of a European woman, whose dresses are few, but good, designed to last, expensive. Even in the warm afternoon, she wore a suit of light gray flannel, pinched at the waist, relieved of severity by a scalloped neckline. Luzzatto hesitated morosely. "Well, for a minute."

Eva had been dividing her attention between Wodzick and a water

175

color of a praying mantis. The model was the grandfather of all praying mantises. It was perched in a rhododendron bush, six inches long, apple green, exercising a unique ability to swivel its insect neck to gaze with shining compound eyes of incredible intelligence at a passing train of red ants. Its serrated forelegs opened and closed, sluggish and devout and voracious. The sketch was done with a light brush. Luzzatto nodded appreciatively.

"That's real good, Evvie," he remarked glumly.

She shrugged off the compliment with the remark that the knack had been picked up in a year's sojourn in Paris. It was really nothing much, she smiled.

Eva's future, Wodzick observed, lay in the field of scientific illustration. He squatted on the sward, voicing the opinion of one who understood the world of business. "What the hell, Dave? The girl's got a commercial gift, why not exploit it? Lots more dough in advertising than the laboratory." He winked humorously. "Why waste those looks on a pack of undernourished, walleyed scientists? Where's the future? I'm only speaking for the conservation of natural resources, honey," he added.

Eva patted a hairy wrist in reproof. "Oh, Bronco," she laughed, "I like the undernourished type."

Still sore at heart, Luzzatto studied the sketch. Since the night at the Puces, he and Eva had worked together, attended concerts, talked endlessly of the missions of art and science in a threatened world, but not again of the past. There seemed no end of things to learn. He said curiously, "Did you go to art school in Paris, Evvie?"

"My God, no!" She closed the paint box with a somber glance of amusement. "I was much too busy scratching there for a living while going for my degree. No, I was tutored in painting in exchange for teaching a dreadful child the elements of biology. Her father was a refugee, a Pole. France was filled with them."

It was pleasantly warm with a moist earthy smell rising from the soil. Wodzick was attentive and thoughtful as Eva established the mood. With her reddish-gold hair she was especially handsome against rhododendron green, with a perfection that commanded respect. He said bluntly, "Are you a refugee, Eva?"

Eva glanced at Luzzatto. "Not any more," she said, quietly.

Without quite knowing why, Wodzick laughed and sprawled back with a lazy gesture. "Eva, how does all this strike you?"

She lifted a shoulder dubiously. He was referring, she understood, to the placid scene, the lazy, untroubled, well-fed students, the innocence and

176

prosperity of a remote, protected corner of the world. "Tell me, Bronco," she said seriously, "can this *last?*"

Wodzick hooted with laughter.

"Have I said something amusing?" Eva eyed Luzzatto curiously. "We were just talking about that B in genetics," she said, sympathetically. "It's a damn shame!"

"God, yes!" said Wodzick, warmly. "I pulled an A myself and I don't touch you, Dave. Everybody knows you're the leader in that class."

Luzzatto plucked a leaf of sorrel and chewed disconsolately. "Ullman doesn't seem to recognize that."

Wodzick leaned back and glanced at Luzzatto sardonically. "Screw Ullman! Who cares what he recognizes? As far as *we're* concerned, you're still the leader."

"Oh, drop it, Bronco," said Luzzatto impatiently. "What's all this talk getting at?"

Wodzick responded circuitously. "What are you doing about that lousy B he slugged you with?"

Luzzatto glowered. "Nothing!"

"Nothing will come of nothing," Wodzick quoted. "You mean you don't plan to put in a beef?"

Luzzatto said venomously, "It's not up to me, Bronco. Ullman knows how I feel. If he wants to do the right thing, he can change that mark. He can't treat me like a child. I respect his dignity as a scientist. I expect him to respect mine. Let him make the first move!"

Wodzick shrugged. "I told you, kid," he said to Eva.

"Told her what?" asked Luzzatto.

Eva exchanged glances with Wodzick. "Willie Tewk's in serious trouble, Dave," she said slowly. "He has some notion that they're ready to give him the sack. We've been talking about how to help the man."

Wodzick said, "I'm surprised you didn't know."

"Tewk?" For a moment Luzzatto was jolted from his own sense of grievance. The recollection of a wretched family situation was appalling, and it was hard to imagine that anyone could wish to shake the poor devil from his niche. He said slowly, "That doesn't sound right, Evvie. How can he be sure?"

Wodzick gazed off toward Davenport Library where a clamor of hammering arose in the air. Workmen were beginning to knock benches together for commencement exercises. He shrugged. "Who knows? The guy's alert to every mood around him. Those attacks give people the creeps, and that makes him hypersensitive. He's always waiting for that

177

look of disgust. Funny thing is that he's a good biologist," he concluded wonderingly. "Did you know he's got a master's from Wayne?"

"I had no idea," said Luzzatto.

"It's only a physical disease," said Eva. "It shouldn't count against the man. Why must it make him unemployable?"

Luzzatto blinked uncomfortably. The secret truth was that Tewksbury still filled him with guilt and fear. Was it right? Or fair? Perhaps not, but revulsion was still there. He said, "I'm sorry about this, but what's it got to do with me?"

Eva said, "Bronco and I feel you're the logical one to head up a committee for the man. The question is how you stand with Ullman at the moment." She paused. "You know what a stick of wood Tewk can be? No emotion? Well, this morning, when I got to the lab, I found the man in tears. He was looking for you to help him, Dave."

Luzzatto frowned with disbelief. "Oh, now, look, Evvie! Bronco! I can't believe any of this. I'm annoyed with Ullman, but why would he want to get rid of Tewk? What reason? The guy's been a fixture for twenty years. Maybe somebody else has the axe out?"

Wodzick shook his head. "It could only be Ullman," he said, giving a number of reasons drawn from reliable sources. Talk of reorganization was in all the powder rooms. Luzzatto listened with growing dismay.

"I thought a group of us ought to call on Ullman," said Eva earnestly, leaning forward. "But Bronco feels that too much pressure might backfire. It would be advisable, I imagine, for you to see him alone."

Luzzatto stared in consternation. "You both know I'm in the doghouse. How can I talk to him at this time about Tewk?"

"How can you compare the problems?" asked Eva quietly. "Poor Tewk is being killed by this thing, Dave. I would do this myself if I could," she added persuasively.

"As a matter of fact," said Wodzick, "you're just the man."

"What makes you think so?"

Wodzick sucked a grass blade. "Well, Dave, in my opinion, Ullman's the type who wouldn't mind a bit of crawling. If that's the case—crawl! It'll be in a good cause. What d'ye say?"

Luzzatto sighed heavily, thinking of his B in genetics. It was thoroughly depressing to end the academic year on a sour note.

Yet it was, in a way his own damn fault! If he had given one day of the Christmas holidays to his parents instead of to poor Jo, Cesare and Nella would not have descended on him for that fatal visit—nor would Ullman have had occasion to retaliate. Every obstinate instinct rebelled at eating crow.

178

A beetle darted across Eva's skirt and he snatched it up. It was a tiger beetle, one of the loveliest of its carnivorous kind, *Cicindela polonius,* he observed, automatically noting its markings and classifications. He thought deeply of all the considerations extending into the future and glanced up finally into the large, green, idealistic and compelling eyes of Eva Bronowski. His heart was throbbing with dread.

"Why must it be me?" he protested.

Chapter 15

IT WAS HOT IN ARGYLE STREET.

After the shimmering pavement, Luzzatto found the shabby, cavernous parlor dim and cool. He glanced about nervously, finding it awkward to sit in furniture swathed and ghostly in white sheets. Camphor was sprinkled on a carpet rolled in brown paper. He placed the briefcase on a side table.

Jo cocked an ear to the sound of a hammer above. "He's nailing up a crate of books."

Luzzatto glanced at the mantel—a figurine of Lao-tse, fat and jolly, sat under a glass bell with a clock in his belly. "But won't he be late? He's due at the exercises."

Jo smiled grimly. "Oh, he'll make it," she said morosely. "Never late to class, never missed a lecture!" She tapped out a cigarette. "Will he make those stupid exercises? God, yes!" She tossed back her head and waited with burning eyes.

He hesitated. She was pale, he thought; the smooth texture of her flat cheeks suddenly struck him as puttyish and coarse, but this might be due to the poor light. He said, "What are you planning to do at Lake Marah, Jo?"

"I'm not sure. Putter around, I guess. I may put in time with the horses, sailing, tennis, things like that."

Luzzatto became aware that a slender beam of sunlight had glanced into the room, lighting up a music cabinet of Italian design. It was moderate in height, gleaming with the richness of fruitwood, with a center tilt tray and shelves at breast level. In striking contrast with the room, it was

180

lovely and old, an exceptional piece. A band of green marble, guarded by nymphs, was decorated with a row of buttons. He turned from the sight back to Jo.

"You don't sound so keen, Jo! Why not take a real vacation? Why Lake Marah?"

A dead, level glance fixed him.

"We always go there. Maine is supposed to be good for me." She resumed smoking, resting an elbow in her palm, meeting his glance of troubled concern with tranquil detachment. "Luzzatto, boy," she sighed. "What brings you here?"

He was surprised at the stir of feeling for this older woman whose deeper glance was dark and mournful beyond description. Would he ever, he wondered, quite be free of her? Even now, finely drawn as she was, every motion—the sinewy gesture, the toss of her head, the nervous lift of her chin—stirred the residues of a sore, past tenderness. He glanced at the briefcase. "I've got to see him, Jo."

"Oh?"

"I've been sending in messages, and Freda keeps telling me they're delivered, but nothing happens. If he won't see me, why won't he say so? I'd know where I stand. He's never done this to me before, Jo. I'm not used to it."

Jo paused in the act of blowing down her slip. She caught, and understood, his glance. He was struck by the translucence and painful boniness of her chest. "I haven't heard any of this, Dave," she said slowly, closing her smock self-consciously. She had not been well, she explained, and had taken several weeks of sick leave. "But I know he's got a lot on his mind," she went on hesitantly. "Some hassel with the front office. Next year's budget, appointments he'd like to make, equipment he thinks he wants, what not! Usual stuff."

At the queerness of the tone, Luzzatto stared anxiously, but there was no follow-up, not of her illness, nor of the extraordinary, biting tone. Was it fair to impose an added strain? He hesitated, then succumbed to a brimming sense of grievance.

"No!" He shook his head doggedly. "He's had time for others, Jo! Why not for me? Just because I sent back that—that snotty letter." He went on emotionally, "Maybe I wasn't politic. Maybe I was stupid, but I don't know how to suck up to anybody, how to beg. I wasn't brought up that way, not in my family." To his surprise, an entirely novel sentiment had been uttered, but as he spoke the words, he knew they were true. Suddenly he realized his pride—pride in himself, his family, his sense of inner dignity—and anger to be put upon. "Why couldn't I show my Pop and Mom around the lab? He's supposed to be a *scientist*. A great scientist! He ought to be above these petty things."

There was a silence.

"Do you want me to talk to him, Dave?" she asked finally. "I will, if you say so."

He shook his head. "No! I'm just telling it to you."

The rat-tat ceased. Jo cocked her head and waited quietly. Heavy footsteps sounded overhead, echoing down carpetless halls. She gazed enigmatically at the troubled youth. "Luzzatto, boy," she said in low, wondering tones of affection. "If you could only see yourself. You're so much like him, I could weep."

The harsh voice called testily down into echoing spaces. "Josephine, dear!"

Jo went out to the stairs. "Yes, Dad?"

"Is that someone down there?"

"It's Dave."

"I should have been told."

"You sounded busy and we had some things to discuss."

"Things? Things? What sort of things?"

"Things."

"What about the car?"

"I'm calling for it now."

"We are supposed to start at daybreak. You shouldn't have waited till the last minute."

"It's only a simple job on the piston rings. If it's not ready, I'll take it anyhow. We'll be shooting oil from here to Waterville, but that won't matter."

"It's absurdly inefficient. I suggest you get the car now. You can drive me to the exercises. Where is my gown?"

"Where it was last year. In the closet in your study. It's wrapped in brown paper," she replied, quite sure he knew precisely where the gown was waiting for its annual airing.

After a silence, the voice said, "Tell Luzzatto to wait. I can give him ten minutes."

Footsteps receded and a door closed. Jo stuck her fists into her pockets and returned to the parlor, muttering. "At least he's not ignoring you, Dave," she suggested grimly, "and that's something. Oh, sure! It would be simple to give you an hour, listen to your grief, then stick it in some— some pigeonhole in his mind. That's no trick. He'll give time to those others because it's the easier way out—but in your case he's interested enough to engage you in a fuss." She tapped his chest. "What you need

182

is a good and satisfactory love affair with a charming girl of suitable age who can fill that aching void. *That's* your trouble!"

"That's not the point, Jo," he protested uncomfortably. "It's a matter of principle. He can't—"

She stood on tiptoes and lightly kissed his mouth. "Don't be so miserable, Dave. You've been sweet to me—far more than I deserve. If ever I can help in any way, let me know." She stood back and clapped her hands. "Now! You look all beat up! Can I mix a cool drink before I get the car? Scotch, bourbon, gin, vodka? You name it, I got it!"

Before he could answer, she was off to the kitchen from whence came a banging of ice trays and fruity swearing. He followed a step into the dining room. "Can I help?"

"Crikey, no!" Her voice was muffled, panting.

He returned to the shrouded parlor and glanced nervously at the clock. Some faculty wit—Puce? Nadine Foxx?—was responsible for a legend that Sophie Ullman had furnished these rooms with a pitchfork, but this was unfair. The heavy pieces were no worse than one might expect in professorial circles. The wall of books was moldering in five languages. Hegel and Wordsworth, Goethe and Marlowe, *Principia Mathematica* and Mme. Blavatsky, *Die Naturwissenschaften,* Rhine and Reich, Wellhausen, The *Upanishads, A Concordance to the Bible, The Light of Asia,* Jung, Bergson, *The Sieve of Eratosthenes,* Toynbee and Velikovsky.

He broke off impatiently and rested the briefcase protectively on his lap. Now how, he wondered moodily, could he best raise the question of Will Tewksbury without prejudice to his own plans for the year ahead.

Jo had already left for the garage, and he was in a most disagreeable state of tension, when finally Ullman strode into the darkened room, somber and abstracted, but gracious enough, and asked him to state the case. The older man listened courteously, but as the import sank in, the lines of displeasure deepened ominously. He glanced up with a stirring of profound anger. "Luzzatto! What has got into this generation of asses? How is this any concern of the student body? The question is absolutely without the slightest importance."

Luzzatto stood his ground. "We think it is," he responded defiantly. "It's a question of fairness. The poor guy is so absolutely depressed that everybody—"

The magnetic hot eyes stared disconcertingly. "That 'poor guy'? How elegantly you put it! Does it occur to you, my dear fellow, that I have as much sympathy and understanding for that 'poor guy' as anyone? Mrs. Ullman has been more than kind to his family. Is there any reason why

I should wish to get rid of him without cause? Answer me!" His eyes were watchful. "Has he perhaps complained?"

Luzzatto paused. "Not to me," he said, then, observing a lowering of suspicion, added quickly, "He feels you're not showing the same interest in him any more. Little things, I guess, but he's hypersensitive."

Ullman considered the point seriously. "I have been very preoccupied lately, I daresay," he finally conceded on an easier note. "That sensitivity you mention, Luzzatto, is characteristic of the dependent personality. Still, you have not really answered the question."

Luzzatto took a moment to control his voice. "It's not just my own idea, Professor. Everybody seems to know that you've got some plan of reorganization that calls for a lot of changes. I mean, if there's any value to our opinions, we'd like to see him get every benefit of the doubt."

"Plan?"

"It's common knowledge," said Luzzatto.

"You take hearsay for evidence?"

"Not exactly, but—"

"No. Go on! I should like to hear." Ullman sat back with a dark smile. "What is this 'common knowledge'?"

"Actually only the part about Mr. Tewksbury. As a matter of fact, Professor, there's a lot of confusion. Nobody seems to know." Luzzatto drew a breath and opened the briefcase. "We drafted a resolution."

"We?"

"A group of us. We felt we ought to go on record."

Ullman said softly, "Did this fellow put you up to it?"

Luzzatto's glance was level. "No!"

"May I?" Ullman put out a hand.

Luzzatto handed over a resolution typed on the department stationery. Ullman brought the paper to the window and raised a shade. "Hum!" He ran down the alphabet from Eva Bronowski's large signature to the copperplate script of Joe Wodzick. Finally he glanced up ironically. "I am disappointed in Prescott."

"Prescott sent a letter from Baltimore," said Luzzatto stiffly. "I've got it here."

Ullman continued to study the resolution, then, smiling darkly, he observed that the student had missed his proper vocation, and crossed to the foyer where he called harshly, "Sophie? Sophie?"

"Yes, Bokkie?"

"Would you be so kind as to come down, Sophie, dear? It is almost time."

Ullman came back to the parlor. "To my wife I am Bokkie," he re-

184

marked, almost to himself. "To my daughter I am Dad. To you I am the learned pedagogue. To this fellow I am a capricious deity scattering doom without reason or justice. Zeus is dethroned, Whirl is king? Eh, Luzzatto?" He stared somberly at the younger man's frown of bewilderment. "Well, well! I congratulate you, Luzzatto. You have got the entire roster to demand justice of higher authority. In the academic world this is an achievement." He laughed with menace. "There are those, I think you realize, who might regard this as an act of insubordination. As it is—" He broke off as his wife appeared at the door.

"Why, David!" she exclaimed. "How d'ye do?"

Sophie Ullman's greeting invariably expressed incredulity and gratification, as though Luzzatto's presence were ever a source of amazement and congratulation. It was an effect she had developed as a child at dancing school, and had not seen fit to change over the years. She paused at the entrance, tugging at the tightly fitted, flowered dress of bright green, then launched herself stiffly across the room. She was a tall, faded woman of conventional prettiness with a spinsterish armature of bones on which the flesh was sparingly hung. A small, neat head was tightly covered with white curls. "You've been quite a stranger, David. Victor," she remarked, turning, "you really must not work these boys so hard before the recess. Now, tell me how you are?"

"All right, I guess," Luzzatto muttered.

"Oh? Am I disturbing something?" Sophie's bright eyes darted intelligently as she took in an awkward situation. "I suppose it's something technical. Well, never mind me! I won't understand a word. We'll be late, Victor!" She lowered herself to the ottoman with a breathless sigh.

"Would you believe it, my dear?" Ullman said sardonically, "Luzzatto is here on a special mission and I gave him the time because I thought it might be important. He is here to bell the cat." He laughed harshly and explained the circumstances. "Here is the resolution. If I were not so amused, I might be vexed."

Sophie read the paper rapidly, blinking at the text. In the silence she cracked a dry knuckle. "I'm not sure I'm so amused, Victor," she said finally, then turned reproachfully. "How could you possibly do this, David? Does Dr. Ullman deserve this?"

Luzzatto flushed under the reproach.

"Nah, nah!" Ullman raised an indulgent hand. "He is showing good qualities, Sophie. This action may not exactly meet the canons of discipline as I learned them, but it reflects a generous impulse. It is precisely what I might have done in my own rebellious period." He resumed smoking with an air of sardonic affection. "*Esel*," he said softly, using the term

185

endearingly. "Silly ass! This elaborate presentation was hardly worth the effort, and you may so advise your colleagues who put you up to it. Your precious Tewksbury can look forward to a tranquil year." He thrust out a finger with a delighted grin. "Ho-ho! Sophie! Look at the expression!"

Indeed Luzzatto was the picture of foolish confusion. Until the final turn, he had felt a strong current sweeping him into a quarrel he could not in honor avoid. And now? It was indeed a dirty trick, he thought sorely, to be led up the garden path, and down. Ullman's grim smile was discerning.

"Did you imagine after all these years that I could be arbitrary in the case of this poor devil? To what end?" he demanded. "How could I act unjustly to his family? Believe me, Luzzatto," he added reproachfully, "it is not my nature. Of all people, you should know better."

"But—but there is a plan?" Luzzatto stammered.

"Ah? The plan!" Ullman raised a melancholy finger. "I am afraid that any plan to raise the standards of our university must be put off for another year. I am not sure—" He broke off abruptly. "Why do you suppose they have brought this fellow Polk from California to deliver the principal address this afternoon? Surely the significance has not escaped you?" Something urgent was in the question.

"Victor!" murmured Sophie deprecatingly.

Ullman caught the signal and halted in mid-flight. "Well—" He gave in reluctantly, noting bewilderment in the younger man's face. "Never mind that now. The point is that there is no plan for the moment. In any case, the Tewksbury problem would have no importance. It hardly rises to the dignity of this discussion. Where is your sense of proportion?"

"I—I accepted this responsibility, Professor," Luzzatto muttered grudgingly. "I don't want you to assume that anybody had to put me up to this."

Ullman made a handsome gesture of dismissal. "Quatch! I refuse to believe it. I'm not such a donkey that I don't understand the psychology of the ambitious young scientist," he said good-humoredly. "Or of his envious rivals. It is fortunate I have this understanding, for otherwise you took a risk. You have a certain naiveté, Luzzatto, a refreshing idealism, of which that bunch took cunning advantage. I know them. I *know* them. Whose axe were you sent to grind?"

"No one's," said Luzzatto abruptly.

Ullman stared a full moment of dawning incredulity, then in tones of shock remarked, "Sophie! I believe this young idiot is angry with me! Eh,

186

Luzzatto? Why?" The younger man shrugged morosely. "No, no! I insist on frankness between us!"

Luzzatto had come determined to act in the iciest traditions of scholarship, ready for anything but the older man's air of amused indulgence, and then, against every vow to the contrary, the floodgates opened in an outburst of temper.

"It's not the damn grade!" he exclaimed angrily, striding about the darkened room. "I don't give a damn about marks, not really, but it wasn't right. How could you penalize my work on a personal basis? Once that's permitted, what happens to those objective standards we're trying to set up? I remember when you said—" And so on, and on, until he realized that the room was quiet. He paused, waiting for lightning to strike.

Ullman said calmly, "But my dear fellow, it was simply to impress on you the discipline of the laboratory. Surely you understood? If you will tell me that your breach of the rules was unintentional, I am willing to forget the incident. What do you say?" He added gently, "I have been quite unhappy about this whole matter too. I was hoping that we might have had it out even earlier than this."

"You never let me know," Luzzatto said resentfully.

"I am the teacher," said Ullman simply. "It is for the student to make the overture."

The two exchanged glances. Sophie Ullman picked up a large handbag. "Please say something, David," she murmured. "You *were* in the wrong."

Luzzatto waited for a long moment. "I didn't think you'd mind just because I let my parents look over the lab. It didn't seem that important at the time."

"Not mind?" Ullman said wonderingly. "But you were aware of my rule. How many times have I stressed the integrity, the inviolability of the laboratory? On this point there can be no compromise."

Luzzatto came to a reluctant decision, and looked up. "I guess I took too much for granted, Professor," he said in a low voice. "I'm sorry. It won't happen again." He stared at the floor, relieved, yet glum, thinking that those words were the last he had ever expected to say. So much, he thought grimly, for the Luzzatto pride!

"I am delighted, Luzzatto." Ullman exchanged a glance of triumph with his wife. Evidently his own expectations had not been too high. "Yes, yes! I am really, genuinely pleased." He smoked with luxuriant pleasure, twinkling at the unhappy youth, then, like a chess master putting forward an unsuspected pawn, came to the move toward which his game had been planned. "I have good news," he cried, rubbing his hands. "First, I am restoring your mark. I never really intended otherwise. Indeed I was count-

187

ing on your good sense. Second, while you were off sulking like Achilles in your tent, I have arranged for you to spend the summer with us at Lake Marah! Eh? Is that a shock?" He smiled broadly. "There's not much there to do but you'll be part of the family. It will let you meet some of the best minds of the country in the proper setting. The contacts, the social give and take, the friendships, the chance to develop oneself—you'll find, there's nothing like it. Maine is most delightful in summer." He sat back and beamed at the picture of spreading consternation. "You can pack and be ready by morning. We have more than enough room in the car."

Luzzatto's mouth refused to close.

"Does it come too suddenly?" Ullman chuckled.

Luzzatto shook his head. "It's not that. I can't go."

"Eh? Why not?" Ullman demanded sharply.

Luzzatto drew a breath. "I'm finally working on my project, Professor," he said. "You recall? That project we discussed last September? I can't let it go, sir," he added with mute appeal. "I really can't."

In the driveway Jo's automobile plunged and squealed to a halt.

"You are of course joking?" Ullman said.

"No, sir."

Slowly, reflectively, Ullman lit a fresh cigarette and examined the glowing tip nicely. "This cannot possibly wait?"

Luzzatto hesitated. "It's not that, Professor. I've run across something that's got me puzzled. We've been plotting curves of bacterial resistance to the major antibiotics—penicillin, streptomycin, isoniazid, PAS, one or two others, you know. We've also been using a modified Lederberg's technique—not that it was strictly necessary, but it's sort of elegant, you know." He smiled nervously. "We've been able to—"

"We?" asked Ullman.

Luzzatto said reluctantly, "Tewksbury's been helping me to cook up media." He described a nutrient infusion of agar, salts, a simple phosphate buffer, and the juices of ground bacteria of known resistance. "We're using four cultures from the stockroom. I hope that's all right?" he asked anxiously.

The harsh lines deepened. "Does anyone else know?"

"No, sir. Well, Katz-Moebius. I had to talk to someone, you see?"

"It is a matter of no importance. What else?"

Luzzatto rubbed his neck. "Well, in one series of cultures I'm getting no curve of resistance at all. Or practically none. I don't know why. I was hoping you would like to review my notes?"

"Victor," murmured Sophie deprecatingly.

"Ah, yes! The time." A glance flickered toward her, then returned.

"Doesn't all this come a bit late, Luzzatto? Can I give the matter proper attention standing on one foot while the exercises wait?"

Luzzatto gazed at his hands. "It's—it's simply that I didn't want to leave these cultures over the summer. I've got to find out what's flattening that curve." He arose unhappily. "Have a nice summer, Professor. You too, Mrs. Ullman. Sorry I barged in."

Ullman stared without expression. "You are, of course, a free agent. Have I ever suggested otherwise?"

"No."

"What then actually do you wish?"

Luzzatto cursed the fullness of emotion that halted words struggling for life. "I—I don't quite know, Professor. Only, I guess, I've got a hunch that I'm onto something big."

"It would be a scandal, would it not"—Ullman gave the word its dry, Germanic pronunciation—"if the teacher, handicapped by age, confused by experience, were to pit his judgment against the student's? Come, I would like to show you something before you go—"

Jo had returned through the rear door. She was in the kitchen, running cold water over her wrists, listening to the voices in the parlor. Occasionally, the younger voice came through, also her mother's, but it was the harsh peremptory tones which echoed through the house. She stared with distaste at strong hands, sunburned to coppery brown, then wearily twisted the tap.

It must be the heat! she thought.

It was an effort to stand, an effort to think, an effort to cross the immensity of space from the sink, to pass the array of cabinets, to open the door.

"Car's waiting," she said.

Ullman held up a restraining hand. "Please!"

He was at the ornate Italian music cabinet, bending forward thoughtfully, counting a row of buttons. One, three, seven, twelve! A finger stabbed, a tray plunged out—cunningly contrived by a cabinet maker in Livorno centuries earlier. Biting a nail thoughtfully, he stalked back to the center of the room, studying a small card of odd design.

"I have waited a long time, Luzzatto," he said softly. "I have never before put myself in this position."

"Oh, Victor!" said Sophie miserably.

Ullman adjusted his pince-nez. He seemed under a goad of deep emotion. "Nah, nah! I am not unreasonable, Sophie! I simply wish to make sure that we fully understand. I wish not to impose my judgment without

189

regard to the views of the student. Believe me, Luzzatto, I have the deepest respect for your capacities." He stared at the card intently, "I too have my limitations. Tell me, what is the master science?"

Luzzatto frowned. "In what sense?"

"Why, in the ultimate sense, of course!" Ullman seemed surprised. "Must it not be the pure science of Number? Mathematics? All the painfully gathered knowledge of our own biological sciences may in the end turn out to be illusory. But never will a rational number turn up that will denote exactly the square root of two. The proof of that proposition was already ancient and classical in the days of Aristotle. The axioms of pure mathematics have an eternal truth, a symmetry which gives a certain esthetic satisfaction." He turned over the card thoughtfully. "This symmetry too is a test."

"Victor," said Sophie unhappily.

"Yes, yes. I tend to stress this aspect too much. It is a bad habit." Ullman glanced up, smiling curiously. "I must be extremely candid, Luzzatto. I am not terribly impressed that you failed to plot a curve, but then, I'm not exactly a chicken at this game, you know? I have spent too many years with these enthusiasms, these 'great discoveries' "—the heavy mouth twisted sardonically, sadly—"to dance with delight like a monkey on a stick. However—"

"But you haven't read my notes yet!" Luzzatto exclaimed.

"What purpose would it possibly serve?" said Ullman irritably. "No doubt your effect is due to some simple contamination in the media." He stared up estimatingly. "Why these looks? You have a lifetime ahead for your 'major discoveries'." He paused. "I was about to make a point. If you feel that you need my help, you may write to me over the summer. I will be pleased to maintain a correspondence. I will, however, lay down some conditions."

"Sir, if it's—"

Ullman cut this short. "First, you will accept an increase in stipend of fifty dollars a month. No, there are no strings." He smiled thinly. "You may suspend the wine project and regard your own project as a substitute. We simply cannot let you go around any longer without income. Mrs. Ullman feels very strongly on that point. I was planning this for September but I see no reason for delay. Second, you will promptly move into my laboratory for the summer. No thanks, please! I have no great expectations for all this, Luzzatto, but I daresay you must get it out of your system. I really could not endure the thought of that hot box upstairs in this frightful weather. I am, after all, your teacher! You are entitled to the best we can offer."

190

"I'm—I'm grateful," said Luzzatto, overcome.

Ullman turned over the card. "Luzzatto, nothing quite happens by chance. There is a pattern, a plan by which events prove themselves. I have arranged certain aphorisms which seem to me to have a pithy applicability to many situations. It is surprising how they stimulate the imagination—how truly suggestive they become when properly arranged. Would you do me a great favor?"

It was a queer reversal of mood, mercurial and confusing, to detect the note of appeal in the earnest, labored voice. Luzzatto had not before seen such a display of emotion. He caught a strange glance of intensity from Jo.

"I would like you to review this chart," said Ullman earnestly. "It's merely an exercise, of course, but I have put a good deal of work into it. Will you let me know your opinion? Oh, not now, of course!" he added hastily. "But perhaps when we return from Lake Marah? No one outside this room has yet seen this chart."

"Of course," said Luzzato.

Ullman sighed and lifted an elbow to mop his brow. "It is time to go," he said finally. "Josephine, dear. Would you be good enough to fetch my gown?"

The academic procession was already in formation when Ullman took his place in the line, wearing the slashings of Göttingen with an air of pride and disdain. He nodded to acquaintances, bowed to antagonists, and kept his gaze ahead. He stirred restlessly as sweat crept down his armpits. Why had he chosen to wear serge under the gown rather than seersuckers? It was vanity for which he would pay. He could think of nothing but the heat—

Luzzatto! Oh, yes! he thought. Well, it all worked out. It will continue to do so. He rubbed himself abstractedly and looked up with attention, having almost nodded off in the sun. There was this fellow Polk to be endured.

The great chorus of *The Messiah* sounded:

Hallelujah! Hal-lelujah! Hal-lelujah!

The procession moved forward. His walk was leisurely, stately as he proceeded with his fellows, conscious of a timeless rite and the deeper significance of the moment. About him a tempest of icy winds was howling, but in the eye of the storm it was still as death.

The truth was that he was frightfully, monumentally bored.

191

In Mackenzie Hall Luzzatto strode excitedly into the laboratory followed by Eva and Will Tewksbury. He gazed about at the plenitude of space and equipment.

"Oh, God!" he said in a small voice. "Oh, God! Tewk! Eva!"

"Very nice," she agreed.

"Nice? It's fabulous! We can work." He paused to listen. In recess all corridors are lonely, quiet, haunted by the wraiths of departed forms. Almost, he could have sworn, a dry, benevolent chuckle came from the empty hall. He rubbed his hands with miserly delight. "Let's begin now."

Eva smiled faintly. "Isn't it stuffy in here, Dave?"

He threw up the windows and gazed at a sea of faces and colors.

Hallelujah! Hal-lelujah! Hallelu-jah!

The challenge to praise Divinity was commanding, peremptory, awesome. In that moment he could have wept with gratitude. When he turned back, Eva's eyes were alight with amusement, his own awash with brine. "I'd do anything for that man," he choked, brimming over. "*Anything!* I can't tell you how wonderful he's acted about everything. Look at all this space!"

"Ayeh," said Tewksbury.

"Well, now!" Luzzatto drew a breath. "Suppose we get those cultures down from upstairs and find out what happened to that curve of resistance. Evvie, would you give a hand?"

"Love to," said Eva, smiling.

Dawn was breaking when Hilda Puce knocked on the bedroom door. "Eva, dah-ling?"

A yawn. "Uh! Yuh? It's only six."

"Telephone! Some insane boy calling—"

"I'll take it. You're a lamb, Hilda," said Eva hastily. She found a robe and rushed to the telephone where she clung, blinking, while a hoarse, queer voice rattled tinnily in the ear piece. "I'll be right there. I'll have a thermos with me," she said promptly, suddenly awake. At Mackenzie Hall, she was met by a tottering figure of fatigue—bearded, hollow-eyed, numbed with elation. "God, Evvie," croaked Luzzatto, scratching his ribs. "Look here!"

At Eva's entrance, Tewksbury, who had been sprawled, flaccid and supine on a cot, arose with embarrassment. "Excuse me, Miss Bronowski," he mumbled, running a furry tongue over his teeth, "I just fell off." In a clutter of criminal disorder, an autoclave was warm, the smell was like a zoo's, a long table was strewn with orange peels and Petri dishes.

"Well, let's see," said Eva with intense disapproval. Luzzatto stood back in quiet triumph.

It looked like nothing much. Several scores of pour plate cultures showed the effects of various concentrations of a dozen antibiotics on four representative microorganisms: *E. coli, M. pyogenes, M. ranae, B. megatherium*. Even in weak dilutions of the drug, the cultures had the appearance of the skies as seen through the telescope. Larger surface colonies like individual stars floated against smaller, lens-shaped colonies of the nebulous background. The effect of limitless depth was striking.

"Mutations to resistance," said Luzzatto briefly. "The bugs are living on the antibiotics."

"Isn't that expected?" she frowned.

"Oh, sure! Look here!" He drew her aside.

Eva stared into the clear jelly and caught her breath with disbelief. In another group of Petri dishes, the lethal effect of the antibiotics was uniform. Out of billions of organisms descended from sensitive ancestors, not one individual had mutated from sensitivity to resistance. It was the factor added to the culture medium that had secured the effect.

"Oh, Dave!" she exulted. "Dave!"

It was inevitable to embrace and kiss in a wild dance of joy that included the hapless Tewksbury whose blushes lent glory to the early sun, and even as Luzzatto gazed into Eva's eyes in transport, almost with dread, dimly sensing the future, he said with awe:

"What shall we call it?"

The Present Resumed

Chapter 16

LUZZATTO WAS ABOUT TO EXPOUND THE CONCEPT OF ALLELISM. HE was facing the blackboard, hoping that the physical motion of writing would prime the pump, that thoughts would flow. Dusting chalk from his fingertips, he turned to the class. "Now, then—"

The door opened and a man wearing a badge entered the classroom. "Luzzatto?" he asked gruffly.

The intruder clumped across the room while the class gazed in wonder, not sure that some psychological experiment was not in progress. "I'm only doing my job, Professor," the man said angrily.

Luzzatto stared at the papers thrust into his hand. The impossible thing had happened. After talks, conferences, sleepless nights, anxieties, optimistic evasions, he had no feelings left for the moment—except disbelief.

"Here! Just a moment," he began.

But it was too late. The man was gone and he was alone, facing strangers. They knew! All pretense was gone, he thought dully. Of course they knew!

The interminable moment persisted.

He had an impulse, instantly quelled, to dismiss the class. Instead, he thrust the papers, unread, into a pocket and turned to the blackboard. A woman coughed, the class stirred, and he came back to a discussion of allelism and its effects on blood groupings in man. His voice was loud enough, clear and high-pitched, but whether in fact his lecture had the slightest coherence he was never to know.

The gong brought release.

Abruptly he fled, out-pacing the students, and hastened to his office where he locked the door. Only then was he able with some comprehension to read the formal complaint drafted by a law firm in New York City.

In a few simple paragraphs he was named defendant together with the directors of the Haverstraw Foundation against a claim for judgment to restore the plaintiff to all prior rights in the biocin patent. The suit was in equity. At stake was more than one million dollars. The summons designated the Supreme Court: Merton County as the place of trial.

"Damn him!" whispered Luzzatto wretchedly. "Did he have to do this?"

But the nagging hurt was for Eva. He would have to break the news, he thought, glancing with dread at the telephone. How would she take it? For himself he had no feelings at all.

On a gray November morning, Eva awoke with a start and found the bed at her side empty and cold. She arose and went to the study. A rank odor reached her sharpened senses. It was the ammoniac smell of an animal cage—a nervous male creature had passed the night in restless prowling, and now was gone. She noticed a litter of ashes, papers strewn with notations, the green hurricane lamp burning on the Winthrop desk. Drearily she turned away.

She was seated in the breakfast corner staring at untasted food when she heard a familiar clap of the brass rapper. Fog and drizzle were wetting the countryside, and a cold smell of woodlands smoke was drifting in the damp air. She shivered. Her shapeless quilted robe was warm enough but every bone ached with strain and fatigue. She gathered her strength and went to the door. It was the postman.

"Professor in?"

"I'm afraid he left early," she replied.

"Well, seems I never catch him in. Say, Mrs. Luzzatto, Mrs. Wilson and me were sorry to read that piece in the papers about the law case. Thought I'd like to express how real sympathetic we feel. Terrible thing!"

"Why, that's very kind."

"Does the Professor think it'll actually come to trial? Or will it be settled?"

"It's not up to my husband, I'm afraid."

"He's up against a tough proposition. Of course, if the university stands behind him, he'll be okay. I don't think the other side has got a case."

"Oh? Why do you say that?"

"Well, I been in business for myself, Mrs. Luzzatto. I know what it is to sue, and to be sued. I sat on juries and I'm a judge of character. I know

198

you young people because every time I deliver a piece of mail, I get a glimpse of your kitchen, and that's what counts—the little things. Like now, you had them sticky little honey cakes that time you asked me in?"

"Oh, those?"

"Well, you let me eat up the whole batch, Mrs. Luzzatto. I was sitting right there in your kitchen, and you never let out a peep how I was ruining the effect of your tea party with all those faculty women showing up. Now, I think that was mighty wonderful and revealing—the little things. No, I don't think any husband of yours could be capable, Mrs. Luzzatto. I know what it means to sue, and to be sued."

Eva considered this last remark with a wild impulse to flee the garrulity, yet the kindly drone held her rooted to the doorway. She asked slowly, "Did you ever know Professor Ullman?"

"Nope. Never delivered to him. He lived on Argyle Street. I never had that route, luckily. I like it out here in the fresh air, although these new houses mean a heavier load of work. Uh. No, the old Professor had this reputation in the post office for getting all this peculiar religious mail from all parts of the world, but you learn to expect that from professors. They're always getting packages from jungles, and chemical houses, and all this free government stuff. I guess you don't have to be nutty to be a professor, but it seems to help. Excuse me, Mrs. Luzzatto, that's just a little joke we have."

"I'm afraid there may be some truth in that."

"I thought you wouldn't mind."

"Did you know his daughter?"

"Doctor Josephine? Well, yes, although she always used to come and go. You just couldn't help notice her, I mean, because she's got this cheerful way. Also, I got to admit that she's surprisingly good looking for a lady scientist. No, I recall Dr. Josephine about fifteen years ago, when she first come back from Wisconsin to teach at the university. That time she stopped living with her folks and took this place in Catherine Street where I used to deliver. Then something happened and she left suddenly."

"Oh? Why?"

"The story they let out was that she was going to some Indian reservation to study their customs. Blackfeet, I think. Some tribe near Canada."

"What was the truth?"

"Well, it's a little embarrassing."

"I wish you'd tell me," said Eva quietly.

"I don't know if I should. On the other hand, considering everything, you might be entitled to this information. Lemme see, now. Oh, yes! I knew she was going with some young man in New York because of those letters. He kept her mighty anxious, on tenterhooks, and she didn't go with anybody else that I could tell. Not that she didn't have chances, you see? When I had no letter for her, she'd close the door with that gone suffering look, and I knew something was hurting. Then when I had a letter, she'd snatch it up and begin to read, but it wasn't much better. Bad situation! Anyhow, the letters stopped, and then for a month she got terribly moody, but in a way I didn't like. One night—"

"Yes."

"This is the embarrassing part. It was long before your time. It seems that she walked into the police station one night about 2 A.M. in a rain slicker. At first they didn't recognize her. It was a wet night, and my brother, Duke—he was desk officer, rest his soul!—he took it for granted she wanted to report a traffic accident, because her hair was muddy, and she had this dopey look. But instead she dropped the slicker and she didn't have a stitch on."

"Oh, dear!"

"Fact. It's shocking, a nice girl like that, but there she was and with the riffraff in the next room. Duke figured she might be drunk, but she wasn't, not even a smell. Fortunately, he had a level head and when she began to yell what she wanted a man to do—it wasn't a nice word, Mrs. Luzzatto."

"There's no word I can't hear."

"No, but there's some I wasn't taught to use to nice young ladies. Well, when she kept yelling this one thing, Duke saw what he had on his hands, and he called the father. Well, he come with some doctor and they got her away. Lucky Duke was on the desk, because not a soul ever got to know, although of course there's been rumors."

"I didn't dream it possible," said Eva slowly.

"Well, yes! To see her now, you'd never tell. When she come back a year later the doctors seem to of worked a miracle. Just as nice and pretty as ever, except every so often she'd take these leaves of absence. Real tragedy, a lovely young woman like that, and who knows what goes on inside? Isn't that letter from her?"

Eva closed her eyes exhaustedly. "Mr. Wilson!"

"Oh, sure! Sorry. I didn't mean to go blabbing, only I feel you're entitled to any morsel I can pass along. You people are young, Mrs. Luzzatto. Just remember that life has a way of taking care of things."

With a friendly nod, the mailman drove off in the rain. "Funny!" he murmured. That likable young woman, he thought, wasn't wearing too well—too much bloat, and those burning eyes. Had he done the right thing? He was not sure, not sure of anything these days, except of that one principle by which his life was guided and organized—a man was loyal to his route, or he was not. Without that rule, what else was he but a hack?

Eva brought the letter from Jo to the light, wondering at the vision of a lovely, naked girl yelling her torment in the dust of a police barracks. A shudder went through her body. Nothing in her life had prepared her for the malignant impulse to turn the information to advantage.

"Oh, dear God," she thought dismally. "How can I think such thoughts? This is Jo! What has she to do with her father? What is this poison doing to us?"

Many things fell suddenly into place. She sank into a chair, staring at the bold scrawl. The amount of cruelty within herself was depressing beyond belief. Then, with a breathless sigh, she picked up the telephone. She had to repeat the number twice.

"Miss Stahl?"

"Yes, Mrs. Luzzatto?" Freda's voice was curiously tight.

"Please tell Professor Luzzatto that I've got a letter here for him. When he comes out of class, have him call me?"

"Sure. Oh, he's not giving that class this morning. Professor Wodzick's substituting."

"Isn't that the fourth—?"

"You'll have to speak louder, Mrs. Luzzatto."

"The fourth this month?"

"Well, yes. He's in conference with Mr. Podell. You could call him there."

"Just have him return this call? 'Bye."

" 'Bye. Oh, say, I've got a note here to thank you for that brooch, Mrs. Luzzatto. It was sweet to remember my birthday. Only I've been so rushed—"

"It's really nothing, Miss Stahl. You can tell me one thing? How are people reacting? I hate to ask, but my husband looks so worried, yet he won't discuss it with me, you see?"

"Well, I think people are being pretty fair-minded. They're waiting to hear both sides before they make up their minds."

"Make up their minds to what? That someone's a thief and a liar and they can't decide which?"

"Please, Mrs. Luzzatto!"

"Sorry."

"Let me tell you, that's pretty wonderful these days to find people

201

ready to suspend judgment. I've been reading about this scientist down in Washington—"

"Goodbye, Miss Stahl."

Eva stood breathing heavily, resisting dishonor, but the impulse was too strong. With an exclamation of self-disapproval, she stabbed the envelope with a paper knife of ivory.

San Martino Oceanographic Institute
San Martino, Florida

Thanksgiving

Dearest Dave:

First of all, I ought to reassure you about myself. I have been living the good, lazy life—eating much, sleeping late, roaming the beach, finding shells for your collection. Anyhoo—I've picked up a Pecten gibbus, a Horse Conch and the loveliest Tulip Band shell which I'll send off along with my next shipment of oranges. (Now, don't scold me on that again—I love to send these small souvenirs of myself, and the small pleasures keep me from mooching around this place in a thundercloud of despair at the queer course my life has taken.) However, we've got 700 miles of coastline curving from Pensacola to the Keys and I mean to search every flea-bitten inch—after, that is, I've put on another ten pounds of this not too, too solid flesh. Although this recent trip out West did me a world of good, I'm still far too skinny to please my medicine man.

Now I must get to the point—with reluctance, you must believe me, Dave.

Some kind soul—out of pure affection, no doubt—sent me a copy of *Patroon* with those black headlines. I can't, I honestly can't understand why Dad had to name *you!* Why, Davey, you poor lamb, you're the last one in the world to deserve a thing like this. I can see now why you haven't dropped me a line for several months.

As it happens, I didn't need a copy of *Patroon*. Last week I had a long chatty letter from Sophie—which surprised me, because months can pass without even a postcard—in which she warned me cryptically not to write to you. To say I was puzzled would be putting it mildly. She never before gave a damn about my correspondents. Aha! Something, methought, is rotten in the state of Denmark—but what? Answer came almost at once. It seems that the lawsuit has been stirring up a witch's brew of talk in circles scientific, although I would be the last to hear, you see? But only last night John Alcock (you recall, he studies glacial lakes? we once talked about his work?) drove down from Miami and opened up with the thought that the volcano was about to erupt in this lawsuit.

Believe me, I was surprised. I argued myself purple that the rumor was a lie. I've known that Dad was unhappy about that whole miserable mess he left at H. U., but I never expected anything like this. I almost called you long distance but I refrained and sat up all night staring at the black waters of the gulf. Oh, Davey! I could have wept! This morn-

202

ing came my said copy of *Patroon* plus the Miami paper with a foul story carried by the AP. In the midst of black coffee I suddenly turned sick and it was a race to the john. Fortunately, I won by a narrow margin. I'm much better now but these neurological symptoms are on a hair trigger and I simply must watch myself.

I know you think I'm over-emotional but I am *not* presently neurotic. I know this because my fits of depression are simply and adequately reactive to a gray, depressing world. What got me was the content of John Alcock's disclosures.

The fact is, you're being marked as a mercenary, crass ingrate, Dave, who's riding a good thing at the expense of an older man. I'm sorry and mad and distressed to report this, but you might as well get the truth from those who love you—if you don't already know. Right or wrong, John's crowd up in Baltimore interpret this thing against you both—Dad is disapproved of for serving that complaint, but mainly you are held to blame for provoking the situation. Oh, Dave! You're the last man to be accused of having a greasy thumb—I remember too many idealistic arguments on that subject with you and Evvie, and I know how strongly you feel about this commercial prostitution of science, but right or wrong, you poor lamb, the feeling is against you.

Nothing is so bad as public name calling among scientists, but it's worse for you because while Dad's career is virtually over—what can he do now but putter and make suggestions?—yours has just begun. You're far too thin-skinned to live under the cloud of suspicion that follows anyone who gets above the level of mediocrity. What a high price to pay for one emotional basket of eggs. It's all too sad. I wonder what unconscious, irrational and symbolic forces have brought us to this point.

The fact remains that Dad assigned his total interest in this hateful stuff to science, while yours is yielding power, position and pots of money. Do you see how that looks?

Some of these views were expressed at lunch today by Dr. Harry Lockridge. He's been teaching me skin diving and in return I've been dissecting a variety of his specimens. I stink constantly of fish, but it's all new and fun and in my better moments I do a moderate amount of work. In fact I like a bit of discipline *when* it has a purpose! (Do I sound bitter?) Well, Dr. Lockridge wondered whether you realized how much damage, right or wrong, has already been done to your reputation.

I felt so miserable, yet what could I say? I can hardly take sides publicly. How can I hurt you? How can I take a position against Dad? It would look so unclean—and besides, he's grown so old, you see? And I don't actually know all the facts, do I? What really happened, Dave? What did you say or do that turned him on you?

I did my best to explain to Dr. Lockridge the whole psychological basis of your relationship to the family. I tried to write it off lightly as a family quarrel arising out of pure clash of temperament. This didn't sound too plausible, I'm afraid, even though everyone knows how really skittery and quarrelsome scientists can get—far worse than artists and opera singers. Harry suggested sarcastically that if you would offer to

203

turn over your interest to science, you might, or might not, look better in scientific circles.

I asked whether that would not look like a confession of guilt. He just laughed in a funny way and remarked that it might be later than you think.

I hope you won't deduce that I accept any of this criticism. If anyone else but my Dad were involved I'd publicly defend you while I have teeth, and when those were gone, I'd chew for you with my gums. I've been walking up and down this cubbyhole fantasying situations in which I am bursting out at the world in your defense with total faith in your integrity, but as it is, what can I say or do?

One other thing I should tell you. Ever since that stuff was discovered, you've been discussed by others, even your friends, about the question of publicity and assertiveness you've displayed. People are jealous and these tendencies have been taken the wrong way. In your case, it's simply a talkativeness that's your attractive feature (to my womanly heart, that is). That plus your eagerness to raise the general appreciation for the biological sciences among the masses.

Well, Dave, I'll close this ramble with a morsel of hard news. Leo the Katz wrote earlier this week with the usual assortment of limericks culled at the sump holes of Brandywine Labs. He's survived three purges and feels safe enough to turn down a juicy offer from California Spray. (They're doing amazing work with plant hormones and pesticides, I gather.) Evidently he's secure, but stultified in that crass atmosphere he pretends to loathe. Poor Leo! He'll never be happy until he marries that virgin of his dreams—age twenty, baby-blue eyes, blond tresses, decadent tastes, and a fiery soul—and he'll never find that combination this side of Paradise. (An interesting spectacle when it happens!) I'll always be grateful that he fixed me up with this heavenly job when the situation for the Ullmans, stock and scion, became untenable. Has he contacted you yet? Unless I misread him, too, I'm sure you can count on him for moral support.

Oh, Dave! Can't this thing be mediated, or compromised, or arbitrated in some way? Must you let these lawyers drag you through the muck? I have such a dreary feeling that you are being sacrificed to the will of others when a simple heart-to-heart talk with Dad might clear up this whole desolate mess! You were so close once that it ought to be possible. I'd hate to see you turned into a scapegoat for the sins of others.

Can that explain any part of the furor? It's always some poor, inoffensive billygoat, without stain or blemish, who must be driven out into the wilderness when the people have sinned, not logically or even because *he* has offended, but simply because he's handy when the high priest comes looking. And isn't that the picture—there's a pervasive, floating sense of guilt in the air for all the sins of commission and omission of science from Hiroshima down? Oh, Dave! Try to make your peace with Dad. We've seen too many sickening examples not to realize what happens to a benefactor when public opinion is whipped against him.

I'm not immune to doubts myself. I have my own moments of wonder.

204

What happened during these past few years that I've been out of touch? The lacunae are vast and I feel so horribly torn between loyalties. Here I am writing to you, counseling, giving advice, moral support—when I can't seem to get myself to write to my own Dad.

There's the dinner bell and my roommate's calling me to a mess of pompano. Tomorrow night we're going out with the shrimp fleet—and who knows what rare specimens along with the lucrative little fellows?

Love to Evvie and I hope she'll have this baby of yours with joy. I have visions that he will be born with that irresistible Luzzatto sense of humor at the spectacle of a world he never made—but will inherit. I envy her. She must be a tower of strength.

Devotedly,
Auntie Jo

P. S. Please do something about this nasty business. It wrings my heart. J.

Dripping with rain, Clara Stokes used her key to enter through the kitchen where she took in the scene at a glance. She studied a memo board, and walked into the living room.

"For Pete's sake, honey!" she cried. "I told you to let them doggone dishes alone. You trying to take away my bread and butter? You rest, I work!" She paused. "Now where are you going?"

"Marketing," said Eva.

"Honey! In this rain? You're out of your mind!"

"I'm bored stiff, Clara. There's so much reading I can do." Eva stalked about the room, straightening pictures, internally torn. "I wish everyone would stop hovering. Besides, I've got to go into town anyway."

Clara hung up a raincoat. "You really got the jitters this morning. Why don't you call up some friend like Mrs. Adderly and play a nice game of canasta, or gin, like any normal woman?"

"Friends? What friends?" Eva muttered.

Clara considered her answer with care. "Honey! You can't let this thing get you so early in the game. You've got lots of friends, but if you want to hide, they won't want to seek. Is that a way for a grown woman?"

Eva stared with exasperation. "Damn it, Clara! Stop talking! Just tell me what to order for dinner."

Clara gave up a bad job. "Okay, I'll make you out a list. Only why bother? Outside of calcium pills, you don't eat a thing I cook. I'm going to report you."

Eva paused. "That doctor's a fool."

"He's not the only one."

"One of these days I'll have to give you the sack," said Eva without conviction. Painfully, she began to climb to her room, but paused to rest, breathing heavily. A lancet of pain, sharper than any cramp, stabbed through her back. In the dark swirling of amniotic fluids, a gentle thump, a ripple was a startling thing. After a moment, she went on, trembling in every limb.

She felt like anything but a tower of strength.

Chapter 17

"COME IN," SAID PHILIP SEIXAS.

It was still raining, but the offices of Seixas and Wyandotte in the Noonan Professional Building remained a retreat of warmth and tranquility. A fire was burning in a coal grate in Philip Seixas's office, lighting up an array of richly bound reference books. A short, plump, intense young lawyer, Horatio Dotson, entered.

"Mrs. Luzzatto is here."

"How do you like her, Horatio?"

Young Dotson, who was less than twenty-three, fingered a mustache with a legal air. He was in fact a good lawyer who longed for the outward assurance and inner ease that his apprenticeship to the firm was expected to bring. That he was content to serve his formative years in East Haverstraw rather than Wall Street or Washington was a tribute to his chief's standing in the New York Bar.

"She's attractive, Mr. Seixas. Bit unstrung now, but she'd make an appealing witness for our side. If you can control her. You haven't made out too well with her husband."

Seixas glanced up with secret amusement, appreciating a hidden point of irony. "*Our* side?"

"Beg pardon?" asked Dotson.

Seixas handed over a memorandum dictated earlied in preparation for trial for consideration, reflecting that in some matters, the young lawyer, who got an honorarium of $30 per week, had a keener eye than his own.

"Well, show her in," Seixas said indulgently.

Eva had withdrawn her arms from the sleeves of a belted storm coat and now she huddled it about her shoulders as she followed young Dotson into the richly furnished room. Seixas smiled pleasantly.

"May we take your rain things?"

"No, thanks. I can stay only a moment."

"Oh? Surely more?"

"No, really," said Eva tightly.

"Horatio, ask Miss Hunter to bring some tea," said Seixas.

"Oh, no—"

But the young lawyer had already left. Eva took a brocaded chair facing a graceful escritoire of inlaid leather. She settled back, pulling off gloves, and stared with hostile deliberation at antiquities which included a Gilbert Stuart portrait of George Washington. Her brows went up. "An original?"

"Oh, yes."

"Where did you get it?" she asked with blunt interest.

The dark, aristocratic face smiled slightly. "Mr. Stuart gave it to a remote ancestor, for legal services rendered. It's been hanging in our offices ever since. This ancestor was the founder of this firm, you see?"

"Legal services?" asked Eva.

"Something to do with debtor's prison. It seems incongruous, I know, but Mr. Stuart had occasion to paint more than a few of these portraits."

"Seixas?" she murmured. "Seixas? It is an old name? I seem to have heard of it before. Now, tell me, Mr. Seixas, why am I here?" Her tone held a note of defiance.

Seixas sat back with the cool, thoughtful glance of a practitioner in the art of listening with the third ear. Her evasions, followed by challenge, were not without interest. His first question as to her age was designed to establish a degree of rapport. She glanced up coldly.

"I am more than thirty."

"You're older than your husband?"

"A bit," she agreed warily. "Why?"

He smiled gently. "I am simply trying to understand certain things, Mrs. Luzzatto. It has no direct bearing on the legal side."

"Then why go into it?" she asked.

Seixas pointed out patiently that in matters of complexity nothing could be taken for granted by a lawyer charged with weighty responsibilities. He put a background question. "What academic degrees do you hold?"

She hesitated. "The system here is not exactly the same. I have postwar credits from Cracow, also from the Sorbonne, but basically I have my master's in science from Haverstraw."

"You did not go on for a doctorate?"

208

"Oh, no." She fitted a cigarette into a silver holder. "I saw no point in that, even if I had the ability, which I felt I did not." She smiled bleakly. "It's widely believed that only the big brains throng the graduate schools, but that's not true, especially at a second-rate school like Haverstraw. Most students, I found, were mediocrities like myself seeking only to qualify for teaching licenses. I was shocked at the standards of admission."

"You believe Haverstraw is second-rate?"

"Who have they got? Tobiansky?" Eva shrugged. "Well, he's got some reputation, but who else? Gordimer Puce? Elizabeth Batchelor? Ah, my God!"

Seixas said quietly, "There's your husband."

"David?" Green eyes held the lawyer in somber appraisal. "Ah, yes! Poor devil!"

"Why do you say that?"

"Oh, please! I'm not a child, Mr. Seixas, even if you feel privileged to treat me like one. His reputation?" A sneer lifted the delicate nostrils. "Oh, he's considered—what do they call it?—a real hot scientist now, successor to Mackenzie, brilliant future, all that. But what are they doing to that reputation? How will he stand when you lawyers have finished with him?"

Seixas's stolid urbanity was a tribute to long years as a trial lawyer. He glanced at his notes. "Did you submit a thesis in fulfillment of your degree in science?"

Eva stared coldly. "I'm afraid that won't help you much."

Seixas lit a cigar. "Mrs. Luzzatto, I can readily get these facts by picking up the telephone. Mr. Gussett is under instructions to give me this sort of help, but is that what you want? I'm simply trying to establish a point of departure." He added easily, "I have nothing up my sleeve."

They exchanged a long glance.

"I was doing research in the incidence of black melanomas in guppies," Eva conceded grudgingly. "The idea was to inbreed the stock to develop strains in which the rate of tumors would be invariant. I'm not sure of the importance of that work, then or now."

"I take it we can consider you a fair geneticist?"

Eva considered the point. "Not really. I gave more emphasis to physiology than genetics, although formally my major work was under Dr. Tobiansky."

"Are you friendly with Dr. Tobiansky?" asked Seixas carelessly.

"I have no idea about these things, Mr. Seixas. Not any more," said Eva after a pause. "I assume we were friends—to the extent such a relationship can exist between teacher and student."

"You don't believe such friendship possible?"

"No more than between man and woman. Other relationships are possible, but friendships? I cannot say. Why do you ask?"

"Would Dr. Tobiansky be inclined to be helpful in this litigation? I'm told he's always been antagonistic to Dr. Ullman."

"What would you want him to say?"

"Anything that might be damaging," said Seixas with a lawyer's smile.

Eva frowned. "Haven't you talked to him yet?"

"Only briefly. Nothing important beyond certain preliminaries. It's a delicate position, you know. I'm not inclined to trust my own judgment."

"What has David told you?"

"He's in doubt. Come, Mrs. Luzzatto, I'd like your opinion."

Eva considered the matter. "It depends on how it strikes him as a scientist. But otherwise Tobiansky will do what is good for Tobiansky. In this respect, he is like everyone else. Ah?" Her glance was cynical with challenge. "The old ones stick together against the young."

Seixas handed over a paper. "Can you tell me something about these people?"

Eva hesitated. "I have only my instinct."

"I'm consulting your instinct."

Eva studied a list of familiar names. "If you get Will Tewksbury to court," she said slowly, "it will be a greater miracle than Lourdes. Surely, you're not depending on him? Or the rest?" She tossed the list back to the escritoire. "Why do you show me these names?"

Seixas spread his hands. "Why, simply to show the need to have our chat. I keep running into surprising areas of silence. Who actually interviewed you for the Fleischer fellowship?"

She thought back, reviving a dim picture. "It was Victor."

"Victor? Is that what you called him?"

She laughed harshly, obliquely amused. "Then? Oh, hardly! No, that came later after David and I got married, and I got drawn into the charmed circle. No, actually, I got assigned to Dr. Tobiansky ostensibly because the grant came within the scope of his seminar in vertebrate physiology. I suppose, looking back, that Victor handed me over because he took a dim view of my abilities."

"Oh, surely not?"

Eva shrugged indifferently. "I can imagine no other factor that would influence the man's opinion. Dr. Tobiansky was my immediate supervisor, Victor was department chairman as well as acting dean. However, I spent little time with him."

"Ah? How was that?"

"For one thing, Victor was rarely available to most of us students. He spent most of his time in that private laboratory on the third floor. He was notorious for that custom of locking himself in. He—" A flush of embarrassment mounted her cheeks.

"Yes?"

"Well, some of the students' comments were rather imaginative—especially the psych majors. When a man locks himself in a room, are there any limits to speculation?" A look of wonder shaded the pale, clear brow. "I didn't like Victor. I avoided him."

"Oh, indeed? I thought there was a close, friendly relationship all around?"

"Not on my part," she said strongly.

"I distinctly got that impression," Seixas remarked.

"No."

"Well, well. Perhaps that question can wait." He glanced at the yellow pad, but Eva, after withdrawing with an air of decision, broke in suddenly. "I—I felt uncomfortable in his presence, Mr. Seixas. He had an intensity I found disagreeable, almost as though he weren't looking at one, but at some surrounding aura in space. I—I don't quite know how to express it."

Seixas waited curiously. "Did you ever tell this to your husband?"

"Tell David?" Startled eyes of green widened with naive surprise. "How could I do that? Oh, my dear Mr. Seixas. It was something I kept to myself."

"Why?"

"Why? Because David's life, his deepest feelings turned on that relationship. Could I take a destructive line? Mr. Seixas, don't you see? The relationship didn't grow up overnight. David's career was involved in Victor's good will. He was completely dependent for advancement, the chance for publication, a job, recommendations, his place in science—those things that make an academic career possible, that put the student in the teacher's power. This went on for several years. Biocin was a great event, but even after the discovery, he was still a long way from his doctorate. We all knew that David had hit on something big, but the true magnitude was not evident. So, you see, I could not possibly interfere."

"I'm not sure I do," said the lawyer slowly.

"Oh, dear!" She made an impatient, helpless gesture. "One might imagine that a major discovery would establish him, but would it? If he had stopped there, people would think Victor, not David, had actually turned the trick. Isn't that in fact what they're whispering behind our

211

backs? No, that whole complex had to persist until he got his doctorate."
As though her tongue were bitten, she paused.

Seixas made an encouraging sound.

Eva threw back her head. "If you'd lived among these young scientists, you'd recognize how naive, how lopsided they can become—especially the talented. The whole sense of self-esteem, of inner—inner tranquility, becomes involved in this frightful business of career. I can imagine no greater dread than this nightmare of a sterile outcome of a lifetime of craving for success." She stared into space. "Am I talking jargon?"

Seixas shook his head. "Not at all."

Minutes passed while a question waited. "Victor fired his imagination, you see? David was filled with such enthusiasm, such absorption! He was to scale the heights one day. He was in a hurry and yet everything seemed to hang forever in the balance. Could I throw the wet blanket?"

The lawyer waited curiously.

"Oh, my God! The idyllic picture of the innocent, childlike scientist! The life of simple, dignified contemplation!" She shook her head wonderingly. "Ah, Mr. Seixas, can you understand? You live in a profession where strife is externalized into the contest for things, but in his world the forces are dark, blind, underground, turned inward. If you could only see what turmoil the insecurity, the anxiety, the subordination to authority can create in these sensitive types! What sleepless nights—" Suddenly, her pale, broad forehead was slick with sweat. "I suppose the emotional outcome for Davey was predictable."

"Resentment?" asked the lawyer quietly.

"No, Mr. Seixas! Devotion! He was captivated by the man's personality. So you see?"

Seixas considered the point with an air of intelligence. "One does not necessarily exclude the other," he murmured.

"Perhaps." She drew a breath and faced him grimly. "Even so, could anyone object to anything so natural? In a way, it was sweet, touching. Besides, what would it do to my own relationship? I had to think of that. No?"

Seixas continued to smoke.

Finally, releasing an inner reluctance, Eva sighed. "I didn't expect to get into anything so personal, Mr. Seixas," she said in a low voice, "but can I tell you something in confidence? I mean, even from David?"

Seixas looked up. "Does it bear on the lawsuit? Because, if so, I can hardly—"

She shook her head. "No. It's simply that I don't want you to feel that I'm a complete idiot about this thing." What insidious force of the

212

lawyer's personality, she wondered, was undermining her resistance? "Victor objected to our marriage."

"Oh?"

Seixas waited with level eyes, not wishing to interrupt the flow. Eva paused, made a gesture, went on. "Well, just before David was about to take his orals, Victor invited him to lunch at the faculty club. I have no doubt he exerted himself to be charming. Oh, yes! When Victor wishes, he can be highly plausible. He can talk a cat out of its pelt." She tapped an ash, then sighed. "Victor warned him against me. Oh, not specifically by name. Victor was far too devious for anything so direct. No, he had that young man at a low point and he talked in generalities about the problems of young scientists—the initial strain of the economic situation, the horrible effects upon marriage of crowded living quarters, the drive to overwork under the pressures of anxiety. He even had examples drawn from the lives of important scientists to show the high price their families can pay for a scientific career—neuroses, suicides, alcoholics, hopeless perversions, real clinical stuff. Some of the names would shock you. I was furious."

"Oh?"

Eva smiled grimly. "Oh, not for myself. No, it was simply that I was aghast at the man's arrogance. How could he, or anyone, dare to play with another life?" Her green eyes widened with outrage. "Well, it doesn't matter except as an example of his approach. Those are real problems, I suppose, but fortunately, we had already had our understanding. We were to get married as soon as David had qualified for a decent job." She glanced at a diamond ring and smiled without mirth. "All that came under the heading of fatherly advice."

"But I don't understand, Mrs. Luzzatto," Seixas said. "Wasn't the success of biocin indicated by then?"

"Financially?"

"Yes."

Eva thought back, biting her lip with the strain of recollection. "Certainly, I had no such notion."

"And did your husband?" asked Seixas quietly.

Eva sat back with a defiant stare. "I have no idea what he thought, Mr. Seixas. It was an area in which we had no interest until much later."

Seixas considered an unsatisfactory situation. "And yet, Mrs. Luzzatto, I have an impression that your husband confided in you to a large extent. This conversation, for example, with Dr. Ullman at the faculty club—"

213

Eva glanced up in surprise. "Oh, but it wasn't David who told me about that! It was Victor."

"Eh?"

"Yes, when Victor came to explain—" Abruptly, she halted, biting her mouth almost guiltily, as a slow flush mounted her neck. "I learned about that conversation much later. It came when Victor had already left the university."

"Why would he tell you?"

Eva hesitated. "He was afraid, I imagine, that I was trying to turn David against him, but that was absurd. I had no inkling from David of what had happened. He would never tell me anything distressing, you see?" The grave eyes grew moist. "No, Victor had already left the university when he came to make amends. He asked me to remain friends."

"How did you feel?" Seixas asked curiously.

Eva gazed off, brows knitted. "Detached."

"Not resentful?"

"Oh, no." Instinctively, a protecting hand covered her burden, but if the older man noticed the gesture he gave no sign. "I was too tranquil to think. It's only now that I begin to understand what was involved."

"Was your husband present?"

Eva returned to smoking. "David was in Johannesburg," she said briefly. "When he came back—" She halted.

"Yes?"

"Well, there didn't seem any point to the whole thing." The crimson tide deepened as she failed to meet his questioning glance. Seixas waited patiently. "Was anything else said between you? I mean, with Professor Ullman? Was there any talk about the financial side?"

She twisted uneasily. "When?"

"At any time," he said.

"I—I don't think so."

"You're sure?"

"But—but what's the point, Mr. Seixas? Aren't the records in your control?"

The lawyer followed her glance to the row of file envelopes stacked on a side table. "I'm not concerned now with the records, Mrs. Luzzatto," he said quietly. "It's a general mistake that every scrap of writing is technically binding on the courts. Well, in a court of law that's true to a limited extent. But we're in a court of equity and other rules control the situation —good faith, fair dealing, honest disclosure, a score of basic principles that businessmen often neglect to their sorrow." He went on gravely with overtones of meaning. "I'm trying to establish your recollection outside of documents. Come, now!"

There was a moment of silence.

"I have no recollection," said Eva in a low voice. She dived back to her cigarette, scarlet, discomfited. The lawyer studied the young woman with some curiosity, noting elegant details of dress—fine gloves, snake-skin handbag, earrings of jade and silver. He drummed the escritoire thoughtfully and came back to an earlier line.

"Would you say, Mrs. Luzzatto, that your husband and Dr. Ullman were friends?"

"Why does everyone keep insisting on that?" she demanded wearily.

Seixas glanced up at the unexpected tone and opened a folder at his elbow. He smoothed out a formal document. His manner was patient and reasonable.

"Because the other side, Mrs. Luzzatto, predicate their claim to this money on the theory of a breach of trust. This breach was committed, they say, by Professor Luzzatto under cover and disguise of friendship. So that friendship, you see, is an essential element of the case? I am only trying to explore that area of dispute." His tone sharpened. "What can you tell me?"

Eva studied the dark, melancholy face, the bony, austere Mediterranean features, aware of an intellectual force herding her toward a terrain of danger. Slowly, her head shook. "I have no opinion," she said defiantly, thickly. A pulse in her throat was beating.

Seixas put the document aside and sat back. "Are you angry with me, Mrs. Luzzatto?"

"No, I'm not angry, but I'm unhappy about the whole business," she said finally. "I'm not convinced that this lawsuit is being handled to David's best interests."

There was a moment of silence in which Seixas made much of adjusting a pair of cuff links. "What an extraordinary thing to say, Mrs. Luzzatto," he observed coldly.

"It was not my idea, Mr. Seixas, this interview. If I am asked questions by a lawyer, I must to answer. No?"

"What is your point?" he asked evenly.

She glanced up cynically. "Why doesn't my husband have his own lawyer to advise in these proceedings?"

"Ah?"

Seixas had once held a post with the State Department where the capacity to keep a straight face in circumstances of guilt was part of an honorable discipline. He set aside papers with an air of deliberation, re-

215

flecting that the attractive young woman showed a stronger grasp of realities than her husband, but this thought was not one to disclose. Whether or not the interests of the two parties were identical was yet to be seen. Almost smiling, he tapped out an ash. "Why, since our fees will be defrayed by the university," he observed drily, "I imagine he's satisfied to be represented by this firm, Mrs. Luzzatto. If not, he's a free agent. Has he ever expressed mistrust?"

"I didn't mean that," she said quickly.

"No?"

"I'm so miserably bewildered," she muttered. "I don't want to create an—an atmosphere."

Seixas accepted this calmly. "Have you ever mentioned these misgivings to your husband?"

"Not yet." She sighed bitterly. "He has such extraordinary notions of human relationships, my husband. He won't listen to me, or his parents, or friends, or anyone with common sense. He's always been inclined to judge men, especially colleagues, exclusively by technical attainments. It's his chief weakness."

"Why is that weakness?"

"Because it stems from a basic error in judgment: a foolish, naive faith that ability in science is related to moral enlightenment, to greatness of mind." She shook her head with dismay. "I couldn't agree less. I've seen too much of the dark side. These people may have their pathetic little proficiencies, but they're timid, envious, highly judgmental. Ah, my God!"

Seixas was silent. "But what is the application?"

"Oh, don't you see?" Eva brought back a glance of surprise. "His whole approach to this—this lawsuit is compromised by this faith. Somehow, somewhere, he expects the scientific community to impose a solution. It's completely naive, I know, but he won't take the legal side seriously. I'm afraid he'll handle this badly unless he takes advice. His insights are exclusively in science. He has almost no capacity to judge the motives of others."

"And you have?" asked Seixas.

Eva seemed to be looking at another world. "Yes, Mr. Seixas," she said defiantly. "I have an instinct. It's something I've been forced to develop."

A coal fell in the grate. Seixas continued to stare, digesting deep currents of emotion he could not understand. Finally he stirred. "I wish you'd believe, Mrs. Luzzatto, that I find this unpleasant," he said, "but I have an uncomfortable feeling that the entire truth isn't in my file."

"In what sense?"

Seixas looked out at sodden clouds drifting over the city. "I don't know," he murmured, almost to himself. "I've had certain preliminary talks with the other side, you see? The usual sparring, lawyer talk. I've been getting hints that certain exhibits are in their possession. This may be the usual bluff. Or, again, it might not. I was hoping you might tell me."

Eva blinked fearfully. "Me?"

"Yes. Have you any ideas at all? Professor Luzzatto, you see, tells me that he's completely mystified. We've gone over all our records, without results. I have a feeling that you might help us out?"

"Could it be the old lab books? Because Victor took some of those when he left the university."

"No. We know about those." Seixas favored Eva with a stolid glance. "It's in the nature of a piece of writing, or writings. Your husband professes not to know what they might be."

"Then how—how can I help? Don't you trust him?"

Seixas brought his glance to a signed portrait of a white-haired chief justice of a venerable court of final appeal. At the moment, he reflected, the remote serenity of Cardozo, discerning, poetical, steeped in ethical insights, seemed to lack application. He sighed and came back to the discussion with a touch of brutality.

"I am merely asking a question, Mrs. Luzzatto," he pointed out. "If there is anything to Dr. Ullman's case—and I must assume that his lawyers would not embark on frivolous litigation—then somehow, somewhere there must be documentation, something in the nature of an admission that supports this claim that he was unfairly deprived of his rights. I should hate to meet with an unpleasant surprise in the courtroom."

Eva stared hypnotically. "I—I don't—"

"Don't what, Mrs. Luzzatto?"

"I must not be involved!" she burst out. "I can't be drawn into this horrible thing!"

Seixas frowned. "Really, I can't accept this—"

Eva began to shake violently. All at once, her control seemed to slip. She arose in retreat, dropping a glove. "I—I'm afraid I must leave now. Don't you understand, Mr. Seixas? I can't have anything—*anything* disturb me. I'm having my baby. I want to help, but I can't—" She waited, flat-footed, transfixed.

"Oh, surely," said the lawyer skeptically. "I don't quite see the difficulty. I've had to deal with pregnant women before. Come now!"

"Why are you so sure I have anything to tell you?"

Seixas measured his answer. "Because of your husband's violent opposition to this interview. I have an obligation to wonder why. Is there something he doesn't want me to know?"

"He is simply trying to protect me from anxiety," said Eva finally.

Seixas digested this remark. "Are *you* protecting *him?*" he asked pointedly.

Eva stared at the rug. "Oh, don't you see, Mr. Seixas?" she asked in despair. "I am torn for David. I can hardly look at him, he is so pinched, so hurt, and he is everything to me. But this other thing possesses me." In the silent moment, her breathing was labored, heavy as she strove for control. "I must ask why—why? And I have no answer. None except this child to whom I must give life. I am guilty, guilty!"

Seixas thought the remark extraordinary. "Guilty? Of what?"

"That I am alive!" she said starkly.

The lawyer waited, smoking, silent. In four arduous decades as a trial lawyer in all courts of the state—years not without reward and interest—he could recall nothing like the naked fear in the dry, glassy eyes. "It's not entirely in my control," he said slowly.

"Will you do your best to keep me out?"

Seixas sighed heavily. "I wish you'd believe me, Mrs. Luzzatto," he said reasonably. "I'd like to excuse you, but how can I bind myself? I'm afraid to tell you how precarious this lawsuit has become—how important to the university, not to speak of your husband. You went through much worse during the war. Is this really so much?"

Her eyes looked up with wonder. "David told you about that?"

The lawyer nodded. "I hope you don't mind?"

"No," said Eva slowly, "but I see that you must have pressed him very hard, Mr. Seixas."

He shifted uncomfortably. "You showed so much courage in that period, Mrs. Luzzatto. Can't you overcome your reluctance in these circumstances?" he asked with a conciliatory air. "I was hoping to persuade you."

She looked aside at a distant, frozen scene in Poland. "Courage?" she muttered. "It was not courage, Mr. Seixas. I wanted only to live. If I went one way, I would die; if the other, I had a chance. I went toward life." Bitterness settled in her eyes. "I have no courage, no strength at all now. It was all consumed in those years. Now I'm afraid of everything—even of my shadow. I want to help but I cannot. Ah, my God! Is it impossible to understand?"

Seixas waited for the spasm of fear to end. "But don't you see?" he explained patiently. "In the last analysis, these issues are so narrow, so personal that they will turn on the testimony of a handful of witnesses. If your husband refuses to call his wife in support of his version, how will that strike the court?"

Eva seemed not to hear. An expression of intense fear and antagonism distorted her mouth. "I am not the only witness," she said finally.

Seixas waited. "Oh. Who?"

She closed her eyes and said, "Why not Jo Ullman?"

Seixas let a moment pass. "Do you know what you're saying, Mrs. Luzzatto?"

Eva faced the lawyer, observing that he showed less surprise than she had expected. Ah, yes! she thought. A lawyer would know about Jo. She nodded defiantly. "Yes!"

Seixas let a cool, wary glance of calculation appear. "Would she be willing?"

"She'd do anything for David," Eva said grimly, "if only he'd ask her. But not me, do you hear? I've got to be kept out of this thing. I've got to—" She sat in blind fear waiting his answer.

"It would be a risk," said Seixas thoughtfully.

Eva sat forward suddenly, one hand clutched to her breast, the other extended in an odd, foreign gesture of urgency. "Listen to me, Mr. Seixas. I'm convinced she will tell the truth if you can persuade David to get her into court. Wouldn't she be far more valuable for your purposes?"

Their glances met with understanding. "If we miscalculate, it can be extremely damaging," he observed. "Not only to our case, but to her as well."

Eva waited a quiet moment. "In that case," she said cruelly, "let Victor withdraw his complaint against my husband. We did not ask for this lawsuit. Why will ours be the responsibility?"

"Because it will!" said Seixas abruptly, tiring of the situation.

"What am I to do?" she muttered hopelessly. "This is my home, my husband, that they are trying to destroy. I cannot stand to see his suffering. I would sacrifice anyone for him, even myself, if I could, or anything, but I cannot command this feeling, Mr. Seixas." A moment passed. "Ah, my God!" she burst out. "Why do you wait to decide?"

Seixas finally put aside his last cigar for the day. He was less than enthusiastic about the suggestion, nor was he sure that Eva understood the implications, but he promised with distaste to consider it. He placed a sheet of paper on the desk and lifted a pen.

"If you'll give me the full truth, Mrs. Luzzatto," he said quietly, "I'll do what I can for you."

"I will try," she agreed finally.

Uncontrollable shaking began again with renewed violence.

Throughout the afternoon Seixas found himself thinking of Eva Luzzatto. He knew the Wessels House—that white sprawling structure on Tynesdale Road. Who could possibly suspect the icy hell of torment within its walls?

"Oh, damn all this!" He scowled, gnawing his mouth, staring at several pages of notes. She had told him nothing, nothing of consequence at all.

Chapter 18

DURING THIS PERIOD LUZZATTO FELT, OR IMAGINED, THAT TONGUES went silent, that eyes turned when he entered a room, and this sensitivity provoked a deep sense of humiliation. He forced himself to take lunch whenever possible at the Co-op.

"Dave? Will you join us?" asked Lizzie Batchelor.

Luzzatto hesitated, tray in hand. In the section reserved for faculty, there was a subdued hum and clatter of forks and the sound of laughter from the clique of regulars who were playing a word game. Some coins showed that a sizable kitty was building up.

"Not today, Lizzie," he said, and turned off.

"I can see you at three. My office?" she said.

"I'll be there," he promised. He forced a smile, and went on. The game continued with intensity.

Joe Wodzick was attacking a bowl of chowder in a quiet corner. He was reading *Patroon*.

" 'Lo, Dave," grunted the Bronco. "I've been reading about you. Did you see this morning's issue?"

"That crap?" Luzzatto sat and handed a tray to an attendant. "No, I'm too tired, too busy, Bronco," he said wearily. "I know all about the prostitution of science. I don't have to buy that brand from Henschel."

Wodzick read aloud from a column called "Bits and Pieces."

> "You cannot hope to bribe, or twist,
> Thank God, the average scientist,
> But seeing what the man will do
> Unbribed, there's no occasion to!"

221

"Very funny," said Luzzatto sourly. After a moment Wodzick looked up with concern. "Aren't you going to eat?"

Luzzatto was holding a sandwich in mid-air, staring into space. "I guess so, Bronc," he whispered, but made no move.

"It's—it's just the lawsuit, Bronc," he said hesitantly. "I'm finding it hard to handle this amount of tension. It keeps on, and on, and *on*—and I don't get enough sleep. Otherwise I'm in good shape."

"Glad to hear that," said Wodzick, unconvinced. He ate in silence and looked up finally at the pale suffering face. "What's giving this kid Henschel all this incentive?" he asked bluntly. "Is there some personal reason?"

Luzzatto glanced at the newspaper. The editorial was well written, he thought, and its sharp evaluations of the intrusion of commerce in university affairs were well taken. The critical views might have been his own. A flush of anger arose.

"No. Nothing personal," he said vindictively. "I think he's trying to keep in the liberal tradition. An idealist, you know?"

Wodzick was not sure he liked the tone. "That's a bitter thing to say."

"I feel bitter."

"Oh, good God," said Wodzick irritably. "Why?"

Luzzatto sighed hopelessly. "Oh, it's not this kid Henschel; it's the general view he represents. Everyone is asked to suspend judgment. Oh, I'm not explicitly called a crook, but there hasn't yet been one solid expression of indignation in my favor. It's frightening what happens when you're marked out for attack. I'll tell you something, Bronco," he added suddenly. "We're beginning to lose our friends. Even Tom Adderly and Barbara haven't got time for us any more and they're next-door neighbors. Barbara and Eva were getting very close."

"Well," said Wodzick comfortingly, "Tom's just a physicist."

Luzzatto sighed, unamused. "It might be our own fault. It's not too comfortable in our house these days." A look of wonder appeared. "Whenever I used to hear of scientists under attack, Bronco, I felt unsympathetic, largely because I felt so—so invulnerable myself. I was part of a big discipline in which my own integrity would be taken for granted. I never expected to face this situation myself, not here, not in science. I thought these people, scientists, my own crowd would know better than to swallow this shit that's going on about me. Don't they know me?"

"They also know Ullman," said Wodzick.

"What about you, Bronc? Where do you stand?"

"I think you know," said Wodzick with a note of anger.

"Yes. Sure," muttered Luzzatto, lowering his eyes. "Only I need to be reassured, I guess." He sighed. "What's happened to everybody? I've done a few things for science. I deserve something in return."

"What would you want?"

"I want some formal expression of confidence," he said in a low voice, "and not from lawyers. I want it from the men who know me, my work, the scientists around me. Is that too much to ask?"

"Maybe not," said Wodzick, restraining an oppressive sense of boredom. "But wouldn't it be better to wait for the trial? If you win the case, you won't need any such thing. If you lose, what would it prove?"

"It would prove something to me," cried Luzzatto.

"Prove what?" asked Wodzick curiously.

Luzzatto drew a breath. "Whether this whole thing is worth fighting for, Bronc," he said simply. "Why must I be the whipping boy for a snot like Henschel? Why don't they close him down? All Foxx has to do is to pick up the telephone and tell a dean to call a dean to get a dean to tie that kid's head in a sack. Why doesn't he do it?"

"I have no idea. Do you?"

Luzzatto shivered. "Bronco, I'm not sure that this rope they're giving the kid isn't meant to hang me. There's just no moral support."

"How do you know what's on Foxx's mind?" said Wodzick roughly. "Or on anybody's? You don't know your own. You keep talking about Foxx, Dave, but isn't that pointless? He's not your target."

Luzzatto blinked. "No? Who is?"

"Ullman."

Luzzatto laughed uncertainly. "Who said no?"

"Who said yes?" asked Wodzick brutally.

Luzzatto started to speak and paused, flushed and suddenly embarrassed. Indeed he had talked of everything but the central object since he had sat down. He looked up with a goaded expression. "What should I do, Bronc?" he asked uncertainly.

"Have you got a plan?"

"I might have." Luzzatto hesitated.

Wodzick glanced across to the table where the word game was in progress. "It's hard to advise you," he said slowly. "You don't seem to be able to command any discipline. You're writing letters all over the country, talking to people in corridors. I understand it, but it doesn't create the right impression. Why not go back to the lab and put this thing out of your mind till the trial?"

Luzzatto stared glassily. "Bronc, I haven't been able to lift a test tube since this thing began."

"You poor bastard!" Wodzick shook his head with commiseration and leaned forward. "Dave, I picked up a rumor that you're playing footsie with Lizzie on getting that vote of confidence from the Senate Council. Is there any truth in that?"

"I've been talking to her. Yes," said Luzzatto stiffly. "I wouldn't call it footsie."

"I'm glad of that," said Wodzick dryly.

Luzzatto lifted a tasteless meat sandwich to his mouth, unable to meet the direct glance of his friend. What had taken place earlier that day in Lizzie's office had in fact gone counter to his best intentions. He had arrived early in a high pitch of anxiety to find Helen Montgomery watering an unexpected lovely vine. With some reluctance, he described a conversation in which Lizzie had come directly to the point.

"Dave, I've been meaning to have this talk for some time. I see that you're asking the Senate to adopt a vote of confidence in you as a member of the faculty. I suppose the purpose is to strengthen your moral position in anticipation of the lawsuit. Is that correct?"

"Not that alone, Lizzie," said Luzzatto uncomfortably. "It would have that effect, but that's not my primary intention."

"I see," said Lizzie. "Let me study it a minute."

"The language is only a suggestion." He glanced at the other woman at her task with the plants. "It can be changed."

"Well, it's moderate. I can't quarrel with a resolution that deplores strife among scholars. Also, it doesn't cast aspersions against Victor— except by implication."

"Oh, no," said Luzzatto quickly. "I'm not asking for that. All I want is a statement on record of confidence in my integrity." He paused. "Why, my God, if I were charged with treason, or something, a thousand scientific nitwits would be glad to give me any character testimonial I could ask. Why not this?"

Lizzie stared without expression. "If we express confidence in you, doesn't that imply lack of confidence in Victor? Isn't the issue between you that sharp?"

Luzzatto controlled himself with an effort. "The resolution specifically says that it's not passing on the merits," he replied.

"Even so," said Lizzie.

Luzzatto drew a breath. "Lizzie, are you turning me down?" he asked dangerously.

"Oh, no!" Lizzie rose and began to walk about her office. "It would need some thinking, Dave," she observed. "I'd like to know why you're dropping this hot potato in my lap. Is it worth the risk? One loud voice in the Council could raise a stink."

"Why must it come before the Council?" Luzzatto put the question carefully. "Why not bring it to the Executive Committee? There needn't be any public discussion."

Lizzie opened and closed a book. "The Executive Committee can't adopt a resolution that's binding on the Council. You know, Dave," she added in thoughtful tones. "I begin not to like the smell. Mustn't a resolution like this come before the full Council to be legal?"

"Lizzie, Helen—"

The women listened without expression as the son of Cesare Luzzatto outlined a parliamentary maneuver worthy of a larger cause. The Council, a body of fifty, would not meet for several months, he pointed out urgently; in the meantime, the Executive, a committee of five, could consider the resolution to frame the larger body's agenda for May. It was all outlined in the letter on the desk.

"So I see," said Lizzie thoughtfully.

"Then what's so hard about it?" he demanded.

She looked up. "What happens in May?"

Luzzatto stared at the women. "The whole damn lawsuit may be over in May," he said grimly. "I don't care what happens by then. Let it be killed, or tabled, or sent back to committee. In the meantime, it might have some effect on public opinion."

Lizzie strolled back thoughtfully. "How can it be made public? The proceedings are confidential."

"We could leak it out," said Luzzatto.

"Oh, now!" The women were genuinely shocked.

"Don't give me that look, Lizzie. I wouldn't affirmatively arrange the leak, but it would be sure to get out. The other side is doing it."

Lizzie glanced enigmatically at her friend. "I don't know, Dave," she said slowly. "I'm not sure."

Luzzatto sat breathing heavily. "Lizzie," he said in a strained voice, "I'd like to bring Eva some evidence that I'm not entirely an outcast yet."

Helen spoke up reproachfully, "You're not an outcast, Dave. That's a foolish remark."

"I'd like a bit of proof to that effect," said Luzzatto.

Skepticism sharpened Helen's mild features. "A cooked-up resolution is hardly proof of anything," she said.

"Maybe not," said Luzzatto, "but at least it looks like proof. Who's on the Executive Committee? Polk, Gordie Puce, Tobiansky, Juliette Bradley? Well, Gordie Puce is an old friend of Eva's. I'm sure he'll go along,

225

and we all know how Tobiansky feels about Victor. Juliette votes with the majority."

"And Henry Polk?" asked Lizzie.

Luzzatto said grimly, "He'll go along with any resolution of good intention. Just convince him it's got ethical implications." He paused. "If I can't get this simple resolution out of that group, I'll know where I stand. I sure will!"

Lizzie strode the room on full parade, hugging her breasts. "Really, Dave," she observed. "You get so insistent about these things. You're beginning to make it uncomfortable for everyone."

"Do I get that resolution, or not?" he demanded.

Lizzie paused to stare at a priapic Melanesian woodcarving, weighing certain considerations in mind. A significant glance at the other woman was taken as a signal.

"Excuse me. Seminar," said Helen. "See you at dinner, Lizzie?"

"Yes, dear," said Lizzie, closing the door. She continued her formidable stroll about the office. "I have an impression, Dave, that you're driving at something. Why not spit it out?"

Luzzatto drew a breath. "There's something else involved," he acknowledged. "Maybe Helen wouldn't understand this, but you were close to Victor and—and to Jo. I know what you were able to do for her."

The strong mouth showed no reaction. "What are you getting at, Dave?"

"Nothing that involves you," said Luzzatto quickly. "Except that you're friendly with Victor and you know about Jo's problem. You carried her on your budget all those years without any real justification. I have some idea why she was lent out to Victor."

"How does this affect Jo Ullman?" she asked in even tones.

"Well, it's not a good idea to let this thing get too far," said Luzzatto. "You may not believe this," he went on with discomfort, "but I'm trying hard not to hurt anyone—especially Jo." He added unwillingly, "It may not be possible to keep her out of the case."

"I see," said Lizzie.

"Well, I don't control the lawyers," he said angrily. "I haven't told them anything that might send them after Jo, but I don't know how long I can hold out."

"I'm not sure I like all this."

Luzzatto sat forward urgently. "Lizzie, a thing like this gets very complicated with all sorts of pressures and I've got more than myself to think of. It's been hard on Eva. Did you know she's been ordered to bed? It's all because of the damn lawsuit."

"Oh, come," Lizzie said skeptically.

Luzzatto held an impulse of anger in check. He said carefully, "I'm trying my best, but if it comes down to a trial, what choice will I have? My wife comes before anything else in the world. That's why I need this vote of confidence. It might have a strong deterrent effect on Victor to know how people feel about this lawsuit. I have a sneaking feeling that he doesn't actually want to go into court with me, but that he's being carried along by the force of events." He paused. "Lizzie, I want that resolution."

Lizzie stared and turned aside. "Oh, say, have you seen these African violets? Aren't they lovely?" The calculating glance returned. "Oh, I'm not turning you down, Dave," she said. "It's just that it needs thought."

Luzzatto arose and went to the door. "Let me know when you're ready to decide," he said despondently. "Goodbye."

The door had already opened on a busy hallway when her voice, almost as he expected, detained him. "Oh, by the way, Dave, I wonder if you'd care to help out on a little problem of my own?" He paused and returned slowly to the office. Lizzie said, "I'm having a little difficulty scratching together an examining committee for Erskine Hubbard. He's coming up for his orals fairly soon. I'd like you on that committee."

"That's not my field," he said slowly. "How could I do an intelligent job?"

"Oh, nonsense! It's only a formality," she said expectantly.

Luzzatto stared for the longest time. "Let me have a copy of the dissertation, Lizzie. I'll have to study it carefully. I'll give you an answer this afternoon."

Luzzatto looked up to find the stare of Wodzick on his innermost thoughts. He had an uneasy feeling that the episode that morning had not been entirely unexpected, either by himself, or by the women, and that the departure of Helen Montgomery from the office had had an element of the rehearsed. What lingered in mind was the glance of understanding between the women. What was that about? Wodzick listened stolidly to an abridged version of these events, masking a growing weariness for these gyrations.

"What made you rush off to Lizzie?" he asked impatiently. "You know how she operates and you walked right in and put your maidenhead on the auction block."

"I thought she could help," said Luzzatto sullenly. "What did I have to lose?"

Wodzick shrugged. "A lot of tracks lead into that den but none lead out."

"Oh, Bronc!" said Luzzatto resentfully.

"Oh, Dave! I gave you the background on Hubbard months ago," said Wodzick. "You had no use then for the lugubrious son of a bitch. Now look at you!"

"I haven't made up my mind," said Luzzatto defensively. "I only promised to read the dissertation."

"Oh, don't tell me! This is Wodzick," said the other with contempt. "I don't see how you'll improve your position by licking Lizzie's feet. What's happening to your sense of proportion?"

Luzzatto closed his eyes. "I'm so desperately worried about Evvie, Bronc," he said suddenly. "Before this pregnancy she was like a rock. Really doing well, and then this lawsuit began— Sorry!"

Wodzick waited quietly while the other blew his nose. "It's all right, Dave," he said. "I did that the day my kid was born."

Luzzatto wiped his eyes, smiling apologetically at the storm of nerves. "I don't know why I can't control this, but I keep thinking about Evvie a lot, Bronc. Everything's piled up on us—the lawsuit, the general attitude, this pregnancy, money problems. She's still feeling the butchery she went through last time with Dotty Applegate." He looked up. "You know Dotty?"

"What about that woman?" asked Wodzick.

Luzzatto sighed. "Evvie's an anxious girl, Bronco, terribly emotional, especially with the importance she attaches to this baby, and everything affects her, even the color of the walls. Turned out last time that Dotty had a real, cruel streak of insensitivity in her—not what you'd expect from a woman at all. She showed that in all sorts of stupid things, like not understanding Evvie's refusal to accept the diagnosis." He thought back, breathing heavily. "You'd think she'd understand the problem, but she was only annoyed because a girl with scientific training wouldn't accept the A-Z tests—although we all know the A-Z isn't strictly infallible by a long shot. In fact, with all the other things crowding me, I had to run a few tests myself—Hogbens, on South African frogs—before Evvie was convinced. She wouldn't take any judgment but mine, you see, although a technician could have done a better job."

"I never heard of that," said Wodzick wonderingly. "I knew you had some frogs, but I thought that was for biocin?"

"No," said Luzzatto grimly. "Dotty's manner was terribly impatient and casual. Or at least so Evvie thought. We were terribly poor and we got a special price—which stuck in her craw because she hates to take favors and she felt the price was reflected in an awful lot of treatment by telephone. It was the diet that got her—stuff she abhorred and found upsetting. That sounds minor but it was a hell of a thing—a real wracking mess—and, oh, a lot of things happened, and then at about six months Dotty calmly told her that the baby had died." He paused and stared at the table.

Wodzick said slowly. "That's a real rough deal, Dave. Were you there?"

Luzzatto shook his head. "I had too much work in the lab. I got the bad news much later. She didn't react at first, except to feel subdued, quiet. She left the office and walked around the streets and went into a movie. God knows what idiotic horror she sat through before she came home to wait for me. It seems that Dotty was kind enough to advise that it was all just as well.

"Evvie got very emotional, bitter at the mistreatment, and later she accused Dotty of a lot of things, mostly that she'd been given dangerous drugs, and she blamed what had happened on the toxic effects. I doubt that because I questioned Dotty closely and she told me she'd only prescribed nembutal and bed rest. But even if she got drugs when she finally went to be delivered, I wouldn't have blamed any doctor because she raised a terrific racket in the hospital. She was an awful patient, very demanding, cranky, crying jags, oh, the works! I blame that entirely on Dotty for being too complacent about the emotional problem, for refusing to abort her at once instead of waiting the full term. Poor Evvie! She carried that dead baby for every minute through one hundred and ninety-eight days before they finally decided to take the thing from her. Totally unnecessary, totally vicious." Luzzatto paused with feeling. "Bronco?"

"Yes, Dave?" said Wodzick quietly.

Luzzatto turned a pale, stricken face of wonder. "I never believed this stuff that Eva was telling me about Dotty until the very end. Do you know what that woman did? With all the empty beds elsewhere, she actually put Evvie into the maternity pavilion. A pavilion filled with women having babies. She was even taken to the labor room where she could hear babies crying in the delivery room—and that's how she spent that night while I was downstairs biting my fingers to the bone—because I was to blame."

"How was that?"

"I should have known better, Bronc! Not to be so damned preoccupied with the lab that I could let a thing like that happen. What was I thinking? I should have intervened, done something, called in another doctor, but we were so busy that I drifted along with the inertia and let that damned woman doctor—" Luzzatto shivered. "It was the most callous, unfeeling example of case-hardened medical sadism I ever ran into in my life. Oh,

229

not the physical thing, because the pains were mild, but I knew—I *knew* what that thing was doing to the girl. And how do I know that it wasn't my fault, not hers? Not some lethal gene of my own in her causing the abortion? Bronco, I've lived with this thing. I know!

"When I saw her, she was barely awake, smelling of ether, still whimpering. Another woman in the room was nursing a baby, something Eva had to watch. Everyone assumed she'd had a normal delivery, especially the other woman's visitors, nice people who kept congratulating her, asking if she had a boy or girl, things like that.

"She had to lie there and take it until I could get the room changed. Of course, she didn't have visitors of her own. It didn't seem congruous to bring flowers—flowers for what? But the other woman had flowers, and stupidly I brought roses, and that only made it worse. On top of everything, Dotty calmly told Eva that she couldn't have another baby. Maybe that advice was fortunate, maybe not, because Evvie felt at the time she couldn't live through the experience twice. The guilt was too much."

"Guilt?" asked Wodzick curiously.

"Oh, don't ask me for what because I have no idea. It's impossible to get to the root of these things rationally. I suspect that guilt is actually a biological reaction—a sense of physiological deprivation—but to what? Evvie doesn't know herself although we've often talked about it. People don't understand her because she's so outgoing and gay and warm—so cheerful with people that she seems invulnerable, but she's not, Bronco. She's just not. I think it's connected with the war."

Wodzick said slowly. "I never thought Evvie was invulnerable, Dave."

Luzzatto was breathing heavily. "Evvie will be all right. She's strong and sound and the baby will make the difference, but she's slipping into that old frame of mind and I worry about her all the time. The terrible thing is that this lawsuit came along to hit her just when she was at her best. I need every scrap of support, and if Hubbard's the price, it's something to consider. Is one incompetent Ph.D. more or less really so serious?"

"This one can't even spell." Wodzick was silent. "Well, Dave," he said finally, deeply affected, "if you want that resolution so badly, I can't criticize, but why not leave these maneuvers to the lawyers? They're better at these things."

Luzzatto gazed off distantly. "They're good lawyers, Bronc," he murmured painfully, "but they don't know or really understand what's involved. How can I give the final decisions to them? They're not scientists."

"Is this a scientific problem?"

230

"Yes. Basically, I think so."

"I'd say it's a dog fight," Wodzick retorted, "and if you've never seen one, I'll remind you that the smart dog snaps for the balls. Has a terrific calming effect. Learn from our dumb friends."

"What does that mean?"

"Mean? Nothing! Except that you're squirming too hard to save the bric-a-brac." Wodzick arose and stretched. "If you've got something on Ullman, use it. Go for where it hurts!"

Luzzatto's voice was low. "I can't be the one to start that sort of thing."

"It's already started," said Wodzick realistically. "Don't wait too long, Dave. You know your own intentions, but you don't know the other man's!" He rose and strolled to the dessert counter where he paused, torn between stewed rhubarb and gingerbread topped with whipped cream. Wodzick thought back to the sunny day when Eva had sketched the praying mantis. Eva had been good-humored and robust, he recalled, qualities which had been fading under the affliction of the lawsuit. He had called at their home more than once with offers of help and moral support, but Luzzatto's pallid, indecisive responses to his good advice filled him with alarm and impatience. He would have liked less of the squeamishness that served only to generate useless high-minded principles far too brittle to resist the impact of strife.

When he returned with his tray, Luzzatto was at the word-game table in earnest, troubled conversation with a complacent Lizzie Batchelor.

Chapter 19

THE FARMHOUSE STOOD ON A RISE AMONG THE CONNECTICUT HILLS BE-
hind enormous old trees overlooking a patchwork of stone fences. Flights
of geese passed overhead as the cold autumn slid imperceptibly deeper
into winter.

On a sunny day in December Ullman gazed at the sky. "I think, Sophie,
we should be expecting visitors," he said thoughtfully. "It is almost time."

"Will you see them?"

"Oh, yes. Why not?"

Not long after, a limousine plunged along the country road and came
to a halt at the mailbox marked: V. F. Ullman. A hooting brought Sophie
from the barn. She was dressed in rough woolens and carried an empty
bucket to which grains of mash still adhered.

"Yes?" She was faintly hostile.

She recognized two of the passengers—Dr. James Fitzherbert Foxx
in a bowler and a hatless Si Podell, but the third was a stranger, a testy
little man who wore an enormous mink-lined overcoat and elevator shoes.
He was introduced as James Strollo on whose behalf many fruitless telephone calls had been made.

"I believe, madam, you took them all," said Strollo disagreeably. "I
ought to be offended."

Sophie's expression did not change. "Professor Ullman hasn't been
taking calls, or seeing anyone, except his lawyer."

Foxx said, "We'd like to see your husband."

"Follow me," said Sophie.

Later, in a carriage shed converted to an office, Ullman seemed not

232

surprised at their arrival. "Well, gentlemen," he said distantly. "Is this entirely proper? I am not represented by my lawyer."

"Neither are we. This will be entirely among ourselves," said Foxx. "Mr. Strollo has a word to say."

"I have no objection to hearing Mr. Strollo," said Ullman.

Strollo was seated on an army cot on which were heaped books and memoranda without apparent order. Despite his fur overcoat, he was shivering in the cold, stroking a waxy mustache with a coarse hand. He spoke with a harsh corvine voice. "Professor, it's our opinion that this thing has gone far enough. We don't like it. We want it to stop."

Ullman turned speculatively, noting the neat manicured appearance of a man of affairs, all belied by gutter intonations. "Tell me, sir," he asked courteously, "does Professor Luzzatto know of your visit?"

"He does not," said Podell emphatically.

Ullman shrugged. "I am prepared to listen." More than an hour passed before the shed door opened and the visitors drove off in anger.

Some hours later, after a silent dinner in the kitchen, Ullman lit one of his endless cigarettes. "Whiskey and chemicals," he murmured, smiling. "A nice combination. And now, biochemicals into which all that tax money has been siphoned. What an edifice of chicanery and deceit! I have smoked them out, Sophie," he remarked with grim pleasure.

"Why were they here?" she asked quietly.

He glanced at her sardonically. "A considerable bribe was offered, Sophie. I could be director of their biggest operation. A large sum was mentioned to withdraw this action. They would have been well advised to remember me better," he added ominously, and remained alone in the kitchen, smoking and drinking tea, until long after Sophie had gone up to bed.

Ullman was in the workroom, when the telephone in the house rang. Sophie raised the kitchen window and called across the yard that New York was on the line. A man named Bergenline Jones.

"I shall take it," he decided.

He crossed a frozen garden, tidied for the winter, and clumped heavily into the kitchen. After a moment, he raised the instrument to his ear. "Yes, Jones?"

A controlled voice invited him to appear on a national television program originating in New York City. Ullman listened without expression.

"Why do you call me?" he asked. "I am a scientist, not a performer."

Since the program dealt in matters of intellectual interest, his dis-

233

tinguished presence, the voice advised, would be deemed an honor. Ullman was silent and the request was repeated. "Tomorrow," he said harshly. "Just now I am in doubt."

"Can't we have an answer now? Favorable, I hope?"

"I must think it over."

"Good enough." The voice paused curiously. "Oh, Professor, I wonder whether you remember me?"

"I recall you perfectly." Ullman glanced irritably at Sophie who was at the doorway wearing a frayed cardigan sweater. He turned back to the telephone.

"You sat in the first row, second seat from the aisle. Bergenline Jones. In your first recital you saw fit to quote *Fletcher on Biochemistry* to contradict a point I had made in my lecture. Chapter 6, page 122, line 11. You seemed to think that a teacher could know nothing outside his specialty. It was my pleasure to point out that the proper title of the work was *Ullman's Fletcher on Biochemistry*. No?"

The voice laughed uncertainly. "I almost forgot that."

"I haven't. Whatever became of you, Jones?"

"I'm in televison. I produce this show."

"I am not surprised," said Ullman enigmatically. "Call me tomorrow."

He hung up and with a rigid expression marking the heavy lines of his mouth, set out in silence for the carriage shed. Once inside he locked the door and gazed upon disorder. Wooden shelves were heaped with memoranda, papers, books, correspondence, photographs, lab notes—anything, everything with seeming relevance to the great task of his life. It was a process growing ever more complex as layer after layer of meaning became exposed in a remorseless examination of past events. He shuddered with the cold and wearily returned to his desk.

In the freezing weather the kerosene stove was less than adequate; on such nights he wore a threadbare overcoat and storm boots as he paced the shed, shivering, while his mind ranged afield and confusion dissipated the ever-growing clarity that seemed to reach its peak with each dawn. Only then was he free to fling himself on the cot to lie in a semblance of sleep. He lay staring at the roof until the sun was at seven o'clock. Soft clucking told him that Sophie was at work in the hen house.

An hour later Sophie filled a plate with a country breakfast of ham and eggs and fried potatoes. He had become a heavy feeder and the food put him in better humor. She put her elbows on the oilcloth.

"What have you decided, Victor?"

"I see no reason not to express my views publicly."

"Must you go?" she asked.

234

"Yes. Yes, I think so," he said thoughtfully. "I welcome this invitation, Sophie. Are you surprised?"

A whistle attracted her attention. She arose painfully and returned with a kettle. Ullman watched the gush of steam with mounting irritation. In a few short years, Sophie had acquired the dress and manners of a farm woman. Heavy shoes and a wool skirt daubed with mud were work clothes, presenting a picture far from the fastidious intellectual woman of their earlier years. She had become creaky with age, he thought. Each limb and socket seemed more calcined and articulated than ever. The remoteness, he reflected, had become incredible.

"Out with it, Sophie!" he demanded with anger.

Deeply troubled, she filled his glass, a tumbler in a metal holder, to brimming. "What has happened to you, Victor? What are you doing?"

The great eyes widened with astonishment. "So! That again, Sophie? All over the country they are writing in this vein. Must I have it from you?"

She finished in silence. "I was thinking of those young people all night. Have you given any thought what it means to them?" She paused. "Or to yourself? Or me? Or Jo? This thing is infecting every relationship you have."

He stared unpleasantly at something he had never before seen. "What is this new mood, Sophie?"

"Is anything worth this price?"

"*Um Gottes Willen!* Do I want this burden, Sophie? Of all people you should know better. Where is your feeling for me? I am suffering too!"

"Why not end this thing? Why not get in touch with them personally?"

" '*Them*'? Who is '*them*'?"

"David and Eva."

"And I do not want to?" he demanded with feeling. "What has got into everyone? Why does no one *see* the issues?"

"What can I say, Victor?" She shrugged hopelessly. "If you must go to New York, then go, for Heaven's sake! But let's not talk. It's too exhausting." She arose and put on a wool hat.

"Where are you going?"

"I'm picking up a load of feed at the Co-op. I'll be back for your lunch." At the door she pulled on gloves, lingering. "Will you sleep in the house tonight, Victor?"

His mouth was pressed with anger and, after a moment, she left. He sat blinking at the oilcloth and finished the tea, hot and bitter, in deep thought. For the rest of the day he worked in the shed, writing to former colleagues and students throughout the country, working late into the

235

night. The complete orderly arrangement of the file was the essential task which nothing could be allowed to divert, not even the unopened, not to be answered, bundle of letters postmarked San Martino, Florida.

Ten days later Ullman sat in the glare of studio lights waiting for questions to begin. He was aware that every pore of skin, every droplet of sweat was exposed to the Cyclops television cameras and the millions of homes throughout the land wherever the network managed to fling its electronic signal. About him was the confusion of television people. For a fleeting moment he regretted his refusal of make-up.

"One minute," said someone.

Ullman assumed an easy pose of dignity and let a grave smile light up his face while commercial events took place. Oh, the debased uses of science! he thought with interest, noting the blinking signal lights on the cameras. He gestured and got permission to light a cigarette from an egg-headed shadowy figure behind the glare. This was the Bergenline Jones personality he had met before the show.

"I ought to warn you, Professor," Jones had said, "that you'll be asked your opinion of Professor Luzzatto." Ullman had replied with gentle deprecation, "I certainly hope that question will not arise." Jones shook a bald pate. "Once you're on the air, Todd can ask any questions he likes. It livens the show when the audience can see that he's freewheeling. I hope you answer whatever comes along even if it seems a bit, uh, rough." "Must I answer?" Ullman asked doubtfully. "No. You're not under any compulsion, but of course a refusal is sometimes, uh, inadvisable." Under the humorless stare, Jones laughed uncertainly. "The only advice I can give, Professor, is to act natural—to answer with sincerity. The camera's got a depth of penetration that's inescapable." Ullman nodded slowly, thoughtfully. "I welcome such an instrument," he said harshly.

George Todd, a hard-faced man with a patent-leather air of acquired culture, swung about with a satanic smile. A surge of alarm warned Ullman of subtle cruelty in the spade-shaped face, and then panic faded in the interesting notion that all this was not unlike hundreds of doctor's orals over which he had presided. He waited courteously, a giant of intellect among Lilliputians.

Todd's voice crashed through a barrier. "Dr. Ullman, we've been reading much in the press about Professor Victor Ullman, the public figure. Let's find out some things about you, the man. Question: what is your special field?"

"My field? I am a professor of genetics." Ullman pondered the question. "Retired, as the military would say."

236

"What is genetics?"

Ullman gave this further thought. "The name genetics was proposed in 1906 by an American scientist for that branch of biology concerned with the elucidation of the phenomena of heredity and variation. It is a complicated name for a very young science," he added with amusement. "I have my own definition."

"Uh-huh," said Todd intelligently. "What exactly is that?"

"I would say it is the study of the gap between those things which are alive and those which are lifeless. A gap which science has not yet bridged." He glanced at the camera. "This is an ultimate realm of exploration, sir." He looked away, pleased with the phrase.

"Professor, in your opinion are scientists different from other people?" asked Todd. "A race apart?"

"No. They are ordinary men," said Ullman slowly, "but they are chosen for extraordinary responsibilities. In this sense they are a race apart—although the term race," he added, smiling, "is not recognized in this context by the science of genetics."

"A chosen people?" asked Todd innocently.

"Oh, that? Yes, if you wish, but all peoples are chosen for *something*," said Ullman instructively. "It is not always clear how this is meant. The original Chosen People, for example, entertained this concept only in the sense that they were chosen to receive from Moses the law of God, and of course this is exactly what happened in history. It was not deemed cause for personal pride but for the humble acceptance of a great burden." He paused thoughtfully. "A burden, I might add, which anyone might shoulder by submitting to the discipline. Yes, in this view, scientists are a chosen group. It is not always an advantage to be chosen, you know. It may even be a curse. The whole business has been widely misunderstood."

"H'm!" said Todd profoundly.

He turned a page and looked up, having thought of a question. "Then anyone can elect to join the group?"

"On one proviso."

"Yes, what?"

"That a certain faith will be served. The scientist must believe that the cosmos is subject to universal laws, that no limits are set to the frontiers of knowledge. Of course," Ullman added, smiling broadly, "one must also have talent."

"But the scientist is not above ordinary rules of conduct?"

"No. Except that as a man of education and intelligence, he should be held to higher standards than others. He should be an exemplar."

237

"Good enough."

Todd went skipping back several pages and read a question. "However, Professor, would you agree with this statement: Quote. It is unseemly and a disservice to science for scientists to engage in public disputes particularly where the motives may be interpreted as mercenary? Unquote." He put aside the page with a blank expression. "Do you recognize the quotation?"

"Yes," said Ullman. "I wrote that statement in the form of a letter to the *Times* at the time of the dispute between Dr. Samuel Culver and Dr. Theodore Harbottle. I must compliment you on your research."

"Thank you. Can you tell us anything about that?"

Ullman smoked thoughtfully. The reference was to a storm which had recently convulsed the world of medical research. It had centered about a young doctor who had developed a method for preventing Shaw's disease, a baffling viral infection of the nuciform sac, by building immunity through repeated injections of killed virus. A publicity campaign of orgiastic dimensions by a sponsoring organization had proved unfortunate, for at countless learned societies, poor Culver had been pursued, and baited, and reviled, and insulted by Harbottle, a lean, white-haired man with eyes burning with contempt and fanaticism, for daring to prevent a deadly disease by the wrong method. Harbottle's rival theory called for the use of attenuated but still dangerous strains of live virus, and the persistence of his attack had driven Culver to Switzerland, where, according to reports, he was at work on the Barrie juvenence hormonal factor in silkworms. It was a disgraceful business, but quite well known, Ullman observed, noting that Harbottle had appeared on Todd's program at the height of the scandal.

"Quite right," said Todd, having listened to the digression like a coiled spring. A finger stabbed. "You disapprove of Dr. Harbottle! And yet, aren't you yourself engaged in a far more serious dispute with a former colleague?"

Ullman calmly restored his cigarette and exhaled a cloud of smoke, vivid on a million television screens. "Isn't that why you have me here tonight?"

"Well, Professor," said Todd, "how come?"

Ullman said, "One sometimes has no choice. No rule exists without its exceptions. None whatever."

"And this is one?"

"Yes."

"Would you care to enlarge on that?"

"You may ask your questions. I will then decide whether to answer. I

238

would be foolish to give you ammunition for my destruction. No?" Ullman chuckled with sudden good humor.

"But—" Todd halted. "Well, Professor, can you tell me what the general reaction is among scientists to this thing? Are they for or against this kind of lawsuit? Or is there some rule that one scientist is never supposed to sue another?"

"The reaction?" Ullman smoked easily. "I would say it is mixed. A small minority disapprove. For the most part, it is realized that I am Victor Ullman." He smiled pleasantly. "I think the circumstances are understood."

Todd turned to a written question. "Professor, let's be frank about this. Is it personally important to you to be known as the inventor or discoverer of biocin?"

Ullman's air of indulgence deepened. "Really. Mr. Todd. Am I a child to be concerned with titles? I prefer the simple designation of scientist. Isn't that honor enough for one man?"

"Let me read this." Todd picked up a typed sheet. "Two years ago you furnished data to *Who's Who in American Science*. According to that work, page 654, column two, you claimed to be the inventor or discoverer of biocin. What about that?"

Ullman said quizzically, "Yes, I gave that information. But it is not a matter of claim. It is a question of historic fact."

Without transition Todd said swiftly, "Have you got anything personal against Professor Luzzatto?"

"I? No!"

"And yet I have it here that you caused a complaint to be served on him in his classroom in the midst of a lecture. Was there any legal reason for that?"

The smile acquired a sudden fixity. "I am not a lawyer, Mr. Todd."

"Neither am I, sir. Was there any nonlegal reason why the complaint was served in public?"

"None that I know of." Ullman leaned forward and displaced a cigarette ash. "I must assume that lawyers know their business, just as scientists know theirs, or you know yours. I would not have done such a thing myself."

"Did you disapprove?"

Ullman stirred. "What has this got to do with anything, Mr. Todd? I am here as a scientist. This is all beside the point."

Todd smiled darkly and turned back to his prepared questions. A few queries brought him finally to a crucial question. "Are you willing,

Professor Ullman, to discuss the financial arrangements with Brandywine Laboratories for the manufacture of this substance?"

Ullman smiled. "Why do you ask?"

"To hear your answer," said Todd. "Will you answer?"

"No," said Ullman gently.

"Why not?"

"Because the matter is in the courts," said Ullman. "It would not be proper to go into such matters, certainly not without my lawyer's permission."

Todd said swiftly, "Did he clear you for this television broadcast?"

Ullman laughed. "I did not ask."

"Oh, why not?"

"I was afraid he might forbid. He has strict notions about these things. He is never sure I will say the right things." Ullman cocked a quizzical eye.

"But you wanted to come?"

"Evidently, since I am here." Ullman was amused. "But not to be misquoted."

Todd sat back with folded arms. "How can you be misquoted on television, Professor?" he asked sharply.

Ullman laughed uncertainly.

Question followed answer in swift succession. The clock raced and gradually as the issues sharpened the amused smile of superiority faded into a frozen wary manner of objectivity. At certain points Ullman hesitated perceptibly and cast his eyes down while considering his answer. Finally Todd sat forward with an accusatory finger. "All right, Professor! Doesn't it amount to this? Either Professor Luzzatto committed a gross fraud as you claim, or you have made a reckless, false charge for which you've got to take responsibility? How about that?"

Ullman wiped his eyelids. "I think that is fairly put, Mr. Todd," he conceded heavily. "However, I have never in my life made a false accusation and I always take full responsibility for my actions."

Todd flipped a page. "Do you regard Professor Luzzatto as a friend?"

Ullman hesitated. "I did," he said gently.

"Then how do you feel now? I mean, in the light of the lawsuit? Is there any special animus behind it? Do you feel some cause for resentment?"

In the control room the director caught the twitch of an eyelid and called for a change of camera. In the pitiless glare Ullman groped for an answer, rubbing the inside of a thigh. The question clearly had shaken him. He shook his head slowly.

"Oh, no. Oh, no. I'm sorry to disappoint you, Mr. Todd," he said

240

heavily. "There's more than a personal disagreement between prima donna scientists. All this has to do with the central problem of our times."

"Oh? What's that?"

Ullman waited an interminable moment.

"It is the moral issue," he said painfully. "I have no feeling against Professor Luzzatto, sir, except perhaps sorrow and regret. We were close once and I hope we can be so again, but he has committed the sin of Prometheus, and this is tragedy, for that sin denies and thwarts the possibility of a rational world order which is the goal of truth and science. I have no choice but to take a position."

"I see." Todd, who did not in fact see anything, assumed an air of erudition he did not possess. "The sin of Prometheus? Would you explain that to our audience?"

Ullman sat thinking deeply and darkness gathered in his face. He said with foreboding, "Prometheus was the Titan who stole the fires of Heaven to give to man. That sin was compounded of pride and—theft. Can salvation come from this?"

Todd stared. "Some last questions, Professor," he said hastily, and final moments were consumed with a request for capsule opinions of fellow scientists each of whom were characterized with deepest respect. As the clock came close to midnight Ullman could not resist a final word.

"I would not like to leave this program, Mr. Todd, without a personal word. I regard Professor Luzzatto as a gifted researcher, a bit young perhaps, but one whose intellectual resources are unusual and rare. Such a person one holds to the highest degree of responsibility, just as I myself would wish to be held. It is a grave responsibility to call into question his moral integrity—as well as the integrity of great institutions with which I was associated for most of my adult life. If any honorable way out could have been found, I would have been the first to accept, but I have searched my soul, and before the entire nation I can only say that my sole interest, God help me, is the cause of truth and the welfare of science."

His mouth trembled through the closing ceremonies, struggling to control the powerful tide of emotions that held him in clutch.

Throughout the ordeal, more painful than anyone could suspect, he had been conscious of all those who were watching in the university town that faced toward Haverstraw Bay.

The genie swallowed a pinpoint glare and the room was dark except for glowing coals in the hearth. Luzzatto said. "It was a mistake to watch."

"No," said Eva.

"You ought not to get out of bed."

"It was something I had to see," she said.

He looked up, troubled. "Let me hold you, Evvie?"

"Oh, yes."

They held each other tenderly, desperately. Their breaths mingled and between them was the life that held them apart. He touched a cold cheek.

"Some day we'll make love again. I wish we could now."

"I miss it as much as you," said Eva. "You don't hate me, dear?"

"Hate you? Oh, why?"

"Because you have every right. You need me and I'm letting you down. In the simplest physical thing that I might do for you, I'm failing you."

"It's not you at all," he said. "You've done everything you could. I made this decision myself."

"You're entitled to my love," she said painfully. "Only now, you see, my responses are frozen. I've been trying so hard to be a full woman." A pause. "I'm such a coward!"

"Coward? Oh, darling!" He invoked the gods against the thought. "If not for you, I'd throw in the towel. You've been more than good." He was silent, still overwhelmed by the shock of the event on the screen, and waited for a moment of panic to subside. "If I could only turn the hose on this—this filth! If not for you, I'd just run off and let them pick up the pieces the best they know how."

"You don't mean that."

"I do."

"How can you walk out, Davey? It's not realistic to think along those lines."

"Maybe not," he agreed despondently.

She waited in the comfort of his arms. "I love you, Davey," she murmured finally. "I feel so wretched when you talk like that. I wish I could help you. If only I could take some of your burden—" Tears of compassion gathered. Then the telephone in the study was ringing. It was Leo Katz-Moebius calling from New York.

"Long time no see," said the familiar guttural voice.

"Long time no hear!" Luzzatto retorted.

"I caught the show. Sexiest thing on television. Were you watching?" Luzzatto shifted the hearing piece. Katz-Moebius struck him as slightly drunk—the thick accent was slurred and a background of juke-box music gave an impression of a sleazy bar. He said, "I was watching."

"You're in trouble, boy," said Katz-Moebius brokenly, and turned to argue with a quarrelsome female voice of someone called Sonia. "Hear me, Davey?"

"I hear you, Leo."

"How's Eva?"

"Eva's fine."

"I hear she's walking around as big as a house?"

"She's pregnant, yes."

"Lucky, lucky David Luzzatto!" Heavy breathing took place. "What's that lawyer's name of yours?"

"Philip Seixas."

"Seixas, Seixas!" the voice pondered. "Will you tell him, for God's sake, not to be such an impossible, *verfluchter*, thick-headed idiot? Will you do that for Katz-Moebius?"

"What are you talking about?"

"He's been writing to me, Davey," said the voice querulously. "Calling me. Pestering. Badgering. What in ten thousand hells does he want me for?"

"What's your problem?" asked Luzzatto. "You never answer."

"True! Have you thought why?"

"It doesn't matter. If he needs your testimony, he'll get it with or without your co-operation."

"You're angry?" Tears and sorrow were expressed.

"I'm tired, Leo. Good night."

"Davey—" Music blared. Katz-Moebius went on to invite Luzzatto to lunch at the Mott Haven plant of Brandywine Laboratories.

"Why?" Luzzatto was surprised.

"Perhaps my conscience irks. Perhaps I am thinking of juridical obligations. Perhaps I want to talk to you about this case. It is conceivable that I am still your friend, you idiot."

Luzzatto studied the telephone suspiciously. "My lawyer is handling the case. Why not take it up with him?"

"Are you so sure he is *your* lawyer?" Ingenious oaths were uttered. "Does he know where the bones are buried, you idiot? Katz-Moebius wants to chat with you! Be so agreeable as to dine with him at his expense?"

Luzzatto was struck by a thought. "Leo, did someone put you up to this?" he asked suspiciously.

"Is that what you think?"

"It's likely," said Luzzatto curtly.

"Then you're a complete ass, my boy," said Katz-Moebius, restored to good humor. "And you have my permission to perform an intricate biological function upon yourself, because my conscience is clear. Hello, hello!"

"I'm still here," said Luzzatto slowly.

243

"My best to Eva. Tell her to have that baby as soon as possible. It will kill Ullman." Katz-Moebius squealed with delight. "It will positively demolish him! Give her my love—"

Luzzatto was shaking with a delayed reaction, not so much due to the harlequin on the telephone as to the recollection of the thing on the television screen. It was suddenly all too much and he stood back, sweating and trembling.

It was too absurd. What had happened? It was years since that day he had walked into Ullman's class in genetics. Since then he had developed into an established figure in world science in his own right. Why then, at the familiar head of authority on the screen, still handsome, still commanding, did the blood freeze in his veins in a familiar, remembered panic which surely he had long since outgrown? It was queer to hear his name uttered in terms of pity and contempt that went over the nation. He felt exposed and it hurt, he thought, oh, Christ, how it hurt! Only now did he begin to realize the hot flame of humiliation. He had had no idea, nor could anyone know, not even Eva, how the sense of shame could squeeze the bands of the heart.

He was aware of Eva stirring. Abruptly he pulled the telephone jack from the wall plug and popped a pill into his mouth before he went back to the living room.

Eva was staring at the television screen. "Would people swallow all that, d'you think?"

"Yes."

"Oh, Davey!" she muttered. "Ah, my God! He was lying. Won't people see through him?"

"He wasn't lying," said Luzzatto wearily.

Her gaze came to focus. "What does that mean now? Ah? You've got such a way of making this thing so complex." She walked about the room, thrusting her weight forward, flat-footed and clumsy. "He talked about wanting an honorable way out," she argued. "Why would he do that unless he were afraid to go ahead?"

Luzzatto shook his head. "He doesn't care about a way out, Evvie. He's constructed a system of ideas about this thing that has got to remain intact. I have no way to reach him. Oh, he puts on a good act—really clever, really convincing, right down to the meek and submissive mask of martyrdom to science." He paused shakily. "I'll have to meet him in court because there's no other way."

They exchanged stares. "You're describing a very strange state of mind?"

"Yes."

"But—" She broke off abruptly. "No, no! It's too pat! Too pat!" Her glance was thoughtful. "How long have you had this notion?"

"The moment we got that letter from Foxx. In a way, I've always known."

"Yet for months you said nothing?"

A long moment passed. "What could I say? Who'd believe me? You're not convinced yourself, are you?"

"I—"

Eva glanced at the television screen, thinking back to Jo and the bleak house of the Ullmans and something once said at her wedding. So many things seemed to fall into place—the baleful influence which infected all seemed clear. She paced the room, hugging her elbows. "I'm not sure what I think, Dave," she said slowly. "But I don't believe your reasons for keeping quiet. Why haven't you let people know your thoughts? What are you afraid of?"

He stared sullenly. "How can I get myself to do this?" he muttered. "Where would it end?"

"Nonsense! Damn nonsense!" she cried strongly.

Luzzatto began to close windows, unable to speak. A fresh cold wind was blowing from the river. He looked up sullenly. "I can't help what Victor does. I'm responsible only to myself."

"You feel you cannot reply?"

The moment extended ominously. "Not yet. Not unless it becomes necessary."

"You have something in mind?"

He nodded slowly, reluctant to deal with the point. "Yes, I've got something, Evvie," he said.

"Why not use it? What prevents?" she cried.

"It's something I'm trying to avoid."

She flung out her hands. "Why? Why?"

Wordless, he turned to the television screen. During the broadcast he had been irritated and made uneasy by the twitch in Victor Ullman's left eyelid. Other signs had caught his attention—enlarged veins, a looseness of neck cords, an uncertainty of movement. "Evvie, he's got so old," he muttered unhappily. "How can I use those tactics?"

Eva's gesture to the heap of papers dealing with the lawsuit was incredulous. "How can you not?" she cried in disbelief.

Suddenly he said an unforgiveable thing. "Evvie, you're still warped," he cried brutally, flaring.

She paused, wincing with pain, holding her burden. "Perhaps I am," she agreed. He walked about the room, glancing sullenly, defiantly, nurs-

245

ing a grievance that came out of nowhere. He halted finally at the chest, irresolute, breathing nervously.

"Sorry, Evvie," he muttered. "I didn't mean it. It was just talk."

"Oh, such lovely talk!" she cried.

She stood biting her mouth, wordless, fighting for control, then turned and fled to the kitchen. Among familiar things—copper skillets, a gleaming freezer—her mouth opened convulsively. An eternity hung at the precipice, and then from the depths spurted the release of tears—hot, briny, burning like lye. She was bathing her face in cold water when she felt a gentle touch. She shivered.

"Evvie, darling," he pleaded softly.

Her voice was low. "I'm not your enemy, Davey."

"What can I say?" He was in despair.

She stared at the sink. "It's natural for you to hit out," she muttered. "It's just that you're still—still in that old relationship, you see? When will you meet him on his own terms?"

"What terms?"

"If you have a weapon, use it! What else did you think?" she demanded starkly.

He stroked her hair, feeling the warmth, the sweet savor, and every protective instinct in his heart ached. What else indeed had he been thinking of?

"I'll do something," he promised finally, sighing. "I hope it doesn't come to that, but you have my promise. I won't let them touch you. In a few weeks they'll take my deposition. I'll have my chance to talk to Victor and that—that lawyer of his. When I finish he'll see that there's no case." He touched her cheek gently and then, inevitably, her breast. "Let's go up to bed, darling?" he begged.

Their embrace was prolonged, warm, loving—but in the end it was no good and she broke off. She paused to look back at the darkened living room.

The lawsuit! she thought.

It rested not, it departed not, but like a timeless, bloodless Presence, it lived in their home, emitting a cold breath of fear like a winter's fog. It was an embarrassment to their intimacy, intrusion to their thoughts, poison to their souls. It towered, shapeless but real, invisible but palpable, glaring with unwinking eyes upon their marriage sheets. In its miasma, they suffocated, thrashed, panted for clean air they once had known. It had form, shape, dimensions, and she knew at last that it would not of itself depart.

"God damn him. I could kill him for what he's doing to you. Oh,

Davey," she murmured exhaustedly, "I wish for your sake you had some of that feeling."

He made a pained gesture. "What good is that kind of talk, Evvie?"

"No good, perhaps," she agreed despondently.

Step by painful step, she turned and went up to the bedroom. She felt small, diminished, incredibly lonely, and the thought of her parents afflicted her. Silent tears ran down her cheeks. She buried her head in the pillow, stifling a frantic impulse to awaken the man at her side. The sense of life within her sharpened her fright and then toward dawn a sedative took effect and she drifted into sleep.

Chapter 20

WITHOUT COMMENT BOTH *Patroon* AND THE *News* RAN A TRANSCRIPT OF George Todd's television interview. Podell promptly issued a formal statement which said nothing. Luzzatto turned over his course in genetics to Wodzick, and for several days clung to a poor pretense of administrative duties. He had formed the habit of visits to Philip Seixas's office where almost daily he rehashed his story in wearisome detail. That morning he sat with the lawyer, staring at the sky and talking about everything but the purpose for which he had come. Another letter from Jo, the second since the lawsuit had begun, was in his pocket.

"You know, Phil, the most gifted researcher can spend a lifetime in science and get nowhere. I suppose that's the ultimate gamble that the researcher takes when he puts everything into the balance—family, money, career, what not. And yet his chances of success are governed by completely external considerations."

Seixas gave no hint of his thoughts.

Luzzatto went on: "Oh, we're always walking the tightrope between alternatives. We're scared of the big project that might take a lifetime and lead nowhere. And so a lot of younger men choose the short piece of work essentially without meaning. The sort of job we're constantly getting from industry. That's an involvement, I'm afraid, where the demands of industry are great and administrative compunctions few. I wish you could understand the threat of that industrial routine. Emotionally the short-term job has the superficial temptation or advantage that it seems to offer a bit of security, a place to run when the money problem gets too much to handle. And even negative results seem to have their value

248

if only to clear the way for the big discovery that counts. Except that no one wants to spend a lifetime in oblivion while someone else gets the glory. We're all glory hungry, I suppose."

Below an intercity bus changed gears in a maddening whine as it made the grade of Main Street. "There's also the grandiose lifetime study routine which really postpones the showdown. It's a great comfort to a man to find an area where he can bury his phobic indecision in the disguise of fruitful work. I'm told that's not uncommon elsewhere, and I can't say that scientists are too different, but the field really does make demands on their vulnerabilities. It's a field where you've got to show the highest capacities to make your mark, but sometimes that's not enough. Ullman used to have a lot of stories on that, and some of the names would surprise you. I remember there was an important physiologist—a Dane, by the way, but I won't mention his name—who kept fudging his data. Quite unnecessarily, I might add. He did a good piece of work on transplanting human tumors in mice, then for no good reason added some irrelevant findings. Fabrications out of the whole cloth. There's an awful lot of compulsive behavior around—because once the choice of career is made there's no turning back. It's the commitment of the scientist to the universe, I suppose—whatever he is, his integrity, his heart, his brain, his manhood he feels are involved in his work. That's the bargain he makes with himself. Isn't that true of lawyers?"

"Of very few." Seixas was drawing little circles on a pad. "How did you deal with these difficulties?"

"You mean me personally?"

"Yes."

Luzzatto pondered the question. "Through faith," he said uncomfortably.

"Faith in what?"

"In science, I imagine. Or in Ullman," he said. "Or in both because the two always blended in my mind. It's not easy to explain, but from the day I walked into his class, he struck me as the personification of science, the embodiment of its moral and intellectual authority. Could you call that faith? Or am I stretching the point? I know only that in my case I was helped by a sense of identification with something external to myself, something out there, something lending justification and sanction to my work. Isn't that what mystics go through?" He glanced at the silent lawyer, smiled bleakly. "I know what you're thinking and I don't blame you. I've always been susceptible to that sort of thing. I used to follow the figure of Einstein voraciously. Nothing that happened in the world, no event of importance, seemed, well, *official* until Einstein had made his comment. While he was alive, there was always the sense that somewhere on earth was an ultimate authority, a mind that summed up things and lent them morality and sanction. Don't ask me to justify that feeling because I can't. Ullman stepped into that position and convinced me that I could conquer the heights and I believed him. He told me what I could do and I followed his line. Except in the case of biocin of course where we had that wine process quarrel that first year. I think I gave you a separate memo on that background?"

"It's in the file, yes," said Seixas carelessly. "I'm not terribly interested in that side issue. We can't clutter up the picture, running down every rabbit that crosses the trail. Too confusing."

Luzzatto waited, wondering that he had let himself be drawn out. In his own opinion, the wine process was indeed significant to the entire background. "The point is that I was able to look outward, not inward. I became interested in science for its own sake, in the thing itself, not in myself. Haven't you ever gone through any of this?" he asked curiously.

"I've got three strapping sons," Seixas remarked humorously, "and two grandsons, so that I've never had to prove my manhood through my work. But I've seen that thing in the courts—the compulsion to find an external locus of authority, usually the bench. But when good lawyers genuflect before some of our specimens in robes, it argues poorly for that emotion." He settled back with a keen glance at the pale, distressed face. "What about Ullman now? How do you feel since that business on television?"

"Is that important? How I feel?"

"It could very well be," said Seixas slowly.

Luzzatto arose suddenly and walked about the room. "I don't know how I feel," he said in a low voice, "except sad, bitter about the whole business, mostly because of what it's doing to the Center. I can't tell you what importance I attach to getting the Center on a solvent basis—to use the royalties to build a staff for pure research. How else have I been able to seduce these hot young Ph.D.'s away from the big schools? Or from industry? It's only the promise of the Center. With the Center we're solvent, free. We can really get into the basic questions and with all these new techniques growing to maturity—x-ray crystallography, gas chromatography, radioactive tracers—we're beginning to breathe. On the university scale of salaries, how could we attract the real talent? Oh, sure! In my time, a lot of us were ready to live on beans, but with all this industry and government cash pouring into research, what can we expect from the younger men? They're marrying, having babies, and the wives have a lot to say. The whole field's changing, getting security-minded, money conscious. What do you think the lawsuit's done to all

250

that?" He paused with a bitter smile. "I've already lost Cunningham—and I'm having a hell of a time with the rest. How do I feel about Ullman? How should I feel?"

Seixas glanced up under frowning brows, as he sometimes did. "Are you still recruiting personnel, Dave? With this lawsuit pending?" Something odd was in the tone.

Luzzatto paused at the note of disapproval. "I can't let every—every diversion interrupt our program," he said obstinately. "We're slated to start work next October and I've got to do my scouting now. I assume we'll win our case, Phil, because we're entitled to the verdict. All I ask is my chance to meet Victor Ullman—to give my side. I'm going ahead on that assumption."

"Is that a fair basis to make these commitments?"

"Why not?"

"I expect to win," said Seixas carefully, "but if we should lose, these people of yours will be in a fix. If the Center can't meet its obligations, they'll be on your conscience."

Luzzatto paused with a show of anger. "If anything happens to the Center, it won't be my responsibility." A strong gesture dismissed the point. "But it's not only the Center, Phil," he added bitterly. "It's everything else that's happened since this thing began. Everyone that matters to me is being hurt or disgraced through this discovery—and yet it was so wonderful when it happened. When I looked at those results, I just couldn't believe it had happened to me. Biocin! All I wanted was to get Ullman on the telephone with the good news—to let him know the wonderful thing that had taken place in his lab. I was sure he'd be filled with satisfaction for my sake. I never tried to deprive the man of his proper share of the glory. If anything, I've always gone out of my way to give him credit."

Seixas murmured something indistinguishable.

Luzzatto went on, unhearing. "Who could know it would turn out like this? When I think of what I've got to do now—to smear my old teacher!" He was unable to go on, fighting recurrent tides of emotionalism. "I've tried up till now not to give in to anger."

Seixas raised his brows. "Oh, why?"

"I'm frightened by that feeling." Luzzatto shrugged hopelessly. "And what's the use? What does it add to what we're already doing to each other? To what we'll do before this is over?" He remained staring. "I'm not the only one frightened."

"Ah? Who's the other?"

"Ullman," said Luzzatto simply. "The last thing he can want is to meet me face to face."

After a moment, he said somberly, "In a way, it's my fault we're here. I should have understood a lot of things then that I didn't." He glanced up with bleak wonder. "You feel, don't you, that I've been holding something back?"

Seixas nodded slowly. "Let me pose the fundamental point again, Dave. Apparently the affection between you lasted for about eight years. During this period there was nothing but esteem and high regard which neither of you deny. Now suddenly Ullman charges that you induced him to part with his interest in the patents by a pretense that you intended to keep nothing for yourself. Why should he do this thing? Is there any reasonable explanation?"

Luzzatto thought deeply. "I've never called the man venal, Phil," he observed after a pause, and came finally to the purpose of the visit. He drew a breath. "Phil?"

"Yes."

"Why must we assume that he's still reasonable?"

The silence deepened while Seixas gazed at his cigar, digesting the innuendo. After a moment he stirred.

"It's a cheap and dangerous accusation, Dave," he observed quietly. "If it's not backed up by proof, it can readily backfire."

Luzzatto nodded grimly. "Everything I do these days seems cheap and dangerous."

"Why haven't you raised this suspicion before?"

A moment of torment passed before the low voice went on. "I'm not sure, Phil. It's just seemed indecent to use those tactics. I was part of the family, I ate in their house, I had their affection and—and love. Could I erase that from my mind?"

Seixas waited in silence.

"It's dirty, dirty, Phil," Luzzatto muttered wretchedly. "It's the last thing I ever wanted—exposing my old teacher to this kind of mud. I know what he's doing to me, but—well, God! It's not only him—it's the family, Sophie, Jo. How could I involve them?" He turned off and strode about the room in agitation, thinking back to the night with Jo at Mlle. Bailleul's. "I've had such mixed feelings, Phil, that sometimes I've felt completely helpless, impotent in this whole welter of mud. I never believed it would get to this point. Now I see there's no way out."

"What finally convinced you? That appearance on television?"

"Only in part," said Luzzatto with difficulty. "Can we possibly find a

252

use for this?" he demanded, handing over a copy of what he had come to call the Truth Chart.

Know the one true God!

Seixas studied the design curiously, frowning, while Luzzatto described the hot morning before commencement exercises when Ullman had taken the chart from the old music cabinet. "Ullman's got a lot of feeling for those verses, Phil. Can't you use this in cross-examination to get under his skin—to get behind that facade, in some way?"

The lawyer shook his head firmly. "I don't see how," he replied, obscurely displeased. "It's an interesting incident, but what does it add to our knowledge? Merely that the relationship between you was intimate—exactly what the other side wants to prove. We can't possibly open the door to this sort of labyrinthine intricacies."

The chart was handed back.

Luzzatto stared with incredulity. "But that's asinine," he exclaimed with growing alarm and anger. "It wasn't my idea to go after Ullman—it was yours. What's happened to that lecture I got on ruthless tactics? I think this chart is terribly important. I say it should be used somehow. I may not know law, but I know Victor Ullman!"

An impatient gesture brushed this aside.

"Oh, please!" said Seixas irritably. "Feeble tactics are worse than none. I'd be much happier if I knew that all the documents were in. Give me credit for knowing some few things about these matters." He glanced at his watch, frowning with displeasure. In the white, angered face, he read an obstinacy of purpose he could only respect and deplore. "Is there anything else you'd like to discuss?"

Luzzatto stared for the longest moment, resisting the powerful controlling personality of the older man, aware of rage at the affront to his judgment. In his pocket was the letter from San Martino. His face darkened.

"I have nothing to discuss," he said thickly. "I'm sorry to take up your time." With a curt nod, he arose and left. Turning over in his mind was a last hopeless expedient to be explored.

Luzzatto arose the following morning before dawn. He dressed quietly, surreptitiously, and tiptoed to the study where he telephoned for a taxi. Eva was still asleep when he returned for a final look—her mouth pouted like a child's, a slight frown creased her brow, a hand bent helplessly at her cheek. He leaned over and kissed her brow.

"Um? Oh?" she murmured.

"Go back to sleep," he whispered anxiously.

He heard the crunch of gravel and got to the door before Tiny Feinberg could beep his horn. He flung a satchel of papers into the back seat and sat beside the driver, breathing heavily. Feinberg pressed the throttle and the taxi slid forward through the mist.

"Railroad," said Luzzatto, closing his eyes in fatigue.

At the foot of the hill Tiny Feinberg slid a friendly glance toward his passenger. "I hear the trial takes place at Salt Hills, Professor. Is that good?"

"It's the county seat. What's wrong with that?"

A massive paw tapped the region of a left pap. "Apple knockers! No heart," said Tiny Feinberg darkly. "In this man's town you made a dent by now, Professor. You're well known amongst the businessmen and there's a lot of local pride. You got friends, too, what I mean. A lot of us, Gus Apostolico, Joe Wilson, Billy Ludwig, old man Pappas, Councilman Fitzpatrick, the PTA, people like that has been talking it up on your side. After all, you're clean cut, you're married with a little one on the way and that entitles you to something. People *know* you, Professor, and that's half the bout. They won't just accept anything some wise lawyer from New York claims about a man who lives amongst them. But in Salt Hills you're a total stranger with a foreign last name. Oh, believe me, I know. You'd be amazed how a busy hackie gets around and senses the pulse. I been living amongst 'em now for many a weary year. I know the type." A grimace indicated a wizened race as flinty as the hills. "What kind of jury can you expect from that kind?" He mouthed the words with loathing: "Salt Hills!"

"Jury? There's no jury," said Luzzatto. "It's a case in equity. It comes up before a judge."

Feinberg turned a long glance and saw no jest in the haggard face. He pulled up to the curb and set the handbrake and slowly lit a cigarette, striving to master a sense of incredulity. He said slowly and distinctly, "You mean to tell me, Professor, that you don't get a jury?"

"Not in this type of case," said Luzzatto.

Feinberg pondered the answer. "You mean to say you got to go before the one man only?"

"That's what I'm told. I'm no lawyer."

"Maybe you're no lawyer but you're an intelligent man. You going to let 'em do that?"

"I have no choice."

"But this judge? Suppose it turns out he's wild? Or something?"

254

"Even a juror might be wild."

"Yeah, sure! But they's twelve of 'em and they can't all be wild in the same way, Professor. One nut's kink is the next nut's hobby and you got a fightin' American chancet. But a judge! Who knows what's on his mind? You're in the one man's hands. Oh me, oh my!" said Feinberg forebodingly. "They wouldn't do it to a criminal."

At the station Feinberg tossed the satchel of papers onto the train and saluted. He could recall the first day Luzzatto had arrived in town, and as the train disappeared from sight, he wished his passenger well.

Luzzatto swayed with the train as it raced along the bank of the river. After a time he became aware of the benign gaze of a portly man dressed in blue serge.

"Could you use an aspirin, young man?" drawled the man genially. "Or a bite to eat? Because my wife don't like that green look around the gills." A birdlike woman smiled. "My name's Marbury. Upton Marbury. This is Mrs. Marbury."

It would be a relief to his burning eyes, Luzzatto decided, to break off his task. He closed the heavy manuscript and within minutes the friendly mood of a railway coach had been established.

"Speak unto thy fellow passenger," said Marbury humorously. "Says so in the Bible. That's how we learn, by exchanging views with our fellow man. What's that you're reading?"

Luzzatto stared at the manuscript on his knees. "It's a doctoral thesis," he said slowly, and went on to describe an involved argument by Erskine Hubbard in the field of cultural anthropology which assigned higher priority to cultural and environmental factors than to the genetic in the evolution of mankind. "Heredity or environment," he said succinctly. "That's the point."

"Well, now, that's interesting," said Upton Marbury thoughtfully. "Fertilizer and feed can work miracles, Professor, but even miracles can go just so far. Seed, not feed! How does this student work it out?"

It was an irresistible situation and Luzzatto found himself expounding the basis of the problem. Two aspects of the individual were distinguished by the geneticist—the inherited constitution received from the parents and the surface appearance as expressed in shape, color, size, and the like.

Marbury said, "Well, isn't skin color something a man gets from his parents?"

Not necessarily, said Luzzatto seriously. A yellow skin might point to Chinese ancestry. Or to jaundice. It was not easy, he pointed out, to know what outward characteristic was inherited, what imposed by environment.

"My husband used to grow freckles when he was a boy," said Mrs. Marbury, "and his father was freckled as a frog but not one of the girls. I suppose that's what you're talking about?"

"Not exactly," said Luzzatto, smiling faintly. It seemed to him that they had long since passed Peekskill. Marbury indicated Hubbard's thesis. "What's that feller got to say there?"

Luzzatto came back to the manuscript. "Oh this? Well, he's got a special orientation, Mr. Marbury. Feed, *not* seed," he added. "A geneticist would have another slant."

"Oh, now, Professor, I thought scientists was supposed to be scientific. Now you tell me it depends on the slant?"

Luzzatto was silent, thoughtful. "That's often true, I'm afraid."

Marbury hitched himself forward. "If a man eats poorly, he'll do poorly, I'll admit, but there's a runt in every litter, although they all depend on the identical teat. Does this man actually claim that a thing like food can decide a man's color?"

Luzzatto forced a polite smile, tempted to go into the matter, but his temples were throbbing, and he had an uncanny sensation that he had gone through this discourse on another occasion. "Yes, he comes roughly close to making that claim." He closed his eyes, wondering if he were doing Erskine Hubbard an injustice. He felt not.

There was a thoughtful incredulous silence.

"Which would be more remarkable to find?" asked Marbury. "That we come out of the womb like nails from a factory? Or each in his individual form and shape? The answer's right there in Genesis. If you know how to read it."

"Oh, how's that?"

Marbury twinkled in coming triumph. "The Book says that man was made in God's image. It also says that God is a Spirit. The simple scientific conclusion would be that man is no product of a factory operation, and he's totally handmade, and bound to come forth a unique individual, and that's how it's indicated. Besides, there's no limit to the kind of things the average human being will eat."

"That's true," Luzzatto admitted gravely.

"If that's the case, why don't we run wild? Why aren't we born with six fingers? Or two heads? Or fins and scales? If there wasn't something that says that each shall bring forth after his own kind? Oh, I guess I heard just about enough, Professor. Everything's in the Bible, if you know how to read it. I know all about this stuff. When I was a boy, I read

256

Darwin and Lamarck and Huxley—I mean Thomas Huxley, not this present pup of his—and Bob Ingersoll and Clarence Darrow and the whole pack. They've got nothing to tell an intelligent man. You talk about evolution? Read Genesis. There it is, right in front of you. Told in the language of poetry, but it says all that Darwin ever said and a lot better and more convincing. Right there's a description of the creation of man from dust. Except that he's complicated, what else does Darwin add?"

Luzzatto stared with a helpless feeling. "Well, Darwin," he said gently, "supplies a few more details than the Bible."

"Details?" Marbury snorted. "Details is just where Darwin's been broke down ever since his book came out. His details have been reversed many times. Isn't that so now?"

"Um. Yes."

"Then where's the advantage? Son, read Genesis! Don't just repeat what the pack are saying. You've got to learn to think for yourself and that's just what the average scientist won't do. He measures things, and he weighs things, but does he ever *think?* If it isn't what the rest are saying, why, it doesn't exist. Or am I being unfair?"

Luzzatto considered his answer. "Not entirely."

Marbury peered closer. "I feel that life is mysterious and wonderful, and we can find the answers, the real answers in the Book, if we look deep, and study hard—and that's the little comfort we've got in this life. All these so-called scientific laws aren't really laws, otherwise why would they be changing 'em all the time? Why, even Newton—" He paused as a warning hand touched his wrist. "Well, I won't go into Newton but I guess the universe is a lot more awesome and reverential than that atheist ever imagined. Read Genesis, son!" He paused. "I guess Mrs. Marbury wants me to explain that I'm not trying to run down your calling, or that dissertation you're reading. Will it be a book? Because I'd like to buy a copy if it ever gets to Watertown. Sort of souvenir, and from what you say, it must be a scholarly work. We're never finished learning."

"Scholarly? This?" Luzzatto glanced up in surprise, and suddenly the moment was not amusing. "It's not scholarly at all. It's the most diffuse garbage I've ever read," he said savagely.

"Oh!" exclaimed Mrs. Marbury.

"And Newton wasn't an atheist," Luzzatto added. "He was a religious fanatic with an asinine set of theological opinions. It may come as a shock but scientists, I'm afraid, are human." He paused abruptly. What exactly was he hitting at?

257

"Uh. Well, you can't say anything worse about 'em to me, Professor," said Marbury, rising and stretching. "Human beings can get real mean, son. Don't take my word. Read Chronicles! It's all in the Bible!" Nodding pleasantly, he turned off. "Can I help with that bag, Mother?"

After a moment, Luzzatto wearily covered his eyes and heard nothing as the swift clacking fled on into the industrial approaches of New York. The weight of Hubbard's dissertation left him with the knowledge that he had been trapped into something distasteful beyond words. It was a dreadful work, really abysmal, woolly, wrapped in the pretentions of a wretched and detestable pseudo-science—everything Bronco Wodzick had prophesied.

As the train crossed a switching point, he put the matter aside and took out the worn letter which he had read and re-read since its arrival three days earlier.

San Martino Oceanographic Laboratory

San Martino, Florida

Tuesday

Dearest Dave:

Haven't heard a word from thee since the pot boiled over and remain perplexed and hurt but imagine thou art vexed by the terrific strain of thy litigation. I pray for an end to these travails.

Oh, Dave! What's happening to us? Is the circle of doom destined to engulf all our lives? Or is there a rational solution? If so, I beg you to find the way, Dave, for all our sakes.

I know how much that is to ask—how mortified you surely were by that travesty on television. I too was aghast, Dave, literally aghast. I could not grasp at first how Dad of all people could lend his prestige to that public display like some lady impersonator or exhibitionist. I blushed for what I saw. And then I sensed an undercurrent of something else. It struck me that he was appealing not to public opinion but to you. Yes, Dave, to *you*—over the heads of the vultures, the lawyers, meddlers, gossips, operators, vested interests, organization men, sensationalists who've stepped between you—appealing for human understanding to the one man who shared a moment of glory.

Did you sense that too?

I decided not to write or call you about the television catastrophe, since I know that you're going through much, but I had a nasty experience yesterday which depressed me terribly—which you ought to know about. A man called after lunch to ask if he could drive over from town to see me for an hour or so, representing himself as a friend of Dad's. I told him to come over, and it proved to be Dad's lawyer—Emil Dirksen.

Oh, Dave! I was completely taken in. I was out in the shed with Honora (Nora) MacLeish (my latest roommate) stringing out the guts

258

of a manatee (100 ft. of sausage casing, by the way) with both of us filthy, hot and stinking, when he arrived. He told me he was there to get the facts because I had refused long distance calls and all his letters went unanswered.

I needn't tell you, Dave, that I was offended by the maneuver. If Dad wants facts, he could write to me, answer my letters, and say so. I can't see myself forced to hurt either of two men who mean so much to me. Oho! methought. He wants the facts? In a pig's eye! I really resented his using me as a catspaw. But what could I do?

We traipsed to my digs where he talked and I played dumb. Present were poor bewildered Nora, Dr. Lockridge, the horrible Emil Dirksen, a vague woman assistant of his, and my parakeet, Dennis, who's been taught to comment at intervals: "Oh, screw!" Dr. Lockridge offered to run interference, but I waived this aside as unworthy of my ancestry. I swallowed my spit, put a clamp on my shaking knees. Believe me I knew dread.

That lawyer is a Gray Eminence of trickery and obfuscation, a horrible parody of justice with squinty eyes and an ingratiating leer out of Dickens. I barely understood the drift except for some platitudes about co-operation and loyalty—and something about a statement in writing before the other side (that's you, Dave) could get at me to affect my clear recollection. Ugh!

I assured him that no one had made any attempt to "get at me," that I had not got even a postcard in months from either party. (Pathetic, wot?) Least of all was I worried about one David L. who would never, I felt sure, put me in an ungraceful or distressing position for the sake of a lawsuit. Which was more than I could say for my own father.

It was a pointed remark, but the lawyer asserted that the visit was his own idea, taken on his own initiative, unknown to Dad. I wish I could believe that.

I finally gleaned what he was worried about, namely, that your lawyers might seek to pin me down to some version inconvenient to his case. Had I said or written anything embarrassing? I searched my mind but found nothing in that empty attic which I cared to divulge. I reminded him however that the entire family had been at Lake Marah when you telephoned about the discovery from Haverstraw. I thought telephone company records would verify the date. He was hardly pleased at the suggestion and we went to other things.

I could hardly contain a snort of laughter when I heard you depicted as an archconniver. I must say however that legal language has a chilling effect on me.

Questions went something like this. I was asked how much supervision the students in the old department ordinarily received. I answered that of course a confused or untalented student might be breast-fed for a long time but who would want to nurse an infant with sharp teeth? One could not generalize.

Altogether I left the impression that to call me as a witness would do no one any good. I hate to be such a snake but what else am I to do,

Dave? I don't want to hurt or help anyone. I want only to be left in peace.

Well, Dave, enough of this. Just thought I'd scribble these lines in all fairness to let you know what's in the wind. That lawyer seemed to imply that I ought to be guided by family loyalty, but that is absurd, for he ought to know, and Dad knows, that I would tell nothing but the truth between you and nothing else, not even to save my life. Not that he asked for perjury in blatant terms, but he did hint strongly that testimony and recollection are plastic things and easily affected by emotional attitudes of the witness. Well, I remember clearly what transpired and I was struck by a singular omission of his—a failure to follow up about your visit to us at Lake Marah the day after the telephone call.

Does he know about that visit? If so, why did he say nothing? I said nothing nor would I mention it here if it were not all too clear in all our own minds.

I'm almost sorry I started this letter. I get such comfort from solitude and the days slip past in glorious sunshine and peace that these agitating thoughts are the last things in life I want. I try to keep out of this. I wrote Dad and Sophie to tell them of my distress at the embroilment, to urge Dad to find some way out of the dilemma but to date I have had no reply other than one cryptic letter from Sophie—and about that the less said the better. Happiness supreme does not seem to reign along the Thames.

I find myself praying that you will find it possible to rise above circumstances for the sake of those who love you dearly. Yes, Dave. I can only tell you what I feel in my heart—that Dad needs your help and understanding more than you need his. Does that sound strange?

Well, that's about all, Dave. I have read this letter over with the impulse to tear it up, but finally have decided to let it stand. I appeal to your love. Can that be so wrong?

That's all I know now. Meanwhile, skin diving, shrimp fleeting, work, the lazy, crazy life of the beachcomber are mine. Dr. Lockridge is a darling. If I weren't in love with Sarah Lockridge, I'd be willing to bunk off with him any weekend to Miami, but as it is I must be a good girl and poach not. Both Lockridges hover like mother hens and for this I am truly grateful.

Hope to hear of the christening—or whatever you Philistines are planning. Also that you are keeping Eva tranquil and insulated from this madness. Let something good come out of this horror.

Fondest,
Auntie Jo

The train swayed and plunged entering the first approaches to New York. Unconscious of the racing coach, Luzzatto placed a hand over his face. Could the cry of despair be resisted? In the dirty business ahead where was his first loyalty?

He sat thinking deeply and came to a decision. Whatever might come, he concluded bleakly, the first intrusion into that protected life had been taken by someone else, not by himself. "Jo! Oh, dear Jo!" he groaned; and then about him passengers were gathering clothes and luggage, saying farewells after a thousand miles, forever to disperse.

"Come to think, Professor," said Mrs. Marbury pleasantly, "Kim, that's our granddaughter, has more than her share of freckles, and some in the identical place. Takes after Grandfather Marbury. My, it's been a nice little visit, hasn't it?"

Chapter 21

THE BIOCHEMICAL RESEARCH PLANT STOOD IN A SPRAWLING ASSEMBLAGE of red brick structures on an estuary of Long Island Sound in the East Bronx. On a clear day one could see Throgg's Neck. Leo Katz-Moebius turned from the view and reached for a meerschaum pipe.

Luzzatto's glance had gone to the picture of James Strollo, that neat, foxy, familiar head on the wall. "How are you getting along with Big Brother?"

Katz-Moebius grinned sourly. "I don't bother him and he ignores my existence. What brings you here, my boy? Don't the aborigines keep you busy enough?"

"This was your idea, Leo, not mine." Luzzatto waited, resisting the rising tide of fatigue. Since morning he had covered a good deal of ground in Manhattan and was paying now in despondency and a weird sense of unreality. "You invited me for lunch," he said slowly. "Something about buried bones."

"Oh, yes!" said Katz-Moebius solemnly. The clack and bang of electric typewriters could be heard down the hall. Luzzatto adjusted his spectacles with distaste. "Leo, I thought you came here to work in research?"

Katz-Moebius shrugged. "The prodigal gets tired, Dave. He learns that the trough is here in administration. Does the great scientist need diagrams?"

Luzzatto flushed. "What does that mean?"

"Mean, my boy? It means I hitched my wagon to a star, a vice-president named Roswell Tibbett. If certain forces have a chance to work out, Roswell can hope one day to become president of this operation. Oh, not that it means too much. Have you any idea what Strollo pays the unfrocked scientist who heads this division?" He went on to observe that the president of Brandywine Laboratories received a straight $15,000 per year.

"That doesn't sound small," said Luzzatto doubtfully. Katz-Moebius laughed unpleasantly. "For a mere biochemist, no!" he said with indulgence. "Our president heads up a subsidiary operation, but above him at the parent corporation level is a vice-president named Dr. Frank Geddes who tells him when to blow his nose." For this duty, he advised, Dr. Geddes received $100,000 per year plus 5 per cent of gross sales plus $5,000 per idea submitted even though found too impractical to put on the market. A fantastic total figure was the annual reward.

"Do you mean that this man gets that percentage on gross sales of biocin?" Luzzatto asked slowly. "For doing what?"

"For having treated Angelica Strollo successfully for the symptoms of her climacteric," said Katz-Moebius slackly. "To be quite fair, he also showed a talent for plausible talk about steroid hormones when that field was still hot. What's wrong?"

Luzzatto was sick with outrage. "That's twice the royalty they pay the university. I had no idea. I'm shocked!"

"A deal is a deal. Besides, it's not added to the price. That's fixed to include such administrative costs."

"Fixed how?"

Katz-Moebius stared at the picture of Strollo. "That's for us to know and the Government to find out. Oh, now! Don't look so stricken. Some crumbs of the feast are falling into your lap."

Luzzatto turned a burning look toward the older man. "I know the rumors, Leo," he said grimly. "Actually the money has no meaning to me personally except what we've spent on the house—and that's something I've had to do. Otherwise, it's all gone for equipment, and other things. I have little idea about the money side. I don't ever carry more than ten dollars in my wallet. Eva takes care of all that, you see." A pause. "It was my own silly fault that made her insist," he added reflectively.

"Something happened?"

"Well, yes! She had a reason to go rummaging and happened to come across a canceled check for an RCA electronic microscope. Well, those things aren't cheap. I tried to pass it off as an item I was buying for the department, but I had to admit it was outside my budget although actually I had every intention of getting reimbursed, Leo. I really did!"

"But you were taking a chance?"

263

"Oh, yes. But I just couldn't wait another year and I seemed to have the money lying around. Funny!" A haggard cheek was touched with wonder. "I had no business getting stuck for that microscope. That's when I gave the bookkeeping to Eva, but not until after a horrible brush with the tax collector. A nice guy, but he had me sweating."

"You went down there alone?"

"Why not? I hadn't done anything wrong," said Luzzatto defensively. "Besides, it's my Government."

"Oh, my boy!" murmured Katz-Moebius with concern. "I am beginning to be frightened."

"Well, anyway," said Luzzatto rallying, "we've got a tax adviser now but it's all royalty income and I'm broke. That's on top of everything else that's gone wrong."

A moment of silence passed.

"Leo? If I had to leave Haverstraw, would there be any place for me here?" Luzzatto asked finally.

Katz-Moebius nursed his meerschaum thoughtfully. "Is it that bad, Dave?"

Luzzatto shrugged unhappily. "I'm afraid the position is getting untenable. Ullman's lawyer's been tackling people in the department and that's creating resentment against me. Me! As though I'm responsible." His head shook in wonder. "Even people who are my friends are getting the infection."

"Aren't you imagining this?"

"I don't think so. Even Tewksbury was pretty much on my side until I went to his house to get him prepared to give testimony, and he almost died—froze up completely and began to shake. I thought he'd have a fit and I didn't press him. Told me he couldn't forget twenty years of association with Victor Ullman and broke down weeping. Next morning we got a medical certificate that excused him for the duration."

"Maybe just as well?" said Katz-Moebius.

"Maybe. Then Freda—" Once launched, Luzzatto talked volubly and with deep emotion about the disappointments of the case. The university had been more than helpful to the other side, turning over records freely for examination, while his own colleagues, scattered over the world, had been guarded, ambiguous, wary of involvement. The big disappointment had been Tobiansky.

"He's supposed to loathe Ullman," said Luzzatto drearily. "I was hoping to get some dirt for use on cross-examination, but he absolutely wouldn't co-operate. If anything, he was offended when I approached him."

Katz-Moebius stared curiously. "That doesn't sound like you, Dave. Dirt?"

Luzzatto was silent. "I'm finding all sorts of surprising things about myself, Leo. I feel so immobilized. I really get upset and angry only when I find that I've done someone else an injury. But when it's the other way, when I'm the victim of name calling and attack, I just get silent and a bit bewildered and cold at first. It's hard to fight in that condition—but I'm trying to learn." His laugh was bitter.

Katz-Moebius studied the pale, angered face. "Have you seen this, Dave?" he asked.

It was a newspaper clipping which revealed that a convention of surgeons in Atlantic City had issued a call for the return by hospitals to the classical principles of disinfection—rules fallen into disuse since the rise of antibiotics. A report to the gathering noted that *Staphylococcus aureus,* Type 42 B/51/81–a, had gone epidemic in hospitals throughout the world. Penicillin was now ineffective against 80 per cent of staph, whereas only a few years earlier it had been lethal against all strains and varieties.

The item called for a return to plain cleanliness and strict laws to control the use of antibiotics, with or without biocin, or equivalent substances when and if discovered.

Katz-Moebius gazed at the ceiling. "Ah, Semmelweis. Semmelweis!" he murmured.

Luzzatto glanced up with displeasure. "Leo, these people expect too much from the stuff. Biocin can stabilize a population of organisms, but it can't reverse an attained course of evolution. It's in the nature of life to find new paths of survival. We've been warning them for years and now these clumsy idiots are beginning to wake up. Surgeons!" The clipping was returned with a sniff of disdain. "I don't see your point, Leo."

Katz-Moebius smiled at the air of conceit. Having come through an appendectomy with flying colors, he shared this view not at all. He said gently, "The last paragraph." A leading surgeon had called for development from the centers of research of new and improved compounds of the biocin family. "Isn't that where your energies ought to be discharged? Why not get back to the lab and the work you understand? You can't coast along forever on one discovery."

Luzzatto arose and walked to the window in agitation. "I'd like nothing better, but how can I work? With all this turmoil, my brains are like sawdust." A pause was filled with emotion. "Leo?"

"Yes, my boy?"

"I'm having a rotten time with this lawsuit," said Luzzatto miserably.

"It looks as though no one wants me to win—not even the university, not this company. But I thought I could count on you."

"Aren't you getting a bit neurotic, Dave?"

"Maybe. But why did I have to wait for you to get crocked in some bar with a whore named Sonia to hear from you?"

"I travel, my boy," said Katz-Moebius with tranquility. "Mexico. A lot of work in connection with our new plant in Matamoros."

There was a pause. "You haven't been to Mexico in a year," said Luzzatto unpleasantly.

"Haven't I?" asked Katz-Moebius, unabashed.

"Leo, in a few weeks I'm going to be examined under oath before trial by this lawyer, Dirksen," Luzzatto said. "I've been struck by something."

"Yes?"

"He hasn't yet gone after Brandywine personnel or records. Why? I've got a lousy feeling about the background—something I still don't grasp in depth. What happened during the negotiations with this company for biocin? I thought you might want to tell me."

"Are you sure I know?"

"No," said Luzzatto. "I'm not sure of anything."

"I like this man," Katz-Moebius cried, addressing an invisible presence at his shoulder. "I like him very much. Very much *indeed!*" He arose. "My boy, this marks your maturity as a scientist. Now! What about lunch?"

"Giulio, this is a friend of mine, Professor Luzzatto," said Katz-Moebius. "Treat him right. Double martinis?"

The small Italian restaurant was a haven of good cooking in the East Bronx, a refuge from the plant across the highway, an escape from spiked fences and locked gates. The smell of cooking olive oil provided a family touch, as did the napkins laid to conceal the stains of yesterday's marinara sauce. The waiter let his mouth drop with an air of intense respect.

"Luzzatto? Luzzatto? Ah! An illustrious name, I believe?"

Luzzatto looked down deprecatingly, wondering at his affinity for waiters. "I'm not sure of that," he murmured modestly, and turned without appetite to a menu card.

The waiter went off to the kitchen where an excited babble arose. A dark, motherly woman with a mustache appeared, gazed at Luzzatto, returned to the cooking area. Katz-Moebius craned about and waved suddenly to a stout, pink-faced man of sixty finishing up at a window table.

"Hi, Douglas!"

"Hi."

266

"How's the market this morning?"

The man passed over an early newspaper which showed that the shares of a rival drug and chemical house, Frisbee, Ltd., had risen steeply despite an announcement of a cut in net earnings to $20 million after taxes on gross sales of almost $200 million. "It's this rumor of a safe oral contraceptive pill," he explained. "Some extract of radiated yams. Anything can happen in Mexico! It's ridiculous-absurd-why-didn't-we-think-of-that-first-oh-lord-what-a-market-in-China!" He smiled and glanced at Luzzatto.

"Hello, Dr. Beekman," said Luzzatto.

"Yes?" said the man guardedly, puzzled.

"Excuse me." Katz-Moebius introduced Dr. Douglas Beekman, formerly director of biochemical research for Brandywine Laboratories. "Of course, of *course*," said Dr. Beekman, snapping his fingers. "We met that day in Dr. Ullman's laboratory, did we not? Yes, yes, yes! Professor Luzzatto! Ah, yes! How is it we never met in these last years? With all our correspondence, I feel as though we know each other. My fault for getting into exploitation!" The feeling was developed at length, and the good doctor went on resonantly. "After all, we do have a special interest in the welfare of the product. I can't tell you how regretful we all feel here about your lawsuit. Most unfortunate. Yes, really. This sort of thing ought to be worked out in some friendly manner. Talks at the summit, so to speak."

"I believe in talks at the summit," said Luzzatto. "But when one gets there, what does one say?"

Dr. Beekman laughed uncertainly. "One always thinks of something."

Luzzatto considered this gravely. "One may not always like what one may be called on to say up there. Tell me, Dr. Beekman, when will you be available for a conference? I mean, with respect to the lawsuit?"

The responsive glance was clear and intelligent and surprised. "But I am always available, Professor Luzzatto, when I'm asked. Although I have no idea, I must say, why we should be involved in a squabble among, ah, university people."

Luzzatto said slowly, "You haven't asked to be excused?"

A shaven lip was thoughtfully touched. "I did tell our house counsel, I believe, that I was too busy to travel, but I made no request to be excused. I'm always available here. What would I be asked to discuss?"

"Don't you know?"

"I have no idea," said Dr. Beekman, bewildered.

Luzzatto bit a thumbnail thoughtfully. The air of amused condescension, the answer, the encounter in the restaurant were indeed unexpected. "Why, Dr. Beekman, hasn't Phil Seixas called you?"

"Who is Philip Seixas?" asked Dr. Beekman blankly.

"Our lawyer," said Luzzatto after a pause.

"Ah? Well, quite frankly, I leave all these matters to our counsel," said Dr. Beekman genially. "But isn't all that stuff in writing? Your people must have that information and I fail to see how it affects us." He shook his head deploringly and returned to his own table, leaving Luzzatto to certain unpleasant speculations. And then the waiter was upon them with tablecloth which he set forth deferentially. "Luzzatto! A great name," he insisted, and stood back panting, hopeful. "Excuse, but you are relate to *the* Luzzatto. Mr. Cesare Luzzatto?"

Luzzatto blinked. "I'm his son."

Katz-Moebius was grinning. "Why, Giulio, this is Professor Da-vid Luz-zat-to," he said distinctly. "The great scientist! Don't you read the magazines?"

"Never heard of him before! But I am pleased. The son of Luzzatto! Only this morning I was thinking of the tragedy," said the waiter. "Such a style, such a quality! I would read every week from cover to cover. I was privileged to be a charter subscribe. To support the brilliance. Who is left with such brio?"

Luzzatto sat breaking breadsticks. Martinis finally arrived, cold and very dry. Katz-Moebius leaned forward, resting on his elbows. "What tragedy, Dave?" he asked with concern.

"Oh." Luzzatto shrugged and gazed out at the traffic thundering past. "Leo. Did you ever meet my father?"

"Could anyone forget?" asked Katz-Moebius with amusement, signaling for refills. "What about it?"

"His paper folded. He finally went broke."

"I'm terribly sorry," said Katz-Moebius.

Luzzatto shrugged. "Don't be sorry. Who knows? It might be the very best thing. The paper never made money and it took every cent out of my mother's business. It was always a begging proposition, scrounging to meet the printer's bill, running those fund-raising affairs. I'll bet he was into every hotel banquet department in the city for thousands. At least this may give him a chance to catch up to himself." His temples were throbbing. "Only he's conscience-stricken about the old crowd. How will Tullio eat if Cesare doesn't put the pasta on the table? Tullio was one of the old gang in Milan. Stupid old man but a hero, you see? Tackled some blackshirts in an alley to protect a printing plant, and they crushed his feet with sledge hammers before they carted him off to Lipari. It was

268

one of the stories I remember as a kid. We always had a lot of those fellows around." A grimace was bitter. "That's where the money always went in our family. We never saw a cent of it at home. When it comes to human relationships, he's completely helpless and emotional—an easy touch, soft as butter."

"And you?"

"Me?" An uneasy laugh. "I'm not like that at all. I take after my mother's side, Leo. More the practical type. At least I try to be. Gosh! Is there any vermouth in this?"

It was important, Luzzatto reminded himself, to bridle his tongue.

"Excuse, excuse," sang the waiter, and put down two more martinis.

Luzzatto sat thinking of his father. He looked up. "I met him this morning in New York, Leo. I was shocked by his looks—oh, not so much his health but his spirits. He's always been so robust, so vivacious, and suddenly all the juices seemed out of him. It was a wrench this morning to see him like that. Isn't it hot in here?"

The cocktail glass, he saw, was magically refilled, and then somehow empty. Another voice, pitched higher and slurred, seemed to be carrying the discourse. The antipasto, drenched in vinegar and oil, was quite good.

"Am I getting crocked, Leo?" asked the other voice.

"—smoked mussels," came a distant reply.

"We were talking about Cesare? Yes, yes! Well, it was tough, Leo," he said thickly. "Really tough. He kept apologizing for not remembering that I've got my own troubles. I told him he was entitled to every cent I've got. What else is it for? Who cares about money? What's this?"

"Pasta," said the waiter. "More wine?"

"Am I drinking wine?"

"Yes, yes."

"Well, thanks. Say, it's hot! I never saw anything more depressing in my life than the shop. I remember a time when it was full of people eating cheese and bologna sandwiches, arguing everything from D'Annunzio's taste for discharging libido behind roadside hedges—wonderful smelly stories about Eleanora Duse right up your alley, Leo—and the outlook in Catalonia. Those old line philosophical anarchist boys are still there, the only force, let me tell you, still holding out—"

"Out against what?"

"—against this, uh, horrible trend to universal conformity, stultification. Worst thing, Cesare always wrote, is this complete rigidity of thought especially in the radical wing. Ever try to say a good word for the Church? Well, Cesare did in his time. This may come as a shock but Cesare Luzzatto really believes in freedom. I mean, he really thinks freedom is a good thing. He's not just talking, it's in his heart. Weakness like that can be fatal. Think for yourself and you wind up a party of one. Lonely old man, Cesare! What were we talking about?"

"—roadside hedges?"

"Oh, yes! Did you ever see an empty printing shop, Leo? Full of dust and tarpaulins and chattel mortgages? It was suddenly squalid, dead. One bulb dangling and deepening the gloom. It was sad, sad as hell. I almost broke down. Especially when he laughed and called it Adam Smith's revenge."

"—cacciatore!" cried the waiter.

Luzzatto was playing a ponderous game, teetering along a line, striving to keep the whirlwind in focus, aware that one misstep would bring dire reprisals from the Unknown. Somewhere in the tangle was a thread of meaning.

"Tortoni, gentlemen? Zabaglione?"

"I brought him up to date on the lawsuit. He told me finally that he never cared much for Ullman. He felt that Ullman had used me for a good thing. I answered that I had used Ullman too. He said 'Wasn't that permissible, Davido? You're young and this man is old. Isn't it proper for the young to exploit the old? But is the converse proper? Only the lowest forms of life feed on their young.' I tell you, Leo—" A painful frown.

"What's wrong with all that?" Katz-Moebius asked.

Luzzatto worked a thick tongue with difficulty. "Don't you see? Even Cesare's got some idea that I exploited Ullman. Everybody's got the impression that he had the main part of the discovery—that I'm some sort of impulsive and erratic idiot who latched on—" He stared blindly. "But that's not the point. The door was plastered with a sheriff's notice of sale and we talked about his financial picture. What could I say, Leo? It came at the wrong time."

"Why is this time especially wrong?"

Luzzatto opened and closed a mouth coated with mucilage. "Because I wanted to help him out, Leo, and I couldn't. I had to tell him I couldn't do a thing. I'm strapped, you see? The Center's in trouble!" A pause of labored breathing. "Did you know Brandywine decided to hold up the quarterly royalty payment? Well?"

"Yes, Dave, I knew," said Katz-Moebius thoughtfully. "I was one of the first to be told."

"Huh? Why—why didn't you tell me?"

Katz-Moebius wiped a greasy mouth and signaled for espressos. "I did tell you in effect," he said impatiently. "I was drunk that night, but not as drunk as I sounded. Why do you suppose I called? Because I am so abjectly impressed by those idiotic press releases of Podell's? Or because I cannot endure the thought of a fish gasping in the net. I warned you to get that lawyer off our backs. Well, you see that industry has ways of striking back. Of course we are holding up royalty payments."

"Oh, Christ! Let me think!" Luzzatto folded his arms and shivered. "You know what that decision means, Leo? Not to get those royalties? Wha'—what commitments we've made?"

"I've got some idea," said Katz-Moebius brutally.

"But why? Why? It's like telling the world that Brandywine is washing its hands of us. Don't they want us to win this lawsuit?"

The question was considered and weighed from many angles. "Yes. But I have an idea they'd rather not see this go to trial."

"But why? What have *they* got to lose?"

An expressive shrug. "It's beyond my limited understanding, my boy. It has something to do with the basic position. A thought has been circulating in our legal department that Ullman can destroy the whole structure of this operation. Our rights are derived through the university. If he can rescind the original agreement, our position is entirely impaired. But there's something more subtle involved." Katz-Moebius paused.

"Subtle? What?"

"The patent application recited that you and Ullman jointly discovered the stuff. If that statement is untrue as to either of you, the patent, I am told, can be declared void."

A wind began to howl in a wilderness of confusion and pain. Luzzatto struggled to understand. "That—that means that I'm precluded to deny Ullman's claim under the patent?"

"Exactly."

"I'm really drunk! Why hasn't Seixas told me this? Or Brandywine?"

"They will in time," said Katz-Moebius grimly. "It's the last thing we'd like to admit—even among ourselves. How would you handle the problem?"

"I'd offer money."

"That's been done." The visit of Foxx, Podell and Strollo to the farmhouse at New London was described. "Three wise men went bearing gifts and came back with empty hands. Ullman has no interest but to recapture the original position."

"How high did they go?" Luzzatto asked.

"He stopped them at three hundred thousand," said Katz-Moebius succinctly. "Aside from his claims against you, he may be able to concoct some future action against Brandywine."

"Action? For what?"

"Who knows? When they start charging conspiracies, where do they stop?" Katz-Moebius waited quietly. "We relied on your warranties, and there's no telling what action we may take to recapture our losses if the patent should prove invalid."

"They'd do that to us?" wondered Luzzatto. "After taking all the benefits of the discovery?"

"Are you surprised?"

"No, I imagine not," said Luzzatto in low, dreary tones. "It's all accumulating at once. How can I go home with this kind of news?" He looked up piteously. "Do you know what else I learned this morning from my father? What precipitated the crisis? It was the most petty, crushing reprisal you can imagine." He swallowed. "Jim Strollo's been his friend for thirty years. Financial anchor for the paper all this time—and just now, when he's really needed, he held up his personal check for the support of the paper. Why? Could only be me!"

"Not reprisal," said Katz-Moebius. "A quiet indication of the position. Didn't you expect that?"

"Yes. In a way, I suppose I did," said Luzzatto after a moment, struggling against a growing sense of nausea. The scrawl from Florida was painful in his thoughts. He said with wonder, "It seems that everyone, everything is to be hurt through me, engulfed in this poisonous thing, even my poor father. Oh, not that he'll understand! He'll never grasp the basic truth that I'm just beginning to see—that in this kind of thing there are no limits. We can't afford to spare anyone, can we?" He paused on the brink of emotion. "Where does it stop, Leo? Where?"

Katz-Moebius shrugged sardonically. "I'm not sure the lunatic wouldn't break the patents if he could. A result like that would dedicate biocin to the public. We're not ready to give up those rights." A meaningful pause. "Are you?"

Luzzatto looked up with a snarl. "No!"

"I seem to recall some contrary sentiments?"

"I was once talked out of that notion by Victor Ullman," said Luzzatto vindictively. "I'm still learning from the man!" An unendurable moment passed. "Leo, if you were me, how far would you go against Ullman in court?"

"The limit," said Katz-Moebius grimly. "Wouldn't you?"

"I—"

Luzzatto put a hand to his mouth and turned green. A whirligig of light began to revolve—

"Behind the partition!" cried the waiter.

In a noisome cabinet smelling of disinfectant a spewing torrent gave up a feast of corruption. He told himself that he was drunk, but he knew that he was not. In the midst of the debauch was a new cruelty that calculated— a knowledge of purpose that would survive to another day.

Chapter 22

THE ORDEAL OF PRE-TRIAL EXAMINATION BEGAN IN THE BAR BUILDING of Salt Hills—a small, pretty town ten miles from East Haverstraw which served as county seat for Merton County. A large, sunny library in the offices of Messrs. Newton, Hatch & George, Attorneys-at-Law, had been commandeered for quick access to the judge sitting across the street in the Supreme Court Building.

Luzzatto took his place at a conference table, flanked by Philip Seixas and Horatio Dotson. Before him sat transcripts of testimony given by several scores of prior witnesses—a collection which now included officials of Brandywine Laboratories. All this prior matter was background, he reminded himself, to be compared with testimony he was about to give. Thankfully, Eva had been passed over.

As to this sword which still hung over them, he had done his best to reassure her. Earlier that morning he had promised again that she would not be called.

"Why not?" she had said apprehensively. "What makes you think I won't be dragged in?"

"Victor doesn't want to open that box," he had replied. "Besides, his lawyer would rather depend on our failure to call you." He had paused somberly. "Phil won't pull that on you either, Evvie. I won't let him."

"How can you prevent?"

"If Phil dares to hand you a subpoena," he said carefully, "or disturb you again in any way, I'll throw the case, Evvie. I swear I will! I can't control the other side, but this is one point where I've got the last word."

"You told that to Mr. Seixas?"

"Yes."

"What if you need my testimony at the trial?"

"That's a long way off," he had replied. "Before that happens, I'll have my chance at Victor. Maybe it will end the case, maybe not." He forced a smile and kissed her. "By that time, you'll have the baby."

"Yes," she said. "Of course," and the conversation had ended with an embrace.

Luzzatto drew a breath and glanced about. Dotson's pallor and excitement, he observed, seemed equal to his own. Seixas was suave and controlled, remarkably silent, wearing displeasure behind an impassive mask. Across the table sat the opposing lawyer, Emil Dirksen, and an attractive woman, Mrs. Harriet Bascombe, who had been introduced as his partner. During the preliminaries, she had passed innumerable notes which Dirksen read and accepted, or discarded with a contemptuous wave of the hand.

Dirksen said. "Shall we begin?"

Emil Dirksen was a small man of calm and dignity who wore conservative clothes and simple gold links in soft French cuffs. An unpleasant mouth was a bloodless, lipless gash that held all emotions in constraint.

Luzzatto scribbled impulsively and with a nervous grin passed a note to Philip Seixas. "Childe Roland has to the Dark Tower come."

Seixas glanced at the note without change of expression and wrote a reply. "I want you to take these proceedings seriously."

"I'm quite serious," wrote Luzzatto. He turned away, offended.

Dirksen said, "Please ask Dr. Ullman to step in."

Mrs. Bascombe arose and rapped twice. After a moment the door opened and Ullman stepped into the room with a quiet manner. It was a nice dramatic touch. A smile hovered as he extended a hand.

"Nah! Luzzatto, can we go through the forms?"

Luzzatto stared coldly and turned his back. There was a frown of disapproval from Philip Seixas. Then began a ritual of courtesies and formalities which, despite false smiles and pretended suavities, told Luzzatto that he was at grips with a final moment of decision.

The following day a newspaperwoman at the Associated Press in Rockefeller Center in New York City handed a telephone receiver to a man at the next desk. "Al?"

"Yes, Adrian?"

"Your friend. Professor Ullman. Long distance."

"You take the pest."

"I told him you were here."

The newspaperman shifted a cigar and took the call. "Hello, Professor. What's the good word today?" Impatience gave way to professional interest. A note was made on a chit of paper. "Yup! Yup! Got it! Will do!" The receiver was replaced and thoughtfully considered. After some moments of deliberation, he called a lawyer in Wall Street.

"Dirksen? I just got a tip you're going to force Luzzatto into open court?"

A voice asked sharply, "Who told you that?"

"Please! I don't want to waste our time. The question is whether to get a man on the job?"

The soft voice advised that no statements would be made to the press except in court.

"Sure. But that courthouse is a couple of hours away from here, and I'd like to save somebody a trip."

A long pause. "There's a good chance of that. It would be unusual, but the judge up there may want to take over the examination, especially if you send a man from New York to cover the proceedings. This young man has been an obstreperous witness."

"I'm told you've been pretty rough."

The same long pause. "Have a man up there tomorrow morning. I don't think you'll waste your time."

The stab of pain struck and Luzzatto closed his eyes. He was sensitive to the atmosphere of a chill, bright courtroom and the faces of strangers turned to the witness chair. A low-voiced conversation was going forward at the old-fashioned bench to his right. Only snatches and bits of the conversation reached his ears.

Judge Willard Cohalan kept two books of minutes at the bench. The larger, bound in red buckram, was an official record. The smaller was a diary for personal edification in which he kept nonlegal observations of future literary value. He was an ambitious young man and the effect of literary output on the advancement of certain colleagues in the First Department had left a deep impression. He made a note in his diary and received a message from his secretary, which told him that a messy divorce matter would require his presence in chambers later in the day. "Gentlemen, you're free to use this courtroom if it's agreeable with the clerk. Meanwhile, I'll be glad to preside for a time," he advised pleasantly.

Dirksen smiled stiffly. "Judge, I don't like to create discomfort," he observed, polishing his glasses. "If you'll admonish this young man to answer my questions without losing his temper and to heed Mr. Seixas's directions, I'm willing to go back to chambers and continue in private. It hasn't been our idea to impose this burden."

Seixas forced the tired smile of a lawyer embarrassed by a difficult client. "I'm afraid this young man has the bit between his teeth, Your Honor. I'm just as unhappy about imposing this burden, but a proceeding in open court might have a good effect on him. He's had no prior exposure to Mr. Dirksen's tactics and he's a bit sore at some of yesterday's questions. They were pretty rough." Genial smiles expressed a level of professionalism. "He's never had the pleasure of having had his motives put in question. It's upsetting."

The judge swiveled about, considering the position, but in fact his decision had been reached. He was curious to see Emil Dirksen in action and a lawsuit of national interest did not often arise in Merton County.

"You may proceed," said the judge.

The lawyers returned to their battle stations. A slight hum of conversation among the spectators subsided. Luzzatto felt a flush of anger mount.

"May I be heard?" he asked resentfully.

"Yes, surely," said the judge courteously.

"Well, I'm ready to answer any legitimate question that relates to the case, Your Honor, but I'm not prepared to go into personal matters."

"Oh, good," murmured a newspaperwoman.

"Sh!" A bailiff strode down the aisle with an admonitory eye, snapping his fingers for silence.

"I see, I see," said the judge with unexpected mildness. "Perhaps I ought to explain the custom, Professor Luzzatto, although I'm sure your lawyer has covered this ground. Objections will be noted by the stenographer, but unless your lawyer directs that you not answer, the testimony should be given without forcing the court to intervene. Is that clear enough?"

"Well, it's clear enough," Luzzatto said finally. "Except that Mr. Seixas is not acting as my lawyer in this matter. He is representing the Foundation."

The judge glanced inquiringly at Seixas.

The lawyer rose. "I'm afraid that Professor Luzzatto has strong feelings regarding his privacy. It has to do with his concept of personal integrity."

"Do you accept this repudiation?" asked the judge.

Seixas replied gravely, "I don't regard Professor Luzzatto's decision in that light. It is simply a refusal to accept my guidance where his personal interests are involved. I can't accept the responsibility of imposing my own views."

A buzz of interest arose among the spectators. The judge tapped the bench and turned to Luzzatto with a stare of inquiry. "Will you explain yourself?"

Luzzatto raised a defiant chin. "I have my position as a scientist to consider. I can't possibly surrender the final decision as to my testimony to anyone. Not even to Mr. Seixas."

The court was suddenly quiet. Judge Cohalan fixed the young scientist with a keen and wondering glance. "These are complicated issues," he said mildly. "Do you feel qualified to assume these responsibilities?"

Luzzatto sat thinking of his answer. "Your Honor, the scientific questions are as complicated as the legal, and a great many of these problems are moral. In those areas, I deny the competence of courts or lawyers to sit in judgment on scientists! It may sound arbitrary, but I will not answer questions which I feel are unjustified."

"Not even if I direct that you answer?"

"But I'm entitled to object before you rule? Isn't that what you said?"

"I've explained that," said the judge quietly. "This is a preliminary examination. An objection reserves the point for decision upon the trial. Meanwhile you must answer responsively. I don't quite see the objection."

"I should think it's obvious. May I explain? At this point Dr. Ullman doesn't know much about the discovery of biocin. If he were called to the stand now and asked to substantiate his story under oath, it would be impossible for him to give a coherent narrative to correspond to the historical facts. His whole strategy is to squeeze out the data from me which he needs to synthesize a false analogue of the truth. He's terribly adept at that process."

At the plaintiff's table Ullman sat with folded arms, erect and unmoved, letting a tolerant smile indicate an amused reaction to the display of emotion. Evidently, thought the judge, the matter would not be as simple as promised. He said quietly, "Professor Luzzatto, you have touched on a point of criticism of this procedure with which I cannot quarrel. However," he added with a glance to the reporters, "you will proceed."

Luzzatto flushed. "I suppose I have no choice, but I regard your ruling as highly unfair," he said coldly.

Judge Cohalan considered the note of challenge at length. After a moment he instructed the stenographer to expunge the last unfortunate and gratuitous remark, asked the bailiff to open a window and turned finally to the lawyers. He said quietly, "I think, Mr. Dirksen, we had better get on and see what happens."

Dirksen arose and walked forward with quiet deference. A memorandum rustled in his hand. "Professor Luzzatto, we managed to identify a number of exhibits on Monday before we began to run into difficulties. I will come back later to the exhibits, but I would like you to advise the court whether you have carefully read the pleadings in this suit?"

Luzzatto gripped the arms of the witness chair. "Yes."

"In that case, you're aware, I imagine, that the complaint recites that the relationship between you and Dr. Ullman during the time in question was one of great friendship and intimacy. Isn't that the fact?"

"Yes, I'm aware that the complaint makes that assertion."

"And it was a period of friendship?"

"No!" said Luzzatto coldly.

Dirksen paused at the jury rail. "Do you mean to state now that you were not friends?" he demanded with an air of utter surprise.

"Would you call this lawsuit an act of friendship?" Luzzatto retorted.

The lawyer adopted an air of courtesy. "I'm directing your attention to a period almost eight years ago. At the time of the discovery were you friends?"

"We were not friends," said Luzzatto obstinately.

"What was the relationship?"

Luzzatto shot a vindictive glance at Ullman. "Friendship is a two-way street, Mr. Dirksen. I was his friend. I'm not convinced that he was mine."

"This is hindsight?"

"Yes."

"You had nothing for Dr. Ullman but devotion?"

"You can ask anyone. Yes!"

The lawyer picked up this retort swiftly. "I can ask anyone because all your expressions regarding Dr. Ullman were invariably those of affection and respect?"

"Yes."

"And never of derision?"

Luzzatto hesitated. "Well, of course, Mr. Dirksen, a certain amount of banter goes on among the students. A professor's foibles get picked up and exaggerated and possibly I might have joined in some byplay. I have no distinct recollection of any such thing."

Dirksen paused. "Who is Mrs. Nakamura?"

Luzzatto was drawn into a brief description of the informal canteen on the third floor. Dirksen asked whether on a certain occasion he had not characterized Dr. Ullman as an intolerable egotist and petty despot. Had not a dozen students and Mrs. Nakamura been present?

Luzzatto said stolidly, "I remember that I lost my temper and sounded

279

off a bit, but that was after he gave me a reduced grade in genetics. I didn't mind the mark so much, but I resented the reason." He recalled the episode that followed the visit of Cesare and Nella Luzzatto to the third floor laboratory, giving this information with an air of amusement, deprecatory of youthful emotionalism. "I thought I was being punished unfairly. It was not inconsistent with devotion."

"You thought it unfair to be punished for violating a strict rule of the laboratory?"

"Yes."

"Although willing to take its benefits?"

Luzzatto considered the point. "Obviously the mark was unfair," he replied, annoyed, "because when I objected, Dr. Ullman raised the mark and told me it was intended as a lesson in discipline. I made an apology and the whole thing blew over. But I really don't see the relevance to this lawsuit," he added, turning to the bench. The judge had been glancing occasionally at Philip Seixas who had assumed a posture of indifference and boredom. Quite swiftly, he observed, a certain atmosphere had been suggested of callowness and immaturity. He nodded slowly. "Yes, Mr. Dirksen? What's your point?"

Dirksen made a deliberate circuit of the arena, apparently studying the pleadings, but covertly observing the reactions of spectators.

"It ought to be clear, Your Honor," he said, "that these questions relate to our basic cause of action. The complaint recites that a close personal relationship existed between the parties which led Dr. Ullman to repose implicit faith in Professor Luzzatto. In due course Dr. Ullman will testify that he regarded Professor Luzzatto as his most gifted student, a young man for whom he felt, and still feels the greatest affection, although not the same credulity as formerly." A smile was permitted to appear. "It is the basis of our claim that Professor Luzzatto abused a position of trust for his own personal advantage. These questions therefore are entirely in order."

The judge made a note and turned to the witness. "Professor Luzzatto, I suggest that you answer without further objection. Mr. Dirksen, you may put the question again."

Luzzatto raised a hand. "Just a minute."

"Yes?"

Luzzatto glanced with resentment at Seixas. "I'd like to know if Mr. Seixas has any objections to make on behalf of the Haverstraw Foundation?"

Seixas looked up impassively. "No."

"I see," said Luzzatto, having established a point. "In that case, I'll

280

register my own objection against these tactics, but I'll answer the question if the court directs."

"The court directs," said the judge evenly.

"Good!" Luzzatto sat forward with anger. "Dr. Ullman bases his claim on the theory that he reposed implicit trust in my integrity. Well, I trusted him in equal measure, so we're quits. I accept that statement as the premise of the action. I hope it will be remembered when we come down to the trial."

The silence was painful, then, "Professor Luzzatto," said Dirksen with an edge, "during this same period were there other occasions when you expressed sentiments of ridicule or hositility against Dr. Ullman?"

The question was put quietly. A slow flush mounted. "I never spoke with hostility."

"Then with ridicule?"

Luzzatto hesitated. "I have no specific recollection," he said slowly. "Over the years I might have joined in bull sessions where the faculty came in for student talk. I just don't recall."

"Oh, come!" said Dirksen skeptically.

"Well, I don't!" Luzzatto stirred with annoyance. "Students are always taking the faculty apart, poking fun. I won't deny that I might have made some lighthearted remarks."

Dirksen returned to the table and examined a portfolio before looking up. "Professor Luzzatto, isn't it a fact that during this period of incubation, so to speak, you expressed your devotion to Dr. Ullman on many occasions in terms which might be regarded as more than fulsome?"

Brows knitted. "Not that I recall."

Dirksen handed up a book. The volume had been published in 1866 and contained the paper read by Gregor Mendel on hybridization in plants to the *Verhandlungen naturforschender Verein* in Brunn. He called attention to the inscription on the flyleaf:

"With gratitude and devotion to a wise and forgiving teacher in appreciation of guidance and much forgiveness."

Luzzatto flushed. "Yes. I wrote that inscription. It was a sentimental gift."

"Was this a sincere expression of your feelings?"

"I'm not sure I recall my feelings."

Dirksen took a step forward. "Well, then, was it meant to be deceptive?"

"No, no! I was feeling emotional, I guess," said Luzzatto uncomfortably. "As I recall, I picked up this book in Provincetown where my wife

281

and I had gone for our honeymoon. I was a bit younger and many exciting things were happening. I won't disavow that inscription. It was how I felt at the time."

A stiff smile formed. "And how you wanted Dr. Ullman to believe you felt? Gratitude and devotion and appreciation?"

Luzzatto shrugged. "I suppose so. I wasn't calculating the effect. It simply shows that I was extremely attached to Dr. Ullman and to his —his whole family." Ullman seemed unmoved, unhearing, at the delicate nuance. "I thought I was sending that to an older friend."

"Ah?"

Dirksen studied his notes. "You seem to stress the fact that Dr. Ullman is an older man. Does this have any significance to you? In the quality of the relationship?" A moment passed in which the lawyer's gaze was unwavering.

"No. Not really, Mr. Dirksen. I suppose, lurking in the back of my mind, I felt that his interest in me was a bit, well, forced. Looking back, I see that the friendship he expected could hardly bridge the difference in age. You're making too much of a single item."

"Oh, I rather think more than a single item. H'm!" A brief search at counsel table, then, "I show you a letter to Dr. Ullman postmarked Johannesburg which refers to a lecture you delivered to a scientific congress in that city. This letter assures Dr. Ullman that you made clear to the delegates his vital role in the discovery of biocin—"

"I know that letter," said Luzzatto abruptly.

The exhibit went into evidence. "Tell me, Professor Luzzatto. Did you in fact advise the delegates that Dr. Ullman's role was vital?"

The exhibit, Luzzatto observed, was a rambling and enthusiastic description of a public triumph for biocin. It was the first such announcement made outside the United States and a lively curiosity had been evoked among the delegates.

"I may have said something to that effect, Mr. Dirksen, but I doubt that I ever publicly called Dr. Ullman's role in the discovery vital."

"Why not?" asked Dirksen calmly.

"Because it simply wasn't true," said Luzzatto with exasperation, observing that the judge had swung about with renewed attention. "I'm sure the transcript will bear me out. You can get it here in three days if you cable Professor Starbuck at Witwatersrand University. I never called his role vital."

"Then if this letter says that you did," asked Dirksen quietly, "it is wrong?"

A greenish tint was showing through the pallor. "I wrote that letter, as

282

I wrote many things, out of regard for Dr. Ullman's sensibilities. I was at the other end of the world with a smashing success. I wanted to share the moment with my old teacher. I might have been a bit effusive in a personal letter. I never imagined that it would be used one day against me."

Dirksen rocked skeptically. "Oh, come! Let's be frank about this thing, Professor Luzzatto. Doesn't this letter show the fact? A spontaneous piece written three or four years before you had any inkling of this lawsuit?"

Luzzatto stared coldly. "What makes you think it was spontaneous, Mr. Dirksen? I had received an airmail letter from Dr. Ullman earlier in the week in which he specifically asked me to stress his alleged role in the discovery as head of the laboratory. That's why I wrote that reply."

"It was a lie?"

"It was a diplomatic statement."

"But not the truth?"

"No."

"Why was it made?"

"I didn't want to hurt his feelings."

Dirksen stepped back and repeated the testimony with incredulity. "Is that what you ask the court to believe? That you falsely led Professor Ullman to believe you had made a public announcement in his favor? That this was merely a silly deception not to hurt his feelings?"

Luzzatto stared. "Over the years I did many things not to hurt his feelings," he said grimly.

Evidently satisfied, Dirksen strolled back to the rail like a matador leaving a bull bewildered by a quick flourish of the cape. A dozen similar forgotten items were explored before a recess was called. Luzzatto stiffly got off the stand and strode into a corridor where he took refuge in a telephone booth. He paused, breathing heavily, before he called home. The line was instantly alive.

"How is it going?" asked Eva anxiously. She listened in silence. "Oh, Dave," she said dispiritedly, "you expose yourself by a show of feeling. You mustn't transfer all this emotion against Victor to the lawyer. Can't you wear a mask like everyone else?"

"I don't care what I'm exposing," he replied, offended. "I won't let them impose these tactics. You recall that volume I sent from Provincetown? He saved up every scrap and bit—even that book we sent from our honeymoon. Hello? Hello?"

Eva was silent. "I feel like a traitor, not being there with you. Let me come out? I won't go into the courtroom. I'll wait somewhere outside."

"No! Don't come here," he exclaimed, and then Dotson was scratching at the window, motioning that the proceedings were about to resume. "I'll call again, Evvie," he said softly, "I love you," and hung up.

Eva lit a cigarette, perplexed and alarmed. Toward noon she dressed and called for a taxi.

Dirksen exhausted the previous topic and went on.

"Professor Luzzatto, in the testimony given by Dr. Wodzick, he stated on page 103, lines 7 to 23 inclusive, that the discovery of biocin did not become a matter of common knowledge in the school until September when regular classes were resumed. He also stated that the matter was never discussed by Dr. Ullman, but that all knowledge of the background was the result of statements and representations made by you to fellow students and faculty. Is that correct?"

Luzzatto stirred restively. "It was perfectly natural to talk about my work with the gang. I regarded them as friends and colleagues who could be trusted."

The issue was explored in detail before an unpleasant suggestion was made. "In other words you discussed this development in Dr. Ullman's laboratory although he had requested discretion prior to publication?"

"Yes."

"Is it unusual for scientists to keep their developments secret in this manner?"

"It is not unusual."

"Yet you disobeyed your chief's directive?"

Luzzatto stared as one might at a distasteful but fascinating organism dragged from ocean depths. "I completely disagreed with the concept of secrecy within the department. I thought that approach harmful and destructive."

"The development was made in Professor Ullman's laboratory? With tools and equipment furnished by him?"

"It was not his laboratory. It was the university's."

"But he had given you its use?"

Luzzatto flushed. "I have never denied that Dr. Ullman treated me generously, as far as that went. I had no thought of obeying or disobeying any directives. I simply felt that he was being excessively suspicious and a little, well, Old World."

"You knew that Dr. Ullman entertained rather strict views regarding the duties and obligations of subordinates to the head of a laboratory?"

"He made that very clear," said Luzzatto coldly.

Dirksen placed the transcript of Wodzick's testimony on the table. "To your knowledge did Dr. Ullman ever discuss the discovery of biocin with outsiders prior to publication?"

Luzzatto glanced quickly at Philip Seixas but found neither guidance nor comfort. He smiled grimly. "Dr. Ullman was extremely secretive. I would be surprised if he said anything at all to an outsider." At a warning cough he went silent.

"Then all this so-called common knowledge of your role in the discovery can be traced back to a limited source—you and Mrs. Luzzatto? Is that a fair inference?"

"And Dr. Katz-Moebius," said Luzzatto.

"Who likewise received his information from you and your wife?" The suggestion lingered. Luzzatto drew a deep breath and gazed at the ceiling while seconds ticked away. "I think that you can forget Dr. Katz-Moebius. He left the university at the end of August. Also I think you can omit my wife from the question. She was an onlooker."

"Then you are the only person responsible for the prevailing belief that biocin in truth was solely your original discovery?"

Luzzato stirred restively. "Haven't you omitted a significant name?"
"Oh? Who?"

Throughout the proceedings Luzzatto had been conscious of Victor Ullman's magnetic blue eyes staring with fixity of purpose. In spite of all preparation, their first meeting in chambers had been a shock. Ullman was looking much older, he thought. A heavy stoop marked the thick shoulders. He now was wearing heavy lenses through which his gaze loomed with preternatural significance. The cheeks had flattened markedly and the lines running from the nostrils were like crevasses. He met Luzzatto's glance with a thoughtful nod which seemed to estimate the scene with scientific objectivity. It was almost as though he would at any moment fish out a kitchen match for the habitual cigarette.

Luzzatto waited quietly. "Dr. Josephine Ullman."

Dirksen stiffened. "Was she present when the discovery was made?"
"No," said Luzzatto evenly. "She was spending the summer at Lake Marah with her parents. But she knew what was going on in the laboratory. Didn't you find that out when you paid her a visit in San Martino last February, Mr. Dirksen?"

There was a pause. "You seem remarkably well-informed," said Dirksen calmly. There was a stir of interest and in the nonplussed silence the judge called a short recess to answer a telephone call in chambers. Philip Seixas arose and strolled to the witness chair with outward lack of concern. He offered a mint and spoke in a low tone.

"Was that clever, Dave?"

285

Luzzatto shrugged sullenly. "Why let him suggest that I went around like a sneak creating impressions?" A handkerchief nervously mopped a wet neck.

Seixas said somberly, "You've got a nimble mind, Dave, but don't let that facility lure you into these indiscretions. Can't you see that Dirksen's baiting you into these disclosures?"

"I just plugged a loophole," said Luzzatto restively. The courtroom now had a measure of informal disorder as reporters and spectators chatted among themselves. "I don't see what harm it did to get this on the record."

"How can I make this clear, Dave? Whatever you say now is for their benefit, not yours. If you've got a point, save it for the trial. Why let them know you've been in touch with the woman?"

Luzzatto said grimly. "You may think you know the case, Phil, but I'm not sure you do. It's important to let Ullman know that certain things haven't been forgotten."

"What does that mean?" asked Seixas evenly.

Luzzatto shrugged sullenly and the judge returned with flouncing robes, looking refreshed. When order was restored, Dirksen reverted to an earlier point.

"Professor Luzzatto, you made reference to Dr. Ullman's views on the conduct of a research laboratory. Were those views made clear prior to matriculation?"

"Oh, yes!"

"What were those views?"

Luzzatto changed an uncomfortable position. "Well, it's so hard to reconstruct, Mr. Dirksen. Dr. Ullman had the general European notion that the head of a research lab is entitled to put his name on all publications coming under his jurisdiction. It's a strong custom for the chief to take credit for the work of his subordinates." A pause, then, "Whether or not deserved."

"That's not the custom here?"

Luzzatto hesitated. "I don't say it doesn't happen. Frankly, there's a good deal of heartache connected with the problem, but in general our scientists are more inclined to be generous about these things."

"What is your view?" asked Dirksen suggestively.

"In my view, the leader of a research group ought to avoid credit where possible for discoveries that arise solely from the rest of the group's activities. In my own practice I try to withhold my name except where it would be wrong not to take credit." A grim smile appeared. "I don't believe in self-stultification."

Dirksen said quietly, "I'm sure you don't, Professor Luzzatto. Can you tell us precisely what position Dr. Ullman took?"

"So far as I can recall, he told me that the policy of the department was to publish all papers jointly on the most generous possible basis to the student. I believe I am quoting his exact words."

Dirksen sauntered back to the rail and contemplated the witness. He seemed to consider a variety of approaches to the next question. "And joint publication would imply joint credit in the eyes of the scientific world? Did you accept that necessary implication?"

Luzzato hesitated. "It seems like a fair inference. I must point out," he added quickly, "that this is only a presumption. It is not necessarily the fact."

"But a presumption which you knew would publicly arise?"

"Yes."

"And you made no objection?"

"I was in no position to object."

"But did you object?"

"No." Luzzatto dabbed the corners of his mouth.

"Was anyone else present?"

Luzzatto thought back to a hot afternoon in September and a door that had opened on a new world of experience. "I really don't recall, sir. It was the first day that I came to see Dr. Ullman. I recall now that he engaged me in a discussion of the metaphysics of science. Science as an instrument of truth. I might add that this was a constant theme. May I have a glass of water?"

Over the rim of the glass he met the stare of his adversary with a tinge of satisfaction. A warning note had been established. He went on with meticulous, challenging detail to describe the first meeting. Dirksen asked quietly, "Why do you tell us all this?"

"Because you're trying to twist the first talk into a form of business commitment," said Luzzatto, vexed. "It was nothing of the sort. What did I know about business?"

Dirksen rocked contemplatively. "Wasn't there an arrangement for a stipend?"

Ullman sat back during this exchange, smiling gravely, deploring the spectacle of a younger, misguided colleague. Pity, tolerance, understanding, gentle irony, reproach were expressed by his watchful manner.

Luzzatto dropped his gaze and came to the question. His stipend, he agreed, had come out of no university funds.

"Did you know that this money came out of Dr. Ullman's pocket?"

"That was not the way it was expressed," said Luzzatto with annoyance.

"I've already given my understanding that it came from a fund at his disposal. He never said it was his own money that I was being paid."

"It was money he might have retained?"

"Yes," said Luzzatto wearily, "but then he couldn't have exploited my efforts for that wine process. I've already explained that I strongly objected to wasting my time on that banal type of work. I made that very clear to Dr. Ullman. He promised to let me pursue my own line of research, but somehow he never found it convenient to give me the time. I was really tied down for that miserable stipend that he got me."

"Doesn't it come down to this, Professor Luzzatto? That you chafed at any sort of control by your teacher from your first interview? That you rejected the ordinary supervision and guidance which a teacher expects a student to accept without demur or rebellious attitudes?"

Luzzatto glanced at Ullman.

"Perhaps," he conceded after a painful struggle. "But quite frankly it was because I then saw that the wine project was empty of value." It was an honest statement and he felt better at once.

"And yet you stayed with that project?"

"Yes."

"For money?"

"Of course!" said Luzzatto, stung.

"At the time you accepted that money, Professor Luzzatto, did you know the terms of the arrangement between Dr. Ullman and Brandywine?"

For the first time in the proceedings Philip Seixas arose quietly and called attention to a rule of evidence against reception of secondary evidence. The objection was noted, the question repeated.

Luzzatto stirred restively. "Well, in general I knew that Brandywine was supporting this industrial project. I assumed if anything of commercial value were to emerge, patent applications would probably be assigned to the sponsor. I had no liking for that situation, but of course there was nothing inherently immoral about it. I simply disapproved the use of university facilities for such purposes." He turned for support to a memorandum which represented the tedious months of effort. He was tiring rapidly as the morning advanced, finding it difficult to keep his thoughts in order.

Dirksen strolled about the room throwing out hard, precise questions to nail down the witness's recollection. "You knew that commitments had been made with respect to the problem to which you were assigned?"

"I assumed so. But I didn't learn the terms of the agreement until later."

"If you had been requested to assign a patent application to Brandywine Laboratories arising from the wine project, would you have done so?"

"Undoubtedly," said Luzzatto restively. "I recognized that the project was Dr. Ullman's personal affair. I had entirely different feelings for biocin."

"Because biocin was a success?"

"No!" Luzzatto removed his glasses. "Because it was mine."

The lawyer's voice dropped to a whisper. "Even though it was discovered while you were accepting financial aid under the basic agreements in evidence?"

Luzzatto searched carefully for words to express a bursting feeling. It was a point which had loomed for months. "I recognize what you're trying to accomplish, Mr. Dirksen. You're trying to bind me to contracts made by the university with Brandywine Laboratories. I think you're overlooking an essential point. Perhaps Dr. Ullman was an employee of the university at the time. I was not. I was a student and my objective was to improve my knowledge of science, to increase my skills and understanding as a researcher, to get my doctorate. I have never heard that a grant to a student gives rise to an employee relationship. I find the suggestion shocking. The university is expected to teach the student, not to exploit him."

Dirksen accepted the outburst calmly. "But in this case you were accepting your stipend from an industrial house?"

Luzzatto shook his head. "I think you're overlooking another vital point. I've already explained that the stipend was made available by Dr. Ullman from the fund at his disposal. He could have kept it entirely for himself, according to his version of the understanding, or spent it on equipment or anything. It was no longer money which belonged to the sponsor. I got my stipend from him just as students have always gotten help from interested persons—just as I was helping my own students before this lawsuit cut off my income. I was hardly bound, legally or morally, by his commercial obligations to others, merely because I was required to work at a lot of dreary routines that led nowhere!"

Dirksen remained rocking quietly and a trace of mockery appeared in the lidded eyes. The next question was put with surgical precision.

"In other words, Professor Luzzatto, you were actually the object of Dr. Ullman's personal bounty?"

"I have never denied his kindness," said Luzzatto, and felt the hot flush mount to his ears as the interrogation went on.

Chapter 23

A LONG DELAY TOOK PLACE DURING THE AFTERNOON SESSION, WHILE the lawyers exchanged jocularities in an empty courtroom. A clerk tipped Luzzatto a sympathetic wink just as the door opened and word was brought by a secretary that the judge would remain occupied in chambers for the rest of the afternoon but that the courtroom would remain placed at the convenience of the parties. With a sigh of dread Luzzatto arranged his notes, striving to keep the thread of recollection in order. Dirksen turned a page of transcript and looked up.

"Professor Luzzatto, Professor Tobiansky testified that important contributions to the literature on bacterial resistance preceded your work by a few years. Can you tell me how old the literature is on that subject?"

Luzzatto stared glassily. "In my opinion the earlier literature is not too relevant. My first ideas on bacterial resistance were formed before I knew that early material."

"Can you tell us when?"

"It's hard to say. I suppose I can go back to when I first got the notion that a percentage of mutations could be attributed to background radiation or cosmic rays. I suppose you know that background radiation is thought to account for at least five per cent of all spontaneous mutations."

"Was that idea novel?"

"It was novel so far as I was concerned. It led to a more important consideration—not the instability of the gene, but rather its relative high resistance to change. Evolution requires mutation, but if the rate were too high, life would be chaotic, impossible. I remember my surprise when I first grasped this concept and began to think of underlying mechanisms that might control the rate of mutation. I arrived at these ideas without regard to the literature."

"And before you met Dr. Ullman?"

"Yes."

"How old were you then?" asked Dirksen dryly.

"Fourteen," said Luzzatto seriously. "No, I think earlier, perhaps twelve. Later I found that these surmises had already received the attention of investigators, especially in connection with microbial resistance. Let me repeat that drug resistance is a subtle problem and even simple principles have been slow to emerge. The fact remains that a wide range of pathogens have learned to resist these antibiotic drugs. Suppose one day these organisms learn to overcome our natural defenses as well? Biocin has come along to give us a first and imperfect method to control this danger. The problem is to bring these fundamental processes of life under control. Now there's an added urgency."

Dirksen waited as a thoughtful expression settled in the pale face. Luzzatto turned to the window, visualizing a titanic thundercloud of mushroom shape, black and orange, lethal against the tranquil sky.

"I'll put it as simply as this. Humanity is also subject to the universal laws of life—and background radiation of the Earth has already doubled. The need is for something to counteract the danger of an explosive increase in the rate of mutation on the human level."

Dirksen consulted his notes. "When you met Dr. Ullman, had you any idea that the rate of mutation could be controlled?"

Luzzatto thought back. "Not at that time, I'm afraid," he said slowly. "What biocin seems to do is to mutate a wide range of these microorganisms to greater genetic stability and to fix their properties to our advantage. Whether a way may be found to extend the effect to humanity is pure conjecture. But can you imagine how vital it would be to control the genetic effects of radioactive fallout in human beings?"

"And profitable?" suggested Dirksen carelessly.

Luzzatto flushed. "Enormously!" he said nastily. "It almost justifies this spectacle, doesn't it? I wonder how you and your client would expect to divide the loot, Mr. Dirksen?"

Impassively Dirksen stared at the disturbed witness and retired for a low-voiced conversation at the table. There were vigorous nods, an exchange of views, and he came back with an air of renewed calculation.

"Professor Luzzatto, will you agree that these were still mere schoolboy speculations when you matriculated at Haverstraw?"

The stare was hostile. "It depends on definition, Mr. Dirksen. Even a schoolboy is entitled to speculate. I don't think my ideas lacked merit."

"I'm sure they had merit," Dirksen turned a page. "In your initial interview with Dr. Ullman, did you express the view that your ultimate goal was to understand and describe life processes in terms of physical and mathematical systems?"

Luzzatto looked surprised, almost amused. "Does your client remember in such detail?" Under the direct reference Ullman folded his arms and sat back. "Um. I may very well have done so, Mr. Dirksen, although I now realize that the idea is remote. On the other hand, some of those concepts are more than useful even now. I remember pointing to the problem of the stability of the gene as an example. According to quantum theory, you know, the large molecular structures of life tend to keep their configurations until the energy supplied reaches a certain discrete threshold figure. This figure, which is always a well-defined quantity, is thought to determine the amount of stability of the gene. Perhaps that notion was floating in my mind from the beginning."

"Did Dr. Ullman accept your general views?"

"He reacted violently."

"How so?"

"I'm not too sure I know what Dr. Ullman was really thinking. I can only tell you that he seemed offended for some reason with my preoccupation with analogues from the physical sciences. He has always argued that there is something beyond the purely physical which is the concern of science. He was expressing, I believe, a form of vitalism—or something beyond vitalism—because he was opposed to any degree of determinism in my thinking. He used to argue, not only that life mechanisms are endowed with direction and purpose, but that they are governed by some vital factor peculiar to life, some mysterious principle which dwells within living forms, which gives these qualities of purpose and direction. It's this principle which he identifies with principles of indeterminism and uncertainty of modern physics. He's often expressed the view that life involves an element of freedom—freedom of will, of choice—a random factor, which departs from the older causal laws of the physical sciences. But frankly, I don't see that our training as scientists qualifies us to make these metaphysical decisions. I feel that the scientist should stick to what he can prove or disprove. Dr. Ullman does not share these doubts."

Did anyone, Luzzatto wondered, sense the applicability of these recollections to the lawsuit? He was now skating on thin ice.

"Dr. Ullman's approach to these problems is nothing new, Mr. Dirksen. The questions of free will and moral responsibility and immortality are as old as philosophy. Besides, I don't see that analogies from nuclear physics have the slightest utility in dealing with problems of soul or deity. Oh, sure, these new conceptions of physics have changed our common sense ideas about the material world on the nuclear level, but what have they got to do with good or evil or ultimate questions of morality and existence? These are value concepts which lie outside space and time and the other abstractions of the physical sciences." He sat forward. "I'm not sure we've heard the last word from physics either. The idea of causality in physical law is far from doomed. Certainly we're a long way from that dead end in biology. The only value to clinging to the primitive sense of the mystery of things lies, I suppose, in keeping us from sinking into mechanistic dogmatism and a pessimistic view of life."

Ullman pulled out a familiar brown cigarette, examined it carefully, recalled his whereabouts, replaced the cylinder with a gesture of interest in the discourse. Dirksen folded his arms and rocked quietly. "Having said all this, Professor Luzzatto, do you still believe that quantum theory explains the rate of mutation?"

Luzzatto was startled into wariness. "No, Mr. Dirksen, I've got to admit that mutation rates found in nature proved lower than those I expected from physical theory alone. The rate seems controlled by mechanisms for which the physical theories have no sufficient explanation as yet."

"Was this pointed out to you by Dr. Ullman?"
"Yes."
"Before the discovery of biocin?"
"Yes."
"Did that modify your views?"
Luzzatto hesitated. "I'm willing to concede that I overstated the case. In that sense I was wrong—in the sense that I was premature—but that doesn't mean that Dr. Ullman was right. Time will tell."

Dirksen looked up narrowly. "Professor Luzzatto, I'd like to go back to the initial interview. Did you discuss bacterial resistance at that time?"

"Oh, yes. I had already begun a series of experiments. I showed my results to Dr. Ullman. He had some biting things to say about my supposed immaturity and lack of preparation for the work."

Dirksen leaned back against a rail and assumed an air of reasonable discourse. "Isn't it for the teacher to decide whether a student is qualified for a piece of difficult research?"

"I would expect the teacher to use good judgment. In my case, Dr. Ullman's judgment was bad. I was fully ready for that project on bacterial resistance as my notebooks will show."

"In your opinion?"
"Yes."

"But not in your teacher's opinion?"

"I don't know what his opinion was." Luzzatto shifted his position. "I know that he objected violently to that line of research. He didn't think it would lead to anything—or so he said. Apparently he has changed his mind since it led to the discovery of biocin."

Dirksen rested an elbow at the rail of the jury box. "When you began your first experiment in bacterial resistance, were you planning to find biocin?" he asked blandly.

Luzzatto drew back from the snare. "Certainly not, Mr. Dirksen. How could I? It was the outcome, not the goal, of that piece of research."

"Then it was luck?"

Luzzatto shook his head. "No, not luck, Mr. Dirksen. The important thing in research is to explore with an open and prepared mind. I had been working over hundreds of cultures before I found this special culture with its peculiar properties. If it weren't for my determination to study the field thoroughly, it would never have turned up. But how does that insinuation help your case? Isn't your client trying to capitalize on my so-called luck?"

The challenge was ignored while the lawyer developed the concept of chance and opportunity in research. He concluded dryly, "In any case, you make no claim that the discovery happened to strike because of your personal brilliance?"

"No."

"It might have come to anyone?"

"Anyone who had the skill to recognize and interpret what he had. I must remind you that cultures have been spoiled in laboratories since the time of Leeuwenhoek but it took Fleming to discover penicillin. I have no objection if you want to call that luck."

Dirksen went on to establish that Ullman had not gone off directly after commencement exercises to Lake Marah but had delayed his departure for a day. "Was the purpose to discuss your proposed technique for studying bacterial resistance?"

Luzzatto's voice was growing unreal in his own ears. "I've explained all that, Mr. Dirksen, but I'll give it another try. We met in the third floor laboratory with Dr. Ullman for a final talk. Dr. Josephine Ullman was present and also my wife. After the conversation the Ullmans left for Lake Marah."

"Dr. Ullman had delayed his vacation?"

"Yes." Luzzatto tried to recall the moment of gaiety and high purpose. A hot sun had been beating on Mackenzie Hall. Vivid in mind was the fever of impatience to start, the sense of things to come. Ullman had been notably pleasant, discussing the concrete problem for the first time, suggesting pitfalls to avoid, writing order forms for supplies and test organisms from the culture laboratory. Jo had been quiet, pale and wan, but attractive in a white frock. Eva had perched at the window, watchful of the mood. Before they parted, the women had embraced. "Watch the lad's diet, Evvie," said Jo with bleak humor. "If he's not force fed, he'll vanish like a snark." "I'll do my best," Eva had replied, smiling faintly. There had been suppressed poignancy in the moment, as though the older were handing something on to the younger, but if this were so, the subtlety, Luzzatto realized, had been lost on him at the time. Jo's parting handclasp had been icy. "I don't care what turns up here, Dave," she had said with sad humor. "I know you'll have a good summer. Don't forget me." "Oh, sure, Jo," he had replied uncomfortably, conscious that Eva had turned away tactfully to the window, that his mind was already on his work. "I'll keep in touch." "Getting late," said Ullman. "You'll keep me advised of progress, Luzzatto? I'll be following with interest. Coming, Josephine?"

Eva's last comment still lingered. "He's so good-natured today, Dave. What's wrong?" The clear face was grave as ever, betraying nothing of the deeper intuition behind the remark. He had turned at once to the series of experiments ahead.

A screech of wood broke the train of thought as the bailiff closed the windows with a pole. The chamber was growing decidedly colder. "It's quite true that Dr. Ullman had delayed his vacation for a day. He seemed to be curious or reconciled to my approach to the problem. I have never denied that he made certain comments which I took into consideration. I would not say that they were fundamental."

Dirksen let a contemplative moment pass. "Wasn't that much independence unusual?"

"I had clear ideas on what I wanted to do, Mr. Dirksen," said Luzzatto. "Dr. Ullman had no serious objection. I think he felt it didn't matter what I did."

"Did he say so in that many words?"

Luzzatto shook his head tiredly. "No, I judged it by his manner. He was entirely too casual and light to show any deep interest on this occasion. If he had really cared about the work, his manner would have been harsh, peremptory. He gave me less than half an hour of his time before he left. From that point, I was on my own."

"Using your own decision as to technique?" asked Dirksen sardonically. "Wouldn't you have missed the biocin effect, Professor Luzzatto, if Dr.

Ullman had not made his suggestion to examine the nutrient media for contamination?"

Luzzatto laughed harshly, glancing with triumphant irony toward Seixas as though an expected point had been made. "Oh, my dear Mr. Dirksen! Is that supposed to sum up your client's contribution?"

"Don't you agree that he made a contribution?"

Slowly, inexplicably, the atmosphere heightened as the unspoken premise of the conflict emerged. An impulsive denial was bitten off. Luzzatto gazed significantly, bitterly toward Seixas, weighing the legal point that a denial of Ullman's role in the discovery could well imperil the biocin patent. He could feel the tension at the counsel tables.

"What do you mean by contribution?" he said slowly.

"What do you think I mean?"

Luzzatto glanced up grimly. "Will Tewksbury happened to leave that flask of nutrient medium in the sun which gave the biocin mold time to develop as a contamination. Dr. Katz-Moebius gave me suggestions for isolating the organism and purifying the active ingredients. Other suggestions came from my classmates. Would you call those contributions?"

"I'm asking about Dr. Ullman's role."

Luzzatto was quiet for a long moment, struggling within himself. "I have never tried to deny that Dr. Ullman made an important contribution from his point of view. On the contrary, I did everything in my power to keep him in the picture. Even after your process server barged into my class, I wanted this case settled on a decent basis. It was Dr. Ullman, not I, who refused to meet Dean Mackenzie, or to explore the matter without prejudice. Why? I think I know the answer."

He went on deliberately. "Dr. Ullman made an offhand routine suggestion that happened to lead me to an accidental discovery of importance. I suppose that's what you want me to admit?" Angered stares were exchanged. "Well, the truth is simple. Your client knows that this discovery came to me in the heat and sweat of work, in the flood of my energies. His own connection was merely technical and rather—remote. He's always talked about the flash of insight, the intuition of the investigator. Well, intuition spoke, but to me and not to him, and that's what he can't forgive. He's resented that fact since the day I brought him the news. How could he face Dean Mackenzie who might discern the truth?"

A chair scraped as Ullman arose and put out a shaking hand. The familiar harsh tones were pitched with astonishment and reproach. "But all these are lies!" he cried with surprise. "I must ask you to withdraw that remark, Luzzatto! When have I shown resentment?"

Luzzatto went white. "I have no intention of withdrawing my remarks, sir!"

Ullman glanced about the courtroom, noting the empty bench, the watchful lawyers, the reporters, and slowly resumed his seat. "I see I must listen," he remarked heavily. "It is to be expected. *Weh! Wer zu spät bereut!*" he muttered under his breath.

Luzzatto turned. "Mr. Dirksen, I have no wish to deprive Dr. Ullman of any credit to which he's entitled as chief of the laboratory. You keep forcing me into these disparaging remarks, which I'm trying to avoid. I can hardly want to retaliate against this stupid lawsuit by petty bickering about credits, can I? Do you actually imagine I am that vindictive?"

"I really have no idea how you feel, Professor Luzzatto," said Dirksen quickly.

"Then I'll be glad to tell you." Anger flooded the sallow cheeks. "I feel sorry for your client, Mr. Dirksen. So sorry for this terrible need of his to twist every bit of forbearance into a confession of weakness. It's rather pitiful for a scientist who once did good work. Why not get down to the real question? The claim that I abused his trust? How? Where? Why?"

"I'll be glad to oblige," said Dirksen dryly.

Philip Seixas arose and walked restlessly to the window during the outburst. Too much! Too much! he thought. It seemed impossible to head off this new and reckless note. Dirksen meanwhile had picked up a copy of the patent application. He stared unpleasantly at the opaque jargon of the patent office. "Whose idea was it to prosecute this application?"

Luzzatto glanced at Ullman. "I give your client full credit for that too. I was too busy in the lab to know what was happening."

"Can you fix a date of any discussions?"

"Oh, yes. I have a clear recollection of Friday after Labor Day when Dr. Ullman returned from Lake Marah with his family. I was terribly let down by his reaction. I was hoping for an open mind, but instead he accused me of messing the experiment, or of showing him wrong figures. That was like charging me with doctoring the results, and I got terribly disturbed and angry. I threatened to chuck everything and pull out of the school, but he brushed this off and challenged me to duplicate the experiment under his supervision. I must say, he had a great technique for putting me on the defensive. I finally agreed."

Dirksen said, "Miss Stahl has testified that she heard you shouting that day in the laboratory, that you slammed the door when you left. Did that happen?"

"That was the first time in my life I had ever been accused of dishonesty." Luzzatto stared unpleasantly. "What would you have done?"

297

"I don't know," said Dirksen evenly. "No one has ever had occasion to make that charge against me. I doubt that I'd slam doors."

"Oh, let's get off this silly line, Dirksen, or I'll have to start making objections!" Philip Seixas came back to the arena. He managed a hard look to the witness. "Let's not build up the costs of the transcript. I don't want to ask the judge to return either." After a sharp exchange, Dirksen picked up the point that Luzzatto had in fact returned to the laboratory. Why?

"Well, I suppose I didn't have enough anger in me," Luzzatto said in a low voice. "It's a weakness, I imagine, to understand too much."

"Oh, what does that mean?" asked Dirksen with contempt.

"Nothing, perhaps."

"Were you actually prepared to leave school?"

"Not really, I suppose."

"It was merely a threat?" the lawyer suggested.

Luzzatto was silent. "I had talked it over with my wife, and I decided that I had too many obligations. Things too important for personal feelings."

Dirksen interrupted to introduce in evidence a letter of apology.

Luzzatto flushed. "Well, I wrote that letter because I knew it was what he wanted, because I had regard for his position as an older man in science. I had no idea it was meant for a dossier marked Luzzatto!" he added vengefully.

"It was not to ingratiate yourself into his good will?"

"No!"

"But you knew it would have that effect?"

"Perhaps!"

Dirksen dropped the subject pointedly. "You were testifying about the patent application?"

Luzzatto held back an impulsive retort. It was all so badly put, he felt, so inadequate to the situation. "Yes. Well, the following April he called me to his office and told me that he had made arrangements to apply for the patent. I was rather surprised."

"Oh, why?"

"Well, he hadn't consulted me about that move—and also because the application had us down as co-inventors."

"Did you remonstrate?" asked Dirksen sharply.

Luzzatto shook his head slowly. "He explained that it had become technically necessary to use both names because our first publication had already described us as co-authors and co-discoverers. It was some quirk in the patent law."

"What happened?"

"He showed me some papers which I signed. I suppose they were the patent application you introduced into evidence."

"Did you discuss those papers?"

"No."

"Did you examine them closely?"

"Only the description of the process to make sure it conformed to my notebooks."

Dirksen strolled back and threw the next question over his shoulder. "Did you accept the implication that you were equal partners? Legally and morally and financially? That certain duties and obligations were implied?"

Luzzatto sank back with anger. "Except that it was not our intention to exploit the patent financially! The idea was to assign the patent to the university or to some foundation that would be set up."

"But in fact you did get a large share of royalties from that patent, Professor Luzzatto? Contrary to that 'idea'?"

"Yes," said Luzzatto grimly.

He went on after a pause. "I'm aware of the discrepancy, Mr. Dirksen. I'm ready to remedy the situation whenever your client agrees to withdraw his complaint and express regrets."

Dirksen waited impassively for the slight echo to die. "Can you tell us about those sums?"

Luzzatto returned the stare grimly, wordless for the moment. "Oh, must we go over that again? I have no independent recollection. I'd have to take it from the books of the Foundation."

Dirksen handed up a photostatic copy of a canceled check. "Does this refresh your recollection, Professor Luzzatto? Take all the time you like."

Luzzatto gnawed his mouth with growing apprehension, frowning at the item. "I got this royalty check of course, but no specific feature comes to mind. It doesn't register."

Dirksen stood closer, biting a thumbnail, head cocked to one side. "Whose endorsement appears on the back?"

Luzzatto stared at the lawyer. "That's my wife's signature. I can see that she made the deposit to our account."

"Is that why this item fails to register?"

"Perhaps," said Luzzatto tightly.

He flared with irritation. "Oh, damn it, I'm not saying I didn't get this sum, or didn't know about the payment! It's simply that I'm unable to reconstruct the specific event in my mind. It probably came in the mail.

I probably was focusing on other things. What possible importance can my recollection of these details have?"

Dirksen stood thinking. "Well, let's say your wife was authorized to make that deposit?"

"Yes?"

Dirksen paused for a pulsebeat. "And to make withdrawals?" he suggested.

"Certainly! It was a joint account," said Luzzatto. "I didn't give her documents to this effect, if that's your point. I admit I got a large sum there."

The lawyer relaxed imperceptibly. "On the other hand, Dr. Ullman received—what?"

"Nothing!" said Luzzatto thickly. "Do you intend to ask how that came about? I'll be glad to tell you!"

Dirksen turned to his assistant for an exhibit. "I show you this paper marked Plaintiff's Exhibit 183 in Evidence and ask if you recognize the instrument?"

"It has my signature," said Luzzatto tightly. "What is the queston?"

"This document is also signed by Dr. Ullman?"

"Yes."

"It purports to transfer the rights of both parties in the patent application for biocin to Haverstraw Foundation, Inc.? In return for which one David Luzzatto was to receive a share of all revenues from exploitation of the underlying patent? Are you that person?"

Luzzatto burst out, "Yes! We've covered that!"

Dirksen went on stolidly. "Kindly examine paragraph 11. Is there any equivalent provision for Dr. Ullman's benefit?" He folded his arms and waited, facing an angered and disturbed witness with an expression of distaste. The courtroom was silent. Luzzatto fingered the instrument with wonder at the remote consequences of legal acts done without thought or prevision of things to come.

"Well, I'm shocked by your question, Mr. Dirksen," he said finally, drawing a breath, "because your client knows exactly how this came about. When this contract was brought for my signature that night, I was dumfounded. Up to that time I had never questioned—"

He paused, gnawing a pale lower lip. "Well, I'll have to go back to the situation with Brandywine. As I've already testified, I had originally questioned the advisability of letting an industrial house like Brandywine handle the patent application, but I went along for two reasons: first, it was a disagreeable necessity, and second, all sorts of technical and legal problems were involved, and I was satisfied to concentrate on my work.

I assumed that the position was being safeguarded, although I was less than clear how this was to be done. All that was being handled by Dr. Ullman.

"I never saw any Brandywine people except at one or two public functions when I went along to beat the drums for biocin, because it took the scientific world a little time to grasp that we weren't just trotting out another routine antibiotic under a specious claim to novelty. I was in a state of exhaustion with all that work, aside from carrying my regular academic load. Besides, I'd gotten married and I tried to give all my spare energies to my wife because she was having—"

He closed his eyes. "When Brandywine offered to produce certain quantities of biocin for us, I felt relieved of drudgery. I accepted the general understanding that they would be involved in biocin on some proper basis when the time came. I had all this co-operation in mind—"

Dirksen interrupted. "Professor, you insist that you never met any Brandywine officials? Then how did you come to know of their offer? Did Dr. Ullman keep you posted?"

"To a limited degree, yes, where it related to the work in the lab. The business side was another thing. I'm sorry I can't be more specific. Yes, Mr. Seixas?" He turned abruptly to the defense table where the lawyer, hands thrust into trousers pockets, had arisen to interrupt.

Seixas said coolly, "I don't want to break in, Professor Luzzatto, but it's late and we'll have to vacate this building shortly. Will you cover one point? During this period were you told of any *personal* understanding between Dr. Ullman and Brandywine Laboratories?"

Luzzatto hesitated for a barely perceptible pause, no more than a nuance. "Well, I know *now* that there was an arrangement, Mr. Seixas. I wasn't then sure whether it was written or oral." He cast his eyes at the floor, troubled at coming to grips with this issue. Ullman's cheeks had reddened with discomfort.

Seixas frowned. "That wasn't the question," he said sharply. "The question is what you were told!"

"Oh!" Luzzatto paused. "Well, of course I learned about a confidential agreement, Mr. Seixas, the night that Dr. Ullman came up with the contract for my signature. I got the impression it was a loose, informal agreement."

"I see," said Seixas heavily. He hesitated and returned to his chair with a thoughtful expression.

"Tell us about that night," said Dirksen quietly.

"This is part of what I'm trying to explain. I—well, I had less time for sociability and although our relationship never got cool, there was a period

301

of hard work when we didn't see too much of each other. I recall the first afternoon I wouldn't stay in the lab for tea, he was quite disappointed and annoyed. I—I, well, I thought it showed a blind spot not to understand any of my other obligations—"

A tired gesture dismissed this point. "The thing is that the old give and take had come to an end. On the surface there still was the same warmth and cordiality, but I had a feeling that something had changed. I almost never got a direct answer to a simple question. When I did, it was with a faraway look and mysterious allusions to things that were supposed to be above my head. All this was supposed to be for my own good, for my advancement in science and the brilliant career he kept promising under his guidance. But I didn't feel like a child. I felt entitled to be treated like a scientist."

Dirksen glanced at the advancing clock. "You stated that Dr. Ullman disclosed his personal arrangements with Brandywine Laboratories."

Luzzatto leaned forward with an air of coming to grips with finality. "It began, I suppose, when I barged in on Dr. Ullman with a complaint. I remember his annoyed reaction, but I was angry and I didn't care. I had just heard of rumors that I was supposed to be making a good thing out of biocin and I wanted to know what was going on. I was getting fed up by then with silences and evasions.

"Also, I had become suspicious that I was being shunted off to one side while negotiations, whatever they were, were going forward. He tried to turn it off with a joking quotation in German. That I could be pure as snow, chaste as ice, I wouldn't escape calumny. Well, I wasn't there for aphorisms. Then typically he got irritable and told me flatly that he would not tolerate any attempt to question his judgment. We had a flare-up and I left."

Ullman obviously liked none of this. He had sunk down on his spine and was staring fixedly under thick brows at a narrative of forgotten events. Luzzatto resumed grimly.

"A few days later he dropped up to our flat ostensibly to give me the names of the committee who would conduct the oral examination for my doctorate, to go over their points of weakness and such last-minute advice—a sponsor can sometimes get more nervous than the candidate, you know. But actually he had come to get my signature to that contract."

"How do you know that?"

"He told me so. When I came out with that accusation he laughed and admitted that he was the clumsiest diplomat in the world. He was quite frank about it."

"Were you surprised to see him at your home?"

"No, I rather expected him. He used to take long walks at night, you see, and our home was a regular port of call. He always said he liked the warmth of our home, the color, the atmosphere. If I were too busy with my other work, or stuck at the lab, he liked to talk to my wife. She was very good with him." A pause. "That night after she had gone to bed he went off on a favorite topic: the problem of truth and meaning in science.

"I sensed that something was on his mind," he went on uncomfortably, "but I had no idea what was coming. He was putting on his muffler to go about midnight when he asked me to sign this contract. Up to that time I signed anything, but there was something too casual—odd—in his manner that made me examine the text. I saw that it called for Dr. Ullman and me to convey our rights to the Haverstraw Foundation, Inc. with the consent and approval of Brandywine Laboratories. In turn Brandywine agreed to handle the manufacture on an exclusive royalty basis payable to the Foundation. It all looked reasonable enough until I came to this clause by which I was to get a share of those royalties. I was completely taken aback. It was obviously the basis of the damaging rumor about me.

"I demanded an explanation, and for the first time I learned about the financial background. He told me it was absolutely necessary to sign to save him from embarrassment. He asked me as an act of faith not to question too deeply but to sign the instrument. He put it as a test of my devotion and trust. I signed.

"I remember his words. He said, 'You don't imagine I'd do anything to harm you, Luzzatto?'

"I said, 'That's a queer remark, Professor! I have no such thoughts in my mind. I just gave you my signature without question. I wouldn't do that for anyone else in the world.'

"He said, 'I am deeply appreciative.'

"It was hot and he took off his muffler. I recall that we were seated at the dining table with the papers lying between us. He said, 'I suppose I owe you an apology, but this tactic became necessary by the logic of the situation. I'm much older, Luzzatto, there are things here—' "

Luzzatto broke off, frowning in the effort to recapture the precise exchange, now seen dimly through a fog of fatigue, and went on in detail. "Well, there was the usual talk about my inexperience in practical matters. I kept wondering what he was leading to, and finally he mentioned an agreement made by him with Brandywine before I came into the picture.

"I asked, 'What kind of agreement?'

"He said, 'The details hardly matter, Luzzatto. The fact is, it had originally to do with our wine project. I was hired for those studies on a financial basis. Did you know that?' He gave me a funny look.

303

"I told him frankly I had assumed that he got paid for that job. I couldn't see why he was so embarrassed about such a conventional arrangement.

"He asked, 'Did you ever wonder about my stipend?'

"I said, 'No, it was never my concern.'

"He said, 'It was very little, Luzzatto, negligible, a mess of pottage.'

"Then he laughed suddenly and said, 'I gave these people at Brandywine a commitment, you know?'

"I didn't know how to take the laugh. I said, 'What kind of commitment?'

"He said, 'This will be confidential?'

"I said, 'Of course!'

"He laughed again and said, 'Well, it seems I am not quite the fox I like to pretend, Luzzatto! I am amused to admit that I agreed to assign all commercial processes developed in our lab exclusively to those people.'

"At first I couldn't see the connection. What had it to do with me? I had no agreement with Brandywine.

"He said, 'Ah, but your stipend, Luzzatto, came from the wine project! Surely you knew that fund was provided by Brandywine?'

"I said, 'I always thought that money was in lieu of a fellowship.'

"He just blinked at this and then asked if I had confidence in his integrity. I replied pretty strongly that I certainly had, and always would have, but I was alarmed by the freewheeling way in which I was being manipulated. I asked only to be consulted, to receive frank and candid explanations. Was that so unreasonable? He replied that this was a fair question. He told me he regretted the need for caution and reserve but that certain matters had to be kept in confidence."

Luzzatto examined his notes, striving to keep the elusive picture in focus. He was not out of the woods, but his testimony, he felt, rang true. He looked up with a glance to Ullman.

"He said, 'I can tell you, Luzzatto, that certain elements in Brandywine are beginning to take a high view of the commercial chances for biocin. I am being pressed now to execute an assignment of rights. These people, you see, feel legally entitled to claim my share of our patent!'

"I said they damn well weren't entitled to claim mine!

"He said he was not so sure they needed my share.

"I asked what the hell that meant.

"I had never used that tone before, no matter how provoked, because of my respect for his position. I was a bit excited, I imagine, but he didn't react in any way. He said finally, 'Once they get the assignment of my share out of me, they can go ahead full steam and tell all of us to go to hell. However there is one consolation, Luzzatto. I have argued that you are still a free agent.'

"I asked what that implied.

"He laughed and said that this was the chink in their armor. We were not entirely helpless. Using my remaining uncommitted rights, we could still knock on any rival door and convey patent rights equal to theirs—or at least threaten such action. That was why he had spent so much time in New York. To convince those people that until all the rights were gathered into one fist they were not wholly omnipotent!"

Ullman's gaze was fixed with penetrating intensity of scorn and disbelief. The testimony at last was drawing blood, Luzzatto observed grimly; Emil Dirksen remained professionally impassive.

Luzzatto drew a breath. "Oh, I learned a lot that night, Mr. Dirksen," he said grimly, "especially about these twists in the patent law. I told him it seemed illogical to destroy the monopoly which obviously is basic to the patent concept.

"He said, 'I quite agree, Luzzatto. That is exactly the point. While you retain your signature, there can be no effective control elsewhere. Would you wish to see these rights assigned exclusively to Brandywine?'

"I said, 'Certainly not. Why should I?'

"He said, 'Exactly what I told them. That you would not consent to deal solely with one industrial house. Nor is it my desire. Did I misrepresent your position?'

"I said, 'No!'

"Then I asked what else he had told them.

"He gave me a funny look, and said that he had advised that I had certain terms in mind.

"I said, 'Terms? What terms? I don't know what you're talking about, professor.'

"He replied, 'I was forced to take this position!'

"I asked, 'What position, for God's sake?'

"He said, 'The position is that you want something for yourself.'

"I remember my exact words. I said, 'Professor, I never authorized that statement.'

"He seemed terribly disturbed by this remark. I knew that mood and I waited. Finally he said, 'Listen carefully, Luzzatto! I thought that things were understood between us, that I had a certain privilege to take all necessary steps in behalf of this discovery. You and Eva have become close, very close, and perhaps I have come to take too much for granted. It's a fault, but if I have gone too far, surely you'll forgive my clumsiness.

305

After all, we agreed to be in this thing together, and I felt I was acting for the common good.'

"I said that I knew this, that there was no need to talk of forgiveness, but that I also felt old enough not to have words put in my mouth.

"He said, 'In God's name, Luzzatto, do you think I like this mess? I feel a heavy responsibility. Is it right that these people should acquire this process for a mere stipend? For a coolie's wage? How else can we recapture the status quo except in this way? For two years I have spent sleepless nights, considering how to put us back in the original position.'

"I asked what else had been said.

"He said, 'I told them you were giving me a great deal of difficulty, Luzzatto. That you were not too easy to influence and that you would deal only with and through the university on fair terms to be arranged. Otherwise I could guarantee nothing. Isn't that consistent with your views?'

"I said, 'But why must I be made the mercenary bastard in the woodpile?' Well, he laughed as though this were terribly callow, and wanted to know if a bit of extra income would be so hard for a married man to take. He told me it was all part of the same tough posture, that the Brandywine people weren't bad fellows, that they were ready to relinquish their claims to the university on some equitable basis, but only so long as they were convinced that we too were in earnest. That's why he kept me under wraps. He'd bargained away his own position, and he didn't dare to expose me as a financial milksop. That the essential thing was to get the papers off without delay. We could discuss details at a future time.

"I had one last question. 'Can I talk to these people if I wish?'

"He said, 'Of course!'

"Then he said, 'Well, it's entirely up to you, Luzzatto, but it will, I'm afraid, show a certain lack of confidence, especially since I've told everyone that I speak for us both. I'd rather you didn't embarrass me.'

"I said, 'Professor, you know I wouldn't do that. But I insist that I want nothing for myself.'

"It was about one o'clock when I signed the paper. I think," said Luzzatto, "I've covered the entire conversation, Mr. Dirksen. If not, you can ask me specific questions."

He paused abruptly with surprise that he was sweating profusely with the release of tension. A tremendous feat of recall had been accomplished, and his testimony was now reduced to the permanency of a stenotype ribbon. Overtones of meaning had been conveyed to Ullman who sat motionless now, working a heavy mouth of anger. It was now dusk, he noted and the bailiff had turned on lights in the courtroom.

Dirksen came forward with a simple question. "So that Dr. Ullman's intention was to restore the status quo—the original position?"

"So he said."

"And so you understood?"

"Yes."

"Was it your final word on parting that night, Professor Luzzatto, that you did not expect to take any share of royalties from the Foundation?"

"Yes."

"Did you stick to that intention?"

"No."

The handkerchief rolled into a wet, nervous ball. "My situation changed, and so did my viewpoint. My wife was having a bad time with her first pregnancy, you see? She left her job and—and I began to feel silly not to take the income. I never expected more than a few thousand dollars a year at best. I can't speak for Dr. Ullman. Perhaps he visualized the potential—I didn't!"

Dirksen put a foot on the platform. His breath had an unexpected flavor of mint. "In the meantime, Dr. Ullman had left the university. Did you notify him when those payments began?"

"No."

Luzzatto added, "I always assumed he knew."

The lawyer's glance was unwavering. "Did you ever, directly or indirectly, acknowledge an obligation to share these royalties?"

Luzzatto shook his head. "I don't know what you're driving at, Mr. Dirksen. I made all sorts of grateful statements, but that's as far as I ever went."

The whisper cut like a whip. "Did you ever make any token payment to acknowledge such obligation?"

Luzzatto loosened his tie. The room was cold, yet he was suffocating in dust. "No."

Dirksen remained staring. "Let me remind you, Professor Luzzatto, that you have testified to your wife's authority with respect to your bank account." A sheaf of papers was produced. "Do you recognize these photostat documents which I now show you?"

In the harsh bleak lighting, Luzzatto stared at disaster. He glanced at Philip Seixas, who meanwhile had come forward with concern, ready to protect the legal position. "I—I didn't—" A venomous glare went out to Ullman.

"Did you have to use this?" he muttered thickly.

The check was drawn in the sum of $2,500 to the order of Dr. V. F.

Ullman. It was the item he had known about, for the canceled original was in a filing cabinet at home; but it was nothing he had in truth expected to encounter in court.

It was the other item which held his attention—a covering letter which urged that the check be accepted in payment of too many benefits to be described. The signature was Eva's bold flourish.

An hour later the torment was still in progress.

A small group drove back from Salt Hills in silence, licking the wounds of battle. Seixas was extremely quiet.

"Why didn't you tell me, Dave?" he said somewhere along the way. "How could you fail to prepare me for that letter?"

"It was my fault."

Eva was seated between the two men, swollen and uncomfortable, lapped in a loose coat of blue wool. She was smoking nervously, staring into the gathering dusk with stricken eyes. Luzzatto was at the wheel. Podell was in the back.

"That damn letter!" Eva muttered miserably. "I had quite forgotten the wording. I kept no copy, you see. Is it so important?"

"It's important," said Seixas coldly.

He smoked speculatively with the massive calm of experienced trial counsel whom the evasiveness of all clients would always dismay, but never quite surprise. A shudder ran through the pregnant young woman at his side, and the heat, the dismay, the body response were contagious. He made an effort at sympathy. "When you came to my office, Mrs. Luzzatto, I pointed out, I believe, that where the issues are in balance any one thing can determine the outcome. This is an area where the legal concepts are not simple. The debate doesn't turn on the actual events, which are largely conceded, but upon their interpretation given at the time by the parties. Until that letter was introduced, our position was sticky but fairly clear. Now? I'm not sure!"

"How has it changed?" Her voice was low, troubled.

Seixas said slowly, "Let me put it simply, Mrs. Luzzatto. This letter looks like an unconscious, but clear admission that you, and by extension your husband, knew that Dr. Ullman was entitled to be paid for his contribution to the development. If not something worse!"

A glance of dismay went out in the darkness. "Worse?"

"Well, Mrs. Luzzatto, you must forgive me, but an unsympathetic court might even regard your letter as a subterfuge of some sort—a feeble sop to your conscience. Why did you characterize the check as payment?"

She waited miserably. "I was trying to make it easy for him to accept. It was only a few thousand dollars!"

"It's not the amount," said Seixas after a pause. "It's the wording of the letter! Our defense is weaker than I ever believed."

"That one bit of paper?" she muttered.

Seixas nodded grimly. "That one bit of paper!"

They came finally to a rise and saw the lights of the river gleaming in the distance. Eva smoked fearfully. "It's not hopeless?"

Seixas shrugged, wrinkling the long aristocratic lines of a weary face. "Nothing is hopeless that can still be explained away." He added, "What made you give him that money?"

Luzzatto said angrily, "Why worry about spilt milk, Phil? Let it go till morning."

"No, Dave!" Eva held up a hand of restraint. "I'll tell you, Mr. Seixas. Victor told me he was in difficulties. He had come up from New London to arrange for a bank loan on his old house. Apparently he had already exceeded the value of the house and the bank had turned him down. He thought David might be willing to co-sign a personal note at the bank. I told him David was in Johannesburg—"

Seixas interrupted. "Didn't he know that? Wasn't he aware of that scientific conference?"

"Oh, of course he was!" said Luzzatto. "I covered all that in my testimony."

"I want Mrs. Luzzatto's recollection," said Seixas coldly.

Eva thought back, coughing on the cigarette smoke. "I can't tell you too much about that, Mr. Seixas, except that he seemed surprised to learn that David was in South Africa. That was hard to grasp, but I put that down, I suppose, to the extent to which we were already drifting apart. Of course he was more than welcome and I asked him to stay for dinner. His mood was strange."

"How strange?" asked Seixas.

Eva pressed the dashboard lighter and brought the circlet of fire to a fresh cigarette. "Well, he kept remarking about the quality of the furnishings, the cost of the house, things like that. Oh, it was all appreciative, but I had a sense of discomfort I had never felt before. It was always expected that the whole Ullman family would be delighted with our success, our new home, our—well, everything. And suddenly I could see all those beautiful things through his eyes. He looked so remote, so down-at-heel, so out of things, that I felt ashamed of all that money I'd been splurging." Her gaze seemed fixed on her dining room with its warm, ruddy pine paneling and the older man with his stony, handsome features alone with her at dinner. She had served a good wine, she recalled: tapers had cast a soft glow, and the salad had come from her own garden. She shivered and turned to the lawyer. "Some people put that feeling into gardens, I put it into my home. It was never David's idea, poor chap. He could live in a tent."

"Evvie," said Luzzatto pleadingly.

Eva decided she was talking too much, too little to the point. She felt breathless with the effort of speech. "In any case," she went on, "he kept talking about his difficulties with some bitterness. He had bought this farm, I gathered, without real preparation and there was a great deal of hardship because of the rains. Nature was in the conspiracy against him. The strange thing—"

"Yes?"

"Well, he never talked once about biocin," she said slowly. "I thought that odd, but then everything was odd. I offered to co-sign his note at the bank in David's absence, and he declined as though the point were extremely delicate. He asked for David's address in Johannesburg and left. I kept thinking about the visit for several days, and then I sent off the check with that damned letter!"

"But why? Why?"

She thought bitterly. "He was on my conscience, Mr. Seixas. I never liked him, you see, and perhaps I felt guilty, ashamed of my thoughts. Then, again, he looked so disappointed with life, defeated, baffled by the outcome of things. Oh, he kept fingering the ornaments appreciatively, making little jokes, taking credit for David's successes, but I could read his thoughts. It had worked out that we had so much and he had so little. I gave way to an impulse of—pity."

Seixas let the moment pass. "You used the word payment?" he reiterated.

"I know," she muttered. "He's rigid, proud. I was sugar-coating the pill. Do you believe that?"

"Oh, yes! Yes," said Seixas slowly. "I quite believe it, Mrs. Luzzatto." He returned to his cigar.

"Evvie, kid?" Podell's growl came from behind. "One thing nobody's mentioned so far. Ullman had to photostat the check before he put it through? Did you expect that?"

"No!" Her voice was low. "But looking back I'm not surprised. I had a feeling he was looking for—something." She shivered. "I don't think he knew himself what that was—not until it fell into his hands."

"What a lovely touch!" said Podell sardonically.

310

Seixas demanded, "Mrs. Luzzatto, when did you tell your husband about the check?"

"When he got back from Africa," she said, "but I don't think he paid attention. He was simply not interested in the money question. As a matter of fact, we both had difficulty recalling the details at first. But I honestly didn't remember what I wrote in the letter. It was one of those loans which grows stale and never gets paid back. I never thought it would come back to plague us."

Luzzatto interrupted roughly. "Oh, shut up, Evvie."

He stopped the car on the shoulder. "Now, listen to me, Phil! You too, Si! I don't want one God-damned question more. I don't want Evvie distressed or disturbed or involved in this mess in any way. I was reminded about the check, but I kept it quiet from you because I never dreamt it would come up this way. It was a simple kindness that had nothing to do with biocin. I didn't think Ullman could possibly use it against us in court. Well, now we know better. How will you meet the issue?"

Seixas took a long time to answer. "But, Dave, you must know," he said with an air of surprise. "I'll have to call Mrs. Luzzatto as a witness. Don't you see that? Unless you have a better answer?"

There was a sound of heavy breathing. Luzzatto glanced at Podell, then came back to the lawyer. Eva was weeping quietly. "Yes! Yes, I might have just that!" he said hoarsely. "I just might! Darling—"

But she was unable to answer. She wiped her eyes, struggling for control, overwhelmed by misery. "So damn sorry, darling," she whispered. "My fault. My fault."

Luzzatto started the motor and the rest of the drive was in silence. At home, in bed, he put the blankets about her and stroked her hair. "Never worry, darling. Never. I'll work this thing out and you'll never face the court."

Sophie was driving the Ford truck along the Throughway to New London.

"Victor?" she said finally. "What really happened?"

The cigarette glowed softly. "Unbelievable!" said the harsh voice wonderingly. "Fantastic! The complete distortion of reality."

A long moment of silence, then, "He accepted responsibility for the letter, you know?"

"You told me that," she said patiently.

The breath sucked in sharply, there was the dry crisp sound of burning. "I am seriously disturbed."

She made no answer.

"This is the last thing in the world I wanted, Sophie. Surely you'd think he'd understand? All this ugliness. It's entirely against my nature."

She twisted a dial and the dashboard lights faded, leaving the bubble of glass and steel to darkness. Except for a squeak in the chassis, it was quiet, but she was aware that the staring eyes, fixed on the highway, were awash with tears.

Chapter 24

THE AIRPLANE CIRCLED WIDE OVER THE GULF OF MEXICO, JOLTING violently against air currents, and dropped into the runway. With a screech of rubber, it taxied to the gate where visitors were gathered. Passengers emerged shakily, blinking in the morning haze.

"Oh, God!" Luzzatto thought. "Let this work out all right!" A baggage carrier passed, and then he saw a thin, sunburned woman in blue denims waiting at the gate.

"Hello, Dave," said Jo coolly, shielding her eyes. "You're a ghastly sight. Why couldn't those damned lawyers work something out?"

"Hello, Jo," he said, restraining a surge of dismay. The sleekness of that small, neat head was gone. The black tresses were cut to a crude bob, heavily streaked with gray. An open shirtwaist showed the jutting of clavicle bones. Her letters had complained of loss of weight, but he had expected nothing like this stringy Amazon with shrunken breasts.

"How's Evvie coming along? When's the baby due?"

"Oh, about three weeks," he replied. Her manner at least had not changed, he reflected. It was still direct and forthright, marked by her familiar accent. "The doctor's satisfied but of course all this trouble is a strain. She sends her best."

Jo grinned crookedly. "Does she?"

"Of course! Why not?"

"No reason, I suppose, except that I'm V. F. Ullman's daughter, Dave, and she's your pregnant wife. I can imagine how primitive I'd get under the circumstances. I'm surprised she let you fly down."

Luzzatto wet his mouth, feeling his way with caution. "My mother's staying with her while I'm gone."

313

"I adore your mother," said Jo.

"Yes. Well, I've got to talk to you. I never thought we'd reach the point where we couldn't." A note of appeal hovered.

She stared at the thin, obstinate mouth, considering the position. "All right, Dave," she agreed finally, succumbing. "Screw all the legal mumbo jumbo! How much time have you got down here?"

Luzzatto glanced beyond the wire fence to the airport building where luggage was being discharged. "There's a flight to Miami tonight that takes me to New York. I'd like to make it if I can."

Jo threw back her head and laughed harshly. "Oh, darling! Is that all I'm entitled to?" Affectionate humor glinted as she patted his cheek. "You haven't changed one bit. Bring your gear to the parking lot while I gas up. Oh, wot a lovely occasion for a visit!" With a cynical grin, she went off.

The roadster skidded wide, rattled, and after taking a curve, swung back into the road. Luzzatto felt the glare of sky and water on his face and sighed. "I'm sorry this couldn't be in a better cause, but I'm damn glad to see you, Jo."

The crooked grin returned. "Luzzatto, boy! It took a long time to get around to that!"

He waited in silence, considering her mood. She had been going at a furious rate since they had met at the airport. She was full of the region, pointing out natural wonders and items of historical interest with unabated drive. She drove her car with expert muscularity, swearing at obtrusive trucks hauling shrimp to market, talking, talking. Everything was exciting from a recent tarpon rodeo to a proposed trip through the Everglades. There was pressure behind her speech, a frantic quality he found disquieting. "I'm sorry to be remiss," he said carefully, "but how do you think I feel, Jo? I haven't changed because of this lawsuit. I hope it hasn't affected you."

"Don't be an ass!" she said crossly.

The sand dunes ended abruptly and the road turned into a tranquil lagoon. An open gate of wrought iron was neatly marked:

INSTITUTE OF OCEANOGRAPHY

SAN MARTINO

Beyond lay a score of pink and white buildings shining in the sun. "Oh, nice!" he breathed.

314

Jo smiled with pleasure. "I'll want you to meet some of my friends, Dave. You'll like Harry Lockridge, and Sarah's a dear. Nora's mad about Harry too!"

"Nora?" asked Luzzatto.

"Oh, you know—Honora. Honora MacLeish," she replied with a trace of impatience. "I wrote about her in my last letter. About three months ago?"

"Oh, yes," he said dimly.

Jo shook a wondering head. "Nora's one of those tall girls who's decided that romance is not for anyone over six foot, but she's quite a guy and we get along famously. She's mad for fish and hasn't read a novel in years. Well, let's roll!"

A short gravel drive led to a cottage overlooking the Gulf. She parked the car and led him to the patio. "You can clean up here if you don't mind the mess. Living room, bedrooms, kitchenette, john. Or would you prefer the guesthouse?"

"No, this is fine," he said slowly.

He gazed covetously at the peaceful nodding scene. "I had no idea it would be so beautiful, Jo. I'm beginning to see what you mean. You could live here forever." He stepped into a cool, dim interior and mopped his neck. Only a few hours earlier he had driven to the airport in New York through cold rain squalls blowing in from the North Atlantic, and now, in a few hours he had crossed into this sun-drenched land under a soft, blue sky. Haverstraw might have been a million miles away were it not for the task on hand. He said slowly, "I'd like that hot shower, and I'll be ready. It's been a long time since we had breakfast together."

"Yes. It has," she said quietly. "While you're cleaning up, I'd like to read that transcript of yours, Dave. Would you mind? I'll wait for you at the dining hall."

"Help yourself," he said dubiously. He added, "It's hardly edifying, Jo. I'm not too proud of everything I said up there. Just remember, I was under a lot of tension."

Jo took the bulky manuscript of the pre-trial examination recorded at Salt Hills. It was formidable, somewhat frightening in its black covers—the color, she thought, of a hangman's mask. "Enjoy yourself," she said wanly, and left for the dining hall where she put on glasses and began to read.

Luzzatto meanwhile began to undress, waiting for his eyes to adjust to dimness. It struck him suddenly that he had never before entered Jo's bedroom, and the intrusion for some reason filled him with vague un-

315

easiness. It seemed an embarrassment, not justified by their old relationship. Yet in fact what was that relationship? What had he expected? He had assumed many things, but after the strained greeting at the airport, the abrupt evasions, the enigmatic silences, the volubility, he was no longer so sure. He was not the same, nor was she, and between them now lay the shadow of hate. He had come in simple need, in desperation, in friendship, and none of these thoughts were expected.

He was surprised by the barren aspect of the room. It was simply furnished with institutional pieces like a barracks, but the bed was covered with a white spread and the chintz curtains were cheerful. It was this cheery note which seemed to reflect Jo's personality—the jaunty swagger he recalled. He dropped his clothes with relief and stood before the triple mirror of the dressing table. The clutter included toilet waters, a comb threaded with a tangle of black and gray hairs, and snapshots in many sunlit poses. Jo with fishing net draped like a sarong, Jo with face mask and fishing spear, Jo on a sailing vessel, Jo grinning with a white-haired giant who wore the authority of Poseidon himself. A signature showed this to be Dr. Harry Lockridge, Jo's chief in ichthyology. It was a good face and one he instantly liked. There were older snapshots, too, notably a group portrait taken at his wedding. The photograph stood in a place of honor.

Of course! he thought with surprise. That picture had been taken by Jo in a hubbub of applause by the wedding guests. Jo had managerially set the pose, in the back yard of the Luzzatto house. Cesare and Nella were strangely stern and uncomfortable, holding aloft tumblers of wine. Cesare had been splendid in the role of professional intellectual, beard bristling, cravat flowing, fingers inky, hectic with talk, while Nella— Nella looked tired and worn yet satisfied in a smart frock and antique silver jewelry. Victor and Sophie were to the right of the bridal couple. They seemed strangely stern, distant and uncomfortable at inclusion in the family group. It had been their first meeting with his parents and the constraint had been marked. Cesare indeed had been abrupt, unimpressed, and beneath a formal politeness faintly contemptuous of the scientist, barely concealing dislike for the challenge to his moral authority in the life of his son.

Eva was smiling from the center. She was pale and lovely in a simple frock without veil, he observed with a pang. She had been thinking, he knew, that no one of her family had been left to attend the wedding, no one alive out of her past, no one to send her off with love, no one except himself and the surrogate Ullmans. It had been Victor, he thought grimly, who had given her away. For the groom, towering awkwardly in ill-fitting flannels, he had no sense of identification at all.

The group were squinting in the July sun backed against a fence denuded of shrubbery. That vandalism, he recalled, had been the triumph of pet homosexual Belgian hares after a series of breeding experiments had ended without results. In that yard had been spent the best years of troubled adolescence, and while Eva left to change for the trip, he had amused Jo by showing off these and other aspects of his earlier life. They were frisky creatures, he had said, who had found the path to exotic delights without the pressures of a cultural matrix, or the psychological traumata of infantile experiences. How account for that talent? Was it perhaps rooted in the genetic inheritance of the species?

"Oh, don't let that thought get out!" cried Jo laughing, squeezing his arm. Her loud voice was drawing attention. She was a little drunk, and her eyes were swimming. "You're being reckless, Dave, hitting the theology of our times. It's dogma that we'd all be normal, healthy, intact and identical if not for the curse of love deprivation in childhood. Didn't you know that?" she laughed, staggering and spilling her drink on his sleeve. "You've got all the answers. How come?"

"How come what, Jo?" he asked uncomfortably.

She stared fixedly and the smile became a grimace. "Oh, this damn compulsion to explain the emotional departure, the tainted wether of the flock in special terms? Who says the deviant is in breach of preordained perfection? No one's less human because he's got six toes! Why this universal search for causal responsibility?" She clutched at his lapels. "Why isn't it *his* fault?" she demanded with intensity.

"Fault? Whose fault? What are you talking about, Jo?" he asked uncomfortably.

There was a sudden silence in which Victor Ullman's harsh, didactic voice was clear. She was about to speak, when suddenly she changed her mind and laughed. "Why—why, His!" she cried, pointing to the sky. "Up there! The Big Fellow! It's His fault, isn't it, Dave?" Her laughter rang incoherently, and then Nella had stepped in quietly, disapproving, to say that Eva was dressed and waiting.

"Anyone for rice?" shouted Jo, and led a scramble of children into the street. It was her battered Chevrolet they had borrowed for the trip, Luzzatto recalled. At the last moment there had been final embraces, laughter, cheers and a pattering of rice. "Take care of yourselves," cried Jo frantically, tears of emotion starting at last. "Dave, Evvie! You kids don't know what you've got! Be happy and find time for a postcard? Do that for Jo? Eh?"

317

At the corner Luzzatto caught a last view of Jo, suddenly forlorn, waving a handkerchief. He drove into Riverside Drive, and at a traffic light turned to Eva with a relieved grin. A clamor of protesting horns brought them out of a kiss, and with a burst of laughter they drove off to Provincetown.

With a depressed sigh, Luzzatto put aside the wedding picture and stepped into the shower. For a moment he clung to the faucets, breathing rapidly, sinking with fatigue, and then the hot flood poured down, bringing relief from the tiring trip and from the shock of Jo's appearance at the airport. What stuck in mind was the comb on the dressing table.

"You know these people?" said Jo.

The giantess put aside a plate of fried ham and eggs to put out a crushing grip and to acknowledge that she was Honora MacLeish, Jo's roommate. She was a blond woman with a mildly studious face and an air of no nonsense. She was precisely Luzzatto's height, and wore large splayed hands and feet.

"Well, you're Luzzatto?" she said, vaguely hostile. "I understand you're not finished with that lawsuit? When do you expect to get through with it?"

"That's not up to me," said Luzzatto. "I'm not responsible for what's happened."

"It takes two to make a quarrel," said Nora coldly.

Luzzatto said evenly, "But only one to start."

Jo broke in to introduce Dr. Harry Lockridge, her chief, a grizzled, burly scholar of sixty. He had finished coffee and was smoking a pipe with a cool estimating air of wisdom. "Are they giving you a bad time up North, Professor?"

"Bad enough," said Luzzatto briefly.

Nora gathered her dishes on a tray, towering with stooped shoulders over the table. "Do you mind if I say something, Jo?"

"I wish you wouldn't," said Jo.

Nora glared with bitter resentment. "Let me tell you this, Professor," she burst out. "We all think a lot of Jo here, and some of us love her. I don't think she ought to be talked into anything for which she'll be sorry."

Luzzatto met the woman's hot eyes. The abrupt attack had taken him utterly by surprise. It was evident that he had stepped into the middle of a violent discussion.

He said cautiously, "Talked into what?"

318

Nora said tensely. "We've got a fair idea why you're here, and I think it's shocking. I for one resent your presence."

"Oh, Nora!" cried Jo, closing her eyes. "For God's sake, don't be an ass. Dave has every right in the world to talk to me. What I choose to do is my own problem."

"And I choose to think that you're a damned fool, Jo! You oughtn't to listen to this man. Coming, Doctor?" said Nora violently. She carried her tray with angry strides to the far end of the dining hall.

"Silly bitch!" said Jo with weary affection, winking at Lockridge. "Nora's a good kid, but full of penis deprivation, and there's no offset for that in that collection of hers of sea cucumbers. Pity! Eh, Harry?" Jo sighed pensively. "I sometimes envy the brutes."

"Why, Jo?" asked Lockridge.

She shrugged, smiling oddly. "Well, they've got no real enemies, and that's good, but they also have a strange and horrifying defense mechanism when they're disturbed. They contract and throw out their poisonous internal organs through a rupture in the body. Did you know that, Dave? Sometimes that's suicidal, but often they survive and regenerate the organs—which is more than we can do! Even when we wish!"

"Don't go on like that, Jo," said Lockridge softly, sucking his pipe.

"No, I won't," she said instantly.

Lockridge turned to Luzzatto. Nora's outburst, he remarked, was not to be taken seriously, or with offense, but still, it represented a consensus. The matter of Luzzatto's visit had been discussed over breakfast, and no one liked the idea of the savage lawsuit up North.

"I don't like it myself," said Luzzatto grimly.

"Nothing personal," said Lockridge. "But we're thinking of Jo!"

"No one asked poor Nora to spill her guts like that," said Jo, smiling crookedly, but a paper napkin was being torn to shreds. "It was a mistake to bring you to this grimy joint."

It was neither grimy nor a joint, but a bright hall filled with a sunburned intelligent crowd, chatting with tranquility and good humor like any institution of learning anywhere in the country—and yet he felt the taint of envy, a dismal mood of alienation from his birthright.

Luzzatto ordered breakfast and found to his surprise that he was famished. "How does everyone know why I'm here, Dr. Lockridge?"

Lockridge waited with cool reserve. "We're not exactly fools in this little backwater, Luzzatto. Your visit has made a bit of a stir, and some of the guesses are shrewd. I'd like to say something."

"Oh, Harry!" sighed Jo deprecatingly.

"Oh, I promise to be good," said Lockridge gently, patting her hand

319

with reassurance, then turned to the visitor. "It's just that we're fond of this young woman, my wife and I, and we'd hate to find her unhappy, or hurt, or involved, or put in jeopardy in any way because of your quarrel with her father. We don't think she ought to be drawn into it any further."

Luzzatto said grimly, "Well, neither do I!"

"Oh?" Lockridge puffed slowly, wondering. "She had a bad time, you know, when that lawyer came down from New York in February to interview her."

Luzzatto said with restraint, "That was her father's lawyer, Dr. Lockridge, not mine. I've been very careful to keep her out of this mess up till now." He paused. "But I didn't know it gave her such a bad time."

"Oh, yes!" said Lockridge grimly.

"I wish," said Jo, addressing the ceiling, "that these giant intellects would stop discussing me in the third person. I'm not deaf, feeble-minded, infantile, or in the next room. I still have a mind." She folded her arms and scowled disconsolately.

Lockridge glanced at his watch with a cluck of dismay. "Well, I think I've said enough, Professor," he concluded on a friendlier note. "No one ever wins a bitter lawsuit like this. No matter what the court decides, it can only hurt a man's scientific reputation. I only hope that's all that gets hurt."

He nodded and strode off. At the door he was joined by Nora MacLeish and together they could be seen crossing the lawn. Nora's gesticulations were violent until cut off from view by a row of palms.

Luzzatto said, "Jo."

"Yes, darling?" she asked lightly.

His face was marked by deepest distress. "Do you feel in any way that I'm a threat to you?"

Jo sat back with a remote look of pain, considering the import of the question.

"I don't know, Dave," she said slowly. "It's something I'll have to think about."

The shore line lay tranquil and untouched by man, peacefully between sky and waters, green in the tidal shallows, blue in the distance. Air and water were pure and delightful, treasures in a land as remote and untroubled as the islands of the South Seas.

"I can't tell you what this means to me," said Jo in a low voice, squinting at a tangle of mangroves which marked a muddy shoal off an island. "I love to come here at night and watch the phosphorescence break."

"Alone?" he asked.

"Oh, yes! Alone," she agreed, "but it's warm on the sands and no one ever comes. There are some squatters down a stretch, but they never pay attention."

"Do you have much time for this?"

"Oh, yes! Why not?"

"What about your job?"

"Oh, that! Well, I'm not called on to do much. Now and then I prepare specimens for Dr. Lockridge, and I do a bit of diving with him, but not often," she said pensively, tossing grains of coral sand at a sand flea. "He doesn't expect too much. It's mostly to give me a small income. I owe a lot to the Lockridges. Did you like him?"

"Very much," said Luzzatto promptly.

"They're good friends," she said quietly. "I don't know where I'd be without their help. Incidentally, living is cheap as dirt. Nora and I pay forty dollars a month for the cottage so it's not hard to manage. The main thing is that I'm free to come and go."

She turned about and lay on her back, face to the sun, and he was struck by the dried wrinkles at her eyes. He said, "Do you play much tennis?"

She laughed. "Tennis? Oh, darling! I'm much too old!"

"Old? Cut it," he said uneasily.

Closed eyelids drank in the sun. "Oh, but I am. The juices are running thin." They both remembered the passion at East Haverstraw that was tennis, the frantic preoccupation with physical sport. It was all gone.

The whispering of air and water over the tidal beach filled the silence. It was hot, hot. A dreamy sense of remoteness, of unreality seemed to fill the moment, and yet he had to grapple with the issue. She rolled on her belly and squinted with sad humor. "Darling, you know I'm older than you, and what's more, I always have been. That's the tragedy of my life."

"I never think of that," he muttered.

"Well, I do," she said lightly.

A light breeze picked up, blowing from land to gulf, ruffling the waters, showing that the afternoon was dying. He covered her hand with his own. It was dried out and warm like an autumn leaf, fragile in the sun. A shiver of dread communicated through the touch.

"Oh, Jo!" he said miserably. "I didn't want to come down on you like this!"

"I know," she agreed in a low voice.

"I can't help this, you see? The whole damn thing got away from me."

There was a moment of silence, an intake of breath; and then, with a violent gesture, she withdrew her hand and sat up, cross-legged in the

321

hot sand, and leaned forward, shoulders bowed, staring into the distance. A halter of silk fell away emptily, and a brown nipple was silhouetted, the smooth point of a childless woman. "Oh, damn!" she sighed bitterly, clenching a fist, then glanced sideways. It was no longer to be put off. "What do you want, Dave?"

"Will you come back with me?"

"When?"

"Tonight. Tomorrow morning. Soon."

"To testify?"

"I hope not," he said reluctantly, then, "Yes!"

"Damn! Damn! Damn!" she repeated monotonously. She shot a dreadful glance of reproach at him. "Why didn't you stay home? Why must I be involved?"

He said simply, "Because no one else can help."

"Help? How?"

Luzzatto took his eyes away and looked at the sand uncomfortably. He was reflecting how to start.

"I guess the only way is to come out and put it to you as simply as I can. The trouble was that I didn't take Phil Seixas fully into my confidence." She was silent, watchful. "Ever since this case began, I've been trying to hold back the truth."

"Truth about what? That letter of Eva's?"

"That was one thing," he admitted.

"What was the other about?"

He looked away. "Your father. He hasn't been a scientist at all for many years, Jo. We both know that." He paused, swallowing.

"That's what I never told Seixas," he added grimly, staring into the distance. "The essential thing I tried to keep out of that public record. I didn't want the defense to degenerate into an attack on his scientific integrity."

Jo went very pale. "Why not attack?"

"Well, I couldn't foul my own nest, Jo. There was a time when it wasn't like this." He hesitated. "There's another reason, too."

"Oh, yes? What?"

He had not expected the harsh croak of cynicism.

"Oh, damn it, Jo. I'm not trying to be mealymouthed. Don't think it hasn't been hard. Many times I've been so enraged that I've wanted to say the first hurting thing that came to mind. I wanted to insult, revile, wound, but I've kept a bridle on because—" He drew a breath and resumed emotionally. "I've also had to think of you, Jo. Haven't I?"

She gazed into his eyes, considering the overtones of meaning, then turned away mournfully.

"Very noble," she muttered.

He put a hand to her shoulder and she drew away. It was suddenly like that freezing night at the window in Brewster.

"Jo, dear," he said softly.

The shoulder resisted. "Don't!"

He dropped on an elbow so that his head was close to hers. "Jo, do you think that I've lost all feelings? That I've completely forgotten? Oh, Christ!" A hand reached up to touch the pitiable face. "You were the first woman I ever loved. A part of me will love you until I die. Is that so hard to believe?"

The mournful eyes stared into his own, lit up by sand reflections of the sun.

"It wasn't love," she said.

She added dully, "It's never been love. Any woman without scruples could have had as much."

A plunging splash in the shoals attracted her eye. The waters suddenly were teaming with fish feeding on bait species coming down the channel with the outgoing tide, and a brown pelican had fallen in their midst like a thunderbolt. After a moment, the bird emerged with a fish struggling in its throat pouch and flapped out of sight. It was a flash of life and death in the brilliant light.

In the same low voice, she said, "I'll tell you what else I think, Dave."

"Yes?"

"It's rotten, just rotten to use these tactics on me. You're talking about something that's dead. Besides, I'm the one person in the world who doesn't need to be corrupted to come to your help."

"They're not just tactics," he choked, looking off. She made no reply to this. He sank back and closed his eyes, overwhelmed with the despair of a lost game. Time passed with only the sound of placid waters on the hot shore.

"What a ridiculous pose," he muttered bitterly. "All this time I've kept up the pretense that this lawsuit had to be kept a search for truth on a level worthy of two scientists of good reputation. Do you remember that first day I came to the lab, Jo?" She nodded. "I was thrilled by your father— really charged by that concept of the discipline of science, of ruthless adherence to truth regardless of consequence. I was impressionable and it sounded good, and it gave me some stupid idea of belonging to an elect society, a sort of inner circle, a priestly cult—guardians of a holy place.

"Oh, not really," he added, smiling bitterly, "but that's roughly the

323

idea. In my own idiotic way, that notion became a rule of life, a guide to conduct, and yet—what have I done? At the first test, all those adolescent concepts were completely junked. Oh, I kept throwing out hints and warnings, begging him not to cut off all lines of retreat for us both, but the fact remains that I did everything I could to suppress the truth. I didn't even play fair with the lawyers."

He paused with feeling. "I can't tell you what it was like to sit on that witness chair, hour after hour, facing those eyes, while that lawyer of his was tearing at my throat. No hint, no allusion, made the slightest impression. Why? Why? He heard—he understood! Why couldn't I get through? And why did I keep out of the case the one thing that brings coherence to the entire picture? I know the answer. In a way, I think that's what's increased his contempt for me—that I lacked the integrity, the guts to follow the truth to its logical outcome. If I'd done that in the old days, he'd have flayed me, Jo. You know that!

"But how long can I keep this up?" he cried. "I'm dragged through the mud, hounded like a thief, and for what? To sacrifice my wife to a lie? To use these tactics on you? All right!" His voice suddenly shook with rage and grief. "I'm rotten, Jo! I'm anything you want. We'll see how rotten I can get before we're through!"

After unendurable silence he heard her voice. "You said there was something that brings coherence to the case?" He nodded. "What's that?" she asked.

"It's what happened that summer when I came up to Maine," he said finally. "You know how he reacted when I brought the news? I've still got that letter of yours, offering to patch things up, explaining that he'd get over that queer mood, begging me not to do anything impulsive or foolish. That's only one of a hundred points you could clear up."

"Letter?" she murmured.

"How could you forget, Jo? You drove me back to the airport at Waterville yourself."

She said finally, "Why is that so important?"

"Oh, don't you see? The whole case turns on the question of my good faith. What happened that night explains why I knew he never expected to share in anything but a teacher's reflected glory. Why I had no reason to doubt that I was doing the right thing. You could clear this up."

A low bitter tone, almost inaudible. "Do you know what you're asking, Dave?"

"I think so."

"No, you don't! You're asking to use me as an instrument to strike

324

back—to testify in public against my father. Is that consistent with all that integrity as a scientist?"

He looked at the sand uncomfortably, searching for an elusive answer. "It's consistent with the search for truth. I don't think he can object."

"Do you really believe that?" she asked with contempt.

"No," he conceded reluctantly. "It's nothing so pretentious, I guess." Her taut dark face tightened, the sensitive nostrils flared without change of expression. "But if I'm corrupted, Jo, so are we all. It's the only way out."

"Oh, how?" she demanded skeptically.

"I'm still hoping that he'll withdraw the complaint if you appear on the scene, ready to give the facts. I don't think he'd care to face that, because that's what this elaborate hoax is all about—a gigantic attempt to pervert and hide from the truth." Luzzatto swallowed. "It's got to come out, Jo. If not through you, then from him at the trial in a more painful way. I'm not prepared to lose the case—for anyone or anything."

Jo went pale. They stared at each other and they understood the truth which lay between them. This creature, for whom he ached, was in his hands; yet a part of his mind thought: one more push and she'll go over. Out of what hellish chamber of his soul, he wondered, could that thought have been engendered? In her dark eyes, once flashing, now more sunken than he liked, lurked a nightmare dread, part of his own. And then she said a strange thing which staggered him.

"You want me to do something unnatural?"

He said uneasily, "Don't look at it that way, Jo."

"Oh, but I must! What else is it? I can't forget my deeper feelings, any more than you. I shouldn't be talking to you at all, should I?" she asked oddly.

She lowered her head, thinking, then looked up and said slowly, "I can't do it, Dave! I'm too afraid of what might happen to me up there. I'm all right down here in this atmosphere, but I can't! I just can't!"

He was silent and she said, "But I'll do something else. If I have your solemn promise that you'll keep me out of court, I'm willing to go back with you to talk to Dad. I really don't know if I can face him, but I'll try. Otherwise I won't leave this place."

He nodded slowly and with misgivings. "I promise," he said hoarsely. "I'll be ready in the morning. Can you wait over for that flight?"

The flight north was quick and easy. Jo was abstracted and silent. She sipped bouillon and nursed cold hands, completely remote. She asked one question as they were approaching. "Are you sure we'll be met?"

325

"You mean by your father?"

"Yes."

"I don't know. Eva told me last night she'd notify Phil Seixas this morning. He's probably telephoned Dirksen to let your father know. It's not too much notice, I admit, but that's legal protocol. Worse than ours," he joked feebly.

She turned to the window.

They came down out of the clear sky into a gray flurry of rain squalls that beat against the window. It was a race to shelter. A grim, familiar figure was waiting at the exit.

"Hello, Dave," said Seixas coldly.

The lawyer made a signal. A man in a shabby overcoat detached a shoulder from the wall and came over.

"Dr. Josephine Ullman?"

"Yes."

"I have something for you," said the man. He reached into a pocket and handed over a set of forms to which two dollar bills were attached. The court order signed by Justice Willard Cohalan sitting in Merton County commanded her attendance to give testimony in connection with the pending case.

"Jo!" said Luzzatto, stricken. "I had no idea! I swear it on my life."

Her composure was remarkable. "No, Dave, I'm sure you didn't. This form of betrayal would never occur to a simple mind. It takes years of training, I'm sure."

"I'm sorry about this," said Seixas, and turned. "I got your message, Dave, but I must remind you that I made no promises to Dr. Ullman of any sort, so none were broken. It was your own idea to act without counsel.

"If you wish, Dr. Ullman, I'll be glad to drive you into the city," he added.

"I think not, Mr. Seixas. I'll take a cab." A hard, trembling smile formed, grim with irony. "Sorry, Dave!" Jo said more softly. "Goodbye, and all my love to Eva. I'm afraid I know what side I'm on."

With a curt nod to the lawyer, she strode off to the line of taxis forming in the rain.

Chapter 25

Foxx LISTENED TO THE DIATRIBE WITHOUT EXPRESSION. HIS MANNER was one of chilling formality.

"I have no intention of taking this up with anyone, Professor. I understand that you're disturbed about Jo Ullman, and so am I, but the matter was turned over to trial counsel for action. I see no reason to interfere."

"I gave her my word," said Luzzatto obstinately.

Foxx shrugged and reached for his pipe. His response was measured. "You had no right to make that promise. The university is entitled to her testimony. I must remind you that the sums involved are large."

"I know all about those sums," Luzzatto said. "It was my work that created them."

Foxx seemed unimpressed. He finished the ceremony of stuffing the briar.

"Oh, really? I don't think you ought to overestimate your contribution, Professor. I quite agree that biocin has its value as a tool in biological research, but as to its commercial value? Oh, come! I've had my own talks with the people at Brandywine. What's really so remarkable about biocin? Without the efforts of Brandywine, it would have stayed in the laboratory, perhaps forever," he added with a trace of impatience.

"They didn't say that when they needed me," said Luzzatto bitterly.

"They're saying it now," replied Foxx.

He eyed the white-lipped young scientist with worldly curiosity. He saw no recognition, absolutely none, that in the marts of commerce the talents of these creative types were deemed fungible, raw material to the superior race whose commercial acumen and skill alone gave monetary value to mere dreams and the vagrant impulses of imagination. The truth was that in that other world these people were held completely replaceable, essential only as a class, and then only in the sense that oxen are essential to leather. He brought the discussion back to Jo Ullman. "In any case how could you give up legal rights to her testimony which belong to the university? No one gave you that authority."

"I expected to be backed up," said Luzzatto.

Foxx studied the younger man stolidly, almost with pity. It took effort to keep in mind the lacunae in useful knowledge which the type possessed. His own mind looked at the world with the lackluster realism of the fund raiser.

"Yes. Yes, I think you did," he said slowly, "but you certainly lost that right, Professor, when you elected to play a lone hand. You damaged the case and now you've put yourself in a mortifying position. Didn't you expect that much when you elected to withhold information from counsel?"

"We're still in the preliminaries. I would have told him everything before the actual trial," said Luzzatto.

Foxx merely grunted and pressed a button. "Mrs. Haggerty, will you bring in my tea?" He turned back. "Will you excuse me now?"

Luzzatto failed to move. "I'd like to put this to the trustees," he said finally.

"Oh, really? Well, that's your privilege," said Foxx in a hard voice. "I can't stop you from approaching the trustees separately, but I wouldn't feel pleased. I'll remind you that the annual meeting doesn't take place until August."

"Suppose I offer to resign?"

"With this case coming up for trial?" Foxx was incredulous. "Do you realize the effect?"

"I'm quite serious," said Luzzatto grimly.

At this point the door opened and Mrs. Martha Haggerty entered with tea and service of bone china for one.

"Mrs. Haggerty?" said Foxx. "Will you bring a sheet of paper? I'd like to have the official letterhead."

When she had left, he added, "Let's see how serious that really is."

Luzzatto sat waiting while the door opened and closed. Moments later he wrote out a letter which severed his connection with the university.

"Well!" said Foxx, almost with disbelief.

A long glance of determination was exchanged, then Foxx picked up the paper, considering the new situation with a curious hard glance of respect. Still to consider would be the effect on faculty opinion. The resig-

328

nation of a distinguished young scientist during his administration could have unpleasant implications.

On the other hand, such a paper could at the right time ease the fellow's exit from the university with the facility of a burial at sea—quick, smooth, improved by a touch of piety.

"This letter has no date," he observed.

Luzzatto replied grimly, "It wasn't meant to have."

"I won't change my mind about this problem with Jo Ullman, you know."

"It no longer has to do with her."

Foxx nodded in reluctant concession. "You're giving me a free hand?"

"Yes."

Foxx crossed the room, rubbing the pipe against his cheek, weighing the matter in its many aspects. Deep wrinkles creased the low forehead.

"Well, I imagine this letter can wait for the outcome of the trial," he said slowly. "In the meantime, it can rest in my safe. May I say something, Professor?"

"Go ahead," said Luzzatto shortly. A mantle of red slowly mounted his neck. Despite everything, he was confounded that his letter had not been promptly refused—a fact that seemed the measure of his plight.

"It's simply this," said Foxx calmly. "The university doesn't stand to you in the role of a loving parent, Professor. Really. It's quite impersonal and it has its own interests. It might be useful to examine the position in the light of that principle. You assigned those royalties to the university by your own decision. You mustn't complain if counsel takes the line that seems best to preserve those rights. Is there anything else?"

Luzzatto drew a breath and looked off. He had a glimpse into a dimension of reality whose existence he had never before suspected.

"No, I think not," he said finally. "Except to thank you for some good advice, Dr. Foxx. I'll try to remember it."

Mortified and affronted beyond words, he turned and left. He was scarlet to the ears.

Eventually the Executive Committee of the Senate Council met to consider Lizzie Batchelor's resolution of confidence in the integrity of their colleague.

George Gordimer Puce telephoned to express regret. "Sorry, old man!" he cried. "One did what one could. One always likes to go to bat for justice, but there's a lynch atmosphere, you know? The whole thing's become too nasty."

Luzzatto hung up without a word.

329

Podell set his brakes and climbed out of his car beside a stone wall several hundred years old. A short walk through a rocky pasture of thistles and yarrow brought him to the bank of a pond.

Luzzatto was seated on a boulder watching the sun setting between hills in the distance. Podell sat quietly and waited for the younger man to take notice. He was struck by lines of strain etched in the thin, sharp features. After a moment of silence, he said brutally, "What's all this about, Dave? Why don't you get back to your wife?"

Luzzatto looked up vaguely, taking a moment to come out of his thoughts. "She's better off without me," he said morosely. "I'm only getting on her nerves. Besides, if anything happens, there's a telephone at the farmhouse."

"I wouldn't do this to a whore," said Podell with feeling, lighting a cigar. "A lot of people are getting pretty sore at you, Dave," he observed. "How can the lawyer do his job when you poop off like a hairless wonder into the hills?"

"Who? Seixas?" Luzzatto shrugged bitterly. "He doesn't need me any more. He practically told me that much at the airport. I can't be a party to those tactics, Si," he added savagely. "I led Jo into a trap—and there's nothing I can do except to let the case take its course. I've got to remember that I'm just a dumb scientist—that I can't run the case because the case is running me. You can tell Seixas that I'll see him at the trial!"

Podell liked Luzzatto more than most of the academic crowd at Haverstraw. Most of them affected different forms of superficial cynicism toward the educational process. He found this brand of self-depreciation shocking. Self-respect, he felt, began at home and he liked a scholar to be a scholar. He had deep regard for Luzzatto's sensitivity, for his serious and exceptional willingness to express the ideals of science without embarrassment—it was callow, perhaps comical, even absurd, but always touching, and it spoke well, he thought, of Luzzatto's family background. He said, "Maybe there's a way out, Dave. You may not have to go to trial with this thing."

Luzzatto stared without expression. "Not go to trial? Why not?"

Podell laughed at the instant cloud of suspicion. "I'll tell you on the way."

"No!" said Luzzatto stubbornly. "Tell me now."

"Come on, you stupid bastard," said Podell in an annoyed voice. "I don't like to keep my car waiting." He arose and stretched and went off and after a moment Luzzatto followed. "Let me telephone Evvie to let her know where I'll be!"

Podell turned. "She knows," he said grimly. "She knows."

In a shabby room lined with dusty scientific periodicals and detective stories, a gaunt old man was staring with boredom at a television screen. Occasionally he nodded and dreamed. A bell sounded in the distance and he awoke with a start as he heard the door opened by his housekeeper.

"Hello, Davey," said Lackland Mackenzie sardonically. "Mahomet's come to the mountain?"

Luzzatto let his eyes grow accustomed to the dimness of the study. "I suppose so," he said shortly. He was waved to the ruins of a Morris chair. In the glum silence, Mackenzie stared keenly. "Mrs. Noyes, I think two stiff whiskies are in order for our guests. Make that three," he added as the woman left. An arthritic hand reached out to a switch and the picture died. He said heavily, "Well, Davey! It's almost a year!"

"Eight months," said Luzzatto.

"Is it now? Time's playing tricks on me. It doesn't seem that long. Oh, sit down, Podell," he said peevishly.

Podell took a rocker and assumed an air of intense respect while Mackenzie put a series of questions regarding old friends and affairs at the university. A tale, he remarked, had been brought of the maneuver in Lizzie Batchelor's department to jockey Hubbard through the defense of his incredible thesis. Was Luzzatto messed up in that nasty bit of log rolling?

Luzzatto said, "I voted to approve the man for his doctorate."

"Is he qualified?"

"Erskine Hubbard? No." said Luzzatto grimly.

Podell remarked that Luzzatto had had the strength to rise above moral scruples. "For a guy who's not used to that," he added seriously, "it's not easy."

"I daresay," said Mackenzie meditatively. The sunken eyes closed, reserving final opinion. A chill seemed to penetrate the room. Mackenzie looked up finally. "What d'ye think brings ye here, Davey?"

Luzzatto said, "I haven't any conception."

Mackenzie reached for a cigar. "Would it be of interest that I've had a call from Victor Ullman?"

A moment of silence, then, "Do the lawyers know?" asked Luzzatto.

"Hey? Why, certainly!"

Luzzatto shot a bitter glance at Podell. "It's logical enough, I suppose. He still holds the initiative." He added, "Nothing Victor Ullman can say has the slightest interest."

Mackenzie stared dourly. "I suppose you'd rather like to meet in open court where ye can flay the man alive? Where ye can revile and be reviled? Sling mud and get slung? Hey?"

"Nothing would please me more. I've had it!"

Mackenzie turned with exasperation. "Podell, I'm almost in sympathy with the farmer who put his idiot boy out of the way on the ground that it didn't pay to winter the lad. Come in," he called at a knock.

The housekeeper brought a decanter of whiskey and glasses.

"Not for me," said Luzzatto tightly, declining an offer.

Mackenzie lifted a glass to the useful eye and stared through liquor. "Ye're dim in this light, Davey. Exceedingly dim, but somehow that makes ye more acceptable. Just remember that there's little friendship in the world, least of all among equals. It's a good point of departure." With a nasty grin, he tossed off the drink and smacked his lips.

More somberly he arose and turned on lights in the darkening room, sensing the resentful eyes of the younger man on his back. Oh, I'm too old for this nonsense! he told himself wearily, staring at journals no longer read, contributions no longer relevant, areas of knowledge beyond his grasp. New mathematics, new chemistries, new physics had come along, establishing a universe whose boundaries continued to recede into mists of uncertainty and confusion. More than half a century had passed since his own arrival at the school which had grown under his care to stature and reputation. Yet none of these thoughts, he reflected, could help the young scientist fighting for career and honor with an intensity entirely to his credit.

He came back to the chair, tugging at the baggy sweater which hung on his frame.

"It's almost incredible how history seems to repeat, Davey," he said finally. "I recall the same bad business with Fred Banting, oh, more than thirty years ago, I think. He had the fool notion he could lick the worst degenerative disease in the history of medicine. Also the simple belief that the world of science was waiting for him with open arms. Made the mistake of knocking at the door of John MacLeod who was teaching physiology in Toronto.

"Well, I don't have to tell ye what happened. That summer when MacLeod was in Europe, Fred Banting killed several dozen dogs but he came up with insulin and saved ten million lives and more to come."

Mackenzie grinned reminiscently, recalling reprisals and counter-reprisals that followed the split of the Nobel Prize between Banting and MacLeod. "It was Banting's discovery, but it was also MacLeod's lab and under the rules he was entitled to claim the glory. Why not? He brought those rules from Leipzig and Berlin where he got his training." The useful eye rested on the younger man. "Fred Banting knew, or should have known, those rules when he took those benefits from MacLeod. Instead, he found the whole thing intolerable. Bitterly resentful to the end. Never mentioned MacLeod's name. Never saw his point of view and never wanted to. And mind you, there was no money problem to exacerbate that situation because there all the revenues from insulin went to that university. But I want to make a point."

Mackenzie stared keenly. "Fred Banting kept his feelings to himself. He understood that he was joined to MacLeod in scientific history like Siamese twins and he nursed his feelings in private. He didn't go rushing off into print. Or the courts. Was he worse off or better? Hey?"

"Really, sir," said Luzzatto stiffly, "I don't see the application of all this."

"Don't ye? Well," said Mackenzie with a sigh. "This feller Seixas tells me ye've got some sort of ace up your sleeve. Something about a chart ye once showed him? I'm told ye carry it around?"

"Only lately," said Luzzatto.

After a moment he opened a wallet and passed over the little chart which Mackenzie studied with interest. "I'll be damned," he muttered.

Against a black field stood seven candles, each divided into five segments, each segment filled with written texts drawn from Scripture. It was apparent that the diagram had taken scholarship and years of toil, for the texts were organized into highly systematized sets of interlocking diagrams.

A crest proclaimed thirty-five Commandments on Knowing given by the Master to the Children of God. Each of seven candles was divided into five segments of appropriate rank. The lowest rank was assigned to the World. The higher ascended in order into the kingdoms of Knowledge, of the Divine Logos, of the Master and the regions of Godhead.

In turn another set of values had been assigned to each candle reading from left to right. Five texts of the first Candle were grouped under Purpose, those of the fifth under Planting Seeds, the sixth under Power, the seventh under Promised Abode.

Seven flames spelled K N O W I N G .

All rested on the arch of S C I E N C E which in turn stood on Pyramids too intricate to be deciphered.

The underlying legend proclaimed that the Master Science of All Science was the Science of the Master. The Master in Whom are hidden all Treasures of Wisdom and Knowledge and Power.

Power!

Mackenzie scowled at the diagram, turning the chart about, examining the crevices with magnifying glass for further relationships. The old man passed the chart to Podell and sat back, smoking. His expression was odd. "Have ye shown this to anyone else?"

Luzzatto nodded. "Yes. I asked Dean Polk to look at it."

"Polk?" snorted Mackenzie, incredulous at recourse to the outsider. "What in God's name would ye want from that woolly-minded old boy?"

"A theological opinion," said Luzzatto.

Mackenzie was brought up short. "Ye've got me there, Davey," he laughed. "What did ye learn?"

Luzzatto hesitated. Staring at the carpet, he described the conversation.

"Oh, this is interesting!" Polk had exclaimed, beaming with interest. "Oh, yes! Yes, indeed!" He was not sure what it meant, but in some aspects the chart resembled systematized diagrams seen in the literature of Gnosticism—a term that designated certain ancient systems of thought that had centered on the belief that emancipation comes from knowledge of essential truth, that truth which saves the initiate from the clutch of matter.

"Do you mean this man's a Gnostic?" Luzzatto had asked.

"No, no! I didn't say that," Polk had replied. "Oh, there were many such schools," he added, twinkling at the chart with the pleasure of discovery. Essential to all those systems was the possession of secret and mysterious knowledge, not accessible to outsiders, not to be proved or propagated, but to be accepted and believed by the initiated, vigilantly guarded as a secret.

"What makes this unique," Polk went on with intense interest, "is the attempt to fuse the rationales of modern science with these ancient systems. Curious! I wonder if I might have a copy?"

They had been walking that day in circles around Davenport Library. Dean Polk was chatting vigorously in a penetrating voice, flailing his arms with enthusiasm.

"Oh, yes! These people, you see, believe that they know something which neither you nor I know. Or can know! Not until we enter the brotherhood, that is." He smiled broadly, genuinely pleased. "This sort of knowledge of God is not the same thing, you know, as the Biblical concept of knowledge. 'For the earth, the earth, shall be full of the knowledge of God as the waters cover the sea!' But of course," he added seriously, "the prophet was referring to ethical knowledge, not mystical, which is entirely another thing."

"Of course," murmured Luzzatto, suddenly depressed. "The man who made this chart? What do you think of him?"

Polk halted in mid-stride. He gazed at the sky, smiling benevolently.

"Think? Well, it's hard to say. This man obviously has something, you see? He's read the literature and he's got hold of an original notion. Original, at least, in this context." Science, he said, was not the only field that prized originality. He tapped the diagram. "Of course, like most of these people, he's trying to construct a technique, not of general redemption, but of redemption for himself. If I grasp this scheme, he wants to do this by locating the logical foundations of science, not within human reason, but within some Indwelling Spirit from which all knowledge emanates. It's simply another attempt to tackle the crisis in religion, which really is the fundamental problem of the age, don't you think? The loss of faith in reason? It's far more serious than mere loss of faith in God, especially in an age of credulity where we believe any miracle provided it's not in the Bible." He beamed genially. "It's the most serious intellectual disease of modern times. This fellow at Harvard, Bridgman, has been pointing out—"

The digression went on with learning and humor, until finally Polk was recalled to the chart. In a world impoverished in spirit, it was rather touching, he thought.

"Don't tell me you agree with it?" demanded Luzzatto.

"No, no!" Polk said. He slipped an arm in the younger man's. "We're worlds apart, this man and I, but I must confess that I have a certain sympathy for what he's trying to do. This chart shows that he wants to enter the unity of God through commands of certain forms of knowledge. You'll notice how he stresses the runic word K N O W. Almost like a sacred tetragrammaton. Notice how arbitrarily he's introduced that word, which he equates with science, even where he's forced to misquote or distort scriptural texts? I think the purpose is to force the issue, to compel the diagram to work out."

"Like cheating at solitaire?"

"What? Oh, yes! Yes," laughed Polk, highly amused. "In many of these schemes, one must have the right word to ascend into the higher realms of being. A philosopher too tries to establish the unity of God, but purely through reason. He finds satisfaction merely in the assertion of that unity. Or at least I do. I can hardly object to these kindred efforts."

Luzzatto was not to be put off. "What do you make of the man himself?"

"Oh, that. It's not easy to say. This man has spent too much time with this diagram. He's trying to compensate, I imagine, for something else in his life, to escape into an abstract realm of intellectual perfection. He's not the ordinary case, because he makes science the basis of the attempt. I mean, the whole scheme shows strong roots in common sense and

335

scientific method, a struggle to remain anchored in the world of reason and logic. It represents an intense mental and spiritual struggle, I'd say, full of internal contradictions."

"Escape? From what?" said Luzzatto.

"Oh, I have no idea. None at all," said Polk, dropping his eyes to the chart. "It's perfectly possible to escape from life into higher things, just as some escape into low and sensual pursuits. It's the great danger, you know. No workable religion can tolerate the flight from social responsibility. For what," he demanded, beaming, "does the prophet require of us, but to do justly, and to love mercy, and to walk humbly with God? But I am struck here by something," he added.

"Yes?"

"These texts grouped under the heading of Power. They contradict the general scheme of the chart. I find that disturbing. The texts which offer power as a shield are merely comforting. But these that grant power over this man's enemies seem assaultive. I'd say that this man has gotten rather remote. But it's fascinating. Yes. Is he anyone I know?"

Mackenzie smoked contemplatively, scowling at a disagreeable picture in his mind. "What d'ye hope to get with this, Davey?"

"The truth."

"Oh, how?"

A bitter look settled in the younger man's face. "I haven't had my innings yet," he said. "We'll see!"

"Bro-ther! Would you like to know what I think?" said Podell, breaking the silence. "I think this guy cleans his own test tubes. I think he polishes doorknobs."

Mackenzie came to a decision. "Suppose I tell ye the purpose of Ullman's call? Suppose he's willing to submit this case to arbitration."

Luzzatto was visibly jolted. "Arbitration?" He shot a glance of surprise at Podell. "So that's it!" he said slowly. "He's turned down every offer till now. Why now?"

"It's this business with his daughter. He doesn't want to put her through that horror," said Mackenzie.

"Oh, no doubt!" said Luzzatto bitterly.

Mackenzie smoked thoughtfully. "Ye mustn't let your feelings mislead ye, Davey. Ullman was always difficult, but he's a decent fellow with good instincts. D'ye think he hasn't any regard for that girl of his?"

"He hasn't up till now," muttered Luzzatto.

"Well, it's hard for a man like that to reverse himself. The patterns of thought are quite rigid, determined. Let me tell you something, Davey. At your age, he was quite different—bit pedantic, but full of promise. He had great capacity for work, strong ambition, keen insight, and he read everything. We all expected he'd make a big splash in science, like you, Davey, but he never did. Something in him just missed. And yet, he often came close to important contributions. As early as 1935 he wanted to show that the gene produces its effects by regulating the output and specificity of enzymes. Never pursued the idea and finally those other fellers published that paper on Neurospora that pulled the rug out from under. He'd simply spent too much time exploring side issues while the central notion stared him in the face.

"Those things happened to him more than once. The university was smaller and we formed a well-knit group. My wife was alive then, and the Ullmans were regular visitors with that little girl of theirs. He had a good baritone and a sense of humor and my wife loved to play German lieder with him. He was very attentive and terribly kind, not only to students, but to anyone connected with science. Well, all that was before disappointment set in.

"I don't expect ye to see all that, Davey," Mackenzie went on. "All ye can see is the old man who made this devious chart. But I see another man entirely, young and bright, like yourself, prepared to shake the world. He was quite devoted to me and that's something I can hardly forget. None of us know how we'll turn out in the end, do we?"

Mackenzie sighed and threw the cigar into the hearth and went on. "I'll tell ye something else about this proposal. Ullman's ready to offer an inducement."

"Inducement? What's that?"

"He'll discontinue the action against the university entirely."

"And the action against me?"

"That goes to the arbitrator."

Podell broke the silence. "It means he'll give up nine-tenths of his claim, Dave. That takes your God-damned Center off the hook. Can you afford to take the responsibility of turning that down?"

Luzzatto shot over a cold glance of anger. "There's nothing to arbitrate. Not any more!"

"This case has got to be decided by someone," Mackenzie said quietly. "Are you sure you want a public trial?"

Luzzatto leaped up and stalked about the shabby room with its high ceiling and reek of stale old tobacco. His mouth worked convulsively. Oh, the cunning stroke! he told himself vengefully. To have squeezed him into this impossible dilemma! "Well, this is perfect," he burst out finally, opening and closing his hands. "I'm already pilloried, disgraced in public, but when his turn comes, I'm to let a small group of men huddle behind closed doors and get rid of Dave Luzzatto. Oh, great! The whole plan is working out. Maybe I need a truth chart of my own! Can't you see that this is exactly what he had in mind from the outset? First, to disgrace me, then, to put the entire blame on me if we go to trial? No, no!" he cried vengefully. "This sweet proposal comes exactly eight months too late. Let's have the whole business out in the open where we can get some light on this mess. What have I got to lose?"

"You've been screaming about Jo Ullman," Podell growled coarsely. "Well? How do you feel today about the poor bitch? Arbitration could get her out from under. Or would you rather leave her to Seixas?"

Luzzatto wet his lips. "You, too, Si?" he burst out. "And you were supposed to be on my side." He sat back, jolted.

He stared at the carpet for a long time, breathing heavily. "Who'd be the arbitrator?" he asked hoarsely.

"I would," said Mackenzie. "If you consent. I thought that was understood?"

"No, it wasn't," said Luzzatto. "I resent being put in this position and I'm not sure I can go along. In any case, I can't give my answer now. I'll have to talk it over with my wife. It almost seems that she's the only one who's with me," he added bitterly.

"Mebbe so," said Mackenzie.

He sat back with his cigar and smoked quietly. A tinge of compassion darkened the useful eye. The sound of breathing filled the room.

"I think I can be fair," he observed finally. "Or at this stage of life don't ye trust any man of science?"

Chapter 26

MIDNIGHT.

In the dark up and point of fire at infinity explodes and swoops imposing on all pain.

Hands clenched and convulsive nails bleeding.

Conviction at the second toning.

Ah! Ah!

Oh, now, now! Lights on the machine. In the road sleeping houses and pain to the birthing house. Bag things chair lift hands ministering in hair scrape and enema gush and tedium of animal wait. Terror and walls alone.

Soon! God, soon!

David where? David?

Crump of thunder shells dissolve of Polish cellar into white and the long surge of pain.

Vigil below and David waiting.

Where David?

Ah! and the reassuring pat of the (nurse's) hand. Now, mother, are we all right? Father? Mother? Nurse? Elzbieta?

My priest? Safe from—

No! (Doctor) Hawkins hands warm and calm and summons of David. (Jokes dirty and tales told of ambulances when horse-drawn.)

A-a-h!

Good?

No, bad!

Oh, very good! And laughter! Hell, Dave, this girl don't need me.

(Nurse) and (internes) and quite a bawl. (Hands hold with David.) Recall bad times of life shrink upset then (non-) maternity clothes resent solicitude and friends pity. Anesthetist late where in hell that guy? Superstition that life pay price. What did? Punishment this? Lord God Master Universe Why?)

(David always!)

And walk! Soon, soon! Pray God no taint, no imperfection, but life!

A-a-h!

Bad?

No, good!

Oh, that's bad. (Oh, that time false imaginary phantom question growth measuring tape sharp pain and the cramped breath and) (in street doctor and abhorred milk eggs refused abort of drugged monster floating in sack.)

Time of the mighty Thing seizing out of Nowhere. Time, at last! (Hold David. Always—)

Possessed of—

—blind Power!

Feet here, mother, and the theatre blaze. Oh, soon, the moment! In the well of pain oh please for the numb of senses quick oh please and the—

Down sinking into black swirling and the drug—

Face looming and (now mother) legs open to water pass and fecal the oh god flesh ripping of blackness again distance and the Thing flailing muscles like snakes thrust and down squeeze then—

A-a-h!

In the deep hoarse groaning the cord, and slime curdled in shells thunder oh the blood-red finger and nuggets of male generation dangling to generation that passeth like time oh David—

The cry!

In the blackest Sanctification of the Name God of our Fathers—

Measureless peace.

Eva was conscious that many hours had passed. An outflung arm felt the touch of metal. About her was the sense of a sunny room and a bed enclosed with rails. Something was holding her wrist. She moved and knew internal padding. Her tongue was bitten painfully, breath was fruity with exhalations of anesthesia, lips felt bruised and then eyelids felt a kiss.

Luzzatto whispered her name. "Darling?"

She looked up questioningly, noting the pallor and signs of strain. At the bright window, Nella was fixing a vase of roses, smiling.

Eva asked weakly, "Is the baby all right?"

"God, yes!" said Luzzatto gladly. It was a fat boy with red hair, he grinned, and a screwed-up parody of Cesare Luzzatto's face. Even the elongated head, he joked, was a sign of future intelligence.

"I want to hold him," she whispered.

"I'll see what I can do," he agreed. He kissed her hand, clammy and still cold, and went off.

Eva said, "Nella?"

"The child's perfect!" said Nella.

Eva closed her eyes. "Well, I'm happy for us all. I'm sorry I put on such a poor show."

"Bosh! When I had David, I screamed all night like a fishwife. You shouldn't mind a little fuss. No one else does," said Nella energetically.

"Dave was wonderful," said Eva.

"He's a lump," said Nella fondly. "Like his father, but he has his moments." She was highly pleased.

"I've been so weak," murmured Eva.

"After this? Oh, dear," said Nella smiling, patting the bluish hand. "Eva, in the end you're the strongest of us all. This was your goal. You let nothing stand in the way. Your trouble is that you make no allowances for conditions," she added, drawing on her own reserves of intuition.

A moment passed while Eva rested, savoring the languor and peace that followed the struggle.

She said, "I wasn't afraid of the pain, you know? In a way, I was looking forward to it. What shocked me was the way my body took over. I was completely out of control. This thing took possession of me. Whether I wanted the baby or not, I was helpless. I had no idea it was like that."

"Oh, yes," said Nella, patting Eva's hand.

Eva closed her eyes and waited. When finally the baby was brought she examined it closely. "Oh, thank God!" she whispered. "Let me?" When the tiny hand with its fingernails of miniature perfection went to her breasts she burst into silent tears. It was nothing she wanted or could control. It was another woman who had travailed. Another who was weeping. Only at the core was herself who had given life.

What strange journey, she thought with satisfaction, smiling and weeping as a tiny yawn formed at her breast.

Clara Stokes lived up to her reputation as a jewel. On the day of Eva's return, the house had been cleaned to perfection and the nursery upstairs sparkled in the sun.

341

"Oh, the house is lovely!" cried Eva, holding the tiny burden lapped in wool. She looked about the room, breathing with pleasure, absorbing its warm colors. "Everything looks so new!" she exclaimed.

Clara lifted the coverlet and studied a pink bubbling mouth. "Oh, my God!" she cried. "He looks like a professor already! What's his I.Q.? How does His Majesty feel about it?"

Eva smiled wryly. "Well, some people take time to fall in love with strangers."

"Is that what he said?" demanded Clara, placing her arms akimbo, incredulous.

"Oh, yes," said Eva, amused.

Clara shook her head in wonder. "Some people," she said witheringly, "have always got to be honest. Those kind are the worst!"

"It's all talk and bravado," said Eva, replacing the coverlet. Luzzatto was parking the convertible, and at the reminder of sounds in the driveway, the smile of satisfaction faded. "Well, you mustn't mind him, Clara, he's not himself. This other thing is still on his mind." She sighed, then rallied. "Well, let's take this young man upstairs now. I'd like to see him in his crib. Then I'd like some lunch. That hospital food!"

"I know, honey! I know!" said Clara with sympathy.

They mounted the stairs slowly. "Wonderful! Wonderful!" said Clara, hovering over the morsel of warmth.

Less than an hour later Eva put aside her coffee and cocked an ear. They were in the dining room.

Luzzatto said, "He's asleep."

She caught herself and laughed. "Can't help it, Davey. I suppose I'll be doing that for the rest of my life. I hope you won't mind?"

"I won't," he agreed bleakly.

"Oh, will I ever be slim again?" she sighed, stroking herself. She sat back luxuriously and contemplated the serious, intelligent eyes across the table, noting the dark rings of exhaustion. She felt again the stir of love and compassion and decided to open the forbidden topic.

"Match?"

"Oh, sure."

She lit a cigarette and stared through wreathing smoke. "I've been a self-centered pig long enough, darling. Tell me about the case. Is there any way I can help?"

342

Chapter 27

FROM THE MOMENT SET FOR THE PARTIES TO GATHER AT THE FACULTY Club (it being neutral ground), Luzzatto was struck with doubt and uncertainty. He arrived early at the shabby Georgian building. The lounge was deserted and he went up immediately to a conference room to wait for the others. He smoked three cigarettes, changed his seat several times, examined faded encrusted portraits of forgotten scholars, left twice to empty his bladder, finally stalked down the hall to the window where he stared moodily at the courts which once had been Jo Ullman's domain. He had a vision of that first year when she still had played a strong game of tennis.

"Oh, Christ! Christ," he muttered nervously. He heard footsteps on the stairs, first a younger, briskly, then an older, more deliberate. Horatio Dotson appeared, followed by Philip Seixas. Without change of expression they entered the conference room. Moments later, Dotson came out and approached Luzzatto.

"The chief thinks you ought to wait inside, Professor."

Luzzatto said, "I'm the corpse at the funeral. I can't be late."

"It's not that," said Dotson grinning.

Luzzatto shrugged and returned to the room. Seixas was seated with his back to the window. He was flipping the pages of a memorandum, looking tired and irritable. He plunged directly into discussion. "Where would you like to sit?"

"Does it matter?"

"It hasn't the slightest importance, Dave. Ordinarily the parties will face each other across the table with the arbitrators at the head. If you'd like to sit next to me, we can create the impression of a united front. If you'd still rather disassociate yourself from the university, that's your affair. I'll be guided accordingly."

Luzzatto shrugged and pointedly selected the far end of the table facing the head.

"Lovely day," said Seixas, removing his glasses.

The day was indeed balmy and lovely. The sky was blue and a soft breeze was blowing. No doubt the track team, harbingers of spring, were circling the cinder track in South Field. Luzzatto folded his arms and presented a stony face to the ceiling.

Precisely at ten o'clock, chapel bells at St. Peter's and St. Paul's began to ring. The door opened and Si Podell entered with a grunt, followed by Lackland Mackenzie, for whom the publicity man stepped back with an air of deference. The old scientist glanced about with a scowl of surprise at the familiar walls. He seemed astonished at his own face in oils under a patina of dirt.

"Is that fool thing still there?" he growled, pulling off a scarf. He stared at himself, entranced. "Thought they'd burn the frame for firewood once me back was turned. Well, well!" He turned. "Hello, Seixas. Where in hell is the other side?"

Podell advised that the local out of New York was late.

"Hump! Should have been told," said Mackenzie, pulling out a cigar. "Is this me chair?" He took a high-backed leather chair at the head of the table, directly facing Luzzatto. "Well, Davey," he said, striking a match, "for a reputedly brilliant young feller, ye've finally decided to show regard for common sense. Hey?"

"I'm here," said Luzzatto, unsmiling.

"Why?"

"Because I'd rather be judged as a scientist by a scientist. You're capable of understanding the issues."

"I'm flattered. I truly am," said Mackenzie dryly, holding match and cigar at some distance to focus. He puffed nicely and looked up with a grin. "Me deeds upon me head," he quoted. "I crave the law. Is that it?"

Luzzatto shrugged.

The old scientist stared keenly, and, sensing something ugly and vindictive, dropped an unprofitable line of banter. He turned to Seixas, was introduced to young Dotson, and wondered audibly how a clean and intelligent young man could enter a profession which required for success the talents of actor, sycophant, hypocrite and parasite. What was the attraction? Dotson flushed uncertainly.

"I'll tell you this, sir," he retorted, annoyed, "lawyers are like scientists.

344

Some are honest, some are not. It's not the lawyers who'll blow us off the face of the earth."

"Mebbe not, mebbe not. But it's the lawyers who'll justify the carnage on some fool quibble about a comma," said Mackenzie. He seemed more amused than offended.

While this went on, Podell strolled over to Luzzatto and started a low conversation behind a cupped hand, the badge of all his tribe. "I ought to tell you, Dave, that the *Times* called this morning," he said seriously. "I don't know how they got this story, but it wasn't through me. I told them a release would come only from the lawyers."

"I didn't give out anything," said Luzzatto.

"I didn't think you had, but it's leaked out somehow."

"Does it matter?" asked Luzzatto.

The publicity man considered the point, breathing hard. "I thought it might."

Luzzatto shrugged. "Not any more. Why not invite them in? I'd have no objections," he said bitterly. He folded his arms and sank back, smoking. He had no clear idea how to take the plunge and he was hoping for inspiration of the moment. The difficulty was that his mind was a horrible blank. Had he gone too far, he wondered, in rejecting the lawyer's help? A secret fear was growing. He felt suddenly alone and utterly wretched.

"Is this the room? Ah, good," said a familiar, grating voice as the door again opened. Impassive as ever, Emil Dirksen entered, followed by his attractive assistant, Harriet Bascombe. Limping after came R. Major Gussett, chewing his sunken cheeks and looking pleased.

"Oh, Gussett," said Mackenzie ungraciously, letting a limp hand get pumped. He nodded briefly, guardedly, as the lawyers from New York were introduced and went back to his cigar.

"I'm afraid," said Dirksen, "that Professor Ullman will be a bit late. He decided to stop off at Mackenzie Hall for a few moments to look at his old laboratory. Meanwhile, if there's no objection, we can cover the preliminaries."

Luzzatto stirred. "Well, there is objection," he said grimly. "Let's wait till everyone is present. Everyone. Later on, I've asked a few friends to view the proceedings."

"Oh, why? Wasn't this to be private?"

Luzzatto hesitated, conscious that no comment was forthcoming from Seixas or Mackenzie. "Since we're not making a stenographic record," he said after a pause, "I've invited a few witnesses. Or seconds, if you'd like," he added with a mirthless grin. "But we can start without them."

345

"Very well, let's wait," said Dirksen, smiling acidly and with confidence.

Ten minutes later, the door opened and Victor Ullman entered quietly. "Ah, my *dear* Mackenzie!" he said sweetly. "I cannot tell you how I regret the necessity. I hope you understand?" He was wearing an amused smile of deprecation and apology and omnipotence.

Mackenzie put aside his cigar.

"Let's get on with it," he said briefly. "Will someone tell me how to begin?"

After a bland opening statement by Dirksen which received a short nod of approval from his client, Philip Seixas outlined the circumstances under which the university had retired from the contest.

"We're no longer a party," said the lawyer bluntly. "I've agreed to guide Professor Luzzatto with respect to procedure, but otherwise he'll conduct his own case."

Mackenzie glanced down the length of the table. "Are you sure you want no lawyer, Davey?"

"I'd like to regard this as a court of honor," said Luzzatto in a strained voice. "I'll ask you to make your own rules."

Mackenzie chewed his cigar thoughtfully. "Well, I've read a mountain of papers in this messy case. Pleadings, briefs, letters, batches of laboratory droppings, exhibits, mainly the testimony of all those poor devils ye both tormented in examinations before trial. Is all that fertilizer legally before me now?"

Both lawyers nodded. Mackenzie studied the list of exhibits attached to the document. "I don't see any testimony by Dr. Ullman?"

Emil Dirksen advised, smiling slightly, that Professor Ullman was prepared to testify at once in chief, subject to cross-examination. Mackenzie frowned.

"I don't know, Davey," he said, glancing at the younger man. "Haven't ye given up an important advantage? It seems you're entitled to advance preparation? The same benefit the other side had?"

Luzzatto shook his head. "I don't think it will matter too much. If any real surprise turns up, I'll take my chances. Or ask to come back another day."

Mackenzie drummed the table and gazed about him. It was Ullman's manner which he found striking. His former colleague sat erect with pressed lips, immobile, remote, letting the smoke of a cigarette arise from flaring nostrils, expressing by each controlled motion an air of humorless condescension. Occasionally an eyelid twitched involuntarily. Not once

346

since entering the room, not during introductions or courtesies, had he glanced toward the young scientist who sat alone at the end of the table.

Mackenzie felt a chill of misgiving as to his own role. He asked to make a statement.

"When I was asked to act as arbitrator three weeks ago—that is, when Professor Ullman telephoned to describe the development involving his daughter—I had strong doubts that I could intervene. As I explained to Professor Luzzatto, I have known Victor Ullman for most of his scientific career. In fact, we met in Geneva during a conference when he was a much younger man. I think it was my own influence which induced him to leave Manchester, to come to the United States, and to specialize in genetics. At that time, the field was still relatively young. In a sense, between us, we span the entire existence of the science in its modern form.

"Well, I regarded Victor Ullman as highly talented. The school was struggling and I was pleased when he agreed to take a position as instructor at the pitiful level we could then offer. Later, when better offers came from other schools, he rejected those offers to stay on with us. I was always deeply appreciative. He was here in good times and bad. Financially, we suffered during the depression with only the compensation of watching the field expand and flower to acknowledged supremacy among the life sciences. Acknowledged, at least, among its practitioners.

"On the other hand, Professor Luzzatto has come along much later in me life, and only after I broke me hip and retired. I've got a different view of him. Nice young feller, and quite attentive, but the fact is that I see him in different perspective. I'm fond of young scientists—they look so helpless, credulous, with no idea what they're letting themselves in for—but they don't engage me feelings. There's a barrier that I've learned to respect." He paused at this to glance at Ullman.

"I'm telling all this because I find this duty damned unpleasant, gentlemen. I'm not a judge. Never took a judgmental position regarding manners or morals in me life. Don't know how far I can detach myself from the personal element. I have no idea how I'll feel at the end of these proceedings, or how I'll decide these issues, or even if I'm blessed with enough detachment for the task. But I'm only human and I want to make one last appeal. Is it too late to reach a voluntary settlement by direct negotiation?"

Luzzatto stared at his notes during the direct warning and appeal. It was quite evident that Mackenzie was setting up a direct signal for his benefit, cautioning against an extreme position. No other voice was raised in response and he looked up.

"I'm afraid, Dean, that Professor Ullman has consistently rejected the only terms I ever had to offer. I'm asking you to dismiss the complaint. If not, then sustain the complaint and award any damages you see fit. I can't see any other way to decide."

"I am waiting," said Ullman suddenly.

Mackenzie turned to the lawyers. "Very well. Do I administer an oath?"

Ullman had been testifying at length with an air of intense objectivity, presenting a complex set of facts judiciously, slowly, correcting himself occasionally as to date, time, place and the precise nuances of words used on remote and forgotten occasions. Luzzatto was shielding his eyes, making an occasional note, matching the narrative to an outline firmly implanted in his own mind.

So far as he could tell, the story was disappointingly accurate. It was a dry, caustic repetition of the known facts. The career of a gifted, but turbulent student was again presented from the viewpoint of a tolerant but disappointed teacher.

"Victor," said Mackenzie, "can you bring us down to the case? You've been speaking highly so far of Professor Luzzatto. I presume you've got another side. How d'ye account for these alleged acts of his?"

There was a general stir of interest.

"A good question. Well, I am no psychologist," said Ullman pleasantly. "I can only give an opinion based on experience. I always felt that Professor Luzzatto was too immature, too emotional to be precipitated into the responsibilities of early success. It was for that reason I took over so much of the practical side. Without my own efforts, as he practically acknowledged, there'd have been no patent—and perhaps no dispute."

He seemed to consider a nice point. "Also, I early became aware of a certain mercenary streak. Or rather, an enormous anxiety regarding the role of money that stems from his background. He is perhaps not aware how much slipped out during our many talks. His father's newspaper, his mother's concern for property, the intense struggle to break away from medical school to follow the lesser rewards of science. It pleased him to play a sacrificial role, but clearly the controlling thought of money was present."

"Can you be specific? Are you charging that his motives were intentionally dishonest?" asked Mackenzie.

Ullman looked up with an air of caution. "Certainly not at the outset," he decided. "I am not discussing conscious motivation—at least not initially. I doubt if Professor Luzzatto was aware of these weaknesses. No, I am convinced that his absurd pretensions came later. They developed

348

over a period of years, after he succumbed to universal flattery. This lack of poise was always his great weakness—the tendency to blow up every incident of his life into matters of universal, cosmic significance. Nothing could be more preposterous." He lowered his head. "In a way, I feel at fault."

"When did he decide to take advantage of ye, Victor? I'd like ye to be precise."

Ullman took a long time to answer.

"I think," he said, smoking thoughtfully, "the idea to appropriate the patent crystallized the night I brought the final papers to his apartment. That was almost precisely two years after the discovery. He was then married and living in a flat on Faile Street. It was small," he added suddenly, "but quite charming. Mrs. Luzzatto was quite pleased with a Winthrop desk we had given them as a wedding gift. It was the only decent stick of furniture they had."

"What papers were those?" asked Mackenzie.

Ullman turned about to stare. "Oh, the final agreements which got rid of the Brandywine claim to this substance, and which gave the royalties to the university. They're already in evidence. No one," he added with a bitter smile, "has recognized the decisive nature of my contribution. Without my grasp of the practical realities, my knowledge of those mentalities, this entire development would have gone up in a puff of smoke.

"It is most important," he went on with precision, "to recognize the important role played by Brandywine. The Brandywine connection, which made all this possible, went back many years before the young man enrolled in our department. It was almost fifteen years ago that they proposed an industrial grant to examine the problems of their industry in the light of my experience in the field. You were present, my dear Mackenzie, on that occasion when Dr. Beekman and Mr. Strollo made important commitments to our work. In return for certain financial aid to us, they were granted exclusive rights to all developments in our laboratories.

"Exclusive rights!" he added impressively, emphasizing the point. "Your own counter-signature is on my personal copy of the contract so that there can be no dispute as to their rights at that time to claim the entire patent from the university. If they had claimed these rights, on what legal ground could the university have resisted?

"And Professor Luzzatto? Could he possibly have engaged these giants of finance in a legal dispute? He would not have known how to begin. And what then would have been the rewards to science from this

349

discovery? A mere pittance of an industrial grant, a trifling fraction of what was gained through my decisive measures. Nah! I alone recognized that the problem was to pry loose the hold of Brandywine for the benefit of science. I alone persuaded them to relinquish these valuable commercial rights to the university. I had to match wits with their cleverest people, not excluding their lawyers, nor Mr. Strollo himself. It was not easy. My greatest problem was to ensure secrecy."

Ullman went on in this vein, covering in detail past conversations, trips, letters, telephone calls, negotiations, reports, and the like, amplifying his testimony in detail. He seemed to be gazing on a vivid reconstruction of the past, living before his eyes. "I cannot tell you, Mackenzie, how I missed you. Your sound practical advice would have meant so much. As it was, I must to have kept these things locked in my breast. At times I had no idea which way to turn, so delicate did the negotiations become. Their lawyers were aware that the patent was in two names— my own and that of a student named David Luzzatto. I assured them that this student was not easy to control—that the patent might slip away entirely unless the university itself were made the beneficiary. Also, that while commercial rewards had no temptation, I could guarantee that he would respond to idealistic considerations. Once the university obtained the patent, a special and exclusive arrangement with Brandywine could always be effected as before."

Ullman paused to smoke reflectively, gazing about with satisfaction. "Believe me, it was not easy to persuade those people. They are completely calculating in their approach. Above all, I must to have kept all this from Professor Luzzatto himself. With his immaturity, his emotionalism, I had to consider the effects on him of premature disclosure of my efforts. More than once, his rather foolish pseudo-altruistic disavowals in public, to the press, to his colleagues, almost destroyed the final result.

"Why did Brandywine finally make this concession? It was precisely because I kept Professor Luzzatto incommunicado to their negotiators. Of course he complains now of my secrecy, but really. Let him examine his conscience and tell whether today there'd otherwise be anything to discuss. Was it so wrong of me to keep an impulsive boy without the slightest experience in practical affairs in the background? I rather think the result speaks for itself. And yet, that night when I brought those papers for signature, I am convinced his attitude was one of deepest resentment. I knew I had made a mistake."

During the extended narrative, Podell had resumed his seat and was staring uneasily at Luzzatto, who had made no effort to break into the flow.

350

Mackenzie finally stirred. "What was there for him to resent?" he asked curiously.

"Oh, my dear Mackenzie," cried Ullman, smiling broadly. "I had come to confer a benefit, had I not? The papers provided that a valuable patent would be conveyed to the university. Also that a share of royalties received by the university were to be made payable to one Luzzatto. What more natural than resentment?"

After a moment, he added, "I was misled by his promise that night not to benefit from the situation. I trusted him implicitly."

"How were you misled?"

Ullman considered his answer. "I explained that night why my name could not appear on the papers. Also, that the difficulty was known to the administration of the university, who later violated all their obligations to me and became party to the deception. All of them together, but especially Professor Luzzatto, understood the situation. It was a technical thing. It had always been agreed that one would not get more out of the discovery than the other. He knew and consented to that condition. He explicitly promised not to take any benefits for himself. Under those circumstances I delivered the papers to the university. You know the result."

Mackenzie slumped on his spine and brought his fingers together. He stared piercingly. "Do you claim he was lying?"

"Consciously?"

"What else would I mean?"

Ullman remained in thought, breathing heavily. "I am not sure we always know our intentions. We can only guess at the rationale of these obscure processes. In my presence, he was always modest, I daresay, but once I was gone, the surge of vanity, I imagine, became irresistible. The role of the teacher faded away; it became all the brilliant young man who confounded the learned doctors of the Temple. No doubt it began with a small pretense, a failure to mention my role, to correct a false press report—the sin of omission, rather than commission. The mustard seed of minor deceit—a mute acceptance of the false, a tawdry aggrandizement of the ego—grew and flourished. Yet in all fairness, I have no doubt that the young man by now has come to believe the absurd legend which he managed to create—with some help from others." A glance of speculation flickered at Podell and back. "Does intent matter so much? I have taken the trouble to copy the following lines from Professor Luzzatto's testimony at page 611. If you will permit?"

Quivering fingers removed a sheet of paper which was read aloud.

351

Q. (By MR. DIRKSEN) So that Dr. Ullman's intention was to restore the status quo—the original position?

A. So he said.

Q. And so you understood?

A. Yes.

Q. Was it your final word on parting that night, Professor Luzzatto, that you did not expect to take any share of royalties from the Foundation?

A. Yes.

Q. Did you stick to that intention?

A. No.

Ullman threw down the transcript with a gesture of disdain. "I should like to ask one question?"

Mackenzie glanced up. "Go ahead."

"Professor Luzzatto has admitted that the intention was to restore the status quo. I am not exactly a child. If not for that promise of his to re-nounce personal gain, what reason had I to take the sacrificial role? What reason to reject scientific honors and financial rewards? To slink off into the shadows like a bloody fool?"

Ullman had spoken with deep emotion, panting with the effort. Luzzatto caught a flicker of understanding between the lawyers.

"I'd like to stretch me legs," said Mackenzie finally, interrupting with a grimace of discomfort. "Sitting gets 'em knotted. Gusset, give me a hand."

During the recess, Si Podell glanced impatiently at his watch. The lawyers were discussing professional matters among themselves. He got up and went out to the hall where he found Luzzatto talking in low tones to Wodzick and Leo Katz-Moebius.

Luzzatto made a tired gesture. "Si, you know Leo?"

"Are these your two seconds?" said Podell, shaking hands with old friends.

"We're merely onlookers," said Katz-Moebius. "What in God's name is the necessity of dragging us into this thing? Why me? Why Bronco?"

Luzzatto hesitated. "I'm trying to make a point, Leo," he said tiredly, closing his eyes. "I need your presence. If you want to scuttle, it's all right with me." He turned. "You, too, Bronco."

"Let's go," said Wodzick resignedly. "What d'you want, Dave? Testimony? Character references? I'll swear to anything!"

"I only want you to sit," said Luzzatto.

"Suits me," said Wodzick.

352

"I could have sat in New York," said Katz-Moebius, following Wodzick to the conference room. At the door, Si Podell drew Luzzatto aside.

"Now, listen," said the publicity man seriously. "That last stunt of Ullman's was pretty well contrived. I got looks passing between those lawyers of his. I wouldn't wait much longer to make my move, Dave, not if I were you."

Luzzatto tightened his mouth. "What do you think of Ullman? Does he impress you?"

"Yeah! Yes, he does," Podell croaked in his frog's voice. "He's a real convincing type, and that's because he believes every word he says. But I'll tell you something. I think you were right, kid. The man looks good, but he's hanging by a thread."

After a moment, Luzzatto returned to his seat and waited for the proceedings to resume.

Mackenzie said, "You can cross-examine if you like, Davey."

Chapter 28

LUZZATTO BEGAN THE ATTACK.

"Professor Ullman, it took you five years after retirement to bring this lawsuit. If you felt aggrieved, why didn't you come to me first?"

Ullman stiffened. "Really, Luzzatto," he said with annoyance. "I had hoped for a better question. I assumed you had calculated your position. I saw no point in such contact."

"Were you afraid to face me?"

"Certainly not!"

"You knew your letter to President Foxx would create a situation from which there could be no retreat?"

Ullman stared. "In my opinion, the situation had already been created by you. You had five years to reflect, Luzzatto. I saw no reason to beg or cajole. It was your own actions that forced the issue. What else could it possibly have been?"

"Wasn't that letter vindictive?"

"Vin-dic-tive?"

Ullman paused in astonishment. He looked about, inviting attention to the incredible. "I? Vindictive? I am not in the least vindictive!"

"What is your present feeling toward me?"

"Ah! That?"

Ullman studied the cigarette, clearly disturbed. An effort brought a measure of recovery. "I feel profoundly sorry for you, Luzzatto. Your gifts are of the highest order. It is a pity you saw fit to advance yourself in science at your teacher's expense. I wish you well, but also there is such a thing as truth."

Luzzatto stared with burning eyes. "Let's go back to the night you came to my flat. Was your attitude then benevolent or vindictive?"

An incredulous smile was addressed to the onlookers. "I have already described my feelings. They were consistent with those toward all my associates—heightened, perhaps, by our intimacy. I felt benevolent."

"Were you equally benevolent toward Will Tewksbury?" Luzzatto put aside his notes and waited with clasped hands.

Ullman stared for a long time. "I had nothing for that man but the deepest compassion, Luzzatto. I think you know how unfair is that insinuation!"

Dirksen raised a pencil. "Does this have any bearing, sir? I know we're not following rules of evidence here, but even in arbitration? Isn't it out of bounds?"

"Mebbe not, Mr. Dirksen." Mackenzie stared unpleasantly at Luzzatto. "Go ahead, Davey," he grunted. "But I hope you've got some purpose. I happen to remember the problem of Willie Tewk myself."

Luzzatto said to Mackenzie, "Did you know that I once headed a committee to save his job, sir? That I was persuaded in his behalf to bring a petition to Professor Ullman? Dr. Wodzick was a member of the committee of students."

"What if ye did? How does it affect this question?"

Luzzatto said evenly, "Professor Ullman states that he feels sorry for me. He also states that he felt compassion for Will Tewksbury. Aren't we entitled to know what he means by those terms?"

Ullman interrupted harshly. "I will answer any questions, Luzzatto!"

Luzzatto turned to a prepared question. "Do you recall the occasion when I brought that petition for Tewksbury?"

Ullman frowned, genuinely puzzled. "I do not."

"It was Commencement Day. Terribly hot. You left the following day for Lake Marah."

"The date means nothing."

"Would it help your recollection to fix the time in May six weeks prior to the discovery of biocin?"

"No," said Ullman uncertainly.

"Would something else that happened that day refresh your recollection?" Luzzatto looked up carefully. "You opened an Italian music cabinet and showed me a certain chart?"

The first mention of the Truth Chart held a flicker of menace. Luzzatto dared not look at his supporters who knew the point, neither at the lawyers, nor Podell; but the corner of his eye caught a frown of displeasure from Mackenzie.

The antagonists exchanged stares, and after a perceptible pause, Ullman said, "I had no idea, Luzzatto, that you were keeping so meticulous a diary. Yes, I suppose such an occasion took place."

"Did you then not tell me that you were not after Tewksbury's scalp? That you had in fact protected his job for years? That rumors to the contrary were false? If there is any doubt, you can call Mrs. Ullman for her recollection. She was present."

Ullman sat thinking. "I am not sure," he muttered. "It does not sound inconsistent."

"And all those disclaimers would tend to show benevolence towards a rather helpless individual?"

"Yes, yes," said Ullman testily.

"And yet only two years later—just before that night when you came to my flat with those legal papers—you sent Dr. Foxx an ultimatum concerning Tewksbury, did you not?"

"Ultimatum? There was no ultimatum," said Ullman harshly. The eyelid twitched markedly.

"You gave him a choice, I believe, to allow you to dismiss Tewksbury, or to accept your resignation?"

Ullman was silent. In the corner, Wodzick shot a glance of surprise at Podell. The official story of Ullman's resignation, fulsome with regret, had been based solely on the question of health.

Luzzatto waited quietly then added pointedly, "I have asked Mr. Gussett to bring that letter from Dr. Foxx's files to resolve any possible doubt. Would you like it produced?"

Gussett limped forward with a pleased air of functional importance. He waited for a signal, sniffing a scrub mustache.

"It is not precisely what happened," said Ullman thickly. "I had no intention to resign. It was merely a demonstration. I was tricked."

"Oh, how?" asked Luzzatto.

Staring eyes turned in anger. "They should have known I meant not to resign on such an issue as Tewksbury. It was necessary that he be retired from a post for which admittedly he was unfit. It was essential to the plan of reorganization for the school. Tewksbury was not of the slightest importance. The difficulty was this. We had gone through the consolidation of faculties, and this fellow Polk had already become dean of the joint faculties. A complete dreamer! Everywhere I turned, I found these obstacles. Over the years, Tewksbury had consolidated himself. He seemed to have friends, influence everywhere. He had become the one grain of sand in the clockwork, impeding the entire mechanism. What choice had I? Oh, I understand your rather clumsy point, Luzzatto, but

356

it won't wash. Truly, it won't. I was *not* vindictive. Never, never! Ask anyone how much kindness I showed him over the years. My dear Mackenzie," he added, turning violently, "I am sure you will recall the true relationship. Why, the fellow was devoted to me. How could I possibly have wished him harm? All this is more than unfair." A convulsive swallow was followed by deepest outrage. "I will remember this insinuation."

Somewhere below a deep gong reverberated. A waiter was strolling through the lounge, signaling the luncheon hour. The sound was remote, lonesome, falsely theatrical. Luzzatto broke the silence.

"Professor Ullman, as a matter of fact, two years earlier, when I brought the petition in favor of Tewksbury, wasn't your plan of reorganization to get rid of him already formulated?"

"Really, Luzzatto! You are trying to disturb me. I will not permit!" said Ullman violently, turning about. "My dear Mackenzie, I must ask you to do something here." With a massive effort, he folded his arms and forced a calmer tone. "Nah! I should have expected something like this. Of course the plan was formulated. It was however waiting for the proper occasion to be launched. It was still hypothetical. It still had no *real* existence. I suppose you are charging me with failure to open my administrative files? Or to confide my future plans like an adolescent? Was this my obligation? Is this at all relevant to the present case?" he demanded with bitter sarcasm.

"Perhaps not," said Luzzatto.

Suddenly the glare of sunlight was disconcerting. Or were fatigue and moral horror, he wondered, playing tricks on his nervous system? "May I ask one other question about the plan? Aside from getting rid of Tewksbury, did it include any other important or valuable proposal to improve the quality of teaching or research of the school?"

"Certainly," said Ullman, deeply vexed. "It was a deeply considered plan of far-reaching consequences. It would have put us into a leading place in the world of science."

"Can you describe one such proposal?"

"I might."

"Was there a measure to close down Mrs. Nakamura's canteen?"

Ullman nodded slowly, darting a glance of dark suspicion about the table. "Yes. Such a proposal was indeed included. It was long overdue to get rid of the slovenliness that the woman encouraged." He turned about with a broad ingratiating smile. "If I may be critical, my dear Mackenzie, you were always too lenient with the woman Nakamura!"

"Was I?" grunted Mackenzie, noncommittally.

357

Luzzatto went on. "You also proposed to eliminate the students' lounge and to modernize the appearance of the third floor?"

Ullman glanced about in bewilderment. "Is order out of place in science? Is cleanliness hostile to our conceptions? Do the opinions of visitors mean nothing? Is not the entire question of endowment funds involved in these problems? I cannot understand the drift."

Luzzatto said, "I've enumerated four main proposals involving canteen, lounge, third floor, Tewksbury." Each item was ticked off. "Have I left any out?"

Ullman stared venomously. "You have left out only the vision, the drive, the inspiration."

Luzzatto raised his brows. "I assume all that took much thought?"

"Yes!"

"How long did you work on that plan?"

"Years!" said Ullman heavily.

"Can you say how many?"

"I have no precise notion!"

"More than one?"

"Certainly!"

"More than five?"

"Really, Luzzatto! What is this about?"

Luzzatto reached to the valise at his feet for an envelope. "This is a copy of your plan to reorganize the faculty of science, Professor Ullman. It runs to three pages. Where is the rest?"

Ullman sat breathing heavily, glaring at the exposure to public gaze of a secret thing. "Mackenzie! Am I obliged to answer?"

Mackenzie's stare was fixed on the younger man. "Go on to something else, Davey," he said quietly.

Luzzatto flushed and consulted his notes. He resumed on another, surer note. "Earlier this morning, Professor Ullman, you took pains to describe your implicit trust in me, especially the night you brought those patent agreements to my flat for signature. I want Dean Mackenzie to know more about that feeling of trust. When did it begin? Or is it something cooked up after the event to justify this lawsuit?" The question was deliberately, offensively put, and a shock wave flowed invisibly through the room.

"Cooked up?" cried Ullman, outraged.

He looked about uncertainly. "It was nothing cooked up, Luzzatto! I trusted you implicitly, but I must to tell the truth. I had misgivings."

"Did you ever express those misgivings?"

"I certainly—" Ullman paused.

"Yes?" Luzzatto's voice was a prod.

Ullman said slowly, "I told my daughter the following night that I was afraid I had made a serious error. By signing those papers, I had perhaps effectively taken myself out of the biocin picture."

"Yet you delivered those papers to Mr. Gussett?"

"Oh, yes!" said Ullman harshly. The staring eyes turned like lamps to the secretary of the university. "But only because I relied on your statement of intention, Luzzatto—which those people in administration well knew. If you would to make nothing, neither then would I. Otherwise we were to return to status quo. I was dependent on your good faith. I felt extremely uneasy."

"You were suspicious?"

"Yes!"

Luzzatto said quietly, "Was that consistent with your alleged feeling for me of implicit trust?" He glanced quickly about the table. The quick thrust and parry had established another tone, a deadly undercurrent of menace. As the painful moment stretched out, beads of sweat glistened on Ullman's high, intellectual forehead, shining in the sun.

"My feelings went far beyond mere trust, Luzzatto," Ullman said with difficulty. "Of all my students, you were nearest, far closer than any disciple. You were like the son I never had. Why else would I now feel so deeply wounded?

"Yet I must to tell the truth," he went on haltingly, pausing with bitter recollection. "I was never completely satisfied that my feelings were returned with equal sincerity. From the first, I had a sense of distance, of reserve, as though calculation was involved. I had a notion that you were thinking: how much can this old man be turned to advantage? How far can he be used? Perhaps logically the two sentiments are inconsistent, but it is not a question of logic. In this case, against my better instinct, trust overcame misgivings. I refused to believe my inner voice. I completely swallowed the pose." A finger thumped the forehead with derision. "Ullman! A great idiot! What is your next question?"

Luzzatto remained torn by indecision, and finally looked up. He spoke painfully on a note of finality and appeal. "Professor, would you accept my solemn statement that I never had any intent to take advantage of you in any way?"

Ullman stared. "No!"

"Is that because your case depends on proving a corrupt motive? Or is that what you truly think of me?"

"Oh, don't play the martyr, Luzzatto," Ullman exploded. He arose, shaking with rage. "It isn't your role. I *know* what you had in mind. I *know* it in my bones. What else was meant by status quo if we were not to go back to the original position?"

Luzzatto glanced with bleak horror at Philip Seixas, whose dark face was averted. The moment drew on, thick, uncomfortable.

Mackenzie scowled. "Go on, Davey!"

Luzzatto nodded with the cruelty of fresh resolve. The next question stabbed. "Under the 'original position,' Dr. Ullman, what were your rights?"

"My rights were quite clear. I have described them. They were established by the patent."

"How did you earn those rights?"

"*Um Gottes Willen,* Luzzatto!" cried Ullman. "The discovery was made in my laboratory by a student doing work under my direction!"

Luzzatto rubbed his nose thoughtfully. "Well, who actually found the biocin mold?"

"Is that important?"

"Dean Mackenzie might think so," said Luzzatto.

"In the correct sense, it was found by me."

"Is there another simpler sense in which it was not found by you, but by me?"

"I do not admit of any other sense."

"Isn't it correct that I alone physically traced the biocin effect while you were at Lake Marah?"

Ullman said scornfully, "Is this the criterion? Suppose I go to the bathroom while the monkey plays with cultures? Would this give the monkey a role in science?"

"Do you put me on the level of a monkey?"

Ullman pressed his mouth. "I am merely saying that the teacher is the fountainhead, the student his extension. On the day you walked into my laboratory, I told you that all work was under my direction, all papers would carry my name. Or have you forgotten?"

"Professor Ullman, if your contribution was superior to mine, why then did you refuse to allow your name to appear on our initial publication in the *Journal of Cytology?*"

"I am appalled," said Ullman finally in tones of shock. "I cannot grasp that a statement so lacking in truth can be made in my presence. It is a scandal! It is an utter and recent fabrication."

"Not recent," said Luzzatto. "Last September I told Dean Mackenzie about your attempt to withhold your name from the *Journal of Cytology.* The conversation took place in President Foxx's office. Mr. Seixas, Mr. Gussett, Mr. Podell were present. It was the day I got your letter."

Ullman gazed about at the persons named, breathing heavily. "It is then an old fabrication!"

Luzzatto shook his head. "No! I also told them that Jo could confirm that I managed to keep your name on the paper after we had quarreled about the matter. It should be easy enough to find out the truth."

"So! Well, I thought it was agreed that Josephine would not be exposed to this filth? I see where we stand," Ullman said bitterly.

Luzzatto shook his head. "I had something else in mind. The *Journal of Cytology* keeps a correspondence file. A telephone call can tell whose recollection is in better order." He paused, having left an open door, a way out of the trap—for a mere failure of recollection was an honorable fault.

"I think I can recall a moment when I was vexed with your presumption, Luzzatto," said Ullman slowly. "Perhaps I acted on some impulse, or threatened to withdraw my name by way of reproof, but it had no importance. I have a strong temper, I freely admit. I was perhaps angry. Yes, yes! I remember some trifling episode. It completely escaped me."

Luzzatto waited. "Wasn't there another reason perhaps not to permit use of your name?"

"I can imagine none."

Luzzatto finished a cigarette. Beneath the table he gripped a trembling knee. "I want to suggest a reason. You felt unjustified in putting your name to the paper because in fact you had ceased for many years to function as a scientist. You were not then prepared to take credit for work you did not do."

"I am in a dream," said Ullman.

He arose and walked about the room, oblivious to the onlookers. A fixed look immobilized his face. "Mackenzie, I am mortified! I cannot imagine where these disordered ideas come from." He halted and stared directly at Luzzatto, breathing hoarsely. "If I had no part in the work, Luzzatto, why then did you insist to include my name? Was it because the absence would have looked suspicious?"

"No, Professor," said Luzzatto painfully. "It was to conceal your condition."

"My condition?" echoed Ullman.

All color drained as the implication sank in. The room became very quiet. He laughed harshly, uncertainly.

"So!" An expression of intense amusement gathered. "I see the plan, Luzzatto, although the dimensions are incredible, even for one of your talents. It is indeed interesting how the comedy plays out. Or is it farce?

361

Let me tell you something. In this country, they have yet to write their first decent farce."

He returned to his seat and folded his arms. "Tell me this, Luzzatto? Can you reconcile this 'condition' with my massive, really fruitful efforts on behalf of this discovery? Is the insinuation consistent with my admitted productivity in science?"

Luzzatto met the force of blazing, amused eyes, wishing he were anywhere else in the world, given any other task but that which lay before him. The agony seemed without end.

"—go on," said Mackenzie's distant voice.

Luzzatto looked up and shook his head. "Professor Ullman, they were not your efforts, but mine," he said in a low voice. "You hadn't been productive for years. Your textbook was ten years out of date. Every other text had been continually refreshed by new editions—but yours? Everything had stopped with the first edition. Why? I think it was because you had already begun to lose interest."

"I? Not productive? Is this your evidence? That I lost interest in foisting an expensive textbook on my students? That I had a minor dispute with my publisher about an unscrupulous system of rebates? But no one can say that I ever exploited my students for petty advantage," said Ullman.

"No one, that is," he added, grimacing with irony, "except my former protégé. It is instructive how the pattern begins to show." He tucked the handkerchief into a sleeve and waited with an air of profound attention. "So they were your efforts? Not mine? And I was not daily in my laboratory? Where is this conversation taking place? On the moon?"

Luzzatto looked at a man who suddenly had become a stranger. Indeed, he thought, the situation had lunar qualities. A harsh, weird light illuminated the scene, the sun white in a black sky. No particle of dust moved in an electrostatic field. Had his point been made? he wondered. He longed for the advice of Philip Seixas, who seemed suddenly beyond access. "Oh, yes! I'm sure you were there in the lab every day," he said slowly.

"Nah! Well? I was not then directing your training? I am bewildered," said Ullman irritably. "If I was there, what was I doing to which you took exception?"

Luzzatto said quietly, "I don't know what you were doing."

"Eh? What? Why not?"

"Because you were always in the inner office, Professor," said Luzzatto, licking dry lips. "You spent endless hours behind that door. Oh, you'd come out for tea every afternoon, and we'd talk, but in working hours

362

I was pretty much left alone with Jo and Freda. But I have an idea you were always dreaming—or working on a certain chart."

At the second reference to the Truth Chart, several of those present looked up inquiringly. Ullman had gone watchful. Philip Seixas was tapping a cheek softly, staring without expression at the ceiling. Dirksen was studying a note passed to him by Harriet Bascombe.

"Can you tell me," said Ullman finally, "what bearing this has on your breach of faith, Luzzatto? On your failure to restore me at least to my original position under the patent?"

"Not your position," said Luzzatto brutally. "Mine."

"Eh? What? More of this?"

Luzzatto glanced about the silent room. A deep sigh marked the gathering of his last resources. "Dr. Ullman," he said with difficulty, "do you recall a conversation that took place in Maine several days after biocin was discovered?"

Ullman looked about, bewildered. "Conversation? Is this something new?"

Luzzatto nodded. "Yes, Professor. New in a way. I said nothing about it in my prior testimony. I want it clear that I'm going into this matter now against my will, Dr. Ullman. Because you leave me no choice."

Ullman stared. "Oh, I should like to hear about this myself!" He looked about in the silence, nodding with incredulity at the spectacle. Seixas turned to Mackenzie with a frown to explain that he had no idea what was in the wind.

"Go on, Davey," said Mackenzie, after a pause.

"Significantly," said Luzzatto, "your own lawyer, Mr. Dirksen, never brought this up during my testimony. I think the records will show the circumstances. You can imagine the excitement," he went on, turning to Mackenzie. "I don't think Professor Ullman really knows what happened in the lab, not even to this day. He was sitting up there in Maine, working on something far removed from science. Dr. Katz-Moebius made the suggestion that I had some factor that was depressing the entire mutation rate of the culture. It really isn't important at this stage, except that Dr. Katz-Moebius was present when I telephoned Dr. Ullman in Lake Marah. He can confirm the fact that all I got was dead silence on the other end."

Luzzatto paused for breath, conscious that he was talking too fast. It was Dirksen who felt called upon to break in.

"What does dead silence prove, Professor Luzzatto? The circuit might have gone dead."

Luzzatto paused. "So it might," he agreed with a trace of sarcasm. "But

363

I wasn't able to get him back to the telephone. Not even a click, or buzz, but only silence—although I knew he was on the other end. Suddenly, I had this horrible feeling that I was guilty of something. I was terribly upset, and then we talked it over later in the lab. Dr. Wodzick and Dr. Katz-Moebius had no idea what could have happened but they lent me enough to take the plane to Waterville. I wonder," he said, not turning, "whether Professor Ullman will concede that I made such a call."

Ullman took a moment to answer. "The incident had not the slightest importance," he said with contempt. "I will concede only that your incoherent telephone outburst was a far cry from the present calculated version. I was certainly not pleased to be dragged away from my dinner," he added peevishly. "Why do you insist always on trivialities, Luzzatto? It is one of your worst traits. Get to the argument. Did you come to Maine? Where did we talk?"

"On the Point," said Luzzatto.

"Ah, yes! The Point!" said Ullman ironically. "I imagine you were interrupting a sunset?"

Luzzatto paused for a moment, "You wanted me to put off the report for the morning. I told you I couldn't wait and finally you let me talk. There was no reference to the telephone call which brought me up there."

"What reference? Allegedly I knew your purpose," cried Ullman. "I am bewildered, Mackenzie, to know where this is driving."

"Go on, Davey," said Mackenzie quietly.

Luzzatto returned a piercing stare and felt an unpleasant, visceral response. Disconcerted, he turned to a page marked in red crayon. "I told you everything about the biocin effect, what I thought it meant, how important it could be. You listened without comment and we stayed on the Point until the mosquitoes got bad."

Ullman stared. "And did I finally comment?"

"Oh, yes," said Luzzatto quietly. "When I finished, you looked at me, and said, 'How quickly can you go back?' I thought you were joking—I was in the middle of nowhere: how could I go back?—but there was nothing funny about it. There was enough light to see that you were in a terrible state of anger. You then accused me of telling an impossible thing.

"Well, I had my lab books with me and I thought you were posing the usual skeptical hard-minded objections to something entirely new. I agreed that I couldn't understand the principle myself, and that, in fact, was why I'd flown up to get your advice. Then you cut me short. You told me your objection had nothing to do with the farrago I'd been mouthing. You said it was simply inconceivable that it should have hap-

364

pened as it did. I was flabbergasted. I wanted to know whether I stood accused of falsifying the data. This is exactly how you answered."

Luzzatto picked up the memorandum and read a question recalled from the gathering dusk by a lakeside in Maine. The bitter, almost uncontrolled voice still sounded in his ears. "You said, 'Can you, Luzzatto, to whom I have revealed that all things follow an inviolate pattern, say that any man can defeat the force of life, or violate the pattern, or cause a thing to happen out of its time? I am astounded!'

"You gave me a shove and walked back to the cottage. You didn't say a word at supper and went up alone to bed. In the morning Jo drove me back to Waterville and I caught the plane for New York. When I got back to Haverstraw, I told the others what had happened." A pause. "Professor, did you make that statement to me up in Maine?"

Ullman was staring peculiarly, twitching an eyelid. He fumbled in a painful, unsuccessful attempt at a cigarette. "*Um Gottes Willen,*" he said finally in an odd, wondering voice, "what has this to do with the dirty question before us? How does this excuse the grabbing of royalties? The failure to restore me to my position? I must insist that the issue be carefully defined!"

"Because you also said something else which thereafter affected my understanding of your position. You told me that you wanted no part ever in the ridiculous bit of fiction I had brought to your attention. You never said anything else to show a change of mind until the day you launched this lawsuit."

Ullman stared in silence. His forehead was suddenly pale and translucent over a fragile skull.

"Even later, when you were finally convinced, when we finally shook hands on this thing, you made quite clear that you wanted no role except that of mentor and teacher. That talk in Maine explained why at the last moment you decided to withhold your name from initial publication. It was a demonstration of continued pique and anger. Jo persuaded you to let your name stand on the publication, but you never, I think, really forgave me. You'd have preferred the grievance, just as you prefer this lawsuit to the simple truth." Luzzatto swallowed painfully. "What's that truth? Simply that you were in a rage because I pulled off something you hadn't done in a lifetime of effort.

"Anyway," he went on, staring through a haze of exhaustion, "that was the true, not fictional position, that night you came to my flat with those contracts. Oh, sure. We talked about going back to status quo, and I freely admitted that part in my testimony. But what did that mean? I can't say what you had in mind, but I know what I understood!

"You see, I clearly remember that you told me up in Maine to take my lab notes and use them for excelsior. You said it in German which made it entirely convincing, and nothing later ever gave me cause to change my understanding. To me the status quo was established by you that night up in Maine."

The two men exchanged glances of mortality.

Ullman pointed a quivering finger. "I begin to see something, Luzzatto! If my role was so parasitic, why does it come out only now? Why connive at deception all these years when the true sentiment was admittedly so vindictive? It is the worst rubbish I have met in a lifetime of rubbish."

Luzzatto asked, "What's your version?"

"I have no version," said Ullman heavily. "You came uninvited. You revealed a set of notes in horrible condition, completely unfit to show a teacher. Your thoughts were in a muddle, which I properly refused to hear. The rest is an unscrupulous distortion."

"In what respect?"

Ullman stared, breathing heavily. "I am not bound to answer!" he burst out.

Luzzatto felt sick. "Professor, two days after I got back from Maine, I got a letter from Jo which urged me not to be upset by your attitude. She promised to patch things up for me. It's pretty explicit that you threw me out of your home on my neck—and why!"

Mackenzie fixed a scowl on the younger man and slowly lit a fresh cigar. Ullman's face was like wax.

"So!" said Ullman heavily. "You intend to produce this letter from my daughter against me? Mackenzie, I want strict attention!"

Luzzatto looked about the room and shook his head. "No! I guess not," he said slowly, coming to the point of dread. He said with difficulty, "It might help, but I won't use Jo's letter. Not if you object."

He paused to select a final exhibit from the valise. "Professor, earlier this morning I mentioned the time I came to your house on behalf of Will Tewksbury. Is this the chart you took that day from the music cabinet?"

The chart attracted all eyes. Black on white, the segments were conspicuously marked, each yellow flame gleaming in sunlight. Ullman sat breathing with difficulty, incredulous, and a glance of pure hatred shot out. "A thing shown in confidence, Luzzatto?" he demanded hoarsely.

Luzzatto sighed and pushed the chart forward. "Professor, I testified that you told me that no man can cause a thing to happen out of its time. Does the chart refresh your recollection of our talk that night in Maine?"

The room was deathly still.

Ullman turned in appeal. "Mackenzie, this is something you permit?"

Mackenzie put aside his cigar with a speculative glance at the antagonists. Withdrawal had begun in the older man's flushed, trembling features, the welling up of fear.

"Well, Victor," said Mackenzie gently, "I think I grasp the point. I might as well speak freely. There's been a lot of niggling foolery on one side, twice that much on the other, but essentially the whole case boils down to a question of good faith. I think the lawyers will agree."

Murmurs of assent, guarded but distinct, sounded across the table.

"You took yourself out of biocin with your eyes open, Victor. You claim, however, that Professor Luzzatto didn't keep the faith, that he aggrandized the credit, that he failed to restore your share of royalties when he decided to retain those benefits for himself—"

Ullman broke in excitedly. "Did I tell him I would *not* look to a share of royalties in case he changed his mind? I find the suggestion rather odd."

Mackenzie stared. "Did you ever tell him that you *would?*"

Ullman said fretfully, "Was it something I must to have put into words? He should have known what I had in mind, Mackenzie. It was implied!"

"Implied? Oh, why?"

"Because—" Ullman halted.

Mackenzie waited as silence gathered, then resumed heavily. "Well, Victor, Professor Luzzatto claims that this chart reflects your remarks about life patterns and things happening before their time—on the basis of which, he claims, you felt incensed at him for making this discovery in your absence. Did you in fact have this chart in mind that night in Maine? Would you care to answer his question?"

Ullman swallowed. "Is it essential?"

"I won't insist."

Having given full warning, Mackenzie sat back. Ullman stared in agonized indecision. The issue was perfectly clear in the room.

"I might tell ye," said Mackenzie, "an affirmative answer will tend to support Professor Luzzatto's version of that talk. Frankly I'm hoping for a negative."

"I quite understand," said Ullman distantly.

Still he failed to answer. He remained immobile, looking into space, while the silence deepened.

"My dear Mackenzie, the whole thing is an exaggeration," he said, compelled by some inner force. "Of course the chart shows that life

367

follows certain pathways, that things must happen in their proper time. Can it be otherwise in a rational universe?" He paused.

"However, the chart itself is nothing. It is merely a convenient device to delineate what I like to call the topography of another realm. I hope not to be criticized for this by purists," he observed with painful humor. "It is a mathematical scheme by which certain truths are systematized in dramatic form. We cannot create truth, but through symbolic devices, we are enabled to penetrate more deeply into its special realm. Against any blurring of vision, the structure of mathematical truth is an eternal rebuke. This is a stupendous implication."

Ullman wet his mouth. He sat breathing with an effort, following his own discourse with interest, almost with detachment. "Let me remind you of something, Mackenzie. When we first met in Manchester, I then argued that our own field was insufficiently mathematical, immersed too deeply in the purely descriptive, and you then agreed—so that this chart surely is not something new to you. I am the same Ullman, I have not changed my views. I may add that these were precisely identical with those which Professor Luzzatto expressed in his first interview in my laboratory. Let him deny if he dares that he stressed an ambition to reduce the life sciences to a mathematical base. I was charmed at the time—strongly attracted to a young intellect so responsive to my own. Even then he was taking my ideas, yet so cleverly that I was completely deceived by the appearance of originality. Now they are thrown in my face as though these tools of mathematics were signs of I-don't-know-what. I have a taste for the theatrical, I admit, but this chart is no more occult than a weather map—which in its crude way also deals with truth."

The brown cigarette trembled. "It is perfectly commonplace to illustrate any possible system, even one of pure values, by an appropriate diagram. I say any possible system, because mathematics takes us into a universe of absolute necessity to which, not only this material universe, but every possible universe, must conform. I see nothing bizarre, nothing without support in the literature."

Katz-Moebius quietly covered his eyes with a palm.

Luzzatto said, "How is this diagram mathematical, Professor?"

Ullman hesitated, flushing with annoyance. "Well, really," he said bitterly, "it should be reasonably obvious, Luzzatto. It shows a one-to-one correspondence between certain texts in Scripture and the structural necessities of science. A profound insight is involved in this diagram."

"Oh, yes? What's that?" asked Luzzatto sympathetically, setting aside his memorandum with a sigh.

368

Ullman sat drumming, hesitating. "Well, it should be clear enough," he burst out peevishly. "You've had time enough to master the chart. Each text contains the word 'KNOW, which is a tetragrammaton, if we accept the vowel for a consonant, which is contrary to tradition, I admit. Four consonants formed the incommunicable name of God, which in later tradition is not pronounced, except with the vowels taken from the utterable names, so that the system is quite clear. I made it practise always to equate KNOWING with SCIENCE in the first lecture of the semester. Can you deny that always I gave this clue to my classes, Luzzatto? Everyone knows this was my custom."

"No. I don't deny that." Luzzatto was silent.

"Well, then!" Ullman arose and in his old manner strode about with satisfaction. "Symmetry does not exist without meaning, Luzzatto, even you must concede. What is all this but applied common sense? I am no mystic," he said strongly, gazing about for confirmation. "I have no belief in charts as such, but is there not something here which tells us that the processes of the universe cannot be evaded and fail to come to light? Did you think, Luzzatto, that this shabby trick could be used to advantage and not be found out? It is the most bizarre notion I have ever met. Mackenzie," he cried suddenly, turning about, "are you following?"

"Yes," said Mackenzie bleakly.

Ullman touched a finger to his mouth, peering at the older man. A gleam of cunning triumph lit up his eye. "Now, I think we are ready!" he cried. "The young man is finally hoist by his own petard. He invokes this chart? Good! Of course the chart shows that life follows certain patterns —that things happen in their time. Possibly I said something to this effect that night in Maine. Have I ever denied? But if the chart means anything, it runs entirely in favor of my claim. I am embarrassed only that something personal should be on display—something which is after all private to myself. The chart is significant simply as vivid evidence of the young man's capacity for gross betrayal of my trust.

"It is the clearest element of the case!" he exclaimed, halting for emphasis. "Why was I induced to part with this chart? Was it because the young man was thirsty for this knowledge? Or rather because he had in mind one day to invoke it against me? I cannot tell how unpleasant I find the necessity to expose this ugliness, but this is the essence: deceit and betrayal in the inception. Oh, it's all the pose of sweetness and light and mild submission, but finally we see what was involved. What but the old hostility without the mask of hypocrisy?

"Now I shall tell you something, Mackenzie!" he added, turning

369

abruptly. "Have you noticed how Tewksbury was dragged in? Why? Because the best defense is attack. Because Luzzatto knows that the man had no place in the department, that his ouster was long overdue. At first I interpreted that show of sympathy in the light of my own grief for the man. I could hardly expect the young man to grasp my heavier responsibilities—but later I was forced to wonder whether it was actually idealistic concern for a mere laboratory assistant—or prompted by an obscure emotion of reprisal for my disciplinary grade earlier in the year. For he forgets nothing, this young man. Every wrong, no matter how trifling or imaginary, festers and gnaws until it becomes a blinding obsession. Truly! It—

"When the decision was to be made, this Luzzatto, instead of lending moral support, joined the Tewksbury clique to embarrass me with that petition. It was a gross affront that I tried to overlook, but the hurt went deep."

His restless walk took Ullman to the window where he stared into the campus, flaring his nostrils, searching for the meaningful word. "You see," he went on painfully, "this defection took on greater significance later when I tendered that formal resignation to Dr. Foxx. It was only meant as a gesture. I never dreamed—I'm sure that neither he, nor anyone else—Mr. Gussett, listen to this, you must bear me out. No one would have taken that letter seriously if not for—well, you must understand, my dear Mackenzie, that my position was seriously undermined by this intrigue among the students—

"Well, I'm rather delighted that the question of Tewksbury has been raised! Yes, glad, because that minor incident, magnified out of all proportion, explains the true relationship. I was astounded that night at Lake Marah when he revealed his hand because the scheme became crystal clear. Having already used the catspaw Tewksbury to embarrass me, the next step was to deprive me of the fruits of my career—to disrupt the wider patterns indicated by the so-called chart. Is it a wonder that I was disturbed? How could I have been so gullible? It was my genuine love for the young man, I surmise, that overcame my common sense. But how could I foresee the future ramifications of the scheme to step into my shoes—to influence those people in administration to oust me on the Tewksbury pretext? It was there from the first—"

He turned from the window with wonder and pain as memory of betrayal came flooding back. "It is unbelievable, Mackenzie, but almost at once, within the first hour, I received an affront which should have warned me. It would mean little enough to others, I daresay, but still— You see, I have deep faith in the insignificant detail which betrays character. On that first day—now listen to this, Mackenzie!—unbelievably, this young man insulted me so grossly that even now I am astounded that I did not grasp the significance."

The hot blue eyes widened with incredulity. "Oh, it sounds like nothing, but you must understand the circumstances. I had remarked that more things were in heaven and earth than were dreamt of in philosophy, you see? And I attributed the phrase to Horatio. It was of course a mere slip of the tongue. Do you know what he said?" Ullman peered earnestly. "This—this young man had the effrontery to correct me. Even before we had a relationship, he presumed to set himself up as a perfectionist in my presence. I would never have dared to put a teacher of mine out of countenance without first asking permission. Even you, my dear Mackenzie," he said ingratiatingly, "even with all our years of sweet, rewarding intimacy together, you cannot recall one instance where I invaded your dignity as my chief by the weight of a feather. In itself the thing had no importance—but I had to ask myself: Why? *Why?* In that instant I saw with dreadful, frightening clarity that he was seething with resentment because of the error about the Fleischer fellowship. Almost at once I tried to make it up with him, even to inventing a stipend to assuage his disappointment—a stipend which came out of my own pocket, but he has never forgiven me. Never! Even now he is filled with bitterness which he is too clever to expose, but I *know*. I know his mind and I am heartbroken by what I see. A mix-up which actually was entirely your fault, my dear Mackenzie, has been the reason all these years why he has excluded me so cunningly from the—"

He turned blindly to the sun. "No, no! It is not the financial benefits which ever mattered. No one can say I have a single mercenary hair in my head. It is simply that the time had come for this discovery to occur in my laboratory. I had waited so long that— Well, then, it happened! It can be demonstrated that this was bound to occur, that it was not blind chance, because blind chance, as the young man was first to proclaim, does not arise in an orderly universe—except that with typical arrogance, he recognizes no plan, no pattern but that which serves his interests. He has wonderful talents, a high degree of imagination, yet all these virtues are subject to a truly terrifying concentration on his internal needs. Then to be excluded by him from—

"*Um Gottes Willen,* he could have declined to act as director of the Center in my favor. Holding the patent, he could have forced the issue. Was that too much to expect? Then— Oh, yes! I must tell you another thing. This question of his scientific style—"

Once started, the flow went on and on. It covered classroom quips,

371

omissions of punctilio, a quarrel with Katz-Moebius, the descent of the older Luzzattos on the private laboratory, the consolidation of the graduate schools under Polk, a gift of clothing, an unanswered postcard. The sun shifted. The story trailed off finally into silence. All eyes were averted in acute embarrassment. Luzzatto stared at his hands, sick to death. Mackenzie stirred and glanced at the lawyers.

"We have no further questions," said Harriet Bascombe. Her statement was for the stunned Dirksen.

Mackenzie stared disconsolately at a cold cigar. "I'd like ye all to leave me here a minute with Professor Luzzatto. Would ye mind, Victor?"

Ullman arose with difficulty. The broad shoulders were bowed, a burning glance of suspicion went to Mackenzie. He said harshly, "Not at all. I must in any case find the bathroom. I will be waiting in the lounge."

It was Harriet Bascombe who took his arm sympathetically and led him out. Dirksen had turned his back.

The club house was deserted when Dotson was sent to summon the rest to return. The conference room seemed curiously vacant; the atmosphere was stale, wearied. Ullman walked in slowly and took a rigid pose in his accustomed seat. Luzzatto's wretched face was averted.

Mackenzie came at once to the point. "I've given this case a lot of thought, Victor, and I've come to a decision. I've got an award in mind, and I'm prepared to hand it down in writing, but I'd rather see something better take place. An award can only hurt one of ye."

The rigid features failed to respond. "You have discussed this with Professor Luzzatto?"

"We had a long talk," said Mackenzie.

Ullman went through the ritual of a cigarette. "I am prepared to listen," he said without expression.

Mackenzie gnawed his mouth, scowling. "Well, it's simple enough, Victor. Professor Luzzatto has agreed to drop his demand for a retraction which he understands would be too difficult for you to make at this stage. However he has agreed to assign his total interest in the patent to the university together with all claims to salaries or royalties on condition that you withdraw this action and join in some public expression of mutual regrets. In that case, I'll make no award or comment."

"I see," said Ullman profoundly.

He nodded mechanically, without surprise, digesting the proposal. "Will the statement recognize my primary role in the discovery?"

Mackenzie shook his head. "No! The lawyers will compose some face-saving device to get this affair decently buried and out of sight. I'll be

372

frank, Victor. It will merely express the thought that this action arose out of a mistake which has been privately straightened out to everyone's satisfaction. Mutual expressions of high regard will be exchanged. However, attention will be called to your role as chief in the laboratory. I'll watch the language meself."

Ullman's stare went about the table and came to rest at the foot. "Luzzatto? You think this is correct?"

"It was my idea," said Luzzatto unhappily.

Ullman turned back to Mackenzie. "And if I press for a decision?"

"Sorry, Victor! I can't give ye the award. Not under any circumstances."

"You have thought this over? Because this has certain implications, you see?"

"It can't be helped. Not that I doubt your sincerity for one minute. It's simply a question of proof. Ye haven't given enough evidence to rest on."

"My testimony is not evidence? Forty years of faithful service is not evidence?" The tone held dignity and reproach.

Mackenzie hesitated. "It's some evidence, Victor," he said gently, "but it's not conclusive. I'm sorry," he added with finality.

The expression did not change. "But why do you apologize?" asked Ullman with surprise. "I am sure you have acted with complete fidelity. As always, I must accept your decision. It tells me what I want to know. Perhaps more than you suspect." With composure, he arose and straightened his cuffs. "I have tried to establish the truth. No one can deny that I tried. I congratulate the young man on his victory."

He paused at the door, facing sunlight, outlined against the dimness of the hall. Except for the gleam of moisture on the high forehead, he seemed oblivious to the shock of decision.

"Perhaps history will have something to say about this curious episode," he remarked, swinging the gold key. "None of this is too surprising. How is it put by Schiller?" A bitter grimace tinged with satisfaction became fixed.

"Mit der Dummheit kämpfen die Götter selbst vergebens!"

A dramatic finger arose. "Even in translation it has a certain pithy applicability," he remarked. "With the Stupid the Gods themselves battle in vain!"

The door closed and he was gone.

They were again alone on the short warm drive to Cobb's Hill. The old man was silent, scowling at the drowsy streets lined with trees. "How d'ye feel, Davey?"

"Rotten!" Luzzatto drove slowly and shivered. "Soiled! It was the last thing I ever thought I could do. I've got no satisfaction out of this."

"Would ye rather have lost?"

"No."

"I'm glad of that. It's a growing up business," said Mackenzie reflectively. "In a way, a certain amount of brutality is to your credit. Not nice! But then, life isn't nice. The smallest organism tends to devour its environment." A pause. "Ye don't seem convinced?"

"I had hoped for something better of myself. How do you feel about it, sir?"

"Never felt worse," Mackenzie replied abruptly. "But it would have been infinitely more pitiful if you hadn't found the resources to defend yourself, Davey. Ye wouldn't have been a man—which means you'd have been no kind of a scientist for my money. Technician, perhaps, but nothing else. Secretly, I think Victor Ullman would agree with me.

"Oh, you're entitled to feel glum Davey," he went on, almost to himself, "but it's not a bad thing to have gone through the muck. When you first arrived, you accepted your elders at face value. You were inclined to take their pronouncements on faith instead of on mature investigation of the thing itself. That's not doing justice to the field of study. What you accept on faith you can also drop on faith.

"In the long run," he concluded as the car drew up at his home, "it makes a better scientist. Your reputation has suffered but that's a transitory thing—and everyone suffers in a thing like this. On the whole you were more than generous. Now I'll say goodbye, and I'll ask ye to bring that nice young wife around with that infant of hers someday if I'm still alive. Oh, and take my advice. Make a hod carrier of the child. Anything's better than this twiddling nonsense!" With a caustic grin, the old man focused his useful eye and navigated the pathway to the door.

Luzzatto waited a long moment and drove home.

The following day Luzzatto went through an accustomed routine. Tynesdale Road was queer and unreal. He still had no pleasure in himself or the return to his former life. The nightmare had lifted but its site was still occupied by—

—vacancy.

He had been relieved and silent through breakfast, eating voraciously with the appetite of convalescence. Eva had never been more beautiful nor considerate of his mood, he reflected; more than once, she had paused to kiss him; and his arm had gone around her waist, and he had clung to her, breathing the warm smells of her body, straining her to himself. For the first time he had gone through the mail with a sense of purpose. Some plans had been made for their vacation in Bimini—

But it was not yet the same. At his side, Tom Adderly, despairing of conversation, was humming a jingle of recent currency in the physics department:

"Round and round and round go the deuterons—"

The drive to the university was a haze and they went their separate ways. Danny Foy was on the elevator, ears expectant and alert as the tall figure came into view. "Hop in, sir!" cried Foy joyously. "Lots of room in the back. D'ye think it'll rain, Professor?"

"I don't think so," said Luzzatto soberly.

Foy squinted. "It's a northeast wind. Usually means lots of rain in these parts—" Nothing had changed, nothing was the same. Other routines were disposed of until the warning gong in the hall.

On the stroke of ten, Luzzatto turned from a diagram on the blackboard, dusting chalk from his fingers. How would his voice sound? he wondered. The array had lost its remembered value as a group. The faces were again those of individuals—curious, watchful, still remote. Suddenly he could recall their names.

"Ladies, gentlemen," he began, turning the pages of the assigned textbook. "Today let us consider the extent to which the unit of heredity may be integrated in and subservient to the structures and functions of higher order—"

As he spoke, his voice strengthened, regained its assurance, bringing the class to attention, and in the flow and transmission of knowledge of the physical basis of inheritance of life he knew that he had returned from a far journey.